Praise

THE SECRET OF

Raven Point

"Unputdownable . . . Jennifer Vanderbes's *The Secret of Raven Point* is strikingly vivid, tackling war's moral ambiguities from the open-eyed perspective of a young American woman on the cusp of adulthood. . . . *The Secret of Raven Point* finds contemporary resonance in classic themes of humanity and loyalty tested by extremes."

—Vogue.com

"Fresh, compelling . . . War gives men and women a chance to become monsters or heroes, and Vanderbes finds her footing exploring these two extremes. . . . [Juliet] is a companionable protagonist . . . She emerges from the experience as someone altered yet not conquered by war. . . . Vanderbes performs admirably."

—*The Washington Post*

"Two separate mysteries create and maintain suspense throughout this gripping World War II coming-of-age novel . . . the solutions to the central mysteries, revealed slowly, are unsettling in their perverse specificity, yet certain aspects of them remain ultimately unknowable. To her credit, Vanderbes doesn't try to make entirely comprehensible the disturbing actions men may take in the midst of war."

—*The New York Times Book Review*

"A war novel written with confidence, knowledge, and insight."

—Phil Klay, National Book Award–winning author of *Redeployment*

"A sweet and sad love story . . . An unforgettable saga."

—*The Christian Science Monitor*

"At first glance, Vanderbes's novel is a touching tale of a sister's love for her brother, but the underlying themes are much deeper. Readers will fall in love with the delightful Juliet, who is a smart and courageous heroine, and other hospital workers as they form friendships and struggle to accept tragedy and loss while treating their patients' physical and mental wounds. While not all the mysteries here are resolved, the only disappointing thing about this book is that it has to end."

—*Library Journal* (starred review)

"*The Secret of Raven Point* is about piecing together meaning in lives and minds shattered by war. It's a meditation on the power of steadfast love in all its forms—romantic, fraternal, platonic, even divine—to restore wholeness out of chaos and light out of unspeakable darkness. Jennifer Vanderbes gives us characters we care about and a story we believe in an engrossing novel that brings home the particularity of war. A moving tribute to a generation of men and women whose stories, and whose lives, for the most part are now lost to us; it's a great read."

—M. L. Stedman, author of *The Light Between Oceans*

"*The Secret of Raven Point* should do for war-era Italy what Hilary Mantel has done for sixteenth-century England. That is, it proves that fiction can be history with blood in its veins, quickening for us the violence and sadness and the awful incongruity of war. A brilliant novelist, and a book to treasure and never to forget."

—Darin Strauss, author of *Chang and Eng* and *Half a Life*

"Vanderbes graphically depicts the gruesome nature of battlefield injuries, both to the body and to the psyche, even as she shows Juliet's courage and strength. The skillful Vanderbes's aching depiction of Juliet's struggle to maintain her humanity amid the army's callous bureaucracy and the horrors of war works as both an homage to our armed forces and a moving personal story of emotional growth."

—*Booklist*

"*The Secret of Raven Point* draws the reader in with evocative period drama and a rich emotional portrait of its heroine. An arresting, exciting journey of discovery from an extremely talented author."

—Matthew Pearl, author of *The Technologists* and *The Dante Club*

"*The Secret of Raven Point* at first seems to be the mystery of a young man gone missing in World War II, but as the pages begin to fly by, the layers become deeper. . . . This novel had me wrapped in the lives of the couple, who endure much personal loss and yet manage to find humanity in the darkest of times. Definitely one of my favorite reads of the year."

—*Historical Novel Society*

"A subtle evocation of war and loss, which Jennifer Vanderbes—with extraordinary cleverness and restraint—explores slantwise, the story coming visible through its glimmering contours like an embossing on fine paper or an impression in snow."

—Lauren Groff, author of *Arcadia*

"When her beloved brother is declared missing in action, smart, flinty Juliet Dufresne, training to be a nurse, goes to Italy to find him, in an empathetic, oblique take on the layers of damage done during war . . . moving . . . turns unusual and affecting as the emotional depths of Vanderbes's story slowly emerge."

—*Kirkus Reviews*

"*The Secret of Raven Point* is that rare book that reminds us of the deep, immersive pleasures of novel-reading: of getting lost in a story, of being transported to another time and place, of growing so attached to characters that they feel as present and real as one's own friends. Jennifer Vanderbes takes a harrowing but little-known chapter from WWII history and through her compassionate and brilliant rendering transforms it into a story that is urgent, personal, and profoundly moving."

—Sarah Shun-lien Bynum, National Book Award–nominated author of *Madeleine Is Sleeping*

"Juliet surprises herself with her capacity for growth and for maintaining her own integrity against seemingly insurmountable odds. The book does not shy away from the horrible decisions that ordinary people must make when faced with war's extraordinary demands."

—Publishers Weekly

THE SECRET OF

Raven Point

{ A NOVEL }

Jennifer Vanderbes

SCRIBNER

NEW YORK LONDON TORONTO SYDNEY NEW DELHI

SCRIBNER
An Imprint of Simon & Schuster, Inc.
1230 Avenue of the Americas
New York, NY 10020

First Scribner trade paperback edition April 2015

SCRIBNER and design are registered trademarks of The Gale Group, Inc., used under license by Simon & Schuster, Inc., the publisher of this work.

For information about special discounts for bulk purchases, please contact Simon & Schuster Special Sales at 1-866-506-1949 or business@simonandschuster.com.

The Simon & Schuster Speakers Bureau can bring authors to your live event. For more information or to book an event, contact the Simon & Schuster Speakers Bureau at 1-866-248-3049 or visit our website at www.simonspeakers.com.

Designed by Mspace/Maura Fadden Rosenthal

Manufactured in the United States of America

3   5   7   9   10   8   6   4   2

Library of Congress Control Number: 2014381868

ISBN 978-1-4391-6700-7
ISBN 978-1-4391-6704-5 (pbk)
ISBN 978-1-4391-6705-2 (ebook)

For Ellery

A hospital alone shows what war is.

—Erich Maria Remarque,
All Quiet on the Western Front

PROLOGUE

THE GERMAN PUTS his hands behind his head, biting at his lower lip, and gets down on his knees. He's looking at the ground, and his helmet tilts forward over his eyes, but he's too scared to move it. "*Nicht schießen,*" he says. "*Nicht schießen.*" He keeps repeating that in these short, stabbing whispers, like he's talking to himself, talking to God. Sergeant McKnight's watching him, kicking at the dirt, that vein in his forehead getting fat. He orders Rakowski and Dufresne to take the Jerry to the rear, so they each grab an elbow and haul the German off the ground and start heading back toward the wall. . . .

McKnight's looking at me. "Stop batting your fucking eyelashes at every Jerry," he says. Just as Rakowski and Dufresne get close to the wall, McKnight signals them to let go of the sniper. So the German's standing there all alone, his helmet still tilted, and McKnight trains his rifle on him. McKnight's just waiting, waiting for him to start moving, and finally the Jerry takes one step, then another, and soon he's walking, walking faster, staring at the ground, breaking into a run, and I hear a gun go *pop.*

PART I

{ 1941–1944 }

WHERE HAD HER brother gone? wondered Juliet, staring out the window at the empty football field.

It was a Sunday afternoon in early December, and Juliet Dufresne was alone in the school chemistry lab, preparing for the South Carolina Science Fair. Tuck had been glancing up at the lab window throughout practice, awaiting her signal. But now the entire team had vanished.

The sky was pale gray, the window's thin glass cold against her palm. A late-autumn chill seeped through the bubbled cracks along the windowsill, and Juliet crossed her arms for warmth. Beneath the pink pillowcase she'd fashioned into a lab smock, she wore a thick cream-colored sweater. Her black shoes were dusted with flour. Tendrils of dark-blonde hair, having escaped her braids, clung to her safety goggles.

Well, he wouldn't go far, she thought. She'd find him in the locker room and tell him what he'd missed. She looked at her watch: time for one more run-through.

Returning to her worktable, Juliet arranged her funnel of flour, the white dust tickling her nose. She struck a match, lit her candle. *Combustion,* she thought excitedly. A complex series of chemical reactions between a fuel and oxidant, creating heat or light. Inert elements, when combined, could generate a wilderness of power, releasing their full potential.

Full potential—Juliet grinned. Having taken second prize two years in a row, she was certain this experiment would win the blue ribbon. She loved being in the lab. She loved the silence of the corkboard walls and the cavernous aluminum sinks. She loved the room's glittering precision: tidy shelves of thick-glass beakers, rows of test tubes suspended in metal drying racks. Bright, orderly, the lab always had the feel of *morning*. Here she could do as she pleased without being shunned or gaped at.

For as long as Juliet could remember, the mauve birthmark on her left cheek had rendered her something of an outcast. The mark wasn't awful—the size of a strawberry, perhaps—and it had faded with time. But in the quiet southern town of Charlesport, it had been enough to elicit exhaustive commentary from classmates throughout her childhood. *Affliction, deformity*. The words still clung to her, although the remarks ended when her peers, struck by puberty, had themselves become pimpled and unpredictably puffed. By then, Juliet had come to take comfort in seclusion. She devoted her time to *Women in History* biographies (having read the Marie Curie volume four times), to "boyishly unwieldy" chemistry experiments, according to Mr. Licata, her favorite teacher (now lurking supportively in his next-door office), and, late at night, she disappeared into the delicious misery of Henry James's heroines. Juliet's sole confidant was her brother, Tuck. "Tuck here!" had been Juliet's first sentence, shrieked through the house, a toddler's garbled and passionate plea for her brother, two years older, to remain constantly by her side.

Glancing once more out the window, clouded with her hand-prints—how could Tuck miss this?—Juliet gently hammered a lid onto the can. "Please be careful . . ." she whispered to the empty lab, "as you witness the power of combustion." She blew into a rubber tube attached to the funnel, and a tremendous *bang* erupted. The can's lid soared in flips and flutters like a giant tossed coin. Perfect! The judges would be dazzled. Tuck would love it.

Juliet mopped up the traces of flour, gathered her things, and rushed down the dark back stairs, across the silent gymnasium. A weak band of afternoon sunlight lit the planks of the basketball court. At the threshold of the locker room she called, "Tuck? You in there?"

Heavy footsteps thudded toward her, and Beau Conroy appeared, his hair wet from the shower, his face scrubbed a raw pink. Beau was the team's linebacker. He had the shadowed, flattened face of a boxer, and his hair had been shaved close to his head. His eyebrows were thick and dark, his eyes a shade of green that Juliet, when first meeting Beau at age ten, had told her brother she thought looked like emeralds. A bright white T-shirt hugged his sloping shoulders.

"Tuck took off," said Beau. "Everyone scrammed in some kind of hurry. Me? I like my showers. Here. He left you this."

As he offered up the folded page of a magazine, Beau studied her.

J—
    Off to see Miss Van Effing!
        Thanks!

Juliet sighed and slid the note deep into her pocket. This had been happening quite a bit lately.

"This Van lady have a first name?" Beau asked.

She did not, because she did not exist. It was a code Juliet and her brother had devised years earlier. To say Miss Van Effing meant, *Help me, cover for me, tell Papa something to keep me out of trouble.* Juliet suspected Tuck had once again gone to hear the radio broadcast at Sammy's Soda Shop. Their father, who had served as an army surgeon in the Great War, forbade listening to broadcasts about Hitler at home.

"You shouldn't read private notes," said Juliet.

Beau smiled. "Then you gotta make them longer. I never read anything long." He lifted his gym bag. "You goin' home? I'll walk you."

"I'm perfectly able to walk home alone."

"Jeez, Juliet, why you gotta be so difficult?"

Juliet did not mean to be difficult. She liked Beau. She liked his deep voice and his big-toothed smile. He lived alone with his grandmother and had even built her a special wheelchair. But she had only ever seen Beau alongside Tuck. If they walked home together, what on earth would they talk about?

Beau blinked hard, his green eyes studying the rim of the basketball hoop above, and Juliet wondered if he was having the same reservation. She inhaled the steamy traces of mildew and sweat seeping from the locker room. From the darkness beyond, a lone showerhead hesitantly dripped.

Beau settled his bag on his shoulder. "You're getting womanly, Juliet; I can see when it happens to the girls. First they get a few pimples and pretty soon their heads start goin' topsy-turvy. Every girl needs a little something to calm her down. To get her on course. A first kiss is like bourbon."

Juliet stepped back, registering what Beau had said. Years earlier a friend of Tuck's had suggested a game in their yard—*Last one to the tree has to kiss the sister!* The sister. The boy didn't even remember her name. Juliet had forced herself to smile, and would have stoically suffered the degradation of his game had Tuck not told the boy to go eat his own crap.

Now, looking at Beau, Juliet straightened her posture. "Beau, I've kissed so many boys"—she worked her jaw in an exaggerated ellipse—"my mouth is sore."

Beau laughed. "So, little Miss Difficult is a liar."

Did he actually find her awkwardness amusing? Charming? Juliet had read of such unexpected attractions but never imagined herself a participant. Beau impatiently adjusted the strap of his bag, and Juliet realized she did not want to lose this opportunity. "Have you brushed your teeth?" she asked nervously.

Beau walked across the darkened gymnasium to the water fountain, gargled, and spit out an arc of water. "Will that do, ma'am?"

Juliet felt her breath quicken. "Let's go outside." Taking the stairs two at a time, she pushed the door open into the chill of the empty parking lot. She set her books on the ground and leaned back against the school, propping her foot on the wall—a pose she'd seen other girls strike. If she could only get *still,* Juliet thought, just arrange her legs and arms in some vaguely mature stance, she wouldn't feel so ungainly.

"Listen, you won't tell your brother . . ." Beau hesitated in the doorway.

"Staring into a dozen barrels of the guns of a firing squad," she said dryly, "I will not speak of this." But there was nothing Juliet didn't tell Tuck, and she was already wondering how she would relate this incident.

Beau set down his bag beside her. "You know, Coach said we got some college recruiters coming to see the state championships. I might get myself an athletic fellowship. Tucker tell you that?"

Juliet looked away and licked her mouth. Her lips gathered delicately in what she knew was called a Cupid's bow, but the air against them now made them feel enormous.

"Look, it's like jumping into a pool," said Beau. "You just gotta one-two-three-*go*. But turn your face in my direction." He leaned into her, and Juliet closed her eyes, her palms stiffening against the rough bricks behind her. The darkness comforted her; she was nowhere, she was in outer space. She could smell Beau's aftershave, thick and lemony, and felt his hand on her chin. His mouth pressed into hers and in a startled gasp, her lips parted. His tongue was warm and alive and insistent, a creature unto itself. She felt the smooth edges of his teeth and worried at the sharpness of her own. Then his fingers, thick and strong, slid up her face, stopping to cover her birthmark.

She pushed him back. "Hey."

"Oh, come on, I thought it'd be nice."

"Nice for who?" she yelped.

"Juliet, it's not even that noticeable anymore. I bet it'll disappear completely."

"And if it doesn't disappear?"

Beau's mouth fell crookedly open, and the thought of what he might say filled Juliet with such dread that she gathered her things and walked off. "Hey, I'm sorry!" he called after her. She wanted to run, but fought the urge. She had two rules when dealing with tormentors: no running; no tears.

In the grainy afternoon light, she trudged through the old part of town, passing the formerly grand homes of Hancock Street. She glared at the ruined mansions, withering under buckled beams; strips of paint peeled off at irregular intervals so that the façades seemed to be suffering from a bout of measles or chicken-pox scabs. Around the turn of the century both a hurricane and a fire had ravaged Charlesport. But Juliet found it difficult to imagine these events—the noisy, wet drama of a hurricane, the roar of buildings aflame. It seemed impossible that a town standing in such dreary slumber had once built massive ships to sail the world.

Nothing here now, she thought, *but small-town bores.*

Soon she passed the thickly wooded area where years earlier she and Tuck had rescued a wounded raven. "Raven Point," they called the woods. Together they had nursed the bird back to health and kept it as a pet. Juliet had grown attached to Cher Ami, who would follow her to school. But at Tuck's insistence, they eventually released the bird back into the woods. He belonged to the wilderness, Tuck had said. But for months afterward, Juliet and Tuck would lie side by side at the edge of Raven Point, staring up at the thick canopy of trees, calling Cher Ami's name. Several times, they thought they spotted him on a distant branch. But the woods had changed the bird; he wouldn't come down. Eventually, when she called his name, Juliet wasn't even certain she could tell him apart from the other birds. She wept at this, and Tuck held her close. He said maybe it was their mother she was weeping for, and Juliet thought perhaps he was right. She had died when Juliet was only three years old. Over the years, she and Tuck grew accustomed to lying at the edge of Raven Point, listening to the scratch of squirrels climbing the bluff oaks, talking into the early evening. It became their secret hideaway. Here they had shared their first cigarette, sipped their first bourbon. Here they had conjured up the fictional Miss Van Effing.

Miss Van Effing.

As Juliet finally ascended the creaking white steps of her house, she recalled her task: "Tuck's practice is running late," she announced, opening the door. "He won't be home for a while."

Pearl, having commandeered the dining table with cards and envelopes, news clippings and pens, barely looked up. Their step-mother spent great portions of her days writing to politicians. Having once shaken the hand of Eleanor Roosevelt, Pearl prized more than anything else the white glove she'd worn on that occasion, now wrapped in a red velvet cloth in her bureau. Never in the history of the world, thought Juliet, had a woman been so undeserving of a name: Pearl was short and bowlegged; her eyes were a luster-less gray. She was several years older than their father, and had married him that March.

Her father glanced up from the coffee table, where he played his customary game of chess against himself. He slid forward a rook, and in his professorial baritone asked, "How was lab, Juliet? Did magnesium and phosphorous behave today?"

Juliet considered confiding everything about Beau. But it would only sharpen her father's guilt. He had always believed Juliet's awk-wardness stemmed from her mother's absence, and tried to make up for it by spoiling Juliet with the one thing he had in abundance: knowledge. At dinner, he bombarded her with elaborate explana-tions of the respiratory and circulatory systems. He sat beside her at her desk and talked her through the dissection of a bullfrog. She was given three stethoscopes, a microscope, a copy of *Gray's Anatomy,* and a teaching skeleton. One evening, her father even launched into a cumbersome explanation of the monthly shedding of the uterine lining, aided by a series of diagrams and charts—only recently, when Juliet woke in the night to a red streak on her underwear, did she realize he'd been describing the feminine "curse."

"The experiment is stupendous," Juliet answered, climbing the stairs. "But I'm coated with baking flour. Practically breaded. When Tuck comes home, would you tell him to come find me?"

Juliet drew a hot bath and surrendered her legs, then torso to the steamy porcelain tub. The water whitened with soap and flour. She stared dully at a spidery crack on the ceiling, chips of plaster dangling precariously. Life suddenly felt impossibly long, impossibly dreary.

The feeling of Beau's hand covering her cheek came back to her. How could she have been so stupid? So gullible? She slid her shoulders down until the water washed over her scalp. She wanted to be swallowed, to be gloriously erased.

But the probing softness of Beau's tongue also returned—the warmth, the startling wetness, the momentary thrill of her parted lips. It was all so vivid, so confusingly tangible. The taste of him—salty? yeasty?—lingered on her teeth. Juliet drew in a mouthful of bathwater, swirled it around, and spat it at the drain.

As she stepped from the tub, she studied herself in the mirror. *You're getting womanly, Juliet.* In the past year she had grown an inch, and the nipples that had once been mere insect bites had acquired a sudden conical alertness. She thumbed them down and watched them spring back. Was she supposed to cover them? Wear a brassiere? The flesh on her hip bones, too, had risen, thickened, so that her hips sloped elliptically from her waist. All that trouble getting people to ignore her birthmark—and now this? She couldn't very well expect people not to notice when she herself found these fleshy additions somewhat mesmerizing.

Leaving a trail of wet footprints down the carpeted hall, Juliet shoved closed her bedroom door. The room was an embarrassment of pink. The princess wallpaper had, fortunately, been lost for years beneath periodic tables and circulatory-system posters. The mauve carpet was haphazardly tiled with textbooks and magazines.

Juliet threw herself onto her bed. It was Sunday, and the realization that she might see Beau in school the next day made her groan. From downstairs she heard her father and Pearl arguing, interspersed with the unusual sound of a forbidden news broadcast. What would Tuck think, coming home to hear the news blaring? Outside her window, wind rustled the massive dogwood and swept coolly into her room, ballooning the graph-paper calendar tacked above her bed. Juliet stared at the Monday three weeks away— already circled with her blue pen—the first day of eleventh grade.

At the suggestion of her teachers, Juliet was about to skip the second half of tenth grade. She was thrilled. She adored the promise of a fresh start, sometimes reading only the first chapter of a book so that her mind could chart its own course through the drawing rooms of London or the dark, crowded streets of the French Revolution. In this way the story never ended; the characters lived in her mind like the cat in Schrödinger's quantum box, in a glorious state of perpetual possibility. Juliet would, years later, think that as she lay there in her room that night, she, too, existed in perpetual possibility. So much was taking shape around her but only touched her once her door opened and Tuck, all hulking six feet of him, stood in the threshold of her room. The moment she saw his face she knew that something serious had happened. He still wore his football uniform, the knees grass stained, shoulder pads uneven.

"*Jules.*" He walked to her bed and sat on the edge, raking his hand through his thick curls. The sight of him always dazzled Juliet. Where she was awkward and sinewy, her brother was muscular, vigorous. His face was broad and square; his dark-brown eyes were set unusually far apart. He was not handsome in the classical sense, but his robust masculinity drew an endless stream of girlfriends. At seventeen, he was the captain of the football and basketball teams. Walking, pacing—even waving good-bye—could be, for Tuck, an athletic display. He always made her feel safe, but something in his expression at this moment made her heart constrict uncomfortably. While the sound of the radio drifted up from downstairs, he twisted the corner of her coverlet.

"It's the news, isn't it?" she said. "What happened?"

Tuck looked at her. "I don't know what's going on now. But earlier today the Japanese bombed some American ships in Hawaii. It's serious, Jules."

"How many ships?"

"Dozens."

"How many planes attacked?"

"I don't want to give you nightmares."

"Come on, Tuck. You should have seen me this afternoon. I'm a maker of explosive devices. I don't scare easily."

"Hundreds. There were people on the ships, Jules. And nearby. A lot of people. Innocent people."

Juliet remembered an airplane accident she had once seen: when she was nine, riding in the car with her father, a biplane above them suddenly growled and smoked and hurled swiftly, nose first, into the ground; it flipped several times, dropping two of its passengers, and finally crashed into a barn from which people ran screaming. Her father had instructed her to stay in the car while he rushed to the flaming debris, hoping to find someone he could save. For weeks afterward, Juliet had trouble sleeping, recalling all those shrieks for help.

"Are we part of it now?" she asked.

Tuck nodded slowly. "The country is at war."

The words seemed to hang strangely in the air. They had discussed so many things over the years—their mother's death, their father's drinking, Pearl's uncomfortable presence in the house—but nothing of this magnitude.

Tuck tugged off his shoes and lay back beside her, sinking heavily into the mattress. Juliet inched close. The radio downstairs had quieted. Her brother breathed noisily, thoughtfully staring at the ceiling.

"I'm sorry I missed the big experiment."

"It's okay."

"Next Sunday."

"Next Sunday."

Outside the light was fading, and a wintry purple sky sprawled beautifully behind the darkening treetops. For a moment the world seemed utterly silent. Entirely peaceful. The thought of a bombing was wildly improbable. Juliet turned on her side, faced her brother, and drew her knees snugly to her chest.

"We're at war," Tuck said again, as though studying each word. He brought his hands together and slowly thrummed his fingers. His eyes narrowed and his jaw worked itself in a tense circle, and she sensed in his expression something more than anxiety. It was the look he had before a big game: excitement.

Juliet closed her eyes.

$$\left\{\text{ CHAPTER 2 }\right\}$$

TUCK RESIGNED AS football captain right before the state championships. Within weeks, he had quit all sports to devote his time to scrap-metal collection; after school he went from house to house wrestling old washing machines and car parts into the back of a truck. He arrived home in rust-smeared overalls, his palms blotchy with engine oil. At night he volunteered with the Coast Guard Auxiliary, monitoring the sky from the cold decks of shrimp boats. Juliet was proud of her brother but saw less of him than ever before.

Normally she would have thrown herself into her chemistry experiments, but the Science Fair had been canceled. The winter carnival, too, was called off. War efforts gripped the town, and it was understood that every event would serve a patriotic purpose. Blood drives, recruitment rallies. People moved through the gray January streets with a sense of urgency, their coats clutched nervously.

Sitting alone in the school cafeteria, Juliet listened as her classmates rattled off the names of boys from the previous year's senior class who were enlisting. They told excited tales of patriotic eleventh graders from Beaufort and Savannah who, having lied about their ages, were shipping off to Africa at a mere sixteen years old. The German family who owned the bakery, they claimed, had fled town in the middle of the night.

By spring, there were whispers of pregnancies, proposals. Everyone knew which boys had been deemed 4-F, and there were endless speculations as to the reasons for these classifications: asthma, shortness, tendonitis, poor coordination.

A boy named Bobby Lee Fincher, after being declared 4-F, was found on the school steps one morning, his jaw bloodied, his nose broken.

Homo, everyone said. *He was a homo.* It was the first time Juliet had heard the word. And though unsure of what the word meant, she felt sorry for the boy; when she was ten, she'd once had her arm twisted by two girls, but nothing was broken, nothing had bled, and the girls had been sent to the principal. No one was punished for hurting Bobby Lee because he wouldn't say who had done it.

June came, bright and muggy. Globular red roses tangled over trellises. The azaleas and camellias seemed to pulse with life, and in them, Juliet couldn't help but feel, nature was signaling her about excitement ahead.

After school, she walked over to the scrap center, where she had decided to volunteer with Tuck. A vast warehouse once used by shrimpers was devoted to sorting soup cans and chewing-gum wrappers and scraps of aluminum foil. The smell of brine filled the crowded space. Seated on an old fish barrel, Juliet scooped kitchen lard into oil drums alongside girls from her school. A Victrola often played in the corner, which, combined with the clank of cans and the occasional ball of aluminum foil sailing through the air, lent the warehouse a sense of boisterous festivity.

But Juliet never quite knew how to join the fun. She had imagined that moving into the eleventh grade would give her a chance to reinvent herself, to be more outgoing, but first she struggled to figure out how, and then the war had taken hold of everyone's attention, and now it was too late. Her classmates were so accustomed to her reserve that they never thought to include her in their conversations. Instead, Juliet worked diligently, scooping lard faster than anyone else at her table, trying to imagine her next beginning.

In a haze of daydreaming she could lose track of her work for an hour, picturing the gleaming lecture halls and vast research libraries of colleges in Savannah and Charleston. Mr. Licata had given her an old brochure, faded and dog-eared, for a girls' college in Atlanta, which Juliet kept in her bag. On her breaks at the scrap center, while the other girls smoked cigarettes, Juliet studied the photographs of the dormitories and the dome-topped Science Hall, imagining life after high school, a life surrounded by people like her, a life where she could meet *professors*—the word quickened her heart.

One afternoon, while Juliet was studying her brochure, Beau Conroy walked into the warehouse. He was holding hands with a cheerleader named Patty, her hair swept back in a gingham kerchief. Over a pink blouse she wore belted gray overalls. She wasn't particularly pretty, as far as the cheerleaders went, but her earlobes and neck glinted with gold, and she leaned flirtatiously into Beau as they both surveyed the center. When Patty pointed out a space where they could work, he kissed her knuckles.

"Hey, Jules, you seen a ghost?" Tuck had come by to say hello. Juliet still hadn't told him about kissing Beau. She sensed that if she told him, he would only say that Beau was a jerk, that he had tricked her and played a mean game. Juliet didn't want it to be true. She wanted her first kiss, she deserved her first kiss; it was the only thing of consequence that had happened to her in months. And having bent and bowed her memory of the encounter, it had become something in those long lonely days she could cling to.

Juliet stared at Beau and the cheerleader and set down her lard scoop. "It's hot, Tuck. I'm tired. Can we please go home already?"

"Rinse up, the both of you," Pearl said when Juliet and Tuck trudged up the porch after work. "You look like you stepped out of a coal mine."

Side by side at the kitchen sink, Juliet soaped the waxy traces of grease from her fingers and Tuck lathered his forearms, scrubbing off the engine oil, playfully elbowing Juliet out of his way. A rainbow soap bubble floated between them, and Tuck stabbed it with his finger.

They settled themselves at the dinner table, where conversation, at their father's request, was to extend beyond the topic of the war. They spoke about radio plays and the new Jimmy Dorsey songs, or about which vegetables were faring well in the garden. They examined the first tomato of the season, passing it around the table, guessing at its weight, then cutting it into wedges so they could each take a dripping bite.

"I actually had a letter from Senator Maybank," Pearl began, serving their father a thick slice of glistening ham. "The senator said he is deeply concerned about safety regulations in the textile mills. . . ."

The overhead fan stirred the window's gauzy curtains, thick gray moths battered the glass, and Juliet could see in the distance the flashing arcs and bands of the night's first fireflies. The clock on the mantel ticked slowly. Soon it would be her turn to describe her day, but what could she report except that she had been scooping lard all afternoon, looking at a college brochure that seemed of interest to no one else, and that her "first kiss" had forgotten her in favor of a cheerleader.

"Pop, I'd like to borrow the car tomorrow," said Tuck, wiping tomato juice from his chin. "To drive to Charleston."

"You taking Myrna somewhere?" Myrna was Tuck's latest girl-friend.

"Actually," said Tuck, "I wanted to take Juliet to the movies. A matinee." He turned to Juliet. "You free?"

They left early the next morning, riding with the windows open, the salt air tangling Juliet's hair. Normally stagnant, the air in motion had a palpable thickness. It pressed against Juliet's face. Past the intercoastal bridge, Tuck leaned into the backseat, rummaging through his bag. "Jules, take the wheel."

"What?"

"I can't steer with my knees!"

As Juliet reached for the wheel, the car lurched before she steadied her grip. Behind her she heard a snap and hiss; then Tuck swung himself back into the front seat and waved a bottle of Coca-Cola. "Beverages!" he announced.

The movie was *Our Town*. It surprised Juliet; she had never seen anything in which the characters spoke right to you, and she liked it. But Tuck, who had leaned far back in his seat as soon as they arrived in the theater, as though the movie had to impress him before he would sit up straight, rolled his eyes as they left the theater. "I wouldn't have driven all this way if I knew it was gonna be depressing!"

"It was thought-provoking," said Juliet.

"The last thing I need are more thoughts. I need ice cream. Want some ice cream?"

"Tuck." She stopped walking. "Are you about to assassinate me? This whole day has a distinct last-supper feel to it."

"Vanilla or chocolate?"

"Chocolate," she conceded. "But if you offer me walnuts I'm going to have to make a run for it."

He bought them each a cone and found a small table by the window of the parlor.

"So I've got something to tell you," he said. "Right after my birthday"—he leaned across the table—"I'm going to Fort Branley."

"Fort Branley," she repeated flatly. "You're *enlisting*?"

"I've got the papers right here. I wanted you to be the first to know."

Juliet felt a sickening disorientation; Tuck would be leaving. For months, perhaps years. The idea horrified her. And yet in his elaborate display of affection, in letting her know that she was the first in whom he was confiding, she felt the hypnotic lure of his undivided attention.

"That's wonderful," she said, staring at the papers but not reading them.

"They'd draft me soon enough anyway, but I've got to get *in* there. *Now.*" He thumped his fist on the table, and Juliet forced herself to nod. "I knew you'd understand," he said. But he looked away, aware of his lie.

Juliet's ice cream dripped onto her hand and he reached over with his napkin.

"And I'll need your help," he said. "On the Papa and Pearl front."

They rode home in silence. Juliet was frightened by the violence of her own emotions. She suddenly hated her brother for his decision; it seemed, if not exactly selfish, so very neglectful of her feelings that she wondered briefly at his love for her. His departure would dismantle her life. He was a *piece* of her, of the way she thought about and planned her days, even if she was, as she long suspected, of far less consequence to him. What would a night at home be like without Tuck down the hall? How would a morning feel without him at the breakfast table? What would it be like to go months without talking to him, while he gallivanted through the world, facing endless new experiences? They would become different people, mere strangers with a vague shared memory of childhood. Or what if he got hurt? Juliet's hands shook in her lap. She was accustomed to hiding her feelings, but she had never before faced such cavernous, looming loss. She stared out the window, wishing they would never reach home.

As they finally stepped from the car, Tuck hurried around and closed the car door after her. He drew her close in a hug. Juliet wanted to hit him. After all these years, he understood his power over her and was using it.

"Here we go." He exhaled sharply and opened the front door.

Their father and Pearl looked up from the dining table. "How was the picture?"

Tuck sat and began to describe the movie. Juliet took her customary seat to her father's right. It seemed Tuck had missed large portions of the story, and in his nervousness struggled to recall the details. In between sentences, he ate ravenously and set his eyes on their father. Juliet, too, watched the exacting and deliberate way in which their father halved his green beans with a steak knife. For the first time she longed for his sternness, for his uncompromising austerity; she wanted him to defeat Tuck.

When Tuck finished his account of the film, he fell silent. Their father turned to Pearl: "Now tell us about your meeting at the Ladies Auxiliary."

"Well, we're planning to make packages for the troops next week. On Wednesday they want us to bring any baked goods and knitted socks. I was going to bake some butter pecan cookies tomorrow. Juliet, would you help me?"

"I'm going," Tuck blurted out, pushing back in his chair so that for a moment it seemed as though he were announcing his departure from the table, "to the front."

Their father set down his fork and knife and surveyed the arrangement of the dinnerware and place mats, as though bodies might soon be tangled across the table.

"Rommel's wreaking havoc across Africa," Tuck continued, his face tightening. "The U-boats are demolishing our ships, the—"

"I read the newspaper," their father said.

"It's the right thing to do," Tuck continued. "I'm not going to hide out and wait for them to draft me. Not when I could help bring this war to an end sooner. Juliet understands. And she supports me."

"I do," Juliet said to her plate.

"*The right thing.* You realize, of course, that grenades have no sense of justice. That bullets and bayonets care nothing for morality. Being right doesn't protect you from having your brain blown to bits."

"Tuck, have you considered," Pearl said softly, "serving as a noncombatant, like your father did? We support the war effort, but there are more sensible ways to help."

"No disrespect to Papa, but in the words of FDR, I would rather die on my feet than live on my knees."

"You are quoting a man who can barely walk," their father said.

"Pop, come on. I'm a quarterback, not a doctor. Look at me." Tuck stood and opened his arms, trying to show his breadth. "You know exactly where I should be."

"It is the hallmark of youth," their father said, "to suffer an inexplicable and desperate urge to die. It is the hallmark of adulthood to feel a desperate urge to live. It seems you are decided in your course; I only hope that you will be an adult in it."

Juliet's heart sank.

It was a solemn few weeks while Tuck prepared to leave, and Juliet numbly accompanied her brother on every errand, sometimes sitting on the floor of his room for hours as he sorted through belongings.

It was only when their car pulled into the bus depot that muggy July day, when the fact of his departure became so sharply unbearable, that Juliet mustered the courage to say, "This is stupid. He shouldn't go."

Her father and Tuck turned around in the front seats with gentle pity, and Pearl, beside her, set her arm on Juliet's back and said, "Sweetheart, we knew this would be hard."

Their condescension infuriated her, and Juliet felt, finally, on the verge of an outburst; the sadness and anger, gathering for weeks, rose to the surface, so visibly, in fact, that her father's expression turned quickly to displeasure. "Your brother has made a decision, and he is standing by it. So we will stand by him. That is the sole way to proceed. Come on, we'll cook in here."

The others stepped from the car and thumped shut the doors, leaving Juliet alone in the back, until finally she opened her door and walked around to the trunk, where Tuck was heaving out his swollen duffel. Though it was well beyond his strength, their father insisted on carrying it, and they all moved to where the brown bus was parked. The pavement smelled of wet tar, peculiarly sweet and fresh, and the air glimmered hazily; the clouds overhead were long and rippled, as though the sky were a reflection of itself in water. It all felt entirely unreal, dreamlike.

"Oh, my brave, brave boy," said Pearl, who had worn her yellow church outfit. She reached into her purse and held out a tissue-wrapped parcel. "I lost my husband, years ago, in the Great War, when he was your age. . . ." Her hand was trembling, and she turned to Juliet's father, as though he might be able to explain her feelings, but he only put an arm around her shoulders; this seemed to fortify her, and she sucked back sniffles with a proud toss of the head. "I would like for you to have this."

Tuck unwrapped the gift: the white glove Pearl had worn when shaking Eleanor Roosevelt's hand.

"Pearl," he said softly.

"It's the only protection I can offer you."

Tuck laughed. "I'll be the only guy in the army with a woman's glove."

"Don't try to joke your way out of this moment, young man. Take it, and put it somewhere safe."

Tuck rewrapped the gift and placed it in the pocket of his shirt. "I'll bring it back."

"Indeed you will," answered Pearl.

Tuck beckoned Juliet forward. "Come on, no sulking. You finally get the bathroom to yourself!"

Juliet struggled to smile. "You won't forget us. . . ."

"Of course I will." He grinned. "But I'll feel bad about it."

He tilted his head to the side so that they stood almost face-to-face. Then he opened his arms and pulled her close. It was a real hug, without guile, and for the first time she could feel his sadness. Juliet sunk into him and closed her eyes. He held her tight and kissed her scalp, and they stood like that for several seconds. When finally his hold began to slacken, Juliet felt such immeasurable loss that she pulled quickly away and swallowed the knot in her throat.

Their father stepped forward. "Write when you get there, son."

"Don't expect Shakespeare. But I'll put a pen to paper."

"Remember, no foolish heroics. I spent two years piecing boys like you back together. Trust me, a bullet is bigger than you."

Tuck saluted him: "Aye, aye, Captain."

Their father hoisted the duffel and arranged the straps over Tuck's shoulders, testing their evenness; Juliet remembered how, years earlier, he would fasten Tuck's schoolbag onto his back each morning. It seemed so long ago, part of an entire life now disbanding in the heat, molecule by molecule.

Tuck got in line to board. He wore a light-blue dress shirt, bright against his summer tan, and had sheared off his curls the night before so that his head now looked square and somewhat severe. He seemed older. The man before him turned to chat, and Tuck engaged intently, appearing to forget that Juliet and their father and Pearl were there. Tuck nodded, his hands moving in an elaborate description. The size of a fish? Something he'd hauled in for scrap collection? Juliet desperately wanted to know. The man smiled and Tuck laughed—a full-bodied laugh that caused him to readjust his bag. She wanted him to turn back and share the joke; she wanted him to tell the man about his wonderful sister standing right over there. But already it seemed as if Tuck had entered a new world. He belonged to the people on the bus, to the people he would meet in the months and years to come. Juliet's head felt heavy, loose on her shoulders.

He stepped forward, turned briefly, and flashed them an apologetic smile before he shook his duffel high on his shoulders and stepped onto the bus; that was it, a smile. It was difficult to see through the windows, but Juliet continued to wave to where she thought Tuck was standing, uncertain whether he was waving back, or even looking. She licked the tears from her mouth.

CHAPTER 3

December 1942
North Africa

Dear Gang,

It was a lonely Christmas without you; I hung the photos from home on the tree and our squad made ornaments from empty ration tins. Thank you for the Nelson's soap and the knit socks; they're getting plenty of use. I wish I could have sent something back.

We're still encamped in the same place. The air is dry and the sun bright. Dozens of cats wander in and out of the tents all day long; I've never seen so many cats in my life! Apparently the KP (Kitchen Patrol) went soft and gave them some SPAM for Christmas, and now they won't ever leave. It's an odd thing to wake up in a tent in a strange country to the sound of endless meowing.

Jules, you asked how things are organized. Well, the best I can explain it is—the division is like a city, made up of maybe ten thousand soldiers, the company is your neighborhood, the platoon is your block, and your squad, well, that's your family. Those are the nine guys you count on to drag you back to safety if you get hit—those are the guys you talk into the night with, pitch tents with, dig trenches with, pray with. I could tell you the names of the streets they grew up on, their favorite colors, their mothers' birthdays. There isn't a thing you don't share, even if you don't want to. All in all, I admire the hell out of these guys.

Sergeant Bruce McKnight, the head of our squad, is a Princeton man. His father was a lumberjack, his grandfather a coal miner, so his intellectual bent makes him something of a family exception—and he seems determined to earn stripes while he's here. He's the only one who eats his chow with table manners, setting his knife and fork just so on the edge of his tin, and we're all trying to follow so he doesn't think we're barbarians. Glenn Mooney, the best rifleman in the company, carries little clippers dangling from his pack and snips off leaves almost every day to press into a book. Rakowski writes poetry—and I'm no expert but I think it's god-awful. I've managed to get a bit of a makeshift football team going here, and there's a guy named Geronimo—a genuine Indian—who manages one hell of a tackle.

Sorry so much got blacked out in my other letters—I'm trying this time to focus on our rec time so you don't have to wonder about all those crossed-out lines.

Nothing to worry about, as usual. I'm fast on my feet, and luck seems to be following me so far. I keep the white glove with me at all times.

> *Miss you all.*
> *Love,*
> *Tucker*

Since he had shipped overseas, Tuck's letters arrived once or twice a week, but Juliet wrote to him every night. Throughout the day she found herself composing snippets, descriptions of the Victory garden or of a classmate, anything that offered a witty or poetic phrase; she jotted these bits on the edge of the newspaper or the back of the telephone book, tearing off the scraps to shove into her pocket and carefully reassemble on her bed at night, working hard to present her thoughts in a precise and interesting manner. She hoped Tuck would see that even though she was stuck at home, she, too, was maturing.

How will I describe this to Tuck? she asked herself throughout the day, trying to fill the long, dark gaps that had opened since his departure. Almost every notable moment of her life had been coupled with the anticipation of relating it to Tuck, so that now, finding a quarter on the sidewalk or sighting a zebra swallowtail in their yard left her feeling empty.

When life in Charlesport felt particularly dreary, or when more than a week lapsed between Tuck's letters, she would sometimes think back to the day at the bus depot: a simple vehicle had carried Tuck to Fort Branley, and from there he had stormed into the world beyond. The globe seemed divided into Charlesport and everywhere else, and while the latter had always lurked at the fringes of Juliet's mind, it had seemed a far-off and forbidden place, fortified and gated. But the gate had now swung open, and what lay beyond enticed her. Juliet had begun to look into colleges far from home, in Delaware and Massachusetts, and she tentatively researched a nursing program. All of which she confessed to Tuck in her letters, though from the cursory postscript on his reply, he clearly had doubts about her intent to leave home.

Don't forget the blue suitcase! he wrote.

When Juliet was younger, on long, muggy days, if Tuck was off playing football late and her father was at his office, she had sometimes packed her battered blue suitcase and left notes explaining, in courteous detail, that she was running away. She'd bought the case at a thrift shop because it held a dazzling collection of rocks and seashells that someone—*A. Burney,* the tag indicated—had assembled over what must have been decades. She had immediately transferred the gypsum and soapstone and agate onto the shelves above her desk, each item fronted by a typewritten label; the suitcase, however, remained beneath her bed, and when she felt forsaken or had fought with her father, she would stuff it with her belongings and set out into the warm night. Twice she ventured to the corner, the heavy suitcase bumping her knees, but grew frightened and set down the bag. When Tuck came walking home, he called out, "Excellent idea! Where are we going?"

The second time he opened her suitcase on the sidewalk, puzzling over her Latin dictionary, atlas, and magnifying glass, explaining that she had packed so poorly—was she running off to catch butterflies?!—they would have to go back home. He did not comment on a string-tied packet of their mother's wartime letters to their father; however, back home he lay down beside her until she fell asleep.

But Juliet was growing increasingly certain of her intent to leave Charlesport; she did not want to be as Tuck had once described her—a girl who curiously opened every door but never walked through one. As she fell asleep each night, she stared at the map that had replaced her calendar above her bed, stuck with blue pushpins marking what she deduced of Tuck's movements in North Africa, wondering about the sounds and sights of all those new cities.

By late spring, as her graduation approached, radio reports said that Axis troops in North Africa had surrendered. Juliet brightened at this news, imagining that Tuck would finally be sent home; instead, a letter from him arrived suggesting that his division was preparing for a major offensive in another region, and that it might be a while before he could write again.

This marked the dwindling of her brother's correspondence. His early letters had been pages long, filled with descriptions of encampment life and squad mates—so much so that Juliet had grown jealous of his new family. She felt as if she knew them all, these men who had become like brothers to him. But when Tuck finally wrote again, he said little about the other soldiers; his letters, in general, grew shorter and he was distinctly less playful in his language. After nine months overseas, his letters had become mere paragraphs, somber and cryptic.

Gang,

Rain every day and Sergeant McKnight and Geronimo have come down with the flu. Rakowski is teaching me piano on a keyboard he drew on a piece of paper. At night, in the dark, he hums the song, and then shows me the notes when it's light.

Sometimes, people aren't what you think.

We live in holes, dirt creeping into every sock and collar. Bombs all night. It sounds like the drummer in the marching band went mad.

Tucker

Her father turned the page over and set it on the dining table— it was Tuck's first letter in months. "That seems to be all for now."

Her father poured a glass of sherry and looked out the window. Gray hairs dusted his part, and his eyebrows had thinned. "Jules, what is going on with you these days?" he asked, but he did not turn from the window.

"I have an interesting brochure here from a college in Sweet Briar, Virginia."

Busy with various patriotic committees and campaigns, her father and Pearl had been of little assistance in her college research. Juliet had sent away for the paperwork on her own and filled out seven applications for schools all over the East Coast, including a nursing school in Savannah—all of which had recently accepted her.

"Terrific," her father said to the window, ignoring the brochure.

Juliet pulled the college materials back toward her and the table fell silent. Pearl and her father began eating the zucchini casserole made with the last of their weekly butter ration.

"He's in the thick of it now," her father muttered. "I don't like it."

Pearl raised her hand for silence. "How is the scrap sorting, Juliet?"

"Excellent," she said, though she had stopped going weeks earlier, tired of sitting in the corner, her hands slick with grease, while
across the room other girls folded gum wrappers into miniature
airplanes and primped for their evening dates.

But for her father and Pearl, the war was all that mattered now,
and whatever Juliet achieved in school or hoped for her future
would be lost in the discussion of events in Tunisia and Sardinia.
US bombers were raiding Sicily in advance of an invasion. It was
announced that children had been evacuated from the Channel
ports in France.

"I'm going to be a nurse," Juliet suddenly said, though she had
not realized her decision until she spoke the words. "They're setting up an accelerated program in Savannah, like the Cadet Nurse
Corps they're talking about. I can be certified in a year and genuinely help with the war. College will always be there."

Her father looked at her with startled affection; he touched his
heart. "Like your mother," he said softly.

A crooked smile lit Pearl's face. "That would be quite something, Juliet."

She arrived in Savannah in June, two weeks after high school graduation. Her sixty classmates were plucky, compassionate girls, the
daughters of bakers and mechanics, girls who could mend clothes
and tie slipknots and mix gimlets over a dormitory bathroom sink.
Juliet spent her days learning intravenous drips, sutures, wound
dressing, and surgical assistance, and, in her favorite class, Patient
Encounters, students role-played nurse and patient under the
supervision of Head Nurse Mercer; somehow Juliet always ended
up with a girl playing the patient a bit crazy, pulling at her hair
and screaming for morphine. To Nurse Mercer's delight, Juliet was
entirely unmoved by the hysterics and delivered her line, "We must

wait until the doctor returns to determine the proper dosage," with such genuine dispassion that even the girl playing patient finally said, "Jeez, you don't rattle easily."

Returning to her dorm room at night, Juliet soaked her aching feet in a metal pan of warm water and worked lotion into her palms and elbows. Despite her exhaustion, and despite the fact that she had not received a letter since starting school, she wouldn't go to sleep until she had written a full page to Tuck.

The school days stretched and folded into one another, punctuated by the fifteenth of every month, when Nurse Mercer would hold a party in her office for the five girls getting degrees. Over lemon cupcakes and white wine, the graduating nurses tipsily boasted of their plans to zip straight off to basic training and then ship overseas. Some had already bought cameras and leather travel journals. This always produced in Juliet a tinge of envy. She'd be seventeen at graduation, so she would have to wait to enlist. Until then, she could work only in a civilian hospital, probably somewhere in Georgia or South Carolina.

She still caught a bus back to Charlesport every Friday in time for dinner. Although she was always momentarily struck by sadness when she saw that the entry table held no new V-mails, her father and Pearl and the house itself were still *some* connection to Tuck. Juliet would sit at the dinner table, describing her classes and instructors, imagining Tuck across from her, his hair wet from his postpractice shower, ravenously shoveling his food; she tried to anticipate the moments in her narrative when he would have laughed or rolled his eyes.

And then, a week shy of Christmas, when Juliet returned home for dinner, she noticed that Pearl—who spent most evenings on the porch rocker knitting socks for Tuck, and who usually called out a greeting long before Juliet had even reached the walkway—was nowhere to be seen. Inside, her father sat by the coffee table, staring at his chessboard; but the board was empty and pieces lay scattered across the floor. A white bishop, stranded beneath the window, rocked gently over the floorboards, caught in a breeze. As she closed the door behind her, her father did not look up.

"Papa, are you okay?"

At the sound of her voice, the kitchen door swung open and Pearl entered with an apron hanging limply from her neck. Behind her, the kitchen was dark, and she looked at Juliet's father, shaking her head.

"Delaying won't help anything, Philippe."

Her father patted at his pockets until from the side of his trousers he extracted a folded beige piece of paper.

"That says nothing, Philippe."

Pearl led Juliet to the sofa and drew in an enormous breath. "This afternoon we received a telegram from the War Department informing us that Tuck . . . has gone missing in action."

"Missing," repeated Juliet. Her mouth felt suddenly dry. She had heard about such cases, had tried, at times, to prepare herself for such an eventuality, but now her thoughts were scampering, trying to make sense of this word that seemed to say everything and nothing. "So this means he's a *prisoner*?" she asked.

Pearl cast her eyes at Juliet's father, who gazed at his empty chessboard. "They can't say what happened," said Pearl. "The telegram means they simply have no idea."

"Prisoner is a decent guess," her father said.

Pearl glanced all around the room, as though somewhere in the corner or behind the sofa she might find assistance. Finally, she cleared her throat. "It is important that we not give up hope, but also that we begin to accept the possibility that we might not see Tuck again."

"They said *missing*. They tell you when they're killed. It's called KIA. I hear these things in school. I'm not living on the moon."

"I understand," Pearl conceded.

"So he's still *alive,* but missing."

"Alive indeed," her father said emptily, and Juliet saw that a tear had welled in his eye.

"Let me see that." Juliet grabbed the paper and studied the words. It was a Western Union telegram, with a few sentences typed in purple. Tuck had been missing in Italy since November 11. "If other information or further details are received," it ended, "you will be promptly notified."

"I know this is frightening," Pearl said. "I know you think I am being cruel, you think I am being heartless. You want me to tell you that everything will be okay. You think *that* is love, *that* is kindness. So that you can grasp at little shreds of hope for years, always listening for the doorbell, always feeling your heart pound as you approach the mailbox, thinking, maybe today, then fighting back tears as you go to sleep each night because you still know nothing. . . . Child, I am telling you a very ugly truth to save you from unending despair. Let us slowly begin to shed our tears, to grieve your brother." At this, Pearl set her hand on Juliet's arm but Juliet pulled away.

"Don't go digging my brother's grave just because you lost your husband."

There was a moment of silence. Then Pearl stood, smoothing her apron. "You're right, I am sure he is fine," she said, with such determined flatness that it scared Juliet more than anything else.

"I'll be in my room," Juliet said quietly, heading slowly up the staircase. All feeling, all life seemed to be draining out of her. In the hallway, she opened her brother's door. The room was dark and shrunken. She heeled off her shoes and padded across the carpet where a year and a half earlier she had sprawled on her stomach watching Tuck remove a picture of her from a glass frame, set it between two folded shirts, and place it carefully at the top of his duffel.

"We'll still be inseparable," he'd said with a grin.

Juliet now climbed into his bed and lay very still.

* * *

Juliet remained at home for several days, seated at her desk, rereading Tuck's letters. The paper gave her comfort—he'd touched those pages—and his descriptions of weather and food made her smile; she could hear his voice clearly. And as she came to the end of each page, Tuck felt entirely alive. Juliet was certain that if Tuck had been killed, she would have sensed some absence, some loss— a glass would have shattered in her hand, her chest would have cramped. A devastation of such magnitude simply couldn't occur without a person noticing it.

Still, the idea of what he might be enduring terrified her. Her mind conjured up images of dank prison cells and rusty shackles. Was he hungry? Sleep deprived? Laboring beneath a ruthless sun? How long before he was set free? And how long before she heard from him again?

By the time Juliet returned to school, she had determined to bury her worries in the daily muck of bandaging and suturing. The first morning back, striding into the dormitory's pale-blue common room, she shrugged aside questions as to where she'd been— "Juliet, we were worried!"—believing that to mention the telegram would only etch it further into reality. She didn't want pity. She didn't want concern. She wanted to live in the world *before* the telegram, the world where Tuck was safe. So fierce was her resolve not to discuss her brother that she was momentarily annoyed when she spotted a letter from him that night on her dorm-room pillow.

Hope surging, she tore open the letter, but when she noticed the date her hands went slack. One month before the telegram. Juliet almost threw the letter down before the strangeness of it being addressed to her at school in Savannah—where Tuck had never written—registered.

Dearest Jules,

It's late here and I'm the only one awake except for the sentry and I wanted more than anything to write to you. It's hard to say much in these letters, to tell the truth about anything, because anything that says too much about our movements or would lower morale will get struck right out. But so much has been buzzing through my head, and I didn't know who else to talk to. Being over here has changed the way I think about so many things, and what I think about people, about myself. I used to believe in everybody's fundamental goodness, and then came the Nazis, who seemed fundamentally evil. I never really believed in God, the idea of a God who made us and everything and watches over us, but now I think maybe we're the ones responsible for making God. We can create justice if we make the right choices. But you have to keep making those right choices, even when it's hard and scary, and it's so easy to lose your way.

What am I saying? I don't know. Do you understand? Is it too much to think we can steer ourselves toward a better world? I thought that's what I came over here for, to get the world back on course, to get history right, but sometimes I feel like the world is steering me.

I wonder what you're doing, Jules. It's been so long since we talked.

Sometimes when I'm scared I remember holding you in my arms when you were little. I remember the way you looked up at me, the trust in your face. That was the greatest feeling in the world. The memory keeps me calm, it keeps me safe. It's why I'm here, to protect you and everything that hasn't yet gone to rot.

I'd really like you to pay Miss Van Effing a visit if you get a chance, show her this letter. Okay? We can't keep Raven

Point a secret anymore. I know what happened to Cher Ami.
We never should have let him go.
                                        Love,
                                        Tuck

Juliet studied the handwriting—uneven, the end of each line sloping downward. Her eyes returned to his final sentences. *Pay Miss Van Effing a visit . . . show her this letter . . .*

What on earth was he talking about?

She set the letter in her lap and gripped her bed. She had the same feeling she once had standing on the prow of a boat, when the ocean unexpectedly surged. After all those dutifully composed letters detailing encampments, after all those months of silence—this. It was confusing; he *sounded* confused. Tuck wasn't one for pessimism, and he wasn't prone to rambling. The only thing that was clear was that he was reaching out for help. The trouble was, she couldn't for the life of her think what it was he wanted her to do. There was no Miss Van Effing to visit. There was nothing she could do at Raven Point. And what did he mean about the secret? And about Cher Ami?

Juliet tried to imagine her brother there in her small dormitory room, seated in the wooden rocker. When he was seven, he had fallen from a tree in their yard, and she remembered now the wild and desperate look on his face as he'd shrieked for help.

She sat down at her desk, pulled the chain on her lamp, and extracted a small envelope from her drawer. The birth certificate was soft, grayish; she stared at it for a moment and then, with an eraser, gently rubbed at the final digit in her birth date until enough of it had vanished so that with a pencil she could change the 6 to a 5.

Then she crouched beside her bed and pulled out her blue suitcase.

PART II

{ 1944 }

CHAPTER 4

JULIET STOOD PERFECTLY still, listening to the scrape of the saw; small metal teeth were tearing at brittle bone. The boy on the operating table couldn't have been more than nineteen. His eyes were closed, his face as pale as alabaster. A beauty mark punctuated his right cheek.

"The limb, Nurse Dufresne."

Juliet grabbed the leg by the ankle, where it was coldest—warm flesh still gave her the willies—and wrangled it across her forearms, making sure its hairs didn't rub between her cuffs and gloves. She hurried to the corner and set the limb in a pail clogged with legs and feet. Jesus, when was someone going to empty the trash?

Back at the operating table, she avoided looking at the boy. It seemed wrong to stare at a patient splayed so vulnerably unless her immediate task required it.

"Blood," pronounced Bernice, the nurse anesthetist, as she plucked the ether cloth from the patient. "These two pints won't cut it." Bernice watched supplies like a sailor watching weather. She was short and pale and kept her red hair cut like a man's. The longtime nurse at a school for wayward boys, she had the rigid stare of a woman prepared, at any moment, to ruler-smack your knuckles.

"I'll go check the fridge," said Juliet, peeling off her gloves. Outside, she loosened her mask to suck in the damp air. Another breath of gangrenous rot and she'd faint.

She gazed out at the mud-splattered city of tents. The field hospital had been pitched thirty miles north of Rome. Having finally claimed the bottom half of Italy, the US Fifth Army was pushing north of the capital, toward the Arno. Along the mountainous route, the Germans had fortified nearly every church and farmhouse, fighting intensely. Further complicating matters were the Ombrone and Cecina—two small rivers—and an elaborate lattice of gulches and gullies, heavily mined.

That morning, the 120-bed hospital had reached capacity, but casualties were still arriving. In the warm drizzle, a double row of litters snaked nearly a hundred yards beyond the receiving tent; Juliet groaned. On shift for more than forty-eight hours, she was about to collapse. Her back ached, her feet were blistered, and her arms were numb from shaking plasma and saline. And when had she last eaten? A deep hunger splintered her stomach, but breaks were only to change clothes (the sight of blood-soaked nurses panicked patients). Just as well. Anything in her stomach might come up during an amputation.

Lowering her head against the rain, she trudged toward the Sterilizing Tent, where her tent mate, "Glenda Texas," stood rattling a steaming pan of needles and scalpels. Over her mouth Glenda had knotted a red silk scarf, a shiny crimson triangle that lent her the appearance of a glamorous bandit. Glenda had taken acting classes and liked to refer to herself as an ingénue.

"Sugar, you tell them they can have their supplies in five. I'm not playing any games with gas gangrene. And tell that hotshot new surgeon this ain't the Mayo Clinic; if he wants to use every last instrument on every patient, he can get his knives from the mess."

Juliet tugged open the fridge. "Only *eight* cans left?"

"I told them to get blood from those prisoners before they shipped them to evac. But Mother Hen sang on about protocol." Mother Hen was their nickname for Chief Nurse Madge Henfield. "Like protocol has any place in this bedlam? And she won't let the staff donate until the incomings quiet down. Not that I'm volunteering. Delicate constitution."

"Too delicate to help with these cans?"

"Not at all, sugar." Glenda Texas flicked off the steam sterilizer and stifled a yawn. "Double double boil and trouble." She tilted the pan, and the needles rattled onto a tray. With one quick yank she loosened her scarf, revealing two bubblegum-pink lips.

Despite Glenda's size, her claims of a delicate constitution, and her holding the tray in one hand, she hoisted the cans with ease. "Every time I carry these on a different side. That way my figure'll stay balanced. Have you noticed Mother Hen's right arm is twice the size of her left? Like it belongs to Joe Louis. Two years lugging packs and bedrolls and plasma cans, she should have thought it through. Anticipation and imagination, my mama always said."

Outside, in the gray afternoon light, they carried the blood across the muddy field. A sudden shriek came from the surgical tent and Juliet dropped the cans.

"I'll bet right now you're wishing you were back in Naples!" Glenda laughed as Juliet wrestled the cans off the slippery ground. "Sug, I gotta say, it takes a real nutter to request a transfer to the front."

Juliet smiled with embarrassment; she could hardly argue.

In late May she had arrived in Italy just before the Americans took Rome. She had been working at a general hospital in Naples when she heard that the Fifth Army was being reorganized for a northern assault. Hoping to get close to Tuck's division, she requested a transfer, which—Glenda was right; few wanted to work the front lines—was readily granted. But leaving Naples had been surprisingly upsetting—Tuck had once been stationed there, and each night Juliet reread his letters from the city, staring out her dormitory window, wondering if he'd gazed upon the same jagged skyline. She wandered the greasy cobblestone streets, hoping she might, by accident or fate, retrace some of his steps, catch a wisp or shadow of him. But her attempts to get practical information— *If someone is declared missing, how often are they found? Where do Germans take their prisoners? How do you find out who, exactly, reported someone missing?*—had met with such uniform failure that she felt she had no choice but to transfer. If not British, South African, or Polish, her patients in Naples were from entirely different divisions or had idiotically, if not intentionally, succumbed to gonorrhea before reaching the front. Any hope of getting information about Tuck depended on her catching up to where his unit was fighting.

In the Surgical Tent, all four operating tables were in use. Bernice, administering drop ether with clocklike precision, spoke without looking up: "Major Decker needs you both to work the line. Pre-op is swamped. And surgeries need to be on the tables before dark. We're low on flashlight batteries. And locate Father MacDougal."

As they left, Glenda whispered, "Our chaplain only administers last rites to bottles of bourbon."

In their tent, Juliet quickly wrapped a blanket over her soiled shirt and Glenda spritzed her with perfume. "In this job, we've gotta look like sunshine and smell like roses." Flicking open a compact, Glenda spoke to her own reflection. "It's the only thing that makes the boys feel safe. Once they see the women going to seed, that's when they know things are, well, going to seed. And what a smile from us can't cure"—she snapped the mirror closed and grabbed a pack of cigarettes and a flask—"a little nip and puff'll remedy quickly enough."

Outside, men lay quietly on litters, their jackets pinned with the battalion surgeon's brief prognoses. Glenda moved to one side of the line, and Juliet to the other, where she scanned each man for trembling hands, a sweating forehead, dilated pupils, blue lips; with a quick touch of their wrists, she checked their pulses.

"Sorry you have to wait out here," she said awkwardly. Juliet had yet to master the motherly tones of the more experienced nurses.

Apologizing for bringing her out in the rain, the men asked nothing, not even how much longer they had to wait, perhaps having learned that answers, on the few occasions they were given, were rarely encouraging. Their only request was that Juliet pull off their boots, which she did, releasing the fierce smell of wet wool.

One man, his boots shredded at the ankles, turned his eyes away in embarrassment and said, "I was stuck in a ditch for three days. Lost my platoon and couldn't move. I ate up all the grass around me."

Juliet slipped him a ration bar, saying, "Can't promise this'll taste much better."

His soft, gravelly laugh gave Juliet a brief sense of triumph before she moved along. Unless he was on the verge of death, she couldn't give him more than a minute's attention, a rule Glenda seemed to know well, outpacing Juliet as she offered each man a quick sip from her flask.

"Nurse Dufresne, you found the action!"

The boy on the next litter stared expectantly at Juliet with bloodshot eyes, but she couldn't place him. Dirt and exhaustion blurred every face, so that sometimes Juliet had the unsettled feeling that the same injured soldier was arriving every few minutes.

"Second Lieutenant Munson," he offered. "Your old truck mate! Don't tell me you've forgotten me!"

Juliet had traveled north from Naples in a truck of replacement GIs, forty new arrivals only a year or two older than she was. During the noisy, bawdy ride several rounds of "Der Führer" had been sung, and three separate poker games played. Only at the end of the ride, when Private Bledsoe whispered, "Damn the royal flush! We coulda been great," did Juliet learn she'd been wagered in all three games, a revelation that sent her awkwardly hurrying from the truck.

"Munson—of course I remember," lied Juliet. Most nurses, when they forgot a patient's name, laid it on thick with endearments: *How we doin' today, honey? Time for your pills, sweetheart?* But Juliet thought it disrespectful to speak that way to a soldier, and didn't want to sound like a cocktail waitress. "How are you feeling, Lieutenant Munson?" she asked, somewhat stiffly.

"A hell of a lot better than when five Jerries were firing at me." He touched the gauze around his forehead, and one end came free, brushing his nose. His nose was broad and flat, and there was an earnestness to his face that she liked.

"Here, let me."

"I've at least decided on my campaign platform: I'm going to propose legislation to have soldiers paid by the bullet. Whaddaya think? Would I get your vote?" Ah, she remembered now—the boy who planned to run as a write-in candidate for the Kansas senate. On the truck they had called him "the Senator."

"Bullets they shoot or bullets shot at them?" Juliet asked, glancing at his tag—*gunshot wound to thigh*—and checking his field dressing. "Munson, you've practically got a lead doubloon in there, but these surgeons are miracle workers. You'll be good as new in no time."

His face tightened as he fought back a wave of pain. "Double pay for bullets that get shot at them," he huffed, "and triple pay if they get hit."

"A flawed incentive system."

"And hard to accurately track."

"Hup two, Juliet!" Glenda called before disappearing into the Receiving Tent.

Juliet slipped two cigarettes into the Senator's jacket and tapped his shoulder. "Quadruple pay if you get shot and have to lie on the ground waiting for a surgeon."

"Amen."

Just then, an ambulance careened past them, kicking up wet earth. The door flung open and a medic frantically signaled Juliet over. "Eight months I'm here," the medic huffed, "and I've never seen such a goddamned pointless mess." A long, warped moan came from a bundled figure.

"What happened?"

"Grab that end of the stretcher. Elmer took shrapnel in the shoulder yesterday and can barely steer the wagon right now."

Juliet lifted one side of the litter, holding her breath to keep her arms from slackening. The medic's shirtsleeves, rolled to the elbow, were crusted with blood; in the cuff of one curled a shiny piece of intestine.

"Still got hellfire in him," the medic said as the patient, like an engine jolted by electricity, suddenly shook. Elbows and knees struggled to break free from the blood-soaked blankets. "Even tried to jump from the ambulance."

The Receiving Tent was pandemonium. It had the sweltering, urgent swirl of a train station; nurses and ward men, rushing with clattering trays, barking instructions, moved among the wounded. Staring vacantly at the ceiling, the men moaned and whimpered as they awaited their turns. Here and there a team of doctors encircled a litter on a sawhorse, ducking and dodging the elaborate web of intravenous and Wangensteen tubing. They quickly incised and retracted and bandaged, discarding instruments into buckets with a noisy clang before they swarmed the next litter. The air, a soupy mix of ether and sulfur, made Juliet cough. This drew the attention of Chief Nurse Henfield, who waded through the sea of patients to inspect the new admission.

Mother Hen pulled back the blanket; "Heavens to fucking Betsy."

The man's face glistened with blood. One eye dangled an inch below its socket, resting on his cheekbone. The other eye darted about wildly. To the side of the chin gaped a crimson hole, punctuated by the bright white specks of molars. Not a single bandage covered his wounds. Though the man's mouth seemed incapable of moving, he emitted a terrible groan. Juliet was trying hard not to register any horror on her face.

"Battalion surgeon wouldn't touch him," said the medic.

"Not even sulfonamide?" asked Mother Hen. "Why on earth not?"

"On principle."

As Mother Hen examined his medical tag, a sad shock of recognition crossed her face. "Oh, it's Private Barnaby."

"Captain Henfield . . ." Juliet offered uncertainly, "our blood supply is extremely low."

"*Extremely* is not a medical term."

"Less than six pints," said Juliet.

"Well, don't piss them away on this yellow belly," huffed the medic. "You're looking at an Article 85." Article 85 referred to desertion.

Juliet watched Mother Hen narrow her eyes, as if trying to locate, on the ruined landscape of the patient's face, some familiar feature.

"Reckless, stupid, idiotic fool," she muttered. Mother Hen was the oldest of the nurses. A maze of wrinkles spread from her outer eyes, and a thick band of freckles, interlaced with sunspots, darkened her cheeks. She looked bronzed, marbled, and brilliantly shrewd. Nothing hen-like or motherly in her manner that Juliet could detect.

"We'll administer six thousand cc's plasma, Nurse Dufresne, one thousand cc's five percent glucose in saline, penicillin, and thirty milligrams morphine; then get him out of those clothes and dress the wound."

Mother Hen left for the supplies, and Juliet began carefully repeating the dosages to herself.

"Got any straps or cords?" asked the medic.

"We've barely got gauze left."

The medic unbuckled his belt and yanked it loose from his pants. "Here. Strap him down best you can. And keep knives away until the sedatives kick in. I've got to mop up the hill."

Just then, the medic noticed the flesh in his cuff, and with his thumb and forefinger flicked it to the ground.

Juliet crouched beside the patient; "Okay, stay nice and calm for me," she whispered. His face was so thick with blood, it seemed like a lunar landscape on which the only sign of life was the startlingly white eye staring up at her. The other eye, drenched with blood, dangled as if it might come loose. Amazing he was still alive. But that was the first thing Juliet had learned in nursing school— appearances deceived. While invisible infections, fevers, and blood clots could be fatal, men maimed or burned beyond recognition all too frequently lived to see the ruin of their bodies.

Juliet glanced at his tag, where one word had been written: *coward*.

"Private Barnaby, I'm a nurse. When I strap you down, it's for your own good." Juliet hadn't yet dealt with a shock patient, but she'd watched other nurses and knew that the trick was to lower his head, raise his legs, and above all else make sure he knew he was off the battlefield. "If you let me push up your sleeve, I'll give you something for the pain." With an alcohol swab, she cleared a white track on his arm. "That pinch is just a needle. In a minute, you're gonna feel like dancing."

Mother Hen returned, rigging the plasma bag and intravenous tubes. "Nurse Dufresne, strip him down now. We need him in the Surgical Tent before lights out."

Juliet cut slowly through his pants with dull scissors, revealing two knobby legs streaked with bruises. She peeled off his jacket and shirt and found, pressed to his chest, two blood-spattered envelopes, thick with papers; she shoved them in her apron before tossing his clothing into a pile at her side. Somewhere beyond this tent sat pails of blood-soaked shirts and pants, of shrapnel and bullets extracted from bodies, of hands and feet and arms and legs. Hospital debris—if the army had any sense, thought Juliet, they'd pack it onto Thunderbolts and dump it over Germany.

Private Barnaby lay naked now, except for a silver Saint Christopher medal at his neck, which she unclasped, and his ID tags. He was surprisingly thin, the arc of each rib visible through his skin.

"Of all the goddamned messes." The hospital's commanding officer, Major Bill Decker, had appeared beside her, gnawing the stub of an unlit cigar. "Pistol in the mouth. One hell of a messy way to desert."

Self-inflicted? Juliet was surprised. She looked down at the naked boy, the pulpy wreck of his face. Men opted for such gory suicides. A bullet in the brain, a plunge from a bridge—always an act of violence. Women, on the other hand, took handfuls of sleeping pills and pretended it was bedtime. She couldn't fathom either.

Juliet grabbed the stretcher, assuming the major would take the other side, but he tucked his cigar in his shirt pocket, delicately, as though it were an heirloom or pet hamster, before lifting the stretcher with dramatic apathy.

"Oh, let's stroll," he sang. "Let's wander. Let's talk about Nietzsche and Heidegger and Bergson. Let's discuss BIG IDEAS, the nature of time, the possibility of life after death. . . ."

This was the first time Major Decker had spoken to her; he generally kept to himself, except when the hospital was swamped, when he would appear haphazardly at patients' bedsides with cups of water or in the Sterilizing Tent, scrubbing down scalpels. It was said he once drove an unattended ambulance to the front, returning with eleven wounded men. His expression was dark and pensive and mildly hateful. Hateful of the war, hateful of humanity—a look Juliet had begun to notice in those who had for too long tended to the dying.

"I think we should bring him to the Surgical Tent," Juliet said softly. "With all due respect, Major."

"The respect is due death. He *wanted* death. It's a rarity in this place, and we should oblige."

Mother Hen's wizened face popped through the tent flaps with a simple, scolding "*Major.*" For two years she had been helping Major Decker run the hospital; together they presided over a staff of 150—litter bearers, surgical assistants, ward men, doc-

tors, nurses, drivers—conducting themselves in a stern and effi-
cient manner; but when engaging with each other, they seemed like
eccentric grandparents.

"*Madge,*" he replied.

She pointed toward the Surgical Tent. "*Protocol.*"

"*Pointless.*"

"*Now!*"

Major Decker rolled his eyes, a gesture Juliet had not thought
commanding officers capable of. "We'll fix him up," he whispered
to Juliet, "and then General Clark will use this kid for target practice. But there's no crossing Madge. Let it be done! *Andiamo!*"

In the Surgical Tent, after Juliet helped set down the patient,
Mother Hen instructed, "Take a rest, Nurse Dufresne." She tapped
her watch. "One hour. And not a second past. We've a bitch of a
night ahead."

Back in her dark, airless tent, Juliet peeled off her damp shirt
and wiped down her chest. After all those broken bones and seeping wounds, her body seemed precariously fragile. There were
bones inside of her, she reminded herself, and on those bones
lay strips of muscle, tangled with veins and arteries. Skin and lig-
aments held it all together, the entirety of the mass of flesh she
called *herself.* But no bone of hers looked much different from
someone else's bone; her femur would roughly mirror the femur
of any soldier on the operating table; none of the flesh she'd seen
in the hospitals—the torn muscles, the exposed stomachs, the broken ribs—had anything to do with the people it belonged to. The
same delicate pieces made up everyone, and if the wrong pieces or
too many pieces broke, the whole person ceased to exist. Juliet had
witnessed this daily for months, and yet the strangeness of it never
subsided.

She tried to clear her mind; collapsing onto her bedroll, she
devoured a C ration can—cold hash and potatoes—letting the
salt and grease melt in her mouth. As rain needled the tent, she

imagined a summer day back in Charlesport. She envisioned the white wicker chaise on the front porch, a row of cool potted ferns. Juliet almost tasted the thick salt air, heard her father's deep voice from within the house. But when she tried to insert Tuck into the scene—maybe he'd be playing checkers with her as they waited for dinner—the image grew cloudy. Whether she was summoning a memory or a fantasy, Juliet could not have said. Seven months had passed since the awful telegram; almost two years since she waved good-bye to him at the bus depot. It troubled her that her grasp on the details of their past was fading.

She thumbed through a dog-eared *Stars and Stripes,* months old, featuring three articles on the Salerno landings, about which she'd already gathered every grueling, useless fact. (She knew that Tuck's division had pushed north from Salerno to Naples, and that he went missing sometime after they crossed the Volturno—but she had little information beyond that.) Juliet surveyed her books and Glenda's pile of *Vogue* magazines, and finally grabbed Bernice's knitting needles and added a few lumpy stitches to a scarf before undoing them and setting the needles beside a box of letters.

Letters. Remembering the patient's envelopes, Juliet dug through her apron. Stiff with mud and blood, the first envelope crackled as she shook free a small, worn photograph of a young woman posed on the steps of a single-story clapboard house. The woman's hair was tied back, and her gingham dress fell loosely, as though trying to obscure any suggestion of a figure. She smiled tiredly and some-what crookedly, one of those smiles, Juliet knew, that came from posing too long. A thin band glinted on her ring finger.

So, the troubled soldier had a wife.

Juliet slid the photo back in the envelope and pulled out a letter; she stared at the address for a moment, taken aback: Private Chris-topher Barnaby, 88th Infantry Division, 349th Infantry Regiment, Rifle Company C—Tuck's company. She brought the envelope to her chest, heart thumping, and then remembered that each company consisted of several hundred men. Unless Private Barnaby was in the same platoon as Tuck was, he'd likely be of little use. Still, it was the first shred of hope in months.

Setting the letter in her lap, Juliet lay back down and smiled.

All sixty cots in Recovery Tent One were filled. The bandaged men, their limbs suspended in bright white casts, looked like creatures caught in a giant web of intravenous tubing. Juliet checked the med schedule on the nurses' desk and then made her way from bed to bed to take temperatures, administer penicillin and morphine, rewrap bandages, offer cups of water. Except for the occasional cough, the tent was quiet.

"Ah, Nurse! I'll die of thirst!"

At the far end, a corpulent man fanned his pink face with a Sears, Roebuck catalog. In the sweat-beaded crescent above his undershirt hung a gold cross, his chest rising and falling with each raspy breath.

"Father MacDougal?"

He seized the water glass from Juliet and with each long sip his Adam's apple bobbed; the glass emptied, he looked despairingly to the heavens. "What's left of me?" he muttered.

Juliet checked the clipboard, where several notes had been scratched out; added in a different script were the words *very serious condition*.

"I told them, malaria or typhoid. The food here, it's entirely unsanitary. Rats everywhere. And cockroaches! Oh, Italian cockroaches are very crafty."

Juliet set her palm on his forehead, warm and sticky.

"I have the chills, you see. And a pain in my right side. And headaches, splitting headaches. A hammer pounding in my skull. But also, I'm burning up, and there are these swollen glands in my throat. Like walnuts. Here." He led her hands to the soft fleshy bumps of his lymph nodes, which made Juliet suspicious. She slid a thermometer in his mouth and checked his bedpan.

"Don't forget to urinate, Father."

His eyes widened. "No, no, no, no. There's *glass* in my urine," he whispered. "They fed me glass."

"No talking until the thermometer is out," she scolded. "I'm going to run a Widal test for typhoid, and draw blood for a malaria test." With childlike terror he watched her shove back his sleeve and insert a needle. "If it's malaria, we can give you Atabrine. For typhoid, the symptoms will generally subside. If any coughing begins, we'll do a lung X-ray for TB."

"Tuberhulohis!"

"Two degrees above normal," she said, wiping down the instrument. She laid a wet cloth on his forehead. "Get some rest, Father. Patients are sleeping and we should keep it quiet."

"Oh, but I need something for the pain or I'm going to let myself swell up like a balloon. I can't sleep. What would really help, what would really perch the angels on your shoulders for eternity, would be a sip of medicinal brandy."

"Have a sleeping pill." From an unmarked bottle of aspirin, Juliet shook out a tablet. "Twenty minutes, and you'll be sleeping like a baby."

As she leaned forward to adjust his blanket, his thick hand landed on her hip. "Such kindness," he whispered, sliding his palm up and down. "The angels are all over you."

"If they are," she said, stepping away, "I'm betting they don't like to be groped."

Throughout the night, the ward was full of breathing, the intimate breaths of human sleep. Juliet paced the dimly lit tent. Here and there a bed creaked as a patient thrashed in the privacy of a dream. Occasionally, she checked a bandage, trying not to rouse the sleeper. As the hours stretched on, her eyes began to ache with exhaustion. Rules forbade sitting down (in case she fell asleep), so as she walked she recited the periodic table to herself, and when in the last heavy hours of darkness her limbs began to revolt, she windmilled her arms. Despite this exertion, her eyes had begun to drift closed when two surgeons appeared with a litter, letting the soft white light of morning spill into the tent.

"No more beds?" asked Dr. Lovelace, his eyes pink and ragged.

"The best I can do is the floor."

"Well, Private Barnaby won't know the difference. He'll be lucky if he has broccoli left for a brain." Dr. Lovelace was the hospital's chief trauma surgeon. Brawny and thickly bearded, he was also, according to Glenda, exceptionally wealthy.

Dr. Mallick stood silently. He was short and pigeon-breasted and had the wide-eyed look of someone holding his breath, perhaps for decades.

"Psst. Is that Private Barnaby?" This question came from the Senator, squinting against a band of sunlight.

"Go back to sleep, Munson," whispered Juliet.

"You can't put Barnaby on the ground. Enough's enough already. Give the poor sod my bed." With evident annoyance, the Senator yanked loose his bedsheet and settled on the narrow strip of floor between cots. He burrowed his face in the crook of his arm, sighing with exasperation. In the silence that followed, he seemed aware of Juliet's puzzled stare. "It's nothing," he said. "I'm used to sleeping on the ground."

The doctors held the litter steady, and Juliet eased Barnaby's body onto the cot. Through the thick gauze, the rasp of his breathing had an insect-like quality; he seemed an entirely different creature from the one in the ambulance. Bandages and casts were like cocoons, thought Juliet, and the person who would eventually emerge would look entirely unfamiliar. From her pocket she pulled the Saint Christopher medal, rinsed of blood, and fixed the clasp around his neck.

"If you'll excuse us," said Dr. Lovelace, "we've still got two thoracotomies, a laparotomy, and one crappy flashlight. Wish us luck." He gave Juliet a sportsmanlike hug, resolutely patting her back. Lovelace was known for this—hugging his entire surgical team after every operation.

As they left, she looked at her watch—thirty more wearying minutes until her shift's end. Around her men lay splayed and motionless in the last firm grip of slumber, and the sight made her desperate for rest. It became an ache. To pass the time, she turned over a page on one of the clipboards and drew a tic-tac-toe board. She had played almost a dozen games when from a nearby corner a voice rose with panic. "Hello? Is anyone there? Please, someone!"

Juliet rushed to the man, whose bandaged head was swinging in desperate arcs.

"I'm here," she whispered. "You're in a field hospital. It's okay."

He stopped moving. His eyes were wide open, his pupils strangely dilated, like the shocked eyes of a dead fish.

"Jesus, I thought I was taken prisoner. When can I take these bandages off?" He touched his eyelids, then his eyebrows, and blinked several times, poking his fingertips at his eyes as terror slowly took hold of his face.

Juliet skimmed his medical sheet. "Lieutenant Geiger. A piece of shrapnel pierced your helmet. It severed your optic nerves."

"Well . . . just turn on the lights."

"That bit of shrapnel, it *tore* the nerves that control your vision."

"But my eyes don't hurt."

"It happened inside your head. I think you're blind."

"How do I know you're not a German trying to trick me? A Kraut nurse who speaks English?" He slowly crossed his arms, raised his chin. "So tell me, Miss America, what's the name of Roosevelt's dog?"

Juliet paused, wanting to give him a few more seconds of hope. But in the uncertain silence, his upper lip trembled, and she finally whispered: "I'm sorry. Fala."

A tear traveled the ridge of his cheekbone and pooled above his lip; he was quite handsome. It was strange to think he would never see his face again; he would never see himself grow old. Years from now, as a man of fifty, he would imagine himself exactly like this.

"Why don't you get a little more sleep?" She handed him a cup.

"Mmmmm. Brandy. At least I can taste."

Juliet hung his clipboard on a small hook on the end of his cot, and at the sound of her leaving he asked, "Would you stay? Just until I fall asleep?"

He had clenched his hands, nervously kneading his thumbs into his fists, and she wondered at the last thing he had seen, if it had imprinted on his mind, like a lightbulb turned off.

"Of course," she said, sitting beside him.

The Officers' Mess surged noisily as a crowd of doctors and nurses came off the night shift. The food line snaked through the dozen long tables, and as Juliet reached the front she ladled four heapings of watery scrambled eggs into her metal bowl, hoping to devour as much hot food as possible before getting some sleep. Settling in a corner alone, she began to ravenously fork the curled wet strips of egg into her mouth, but when she saw Mother Hen approach, she slowed her intake.

"Lieutenant Dufresne!" Mother Hen slid beside her on the bench, hip to hip, and gazed wearily at the bustling tent. In a somewhat devious whisper she asked, "How did your overnight shift go?"

Juliet's mind quickly scanned the night's events to see if anything she had done might be a violation of protocol. "Just fine," she answered uncertainly.

"And you're settling in well with the unit?"

"Yes, Captain Henfield."

Mother Hen turned toward her. "I've been watching you, and I think you've adapted quite well to this new environment. I can see you've got character, and grit. You can't teach grit." Mother Hen reached for Juliet's piece of toast. "May I?"

"Of course, Captain Henfield."

Mother Hen narrowed her eyes reflectively as she chewed. "In 1854, Nurse Dufresne, when Florence Nightingale arrived in Scutari, do you know what she saw? Men wrapped in filthy bandages. Men lying all day beside overflowing bedpans. Injured men abandoned on the battlefield for days. Misery you cannot possibly fucking fathom. Why? Because in the midst of the Crimean War, no one knew what he should be doing and when. But since she revolutionized nursing, hospitals are arranged so that we all know what we should be doing at any given time. It's not a thing to take for granted. And it's crucial to the war effort that each of us knows precisely what we should be doing and also that we should be assigned the tasks to which we are most naturally suited. It's hard enough fighting the Germans; why fight our own natures? Nurse Dufresne, when I saw you with Private Barnaby, I saw attentiveness, commitment. I'd be remiss in my job if I ignored that. So I have decided to promote you. I'm assigning you as Private Barnaby's personal nurse. You alone are to deal with his wound dressings, his bathing, his intravenous feeding, his defecation, his urination needs, at all hours necessary. Don't let any of the ward men near him. Are we understood?"

"Yes, Captain Henfield. Thank you." Juliet blushed with pride.

"I knew you would respond to the call of duty." She slid off the bench and brushed crumbs from her uniform. "Carry on."

Glenda Texas, carrying over her breakfast tray, raised an eyebrow as the chief nurse left.

"You in trouble already?"

"I've been promoted."

"Oh, no, the promotion demotion!" Glenda settled across from Juliet. "The woman is a master."

"You're saying I haven't been promoted?"

"Promoted to do whatever job the rest of the gals don't want. A true bedpan commando."

"I'm supposed to care for the soldier who shot himself."

"Sugar, it's like the biggest bird in the world just took a crap on your head."

Juliet looked dejectedly into her eggs. She felt stupid. "Well, someone needs to care for him."

"You've got to admire her, really. She pulls it off every time. *This* is how people win wars. The woman was born into the army. She's got one sister in the Philippines running a field hospital. And another sister somewhere here in Europe working as a nurse. Her brother was in North Africa with a cav division. Her mother was an army nurse in the Great War. And there are rumors she's a real flesh-and-blood *dee*-scendant of Miss Florence Nightingale herself."

"Except Florence Nightingale never married," said Juliet.

"That never stopped the gals in Texas from bearing progeny."

"Who's bearing progeny?" asked Dr. Lovelace, joining their table. Dr. Mallick sat beside Juliet. Stubble matted his face and gray sideburns sprouted below his ears. Lovelace raised his cup: "To the graveyard shift."

Dr. Mallick probed his food with his fork. "I've never seen a foreign object lodged in the cerebral cortex without causing devastating tissue damage," he said. "Astonishing recovery taking into account Private Barnaby's cerebral hemorrhaging."

"They should have shipped Humpty Dumpty home the first time he cracked," said Dr. Lovelace.

"The first time?" asked Juliet.

"That's right, you missed the sordid tale. This was maybe seven or eight months back . . . where were we, Glenda?"

"Near Monte Petrella. Or maybe Monte Fammera. At the base of one of those massive Italian granite *montes.*"

"Monte Fammera, that's right. When Barnaby was in McKnight's squad. The boy took a bullet in the shoulder. Minor musculocutaneous injury, nothing ten minutes on the table couldn't fix. But whatever he saw *before* he took the lead scared the hair off him. He had a set of shakes like I've never seen."

Much of what Dr. Lovelace said was lost on Juliet because she'd been immediately struck by the name. "He was in Sergeant *Bruce McKnight's* squad?" she asked.

"Affirmative. And when Captain Brilling came to visit, the kid had some kind of breakdown and tried to run. Brilling thought he was going to desert. That was a sight. Brilling reassigned Barnaby to a different platoon, as BAR man. The canary in the tunnel. Those kids last an average of ten minutes in combat. I'm amazed he made it this long. But I guess he couldn't take it anymore, tried to do himself in. Sadder than Samson, if you ask me."

"How long was he with McKnight's squad?" Juliet asked.

"My, my, Nurse Dufresne. You sweet on Bruce McKnight?"

"I've just heard of him, that's all."

"Well, I'd be glad to make an introduction. Anyway, I wouldn't be surprised if Barnaby got a court-martial for desertion. They're trying to crack down, starting to issue death sentences."

Juliet shook her head in disbelief. "But we just worked all night to *save* Private Barnaby—they can't sentence him to death."

Dr. Mallick set down his fork and slowly clapped his hands; then Dr. Lovelace clapped, and Glenda joined in. People at nearby tables—half-tired, half-bored, intrigued by the bewildering scene— began to clap as well.

"The new arrival has fully joined us!" said Dr. Lovelace. "Welcome to our absurdist little field hospital! We also go without sleep for days to save men so they can go get shot again. Very rewarding work, indeed."

Embarrassed, Juliet struggled to say something articulate, something to mask her inexperience. "Well, it strikes me as unjust that boys who try to serve, who ship over here but maybe can't hack it, end up sentenced to death, when the conscientious objectors stay home doing volunteer work."

"Truth be told," said Lovelace, "not a single desertion death sentence has been carried out. *Yet.*"

"Everyone objects to dying, Nurse Dufresne," said Dr. Mallick. "Conscientious objectors object to killing. The medics here get picked off faster than BAR men. They are quite courageous."

"Have y'all forgotten?" Glenda clucked her tongue and pointed at a handwritten sign taped to the side of the tent: *No politics before noon.*

"Then let's talk about the Goumiers."

"Again?" sighed Glenda.

"Maybe the new girl hasn't heard the story. Juliet, may I call you Juliet? Juliet, do you know about the Goumiers? The Goumiers are from the Atlas Mountains in Morocco. Now you know we were stalled at Monte Cassino for months, but these men, these African climbing geniuses, scaled a five-thousand-foot peak in the Aurunci Mountains just south of Cassino to single-handedly break through the Gustav Line. What took the rest of the army months, they did in three days. Three. Chasing the Germans into the Liri Valley."

"Goumiers," Juliet repeated vacantly, distracted by the fact that Private Barnaby had once been in Tuck's squad. This was the closest she'd come to finding someone who might know her brother. She noisily scraped up the cold remains of her eggs, shoved them into her mouth, and stood.

"I almost forgot," said Glenda, grabbing Juliet's wrist. "Did you see our poor ailing Father?"

Lovelace palmed his forehead in exasperated disbelief. "Typhoid. Malaria. Chicken pox. The man claims to have everything."

"Well, he's sick all right," said Juliet. "So, I ran some tests."

"You mean he's not goldbricking? Well, I'll be darned."

"As it turns out," Juliet said, "the chaplain has syphilis."

Dr. Lovelace set his fork decidedly on his plate. "Sometimes I just don't know whether to laugh or cry."

In her tent, Juliet resisted the urge to throw herself onto her bedroll and instead rummaged the depths of her musette bag. She'd brought every letter Tuck had sent, and now shuffled anxiously through the pages, scanning the names: *David Rakowski, Dick English, Geronimo, Dudley (the Duke) Draper, John Kendall, Rex Appleyard, Glen Mooney, Sergeant Bruce McKnight.*

No Christopher Barnaby.

She set down the letters. She lined them up and flattened them as though that might order her thoughts. Dr. Lovelace had said Barnaby was in Sergeant McKnight's squad seven or eight months earlier—close to the time Tuck disappeared. Tuck, who'd made a point of writing about every man he served with, hadn't once mentioned Barnaby. Was it possible, she wondered, that Lovelace was wrong about when Barnaby had been shot? Or was her luck so abominably rotten that she'd found a man who joined her brother's squad just after Tuck's disappearance?

The thought struck her with a thud: Was Barnaby her brother's replacement?

Replacement.

The word brought flashes of Barnaby's ruined face. Bone, blood. The disgorged eye. If Tuck's replacement had done *that* to himself, then . . . No. The possibility her imagination had let loose made Juliet so uncomfortable that she stuffed the letters back in her bag.

She sat very still. Thus far, she'd prevented her mind from wandering gory paths, and she wasn't going to allow it to start now. Barnaby was a connection, a link, to Tuck, and she simply had to utilize that.

Juliet took out a clean sheet of V-mail.

Somewhere in Italy

Dear Father & Pearl,

My request for a transfer came through and I'm at a field hospital about five miles from the front. All the tents have big red crosses on them, so you can sleep peacefully. This hospital is much smaller than the one in Naples—only eighteen nurses for about 120 patients, though right now we have almost 200. The evacuation hospitals farther back are overflowing, so we just set the men on the ground and wait. The doctors have been performing about eighty operations a day and everyone shuffles around like sleepwalkers.

Was it like this when you were in Belgium, Papa? Is this why you never spoke about it?

I'm living in a pup tent with two other nurses: Glenda La Bouvier from Abilene, Texas, and Bernice Murchstone, an anesthetist from Iowa. Glenda is definitely the belle of the ball here; she can tap-dance and sing and knows the words to any song you can think of. She tracks everyone's birthday in a calendar and arranges festivities.

Bernice keeps to herself and suffers from awful insomnia. She seems to knit herself to sleep. My first night here, before bed, her face all greasy with cold cream, she sat there for hours with a ball of yarn in her lap and two knitting needles clicking and clacking like they were having a sword fight. Everyone calls her "Bernether." But Glenda loves her. She told me that

Bernice lost her parents to the influenza epidemic in 1918 and grew up in orphanages. So I try to be as forgiving as possible.

The girls swear this tent can be collapsed and packed in under an hour, but from the look of it, you'd think we were settled in for the long haul. Glenda decorated it with purple and yellow silks she bought in Rome and some silver trinkets from North Africa.

It's been raining nonstop, so Glenda put Vaseline along the tent seams and that stops the dripping for a few hours at a time. It's cozy. We have a little woodstove, but haven't had a moment yet to cook so we make do with rations and what the mess gives us.

Forgive me again for the way I left, but here is where I can make the most difference.

Love,
Juliet

Juliet studied her final words. She had never told her father and Pearl that she enlisted to try to get close to where Tuck went missing, and if they guessed it, they had opted to avoid a confrontation. When she had written from Basic Training, they accepted her explanation of patriotic duty. And she had dutifully written once a week, sometimes twice, always careful to clarify she was in no danger, and always careful not to mention Tuck. Yet it was now unavoidable; the question was crucial. She added:

PS: I've a new patient who served in the same unit as Tuck—Private Christopher Barnaby. Do you recall Tuck writing about him? It's possible some old letters arrived since I left. Please let me know.

She sealed the letter.

Outside the rain had lightened, and in the gray mist Juliet trudged toward the Post Exchange, where a small supply convoy had parked in a tidy line. Empty barrels flanked the massive water truck. Beside the mailbox, where she slipped her letter, a stocky young man jumped down from an army truck. He reached back for two black suitcases, a white cross on the side of each, and curled them to his chin like free weights.

"They sent a new chaplain before they sent plasma?" Juliet blurted.

"Reporting for duty with the 42nd Field Hospital." His hair was dark brown, neatly combed, thinning slightly at the front, though he couldn't have been more than twenty-five. His nose was large and beak-like, his eyes small and dark and alert. Pinpricks of acne clustered beneath his temples.

"Father MacDougal fell ill just a few days ago," she said.

The chaplain tilted his head. "My understanding is that Father MacDougal fell ill a very long, long time ago." He set down his cases and surveyed the area. The silver crosses pinned to his lapels glinted in the light. "Tents, tents, and tents."

"Just try not to confuse the outhouse and the shower house," she said.

"Simon Reardon." He extended his hand. "Army Chaplain Corps."

"Juliet Dufresne. Army Nurse Corps."

His handshake was authoritative, but his smile was boyish, buoyant. Around his neck hung a long, thick chain with an ornate crucifix, nearly the size of her index finger. She'd never before seen anything like it.

"The abbot lent it to me," he explained. "For protection."

The abbot. He was a monk, then. Juliet didn't quite believe in God, and certainly not in all the hoopla of Christianity, but it seemed wise to be friendly to a chaplain—just in case. She worried her haggard and sleep-deprived stare had been impolite.

"If you'd like, I can show you to Major Decker's tent," she said.

"I'm here to tend to the soul," he said, "and the spirit and essentially whatever else pops up before me. You, though I've never met you before, would, I think, be well served by finding your way to *your* tent. I'm no doctor, but I'd say some rest is in order."

The mere thought of sleep made Juliet break into a yawn. She felt as if she'd been awake for days, moving and working and worrying for months. "Rest would be good," she said. "Chaplain's orders?"

The chaplain nodded. He took her elbow and walked her quietly through the drizzle to her tent, where finally Juliet slept.

CHAPTER 5

NEWS CAME THAT the division had pushed the Germans farther north and several battalions were being rested. The rain ceased, and a pleasant silence settled over the landscape. In the distance, the trees were thick and green, and the mountains beyond looked beautiful against the sky.

Assigned to a seven-hour daytime shift, Juliet took her breakfast at dawn in the Officers' Mess, and as the sun's rays, like the limbs of a waking sleeper, stretched slowly over the encampment, she began her rounds.

By noon the glare was hard and bright, and inside the Recovery Tent the canvas walls gathered the hot air and held it very still. Juliet moved slowly; with each step her ward dress stuck to her sides. She fanned patients with magazines, laid wet folded cloths above their brows, flicked flies from their wounds. The worst off were the men in casts, whose necks and chests she doused hourly with a pitcher of water. "Holy Mary," exclaimed a man in a full-body spica cast, "I'm cooked like a casserole!"

Slowly the mud dried and the bald patches of earth grew cracked and dusty; a tan soot rose from the ground and found its way into the creases of her clothing.

The most critical patients were trucked to Naples for evacuation, and soon the hospital took on the feeling of a resort; two by two, patients on crutches hobbled together around the lush grounds, speaking in low, intimate tones, smoking cigarettes while staring off into the mountains; young Italian girls waved empty baskets over the hospital fence, eager to do laundry for pay. A female reporter from a Chicago newspaper arrived; having been denied access to the front lines, she huffed around the recovery ward trying to coax patients into dramatic quotes—"You must have been terrified. . . . You must have felt trapped. . . . You must have been feverish"—which, theoretically, would bring home to her readers as palpable an experience of the front as did Ernie Pyle's reports. Feeling sorry for her, the men invented tales of reckless heroism, of distant cousins reunited on the battlefield, ridiculous yarns that they referred to, among themselves, as *must-ofs* or, soon, *mustaffs.* "I've got a good mustaff."

Members of the nearby British air force squadron visited, including a pilot Glenda knew from North Africa who arrived one evening in a jeep with two friends and a bottle of grappa, insisting the nurses come to an Officers' Club dance.

Returning from her rounds, Juliet found Glenda on her back, studiously penning a black web of fishnet stockings across her legs.

"I hope it doesn't rain," Juliet laughed.

"Want me to do yours?"

"I'm not going."

"A little roll in the olive grove could do you good. It gets my circulation going, and that, sugar, does wonders for the complexion."

Juliet bent to unlace her shoes. "You're forgetting my special patient."

"Private Cyclops?" Glenda pointed her toes and examined her handiwork. "He won't know if you're gone."

"Mother Hen will."

"Then we'll sneak a chum back for you! *One for you and one for me! Share alike for Victory.*" Glenda scissored her legs. "Just give me some guidelines. Tall and dark? Short and athletic? Freckled? Bookish, I bet."

"Hunchbacked and pockmarked," said Juliet. "With a speech impediment."

"Hell, that's my first husband. Come on, I'm offering you my extraordinary powers of discernment."

"Thank you, but it's unnecessary."

Glenda flipped onto her stomach and narrowed her eyes. "Sugar, you're not *inexperienced,* are you? 'Cause if that's the problem, Glenda here can talk you through it. I know very little about most things of worldly consequence, but I'm encyclopedic in the boy department."

Juliet had not, in fact, kissed anyone since her failed attempt with Beau Conroy years earlier. Just as she began looking at boys with greater interest, most in Charlesport had shipped overseas. And by the time she'd arrived in Naples, the soldiers there were endlessly claiming they were "pissing fire." She'd tired of handing out condoms and brochures on syphilis. One more short-arm exam and she'd have joined a convent. (*Short arm* was army slang for the male organ, though most men, as they sat half-naked before her on the hospital beds, trying to mask their shame with wisecracks, claimed *short arm* was a misnomer, suggesting that for medical and historical accuracy, Juliet should note their manhood as *long arm.*) It was, Juliet realized, an unfortunate introduction to the male anatomy.

"I've sort of got someone back home . . ." Juliet fibbed.

Shrugging, Glenda stood to smooth out her dress. Glenda wasn't exactly beautiful—there was a thinness to her lips that made her seem old, and a slight crook at the bridge of her nose; one eye even seemed slightly smaller than the other—but she gave the dazzling impression of glamour.

"This pilot," said Juliet, "is he your sweetheart?"

"Oh, I got more sweethearts than I can count. None of them worth a horseshoe, though. As my momma likes to say, they are *phi-landerers.* You know what that means? It's from Latin. Latin for stickin' your hand in too many cookie jars." She hopped into one of her pumps and was about to duck through the canvas, when she turned back thoughtfully. "Look, Juliet, you got a real nice face, you know. Don't be fussing about that there birthmark. It makes you distinct, distinguished. The first time you walked in here, I thought, *That there is a special gal.* You should be out there dating. They got ten boys here for every girl, and half these boys are missing *essential* parts! They aren't exactly in a position to be picky."

Glenda exited at the onset of Juliet's blush. Since Juliet entered nursing school, no one had mentioned her birthmark (nurses and doctors were wonderfully delicate about such matters), and the absence of mirrors in the hospitals had allowed her to forget it. But the sudden recollection of the attribute that had for so long compromised her self-confidence stung her: she was an army nurse, she was serving on the front lines in Italy, but to plain sight she still seemed the same odd-looking girl she'd been back in Charlesport.

Juliet felt *different,* though. Inside her resided a new, unflappable sense of triumph; after all, she'd worked tirelessly to get her nursing degree in under twelve months; she'd studied enough Italian to ensure a posting to Italy; she'd endured five grueling weeks of Basic Training and eight blazing, seasick days aboard the HMS *Mayflower* to arrive in Naples. She was now closer to her brother's last known steps than she'd ever imagined possible. *I've been tested and I succeeded,* thought Juliet, and nothing—not even the blemish on her face that she'd so long wished away—could take that from her. Was it too much to hope that this whole experience would transform her in a way others would find attractive? All she had ever wanted was to come across as a person of substance. Perhaps Glenda was right; maybe the boys here wouldn't make a scene over her birthmark as Beau Conroy had. Plenty of nurses were heavyset, even mannish, and they didn't seem the least bit shy about prancing off to dances.

Juliet lay back and imagined the Officers' Club. She envisioned ivory tablecloths, yellow wildflowers in empty wine bottles, lipsticked nurses sipping champagne from tin cups. A makeshift band would be playing—maybe a pilot with a saxophone who loved Glenn Miller—and in a swirl of cigarette smoke a group of clean-shaven officers would pull the nurses by their fingertips onto the dance floor. Juliet eventually drifted off, awakened by the sharp white glare of a flashlight. In the semidarkness, Glenda blinked forcefully, as though to orient herself, releasing a deep-throated moan. "What . . . a . . . night."

Her mouth, smeared with lipstick, looked bee-stung; her platinum curls had wilted. She flung her hands behind her back and struggled so noisily and strenuously with the zipper on her dress, it seemed she was fighting handcuffs. In final surrender, with the dress half off her shoulders, she plunged her fingers into a vat of cold cream and worked it sloppily into her face.

"How was it?" Juliet asked tentatively.

Glenda flicked off her flashlight and let her head thump into her pillow. "Sug," she sighed, "wake me when the war's over."

In the morning the world was bright and green and frenzied. Supply trucks rolled noisily into the encampment and crews of ward men unloaded crates of surgical supplies. Cigarette packets were distributed; the bugle sounded for mail call. The clank of the weekly crate of Coca-Cola bottles elicited wild applause.

The sky was cloudless; the day blazed.

In the shade of the Recovery Tent, Juliet was reviewing the medicine schedule. She stood at the nursing station, flipping through the clipboard, when she felt the dark weight of someone staring at her. In the entrance of the tent stood a man she suspected to be Captain Brilling, the commander of C Company. A few minutes earlier, she had heard his arrival announced over the megaphone. Three thick lines traversed his leathery forehead; a gray mustache topped his lips, which were thin and dry and seemed to be working over a deep annoyance.

"You're in charge?" he asked.

"Well, I'm the senior nurse on duty at the moment." And that was only because Mother Hen had briefly gone to the quartermaster to complain about the gauze that had arrived. "But I think you'll recognize most of your men. And for the ones with head bandages, you can check their tags. . . . Everyone is doing pretty well."

"*All* the beds are full?"

"Yes, but a lot of the patients should be up and walking in no time."

"Walking? I need them climbing, kicking, fighting." He made a fist, and Juliet noticed the heft of his hand; a large gold ring shone from his forefinger. "The Krauts have dug in like moles. It took half my men to get them out of that godforsaken town and now they've dug into the next." His dark eyes roamed the cots. "Where's the Nervous Nellie?"

"Private Barnaby is—"

"Christopher Barnaby."

"He's been discharged?"

The captain stepped toward Juliet with such slow deliberation that his very lack of speed felt menacing. Juliet noticed a thin scar across the left side of his face, from the corner of his mouth to his ear. Not a speckled scar from shrapnel, or the clean entrance wound of a bullet; this scar had been carved at close contact. He would have seen the blade traveling his face. Once, when she was a child, she had willed herself to imagine the face of a convict, because she and Tuck had heard a report of a man escaping from a nearby jail; this was the closest Juliet had ever come to seeing an embodiment of her childhood terror.

"He's in the far bed on the right side," she said timidly. "But he's sedated. And the doctors aren't certain he'll be able to speak."

Captain Brilling remained entirely still, as though challenging her to say more. Juliet could smell his perspiration, could hear his unnervingly long breaths. Finally, he crossed the ward in the direction of Barnaby. From all sides of the tent, men looked up from playing cards and sheets of V-mail, muttering, drowsily and morphine slurred, one hesitant, affection-filled word: "Captain."

Juliet slipped out, entirely against protocol, and ran to the Sterilizing Tent. "Glenda, get Mother Hen. The commander of C Company is here to see Private Barnaby."

Back at the tent, Juliet saw the captain standing over Barnaby, studying his cocoon of bandages. He waved his hand in front of Barnaby's mouth; he snapped his fingers beside his ear. He shook Barnaby's leg. Finally, from his side holster the captain pulled a pistol and held it just above Barnaby's face; he cocked and released the weapon several times. "So you like the sound of this? This sound brings you comfort?"

When Brilling noticed the uneasy stares of the other patients, he reholstered his pistol. "Men, five miles north of here, forty-three men in our company lie in the cold ground." He twisted the ring on his finger. "I planted the crosses myself this morning. Forty-three. Men who died fighting for their country, and for you. This *Nellie*"— the captain kicked Barnaby's cot—"couldn't even fire on the enemy. He fired on himself. But when he wakes up, mark my words: If he wants a bullet, we'll give him a whole goddamned firing squad."

He spat sharply on Barnaby's head, and several patients, including the Senator, turned away.

"Captain, step back from that patient." Mother Hen bore down on Brilling from across the tent, holding her clipboard like a shield.

He studied her lapels. "A silver star, Nurse?"

"Anzio," said Mother Hen, and the word hung in the air above the patients, some who had been there, many who had lost friends there, and for a moment Brilling was silent. Anzio, Cassino, Salerno—the names conjured up smoky heaps of bone and earth. Brilling and Mother Hen stood face-to-face, and her proximity seemed to unsettle him.

"Then you know how criminal such actions are," he said.

"War is the criminal. We're all its victims. We treat everyone, even enemy soldiers, with mercy. Now come."

The weakened men, limp in their beds, gazed at Mother Hen with dazzled gratitude. In the middle of nowhere, here was a woman who would protect them no matter what gory messes they made of themselves—she was their proxy mother. And while their love for the captain was evident in their faces, it was the love a child has for a stringent father, fearful and irregular.

Juliet heard the slap of tent flaps opening and turned to see Major Decker, followed by a tall, broad-shouldered man. The man carried a black leather bag and stepped awkwardly into the tent. He was unremarkable but for his height; his face was long and plain and pale, the face of a bank teller. He tapped his gold-rimmed glasses into place and offered Juliet his hand. "Dr. Henry Willard. What's the situation?"

Juliet did not sense the doctor wanted personal impressions. "Captain Brilling came to see Private Barnaby," she answered simply. "A conflict of sorts has ensued."

Willard turned to Major Decker. "The attempted suicide, correct?"

As Dr. Willard crossed the ward, Juliet saw that he was not merely awkward in his gait—his right foot seemed to drag slightly against the ground. He approached Mother Hen and Captain Brilling, and the three stood at the far end of the tent beside Barnaby's bed under the rapt gaze of the entire tent.

"Captain Henry Willard," the doctor announced. "I'll be looking after this patient now."

"Dr. Willard, I know about your work at Monte Cassino." Mother Hen reverentially pumped his hand. "You've done great things for our boys. I'm honored to have you with our hospital."

"Ah, the fancy *head* doctor." Brilling patted the doctor's shoulder with slow, deliberate condescension. "Well, hypnotize, anesthetize, take his cowardly pea brain apart and put it back together again. Still, this man will be court-martialed as soon as he's fit."

"Captain Brilling, I just traveled a hundred miles over some very unpleasant terrain to determine if my patient was *ever* fit. The mind can bleed, just like the body."

"Willard, you want to hold this kid and tell him it's all okay and cradle him close to your psychiatric bosom? Excellent. Then come to a dugout in the deep of night and explain to the four soldiers there, they're about to get their heads blasted off because their forward scout decided not to do his job. If we don't stop this kind of idiocy, we will lose this war."

"I couldn't agree more. We merely have different strategies for ending what you call idiocy, and what we medical professionals call battle fatigue." Dr. Willard knelt to open his black bag and then, with a stethoscope in hand, sidestepped in front of the captain. He hooked the rubber-tipped horseshoe into his ears and leaned close to Barnaby, pressing the disk on his chest.

"Alert me as soon as this man can stand trial," Brilling instructed Mother Hen. "He's not going to prance around this hospital like it's some goddamned Hilton; he's going to division stockade."

"We'll keep you fully apprised of Private Barnaby's recovery, per regulation. Now"—taking Brilling's elbow, Mother Hen eased him back across the tent—"wouldn't you like to visit the rest of your men?"

Slowly, one by one, the patients mustered the courage to converse with their formidable leader:

"How are ya, Cap'n?"

"Heard we finally took the town."

"I swear I'm gonna get right back up there soon as I'm fixed up."

"Break me outta this cast and I'll get back in the lines."

Juliet noticed that as the captain made his way along the beds, a few men stayed silent. The Senator lifted a magazine and began to read intently.

As Captain Brilling surveyed the men frozen in casts, the men squinting through head bandages, despair washed over his face. He drew his thick hands together as though in prayer—suddenly an entirely different man, Juliet thought, from the one who'd spat on Barnaby. This man looked heroic, and utterly tired.

"Men," he said. "My brave men."

By lunch that day, the Officers' Mess buzzed with the tale of Mother Hen's row with Captain Brilling.

"If I had to be in a hospital, I'd wanna be one of Mother Hen's patients," Glenda said to Juliet across the table. "She'd wrestle a bull to the ground before she'd let anyone touch one of her charges."

"She really got a silver star at Anzio?" asked Juliet.

"Buried three of her own. Gals just like us. She stayed in the tent with her patients, the ones who couldn't move, while bombs were dropping, and the tent got blasted."

Juliet smiled. "Is that true in the way her hitting Captain Brilling with a clipboard is true?" Glenda had been happily embellishing the story with each retelling.

"Oh, sugar. It's the *gist* of the thing that matters. Sometimes a little embellishment gets the point across better. Ooh, look, that head doctor is coming. Quick. Give me the lowdown."

"Lowdown?"

"Wedding ring?"

"I didn't notice."

"Sugar, you oughtta be dishonorably discharged from the nursing sisterhood! Haven't you heard of *recon*? All the other white coats in this hospital are hitched. Anyway, what *did* you notice?"

"Well, he's very tall."

Glenda impatiently drummed her fingernails on the table.

"They say he's been running a battle-fatigue hospital near the coast with the Eighth Army," Juliet offered. "And Mother Hen mentioned his work at Monte Cassino. I think he's here to study neuropsychotic patients and get them back into battle."

"Bingo," she whispered, wiggling her fingers as she peered over Juliet's shoulder. "No ring." Glenda did nothing so obvious as powdering her nose or fixing her hair, but as Dr. Willard approached, Glenda's eyebrows arched with delighted astonishment. "Why, it's the famous Dr. Willard." She smiled coyly.

"Good afternoon, ladies." Dr. Willard paused uncertainly beside their table, stiffly holding his tray.

"Well, Doctor, don't stand there like a sniper target," said Glenda, sliding over on the bench. "Join us!"

"I'm not intruding?"

"Not at all. We're all done discussing lingerie and menstrual cycles. I'm joking! Please, we'd love your company." She extended her hand, palm down, as though he should kiss it. "I'm Glenda La Bouvier. But just call me Glenda Texas. Or the Yellow Rose. There are two other Glendas here, and the one thing I cannot tolerate is being confused with someone else." Juliet had noticed that Glenda was always announcing a different "one thing" she couldn't tolerate.

Dr. Willard nodded hello to Juliet as he settled opposite her, then gazed blankly at the steaming contents of his mess kit.

"Spice it up," whispered Glenda, pulling a small red bottle from her pocket. "*Tabasco.* Around here, this stuff is more valuable than single malt."

"Ingenious." He studiously tapped out three drops, and Juliet detected wisps of gray crowning his hair. How old was he? His sheer height created the impression of authority, which she associated with adulthood. But there was a smoothness to his face that made him seem younger than the other doctors in the hospital.

"You're Private Barnaby's nurse?"

He had fixed his stare on Juliet. "I'm Juliet Dufresne," she said, realizing immediately that it was not the question he had asked.

"Well, I'm eager to get hold of Private Barnaby's medical records. From his first admission."

"I could look for them this afternoon," Juliet offered, realizing this might confirm when, exactly, Barnaby had been in Sergeant McKnight's unit.

"How long was he here?"

"Two crazy weeks!" Glenda chirped. "A lot of patients you forget, but not Christopher Barnaby. There was something different about him, something gentle. He was sweet, polite, smart, clean. He'd make his own bed for the nurses, and you *never* forget that. But he was frightened, frightened more than you usually see. He didn't want to talk to the other patients, didn't even want to look at them. He kept to himself. His neighbor had a banjo and everyone would sing, but Barnaby wouldn't even hum. . . ." Dr. Willard pulled out a notebook, and at the realization that he was documenting what she said, Glenda became even more loquacious, detailing the meals Barnaby had eaten, the magazines he had read, and how she had nursed him with unparalleled skill and tenderness.

When Dr. Willard finally closed his notebook, Juliet asked, "So, Barnaby's condition . . . is it caused by some event, some trigger, or are certain people predisposed to it? And how soon will he come out of it?"

"That's precisely the nail I'm trying to hit on the head. Battle fatigue has been around for ages but wasn't really studied until the last war. Those trenches at Verdun and the Somme rendered thousands mute, sometimes paralyzed. But war neurosis goes back centuries. Herodotus wrote about Epictetus, who in the midst of the Battle of Marathon went blind though he wasn't struck or injured."

"Psychosomatic illnesses," Juliet offered.

Dr. Willard smiled with surprise. "Indeed."

Glenda yawned, her fingertips patting her outstretched mouth. "It sounds like you'll be staying for a while, then? Examining the men and whatnot?"

"I'll be here as long as it takes. The army wants the field hospitals better equipped to diagnose and treat battle fatigue. Of course, now I'm interested in Private Barnaby. He's the first known attempted battlefield suicide in this campaign. We had two suicides last year in North Africa. But those men succeeded. If we can figure out what drives a man to that kind of an act, we might be able to prevent these breakages in the mind. Self-preservation is man's strongest instinct, so when that cracks, you want to take a good long look."

"Well, Eisenhower says this whole mess'll be done by Christmas," said Glenda. "If it goes beyond that, I think *I* might crack!"

"We can always hope for a swift end, but I am temperamentally inclined to prepare for the worst," said Willard, spooning the last bit of food into his mouth. "If you'll excuse me."

They watched him carry his tray to the far side of the tent and plunge his mess kit into the steaming barrel of soapy water. Glenda rolled her eyes. "Herodotus? Epiwhatever? Have you ever met such a Sergeant Boring!"

"You seemed quite interested," said Juliet, surprised by the accusation in her voice.

"That's how I behave with all men, sugar. Frankly, I thought *you* seemed interested. 'I'll get you those records, Doctor, just as soon as I slip into something more comfortable. . . .'"

Juliet nervously looked away. "His work is interesting. And Barnaby *is* my patient."

"Sugar, he's a head doctor. Never, and I mean *never,* trust a man who can understand what you're thinking."

* * *

After lunch Juliet returned to the recovery ward, where Barnaby lay quietly gurgling in his sleep. His arms, covered with a fine layer of chestnut hair, were crossed at his chest—a coffin pose. Had someone placed them that way or had he done it in his sleep? Juliet looked around, but none of the nearby patients seemed to be paying him any attention. His head had been shaved and his face was practically mummified except for his mouth and his one good eye. Since the surgery, though, his eye hadn't opened; he seemed to be in some sort of coma.

Snipping the thick layers of gauze from his head, she cleaned the blackened blood from his face and smoothed in sulfonamide ointment before redressing his wounds. She wheeled two screens around his bed and, holding her breath (Juliet could do this for exactly thirty-seven seconds, long enough to flip, clean, and change a patient and carry a soiled diaper to the garbage), turned him on his side, removed his diaper, and sponged him clean. *Twenty-two, twenty-three, twenty-four.* She laid down a new diaper, rolled him once again onto his back, and taped closed the sides. *Thirty-four, thirty-five.*

"All better," she huffed. She watched the rise and fall of his chest, his Saint Christopher medal nestled just below his Adam's apple. From the neck down he looked entirely normal. He was tall—over six feet, she guessed—and a bit lanky. He looked perfectly healthy. Perfectly young. She wondered where he came from, what he'd done before the war. She recalled what Glenda had said—*There was something different about him, something gentle. . . . But he was frightened.*

Settling on the floor behind one of the screens, out of view of the ward, Juliet pulled out the thick envelope. Once again, she studied the photo of the young woman, this time noticing the sign behind her: *Betty's Beauty Shop.* She had a hunch this wasn't Betty; this woman looked too glamourless to be running a beauty shop.

Of the dozens of letters, Juliet removed one that had been

folded, like an accordion, many times; she had to pry apart the pages, gray with fingerprints.

Dear Christopher,

The days are long and the news keeps saying this isn't going to be over anytime soon. I'm having a hard time. When I wake each morning I just hold my breath and count the squares on the bed quilt until I get to one hundred. I'm afraid this war is determined to steal everything I care about. I wish so much you were back home.

I make a point of reading the paper every day, top of the front page to the bottom of the last, but it makes me sad to know it wasn't you setting the type.

I write down the words I don't know, just like you, and get out the Webster's and look them up. Anything to stay busy.

I've been sick a good deal, but I don't know if it's from nerves or the baby or flu. But I'm still on my feet, working every day.

I asked Betty about the raise and she said until more folks come home and need haircuts, there isn't any extra money to be giving away. I know she's right. Most of the gals don't even bother getting their hair done since the men are gone. Pinching pennies. I think it'd be pretty funny if all the men just showed up home one day. Boy would they be in for a surprise! All the girls with mussed-up hair and not a hint of makeup. Eyes puffy from not sleeping and crying. The houses needing dusting. Dishes needing washing. Betty said, "Well, them's the blues, Tina. It's the blues makes you not want to do the things you usually do." And then she said, "Tina, just like you're not doing good with the sweeping up. Look at the floor." She handed me the broom and said, "Go on, it'll help clear your blues." Betty is still Betty.

I'd really like to get one of the factory jobs, be a real Rosie

the Riveter. The mill is hiring girls, but those jobs aren't safe
for girls in the way like me, so for now I'm stuck.
    I know I'm supposed to be proud of what you're doing, and
I am. But I'm scared for you, Christopher.
    Be safe and write soon.

                    Love, as always,
                    Tina

    PS: I put some cocoa mix in this time for you, the kind that
doesn't need milk. It's the best I could do.

Juliet slid the letter back in the envelope.

So his wife was pregnant; this made everything exponentially worse. Hopefully the woman wouldn't get a heartless army telegram informing her of his suicide attempt. What was the protocol with this kind of injury? With a man who was alive but couldn't put a pen to paper or even dictate a letter? With a man whose injury was considered desertion?

Juliet looked at the date—April 23. Just two months earlier. Even in the most dire of situations, wouldn't Private Barnaby have tried to make it back to his wife and child? Had he just aimed at his foot, he'd have been shipped home—with charges, maybe, but he'd be alive; he'd be a husband and a father. It made no sense. She thought about what Dr. Willard had said to Captain Brilling: *The mind can bleed.* Perhaps. But had his reason and love and sense of duty hemorrhaged entirely away? What could do that to a person?

She took his hand, warm and soft, and pressed it to her cheek. "What happened to you, Christopher?"

CHAPTER 6

AS THE AMBULANCE bucked and bumped along the rutted dirt road, Juliet held tightly to a beam beside her to avoid swaying into Dr. Willard. The back of the vehicle had been designed to hold six litters, with three folding racks suspended on either side of the narrow space. Having fastened the racks to the walls, the group on furlough sat on the floor, cross-legged, in the cool shade of the metal enclosure. The vehicle groaned as it tackled each steep incline through the hills, and whenever the road curved sharply, Glenda Texas flung herself laughingly against Bernice. When they finally entered the valley and the road lay flat and wide, Juliet pulled herself up and stood looking out the two small glass windows of the back door. It was thrilling to travel through that strange land; despite the war, despite the pressing mystery of what had happened to Tuck, the simple pleasure of seeing new parts of the world intoxicated her.

"How are we doing back there?" Dr. Lovelace called from the driver's seat.

"Impressive driving," said Glenda.

"Rodeo-style," yelped Lovelace, leaning his head out the window, the wind in his curls.

"I don't think army insurance covers road accidents on leave," Bernice said.

"Don't worry, Bernice," said Glenda, "you've got a surgical team right here. We'll fix you up for free."

Before the Division's next push forward, some of the hospital staff had been issued twelve-hour leaves. The day promised to be hot and bright, so at breakfast they voted to ride to Lago di Vico to take a last swim before the hospital moved north. Dr. Lovelace borrowed a map from a division commander who charted a route for them. The lake was about twenty miles from the Tyrrhenian coast; the commander assured them the area had been swept for mines.

Beneath a cloudless sky, the road behind them lay like a ribbon of dirt. In the bright morning light, an abandoned olive grove cast beautiful tangled shadows across the road. In the distance, there was a line of what Juliet thought were oak trees, but they looked smashed and frayed. On the broken branches birds had gathered thickly, as though in sympathy. At points in the road the earth had been entirely disgorged; beside these pockets of darkness lay an unsettling array of items: a broken wheelbarrow, a boot, a muti-lated suitcase. She noticed an abandoned farmhouse fronted by a dozen corpses—cattle and horses, withered and blackened. The sight jolted her, but through the small windows it all had the far-away feel of a movie scene, the images clouded by the thick worn glass, bounded and circumscribed by the dark metal of the door.

Juliet returned to the floor of the ambulance, where Glenda and Bernice were intently playing a hand of poker. Bernice was a wiz-ard at cards and played only for money; between the women lay a pile of tattered lire. Hoping to learn a thing or two, Juliet settled in beside Bernice. At the front end of the compartment Dr. Willard presided, having repositioned himself so that he could stretch his legs. The ambulance groaned once again as it tackled an incline, and Juliet felt the rumble of tires through the floorboard. Bernice was gleefully winning her fifth hand of poker when the vehicle slowly ground to a halt and Lovelace called, "Ta-daaa."

The lake was stunning. Sunlight skipped along the vast surface like a thousand tossed stones. A line of dense forest surrounded the water, a border of green velvet against the sky. They stood silently beside the ambulance, finally muttering, "Jesus" and "Amen" and

"It's like a fucking postcard" before making their way to the bright crescent of sand.

Juliet spread out a hospital blanket, and they all began to excitedly unlace their boots.

Dr. Lovelace, stripping down to a pair of red swim trunks, called over to Dr. Willard: "Shall we scare away the lake monsters for the ladies?" Without awaiting an answer, Lovelace dove in. Juliet watched as Dr. Willard hesitantly followed, pausing at the lake's edge to study the horizon.

Glenda stood, unbuttoning her shirt with a languor that suggested she was accustomed to an audience. Juliet instead wrestled off her shirt and pants while sitting on the blanket. In their swimsuits they eagerly made for the water, leaving Bernice fully clothed on the grass, gleefully counting her poker winnings.

Juliet shuddered as the icy water bit at her calves, but forced herself farther in. Glenda paused waist deep, her face to the sun, a gold bobby pin in her teeth, arranging her curls. Her hair finally fastened, she flung both arms behind her, puffed out her chest, and threw herself in, up to her chest, with a *whoo-eeee*.

Dr. Lovelace emerged on the shore after a spectacular and noisy circuit of aquatics; his beard dripping, he inflated a rainbow beach ball, tossed it straight up, and caught it with a thwack. "Now, ladies," he called as he strode back in, "I realize this may look like child's play, but this is actually an advanced exercise in hand-eye coordination. Heads up, Texas. . . ." Dr. Lovelace tossed the ball so that it splashed just in front of Glenda.

"*Clifford.*"

Glenda had been assisting Dr. Lovelace for a year, and Juliet thought she was sweet on him, though Glenda seemed sweet on most men. Lovelace was easily twenty years her senior and had a wife and three teenage children back in California. Juliet suspected it was a flirtation to pass the grueling time, something to take the edge off sawing gangrenous limbs all day long. Who could blame them?

Pawing the ball toward herself, Glenda turned to Juliet. "Sugar, why don't you show the boys a thing or two?" The ball sailed through the air and Juliet caught it securely, just as Tuck had tried to teach her hundreds of times but which she'd never quite mastered. Delighted with her feat, she excitedly threw the ball to Dr. Willard, who, taken by surprise, swatted it away.

"I did not miss my calling," he said, staring dolefully at the drifting ball. "Nurse Dufresne, on the other hand, should go pro."

He turned to Juliet with a dazzled smile, and Juliet's stomach fluttered. Without thinking, she flipped onto her back, scissor-kicking hard through the black and icy water. He made her nervous, the psychiatrist. Far from the group, she lifted her head and looked back. Willard had thankfully turned his attention elsewhere, so Juliet eased into a slow, measured sidestroke.

Gliding alongside the overgrown shore, her body passed through unexpected patches of warm water in the cold. Shallow spots, she thought. In the distance, a procession of ducks slid along noiselessly. And what she believed to be a cormorant studied her from the perch of a mossy rock. The shimmering sprawl of the lake, the primeval elegance of the birds—the panorama tightened her chest: here was the most beautiful landscape she'd seen in years, and she couldn't help but think, *Tuck would love this.*

It was a thought that did not come often these days, so it had the power to disorient her; once again, Juliet had to remind herself of the telegram, of Tuck's mysterious last letter; she had to acknowledge that the person with whom she had shared almost every experience of her childhood, the person she assumed she would speak to for the rest of her life, had simply vanished.

He's gone, Juliet told herself. *You can't talk to him, you can't write to him, you can't tell him about this beautiful lake. You're alone now.*

The feeling moved through her sharply, and Juliet dove under the water and swam. Holding her breath in the darkness, she counted—*one, two, three, four.* She imagined fetching a bedpan, carrying it to the washroom. *Twenty-three, twenty-four, twenty-five.* . . . She wanted to break thirty-seven seconds; she wanted her lungs to burst.

"Ahoy!" Dr. Lovelace called when she shot up, gasping for air. "We thought you were trying to swim to Switzerland!" He and Glenda were wading in the shallows, tossing the ball back and forth. On the beach beyond, Bernice was doing calisthenics: squatting and standing, squatting and standing. Dr. Willard lay nearby with a book propped before his face.

"Let's see you jump for it, Cliff," Glenda called, and the ball sailed in a vast arc over Dr. Lovelace and past Juliet, disappearing into the woods. "Whoops, sugar, can you grab that?"

As Juliet swam toward the ball, Dr. Lovelace called, "Willard, can you give the girl a hand?" Dr. Willard set down his book, tugged on his boots, and knotted a towel around his waist, heading dutifully toward the woods.

A thicket of leafy birch trees shaded the area, and twigs blanketed the ground. As Juliet pulled herself onto the mossy shore, she could hear the crunch of Willard's approaching footsteps. She straightened her bathing suit straps and quickly thumbed the bottom into place. But when she turned to face Dr. Willard, he was staring at the ground. She followed his gaze to the curled-up body of a soldier, the face blackened with dried blood, a swollen blue tongue protruding from the mouth. A German, it seemed, from the uniform, which was oddly pristine. The man's hands, however, had been pecked and gnawed, and a curious cormorant now poked its beak at the pulpy remainder of one thumb. Juliet shooed it away and dropped to her knees beside the body, gently touching its shoulder: "Oh, God, the poor thing."

Willard looked at her quizzically. "It looks like one shot to the temple," he said. "I doubt he suffered much."

Juliet shook her head. That wasn't the matter at all.

She looked at the boy, or the man, and all she could think was, *Here is someone who went missing.* Surely his squad hadn't seen him shot, hadn't just left him to die in the woods—even Germans weren't that disloyal. Burial mattered; the ritual, the ceremonial good-bye, meant something to everyone in the world. The Neanderthals had buried their dead. No one just left the dead to rot in the woods. But as far as the world was concerned, here was a young man who had, like Tuck, simply vanished. And so what Juliet wanted desperately to do at that moment was to carry the body out of the woods and find out who he had been and who he belonged to, so that those people—his mother, his wife, his sister—could say good-bye and find some peace. But she knew that was impossible, and certainly irrational and impractical enough to prompt the concern of a psychiatrist if she voiced the thought. So she gathered some branches and laid them over the corpse, then gestured to the towel around Dr. Willard's waist. "We need a shroud," she said matter-of-factly.

So what if he thought she was sentimental and crazy? She was certainly a lot more sane than the soldiers he dealt with.

Willard removed the towel and studied her as she laid it over the man. "Most people these days spit on German corpses," he said.

"If you need to spit, I won't stop you."

He smiled. "I much prefer shrouds."

They walked in silence toward the beach, and once again Juliet was aware of the slight unevenness of his gait.

"We couldn't tell if you two were stealing our ball or stealing off!" hollered Lovelace.

Juliet looked at Willard, and between them emerged the shared realization that they had forgotten the ball. Juliet glanced back toward the woods, and her face must have shown unease in returning there.

"To hell with the ball," Willard whispered.

"To hell with it," she agreed.

Together they settled themselves on the blanket and Juliet squeezed water out of her braids and stared contemplatively at the tree line. Dr. Willard picked up his book, began reading, then set it in his lap. "So, Nurse Dufresne, where are you from?"

Having collected dozens of cigarette packs and cans of Spam and 40,000 lire from the other nurses and doctors that morning, the travelers had decided in advance that the afternoon would be given over to buying wine. So, in the town of Caprarola, the group went from house to house bartering for libations, but it took longer than expected. Hoping to sell as much as possible, the Italians lifted framed paintings off the walls and urged them on the visitors; they emerged from their attics with dusty brass candlesticks. Given the sparse look of their homes, it seemed to Juliet that they had already sold most of their belongings; they stood gaunt and bony and worried, keenly eyeing the cans of Spam. The hospital staff had little interest in the curios, but Glenda purchased an alabaster elephant from a young woman who, when she realized the group wanted only wine and she had none to sell, began to weep. They eventually collected thirty-two bottles and, at Lovelace's suggestion, opened two of the folding litter racks and laid the wine bottles on their wet towels; they put hospital blankets on top and fastened everything with rope. All of this was done quite slowly, for they were all saddened by the threadbare homes they had seen, the desperation of the Italians. By the time they climbed back into the ambulance and set out on the long, winding roads to the hospital, it had grown dark.

"Exactly how lost are we?" asked Glenda, leaning into the front and shining a flashlight on the map beside Lovelace after they had been driving an hour, intermittently singing "*Thirty-two bottles of wine in the truck, thirty-two bottles of wine . . .*"

"Well, I know exactly where we are," said Lovelace. "It's just unfortunately not where we want to be. All of these signs are a mess."

"The Krauts love that game," said Bernice. "They spin them like weather vanes. We'll be halfway to Sicily soon."

"If anyone learned anything about dead reckoning in Basic Training, now's the time to speak up."

For the next fifteen minutes, they rode along in alert silence, the ambulance groaning as it climbed the dark hills. They had switched on the surgical light in the back of the vehicle, as though the hard white glare might help them concentrate on finding their way home. They stared anxiously at one another. It was impossible, thought Juliet, to just sit in the dark and relax. Juliet had heard the awful stories of deadly furloughs: one wrong turn and they could drive over a mine. But she saw there was no point in discussing it. Bernice and Glenda and Willard sat quietly, their jaws clenched, dutifully accepting the risk, as they had done when deciding to enlist, of what it meant to be in a war zone. Following their lead, Juliet leaned back against the cold metal cabin, the faint scent of lake water drifting from her hair.

Soon the ambulance lurched to a halt, and Lovelace's voice startled her: "Turn off the light!" he snapped.

Willard reached up and switched off the surgical light, stranding them in a thick blackness. Juliet could see nothing, but she heard Lovelace wrestling with the gearshift. She was aware that they were slowly beginning to move backward, when suddenly a bright light pierced the back window. "Bloody fuck," Lovelace huffed, stopping the vehicle. "I'm sorry, gang."

Again they were in darkness, but then the light returned, illuminating the crowded compartment in irregular surges. In one quick flash, Juliet saw Willard's face, looking around at everyone's shirts. "Does everyone have their Red Cross armbands?" he whispered.

Amid the quick chorus of yeses, Juliet's mouth went woolly. She had forgotten hers.

"We've got a Jerry coming up right behind us," said Lovelace.

A beam directed at Juliet's face forced her to turn away. There was a slow knock on the door—one, two, three—and then only the sound of the engine rumbling.

"Are we supposed to open the door or do they open the door?" whispered Glenda.

Willard, seated at the head of the compartment, climbed over the nurses so that he was the closest to the door. He raised his hands in front of the windows and called out: *"Bitte nicht schießen! Wir sind Ärzte und Krankenschwestern!"* Slowly, he reached down and opened one of the doors, gently pushing it open.

Two men in German uniforms stood staring at the ambulance, each clutching a flashlight and a pistol.

Willard gestured for the nurses to raise their hands, and Lovelace slowly climbed into the back.

One soldier stepped forward and barked at them lengthily in German, to which Willard replied, simply, *"Nein."* Willard then turned to the nurses and said, "Stay here." Stepping slowly from the ambulance, he kept his hands above his head. *"Wir haben uns verfahren. Wir sind auf dem Weg zurück ins Krankenhaus."*

Glenda and Bernice fumbled for their armbands, and Juliet drew her knees to her chest. Willard was soon led away, out of sight, though beside the vehicle Juliet could hear fractured bursts of an argument in German. She told herself that if she could still hear Willard speaking, everything was okay. She listened intently for his voice.

The remaining soldier trained his weapon on the nurses. Juliet closed her eyes and forced her mind through the periodic table. She'd run through it twice and was slowly mouthing "Radium" when the second door of the ambulance flung open. The other soldier had returned with Willard, and his flashlight beam traveled from face to face, armband to armband, stopping on Juliet's bare sleeve.

"Wo waren Sie?"

"Schwimmen. An einem See," answered Dr. Willard.

The German signaled everyone to get out. "They want to inspect the vehicle for weapons," said Willard.

Juliet followed Glenda and Bernice and Lovelace to the side of the road while the soldier leapt into the ambulance, noisily upturning bags and shaking towels. Behind them, a dark and forested hill sloped toward the night sky; its treetops barbed the low crescent moon. On the other side of the road, heaps of deadfall were piled between skeletal bushes. Through this, Juliet saw a glint of eyes: someone was crouched in the overgrowth, his gun trained on Dr. Willard. Up and down the road, she now noticed, behind the deadfall, every few yards lay men with rifles. Juliet tasted bile rising in her throat.

Stepping out of the ambulance, the German soldier shook his head at his compatriot and began a serious discussion. The pitch of this debate wavered and surged, each man shaking his pistol while trying to make some passionate point. Eventually, a resolution was reached and a pensive silence ensued. The first soldier climbed back into the ambulance, reemerged with a folded litter and disappeared into the overgrowth.

A minute later, he lumbered out of the darkness with another soldier, and between them hung the litter, now topped with a man who had damp black hair, a face that was pale and waxy. His eyes were gummed shut. Over the litter's side, his bloodied leg dangled limply.

"Helfen Sie ihm," the soldier announced, sliding the litter into the back of the ambulance and gesturing the doctors over. Willard and Lovelace hesitantly obeyed.

"Is he shot?" asked Lovelace, gently lifting the man's leg.

"Maybe septicemia?" Willard took the man's pulse.

"Or malaria. He probably needs Atabrine. And this leg is infected."

Willard spoke to the Germans: *"Wir haben nicht die nötige Ausrüstung dabei. Wir werden ihn mitnehmen müssen."*

The soldiers nodded. *"Sie können gehen."*

"Start the engine, Lovelace," Willard said. "And get in, ladies."

Juliet helped Willard arrange the litter on one of the racks, a matter complicated by the layers of wine suspended overhead. Glenda and Bernice climbed in behind. There was little room for anyone to move. As the wounded German moaned from his litter, his teeth began chattering, and Juliet reached for a towel to wipe down his forehead, knocking into the overhead rack, sending two bottles of wine crashing to the floor.

"Why don't we just *give* them the wine?" said Willard, glaring at the shards of glass floating in a pool of red.

"Thirty-two bottles?!" said Glenda.

"They'll think it's poisoned," said Bernice.

Without waiting for further instructions, Juliet began removing the wine on the rack above the German, bottle by bottle, passing them to Willard.

"Ein Moment. Ein Geschenk!" Willard called to the Germans, setting the bottles on the ground.

One soldier approached, offering a suspicious half smile. *"Ich hoffe, daß es nicht vergiftet ist,"* he said.

"What did he say?" Juliet asked as the ambulance slowly rolled away and they closed the metal doors firmly behind them.

Willard said, "He hopes it's not poisoned."

As the ambulance crept carefully along the winding roads, Juliet fed the German mashed K rations while Bernice held a flashlight close.

Finally Glenda, who had joined Lovelace in the front, whispered, "Clifford! That's the *tree*. We're close."

Within minutes they'd given the two-word password to the hospital sentry, and their ambulance pulled up to the quartermaster's tent, where Lovelace and Willard wearily unloaded the stretcher and began carrying it toward the Receiving Tent. The nurses followed, lugging their packs and canteens across the dark and silent hospital encampment.

"Good God, who got hit?" Major Decker, smoking a cigar beside his tent, had spotted them.

Dr. Lovelace answered: "We were given a German."

"Who, exactly, is handing them out?"

Glenda shook her head as though trying to shake off a headache. "We traded very good wine for a malarial Kraut."

"Perhaps I should have been more clear. As noncombatants, you know there's no need for you to collect German prisoners. They aren't souvenirs."

"We'll get him into surgery and he should be ready for evac to a POW camp by morning," said Lovelace.

"Make sure it's by 0700 tomorrow," said Major Decker. "That's when we start packing up. The front is in motion." He turned to the nurses. "Ladies, say your good-byes to the bandaged boys."

"All of them?" asked Juliet, thinking of Barnaby and everything she meant to ask him.

"Anyone who's getting sent back into combat stays with us. And we've been ordered to hold on to Private Barnaby. Brilling wants him close, and the army wants him with Willard."

"Then I move forward with you," said Dr. Willard.

Juliet smiled in the dark.

In the delicate seam between night and day, the bugle sounded; surrounded by semidarkness, the nurses tugged on their uniforms, packed their musette bags, rolled their bedrolls, and soon lugged the entirety of their belongings outside. One by one they eased the tent stakes from the ground and watched their homes billow and flatten. All across the encampment, as the sun rose, the same was happening, and soon the hospital looked to Juliet like the remains of a massacred giant—canvas skin strewn across the grass, a skeleton of wooden poles.

While the hospital staff loaded the dozens of vehicles, vague figures began to emerge from the hills. A swarm of women and children and elderly men soon descended on the camp, poking through the abandoned barrels and oil drums, the trash heap; any scrap that had been left on the ground was stuffed into a pocket or laid in the bib of a shirt.

As the morning shadows slowly lifted, the convoy of half-tracks and ambulances set off into the hills. Juliet sat in a truck with a group of nurses she did not yet know well, but when artillery rumbled in the distance, they began to sing, *"Over hill, over dale, as we hit the dusty trail . . ."* and the reassuring smiles that always bridged unfamiliarity across an operating table were exchanged. Along the road lay abandoned tanks and overturned trucks, heaps of torn and rusted steel. Everywhere, metal was strewn across the ground as though scattered by a tornado. It unsettled Juliet to think that this equipment might have been built from all those washing machines and car parts Tuck had gathered back home, the balls of aluminum foil playfully tossed around the scrap collection center. *Just give us the scrap. We'll turn it into tanks. We'll turn it into planes. We'll turn it into jeeps. We'll turn it into guns.* Such a boisterous effort had gone into building machinery they all believed would be indestructible.

Within an hour they had arrived in a two-acre field. Before the convoy came to a stop, Major Decker leapt from the lead truck and began barking orders. The assembly of the hospital, it seemed, was much more complicated than the disassembly. Climbing groggily from the truck, the nurses made their way to the ambulances to check on patients, while around them the engineers staked flags into the ground as they swept the field for mines, and the enlisted men, moving close behind, hacked away at the overgrowth. By lunchtime, tarps were laid on the ground, where the nurses ate quickly, and when the ward men finished pitching the Recovery Tent, the nurses scraped their mess kits and carried in stacks of linens to make the ward beds. As they carefully transferred all the patients from their litters, Juliet arranged Barnaby on his bed; a downy layer of chestnut hair now covered his scalp. His neck had thickened, and a ruddy flush brightened his chest. "That's it," she said, arranging his feeding tube. "You're on the mend." But his eye remained closed, and he appeared lost in his silent slumber.

As the day wore on, Juliet, Glenda, and Bernice pitched their own tent, unpacked their bags, and hung mosquito netting at the entrance. Outside their tent Glenda attached a sign she had been carrying since North Africa: *Waldorf-Astoria*.

By the time the sun began to fade, dynamos whizzed to life, bare bulbs flashed on, stoves were lit; once again, the hospital began to glow and thrum like a carnival. Sweaty from the day's exertion, Juliet searched out the shower house, an uncovered wooden room with benches on either side.

"Oh, no, what's this?"

Glenda sat naked on a bench and from a large metal drum scooped water with her helmet. Juliet had grown unexpectedly fond of the perforated beer cans that dumped water when she tugged a rope.

"No showerheads until tomorrow," Glenda explained. "The engineers had to go to the front for a mine sweep." As she doused her shoulders, the water sloshed onto the wood planks and steam swirled from the wet timber.

Juliet unfastened her braids. The ends of her hair were dried and split, but her scalp was oily from lack of washing. Using her fingers, she worked through the tangles, tugging hard at several knots. "Birds could lay eggs in this mess," she said.

"Wow, you look older with your hair down. *Womanly*. It frames your face real nice. You should let it hang long, put some curlers in."

"The braids are easy," said Juliet. "I've been wearing them forever."

She peeled off her clothes, hanging them on a nail, and sat on the bench beside Glenda, who had begun intently soaping her breasts. Something in the way Glenda flaunted her body perturbed Juliet. It made her aware that she didn't, or *couldn't,* flaunt her own, that she was cursed with being awkward and demure. *Prudish* was the word; she was prudish without wanting to be. But growing up without a woman in the house, she never learned how to primp or prance about or even pluck her eyebrows. She feared her inexperience was feeding on itself: Was she too priggish even to be at ease near a woman who wasn't?

"What do you think of Clifford?" Glenda asked.

"Dr. Lovelace? Well, he's a lousy furlough driver, but he seems like an excellent surgeon. He did an amazing job with Barnaby's face."

"I mean *personally.*"

"I've only known him a few weeks!"

"But a girl gets impressions, feelings. . . . You seem observant. Don't be stingy with your smarts!"

Juliet plunged her helmet into the bucket and doused her shoulders, rubbing at the dirt on her arms. "He seems like a good man."

"He's going to make me a plaster cast for my alabaster elephant so I can ship it home to my momma in Texas."

"That's very sweet."

"That's what I thought. Beyond the call of duty." Glenda nodded slowly, and the soap slipped from her hand. As she retrieved it from the wet planks, her bare bottom rose momentarily, and Juliet turned away in politeness. Glenda laughed and offered Juliet the bar. "Here, you'll smell like strawberry shortcake."

The soap slid smoothly across Juliet's stomach, and she practically drank the fruity musk.

"Now, don't forget to go down south." Glenda gestured between Juliet's legs. "You never know when a visitor might drop by."

"Ugh." Juliet dramatically shuddered with disapproval. "Trespassers will be shot."

"A girl should never waste her pink parts."

Juliet vigorously soaped her arms and chest and waist—but avoided her thighs. Shrugging, Glenda yanked a bedsheet from the nail and loosely knotted it at her chest. Juliet doused the suds from her body and reached for her own towel. Taking in the last glimpse of Juliet's nakedness, Glenda grinned.

"You know, sugar, if you won't touch it, who else will?"

Juliet sat on her helmet on the ground amid a circle of nurses and doctors; the sky was black, the first night stars punching through the darkness. Her hair still wet, the air cool, Juliet clutched a blanket over her shoulders and sipped slowly at her "moose milk," a pungent cocktail of medical alcohol and canned grapefruit juice. It surged through her head and tickled her scalp, but she was afraid to drink water since she loathed the makeshift latrine—a bucket encircled by a shower curtain. She'd been avoiding fluids all day, hoping to wait out the construction of the outhouse.

In the center, where a campfire should have been, sat a small radio. Dr. Lovelace crouched over it, fiddling with the dial. His shirtsleeves were rolled above his broad forearms. His wristwatch gleamed in the moonlight. He was trying to tune in to *Blind Dates,* a show in which women read letters to their sons overseas. Meanwhile everyone drank and stared at the sky, debating the names of obscure constellations. Another nurse, Avis, asked Juliet how she had survived the decampment; Avis swore Juliet would be able to single-handedly pitch a tent within weeks. Everyone talked to her, asked how she was settling in.

Almost all of the doctors except Dr. Willard were there; Juliet wondered if he was working, or if he didn't like socializing.

The smoke from their cigarettes drifted toward the green tents beyond. Juliet was amazed by how closely this encampment resembled the previous one.

The radio suddenly blared as it picked up the end of Radio London, reporting on the landings at Normandy. Juliet and Avis leaned in, and then the broadcast cut to noisy static.

Lovelace checked his watch. "It's only our gal Sally now."

"Turn that crap off," said Major Decker. Major Decker had carried a chair from his tent and presided over the group in a kingly fashion.

"But she plays the best tunes," said Avis.

"I ditto Major Decker," said Mother Hen, swigging a bottle of beer. "Morale is in the ditches."

Juliet leaned toward Avis. "Who's Sally?"

"An American who broadcasts for Radio Berlin."

"She's our enemy on the airwaves," added Lovelace. "The nastiest, most pessimistic siren that ever spoke—with exquisite taste in music." He turned the dial, and a woman's voice, deep and smoky, crackled from the radio:

Well, fellas, this is Axis Sally talking to you Yanks in Italy. Why are ya here? We know why. You do, too. To fight for those Jewish bankers and Wall Street stockbrokers. That's what for. To make a little money. You're gonna die out here for that, ya know? Now that's a silly thing for you to do, Yank, but you're in a war for them now and you won't make it one inch farther. But we'll play a nice song for you now and listen to some of your favorite music. Remember those nights you sat in the evening with your girlfriend, those summer nights, she'd be in your arms and she'd say "I love you" and you'd say "I love you, too." And you'll never see her again. You'll die here.

Then "Good Night Sweetheart" came on.

"The troops *listen* to this?" asked Brother Reardon.

"They can practically recite it," said Lovelace, drawing Glenda up into the middle of the grass. Glenda kicked off her shoes and rose to her toes and began sidestepping and twirling with sensual grace. Her hair was wet and loose, her mouth shimmering with lipstick. As "In the Mood" came on, and others got up to dance, she sashayed into Dr. Mallick's arms. Juliet watched her move from man to man, eventually dancing happily alone at the edges of the circle, eyes closed, chin to the moon. Juliet slid back to make room for the dancers and quietly sipped her cocktail, tapping her foot to the song.

"It's a sin to leave a beautiful young lady without a dance partner."

Before Juliet could respond, Brother Reardon set her drink on the ground and drew her into the circle. An inch shorter than she was, he placed his arm stiffly around her waist. He moved almost athletically to the music, his feet shuffling out two to three steps for every beat. Juliet tried her best to follow; when she faltered, he pulled her close and loudly counted out his steps. She had never danced with a man before; she had never, in fact, been so close to a man for that length of time. It was nice. *Just my luck,* Juliet thought laughingly. *The chaplain!*

They'd barely spoken since their first meeting. But she had watched him dart endlessly between patients; crouched at their bedsides, a Bible in his lap, he held their hands and anointed their wounds. Behind screens, he "specialed" men through their dying hours, and he spent several evenings with Barnaby, reading aloud psalms. She learned from the other nurses that he belonged to a Benedictine archabbey in Pennsylvania. He had been a monk for only one year before volunteering for the war effort. Was this dance just another act of charity? Although Juliet loathed the idea of being pitied, she was glad not to be left on the sidelines.

He swirled her through the crowd, bumping the other dancers, laughing. At the song's end, he dramatically dipped her, and her wet braids swept the grass. "Sorry, I'm out of practice."

"It's all right," she laughed. "I've never been *in* practice." She stepped back so that he knew his responsibility was over.

How'd ya like that one, boys? Did it make you miss your gal back home? I hope you got a nice moment in, because it will, sadly, be one of your last. We're getting ready for you on the coast of France. Yup. We know all about your secret little landing. And we're ready for you in the Italian mountains. It's a shame you have to march your way into certain death, but our spies amongst you are doing a swell job of letting us know exactly what you're up to. We'll try to be nice and kill you quickly.

This is Axis Sally, signing off.

"They really have spies?" asked Juliet, picking up her drink.

Glenda drew up close. "When you think about it, it's kind of heartbreaking. Spies are the best actors in the world, and nobody ever knows their talents."

"Spies don't have talents," said Avis. "They're just spineless."

"Soulless," said Brother Reardon.

"Okay, okay, we don't need to write a treatise on treachery," Major Decker bellowed, gnawing on his cigar. "There are no spies. That's exactly why this crap shouldn't be playing." He switched off the radio. "Don't you people have work to do? I'm ordering you all on duty right now."

"But, Major," said Dr. Lovelace, "we've been drinking."

"Then try not to cut anyone open. And you, Nurse . . ."

"Dufresne."

"Dufresne, go check on your patient. You can babble to him about spies."

Major Decker set the radio at the foot of his chair and propped his boots on it. Closing his eyes, he smoked into the night.

Juliet found Dr. Willard in the recovery ward, seated beside Barn-aby's bed, an open notebook in his lap and a cup of coffee on the floor. An oil lamp cast a soft glow on Willard's face. The nearby beds were empty.

"You missed the dancing," said Juliet.

"Bum legs make for bad dancers."

She wandered close and looked down at Barnaby.

"How are you?" Willard asked. "I'm sure meeting those Germans last night was a fright."

"I've had better nights' sleep, but I'm all right." She wanted to thank him for saving them but worried it would sound melodramatic; Glenda and Bernice had taken the ordeal in stride, and Juliet aimed to do the same. "You speak German," Juliet said.

"And French and Latin, though they're of less use here."

"Wow."

Seemingly uncomfortable with her admiration, he began to peel back a portion of the gauze over Barnaby's chin. "See how well he's healing? He'll be missing the one eye, but other than that, there may not be anything physically wrong with him."

"Except that he won't come out of his coma." Juliet felt lightheaded. She gripped the end of Barnaby's bed and settled herself, Indian-style, on the ground. She pressed her hands to her cheeks; they felt hot.

"Well, there are many types of comas. It's more of a continuum than a dichotomy. Watch." Willard clapped his hands, and Barnaby flinched. "*Auditory startle*. Auditory startle is excellent. And if I scratch his foot, his leg moves. With proper stimulation, he can open his eye and track an object. Visual pursuit is extremely promising. But it's more than his reflexes. He can actually hear us. His heart rate changes, depending on what I say to him; he just doesn't seem to want to open his eye."

"So he knows what's going on around him?"

"Not like you or I do. It's a neurological limbo. His mind absorbs information; it's just that it doesn't necessarily process it fully. I've talked to some patients after they've emerged from these states who claim vague memories. Most, however, recall nothing."

"I've been trying to say nice things to him, just in case." She rubbed Barnaby's foot. "Nurse flirting." She giggled and exhaled quite loudly, swaying backward for a moment. "Sorry, I'm a little drunk."

"Yes, I can tell." Willard returned his attention to his notebook, turning several pages in search of something.

Juliet straightened her posture. "So what do *you* do in the meantime? Until he wakes up?"

"I train the staff in the treatment of battle fatigue. And I help the other men who come in."

She gestured at his notebook. "What's in there?"

"Thoughts, impressions, ideas." Willard slid on his glasses and lifted the book. "For example."

When the furious struggle of the present war has been decided, each one of the victorious fighters will return home joyfully to his wife and children, unchecked and undisturbed by thoughts of the enemies he has killed whether at close quarters or long range. It is worthy of note that the primitive races which still survive in the world, and are undoubtedly closer than we are to primaeval man, act differently in this respect, or did until they came under the influence of our civilization. Savages . . . are far from being remorseless murderers; when they return victorious from the war-path they may not set foot in their villages or touch their wives till they have atoned for the murders they committed in war by penances which are often long and tedious. It is easy, of course, to attribute this to their superstition: the savage still goes in fear of the avenging spirits of the slain. But the spirits of his slain enemy are nothing but the expression of his bad conscience about his blood-guilt; behind this superstition there lies concealed a vein of ethical sensitiveness which has been lost by us civilized men.

"Any idea who said that?" he asked.

"Dr. Henry Willard?"

"Ah, how I wish. I must, however, cede the honor to the great Sigmund Freud, writing in 1915 about the *First* World War. Of course, none of those men returned home joyfully. But we expected them to; people still expect them to. Unchecked and undisturbed."

He removed his glasses. His eyes were intricately threaded with green and gold and brown. They were thoughtful eyes, beautiful eyes. Juliet felt momentarily speechless. He looked at her as though awaiting her response, then closed his notebook firmly.

"Well, if he can hear, I wonder . . . I mean maybe . . ." Juliet stammered, rifling beneath the cot for one of Barnaby's letters. "Maybe if you read this to him? It's from his wife. Would that help?"

Without glancing at the letter, Willard pressed it back at her. Juliet felt a momentary dejection, which must have been evident, because he shook his head. "No, no, I only meant it needs a woman's touch. Please. Go ahead. You."

Juliet flattened the pages on her thigh, and Willard parted the *V* of Barnaby's hospital gown and arranged the stethoscope.

Juliet cleared her throat:

Dear Christopher,

I got the money you sent, and thank you as always for that as I was able to pay the bank on time and didn't have to get another one of Otis Rattmeyer's huffy telephone calls. That man has lungs so big I swear on my socks you can probably hear his mean old clattering all the way where you are. Though I don't know where that is, Christopher. It's killing me. I know they won't let you say anything but it hurts to think of you and not know where to put you. I'm not used to it. So I imagine you all the way in Africa, because Betty says that's the most exotic place for a soldier to be. When I picture you, just for fun, I have you sitting on a camel.

I take all the vitamins, big as gobstoppers, each morning gulping one down with my coffee. Then I rest for a minute since that's the time of day my stomach starts tumbling. You don't have to worry because I'm taking everything real slow. I'm getting fat and lazy and loving every minute of it.

"See?" Juliet interjected. "Your wife is taking good care of herself."

I only go from the house to Betty's and then stop at the grocery on the way back, and little Billy Sudner (remember him?) walks right beside me and carries the bag home so I don't put a strain on my back. People are being nice. I guess everyone feels sorry for me, and since there are no men around everyone's pitching in best they can. Betty told me that Eunice Cartwright came over last week to fix that Chevrolet of hers. Who knew Eunice was so mechanically inclined?! But Betty said Eunice marched right up to the car, popped open the hood, then went crawling and squirming underneath the whole thing, fiddled with some pipes, and poof: a working Chevrolet! I told Betty how I was worrying about you, and she said, "Tina, you call me on the telephone if you need someone to talk to." But the telephone is pricey, and I know if I got just one word out I'd keep going all night, so I'm just going to pretend like Betty never said it. I'm getting used to the silence. Instead, I pull out my paper and pens and get to writing you a letter like you insisted I do.

Juliet rubbed Barnaby's hand, kneading the knuckled warmth of his long fingers, hoping for some small response, but his eye remained closed. "Tina misses you. Remember Tina?" Finally, she folded the letter and shoved it back in the envelope—had she really thought she'd be able to rouse him?

"Well," she said shyly, "it beats changing bedpans."

Dr. Willard removed the stethoscope and lifted his notebook. "Come on, let's give him a little room."

"I guess that was silly," Juliet said as they exited the tent.

"Hell, if I thought it would help, I'd tap-dance. Here, it's chilly." Willard took off his jacket and placed it over Juliet's shoulders. He pulled back her braids so they fell above the collar.

"I've never met a psychiatrist before," Juliet said as they walked along the darkened hospital grounds.

"Now, that seems the precursor to an observation about my profession."

She wanted to say something clever, but she felt uncertain of herself, and the awkwardness that had always plagued her tangled her thoughts. "Complicated," she mustered. "Interesting. I think it's really complicated and interesting, what you do."

"Interesting enough for you to want to assist me?" Willard stopped and turned to her. "Don't get me wrong, you're no Lana Turner with those letters. But I like your instincts. You were right— it *is* the kind of thing that can help bring someone back. I found some other things in his musette bag: good-luck charms, talismans. Barnaby will need a lot more reminders of his real life. And you have a good rapport with him. Well"—he flashed a grin—"as much as one can with a man who doesn't speak."

Juliet thought about Tuck, and all the things she wanted to ask Barnaby if he ever regained consciousness. She thought about working closely with Dr. Willard.

"You're smiling, young lady. Is that an affirmative?"

CHAPTER 7

RAIN FELL IN thick sheets the next evening, hitting the mud so forcefully, the ground seemed alive. Juliet met Dr. Willard in the Recovery Tent, where they lifted Barnaby onto a litter and draped him with a poncho before carrying him through the rain to the Isolation Ward. The tent was small and dark and smelled so fiercely of bleach that Juliet coughed. She stared at the rectangular shadow of the single bed, empty since Private Blakely had succumbed to pneumonia that morning. This was her least favorite area of the hospital; this was where people came to die.

They set the litter atop the bed, and Dr. Willard lit a kerosene lamp. In the corner sat a glass-covered contraption the size of a typewriter. It was plugged into the tent's sole electrical cord. Juliet toweled the rainwater from her face and studied the machine.

"That," Willard explained, "is so that we don't have to rely on memory." He sifted through his black bag and extracted a syringe. From a small, velvet-lined box he took a glass vial labeled XR-529 and handed it to her. Willard had explained little to Juliet ahead of time about the nature of what they would be doing with Barnaby, and she now felt entirely bewildered. She had assumed they were going to be reading him more letters. She didn't want to reveal her utter inexperience, but she also didn't want to make a mistake. Not with a patient and a dosage.

"We inject him with this XR-529?" she asked, studying the vial. "Five milliliters?"

"Sodium Pentothal. You've seen it used for anesthesia, but in large doses. Five milliliters will slow his respiration and pulse just enough to make him suggestible. I want to start with a low dose to see how he handles it, so we may have only fifteen minutes. You monitor his vitals; I record and take notes of what he says."

"What he *says*?" She studied the vial. "*This* will wake him from his coma?"

"If I'm right, that we're not just witnessing the effects of a brain injury, but that much of this coma is actually a psychosomatically induced withdrawal—and let's hope I'm right—then the Pentothal will temporarily ease him out of that withdrawal and allow him to talk. *That* will begin the process of rousing him from his coma. Imagine it this way: His mind has hundreds of doors, doors to all kinds of memories and experiences. Right now, many of those doors are locked. But when we ask him questions, slowly, one by one, some of those doors will come unlocked. Our questions are like keys. We don't know, of course, which door is the real problem, the largest door, the one sealed so firmly that even he can't will it open. But by process of elimination we may find it, and can then concentrate our efforts. . . . After the Pentothal wears off, he won't even know we were looking. Now, let's get him upright."

Together they propped Barnaby against the wall of the tent. Willard drew up a chair to face Barnaby and flipped open the glass-covered contraption. He unwound a cord from a microphone and laid the microphone on Barnaby's chest. He gestured for Juliet to sit on the bed beside Barnaby, then handed her a stethoscope, needle, and syringe.

As rain drummed on the canvas overhead, she carefully injected the Pentothal into Barnaby's arm. She held his wrist to monitor his pulse. She wanted to believe what Willard had said, but something in her doubted a mere injection would rouse a man who had been unresponsive to all human interaction, to the entire world, for more than a week. And who knew what permanent damage lurked in his brain? A gunshot wound to the head could leave a man with normal reflexes but cognitively vegetative.

Dr. Willard leaned forward. "Private Barnaby," he said calmly, "you're going to relax now and feel very calm, absolutely at ease, not a care in the world. Private Barnaby, can you hear me?"

Barnaby remained still, but Juliet felt his pulse begin to slow. He released a long, noisy exhalation, and then, from the depths of his thickly bandaged face, like a righted doll, his good eye flashed open. Startled, Juliet dropped his wrist. His iris was a dark mahogany; the upper lashes were short and thick but the lower lashes were pale and thin, and beneath the eye spread fine, papery wrinkles. She stared at this one piece of him, trying to grasp the whole: it was like looking the wrong way through a peephole. Finally his gaze moved toward Dr. Willard, who offered a proud smile, as though Barnaby were a student with a correct answer. "Hello, Christopher," he began. "Could you tell me where you're from?"

Barnaby's lips fluttered, light as butterfly wings, as if trying to remember the shapes of words. "Bur . . . ling . . . ton," he slowly said. "I'm from Burlington, Ver . . . mont."

It was strange to hear his voice—husky and soft. He spoke in the long warped tones of someone with a toothache.

"Your rank?"

"Priv . . . ate first . . . class." The words came gradually, unsteadily, and Juliet wondered if something in his mind wasn't working properly.

"So I'd like to talk a little, get to know you. Is that okay?"

"Uh-huh."

"What did you do before the war, Christopher?"

"Worked at the pap . . . er. The local paper. Setting the type."

"Did you like that?"

"I liked reading the articles before anyone else. And I liked figuring out how to change words here and there so they fit. It was like a puzzle. I was good at it." His speech began flowing easily, quick and confident.

"You're in a hospital right now, in Italy, making a wonderful physical recovery from a gunshot wound. Do you recall your injury?"

"I've been to Italy?" He scratched at his head—a small, simple gesture, but the motion stunned Juliet. It was the first time she'd seen him voluntarily move. "Christopher, would you raise your right arm for me? Excellent. And now your left? Brilliant. Let's continue. . . . You came to Italy with the United States Army."

"Screw the army."

"You don't like the army?"

"I don't like what I ate and I don't wanna talk about it. Stop making me talk about it."

"What you ate?"

"It was right there in my meat tin. I swear." Barnaby winced as though he were smelling something rotten.

Willard moved the recording device closer. "Can you tell me about this meat tin, Christopher? You don't have to tell me what you ate, just tell me what was happening before."

The yellow lamplight wavered across Barnaby's bandaged face. His eye seemed mildly bloodshot, and an ash-gray half circle cradled the skin below. He looked harried, exhausted, which was strange, thought Juliet, since by all appearances he'd been asleep for days.

Barnaby blinked several times, thoughtfully, dreamily, and Juliet felt uneasy. The violations of privacy that came with her job always made her uncomfortable. Often, when cutting the clothes off a patient and stripping him down to nothing, she felt a deep sense of transgression. But this was worse. To have a conversation with a person who didn't *know* he was having a conversation, who might confess his darkest fears and later have no recollection—what right had they?

"The whole company's encamped in a forest one night," Barnaby continued, "and Captain comes by to visit the squad. We're all eating dinner, sitting on logs and packs, having a hot stew for the first time in weeks, and suddenly I get up to go take a piss. Captain calls out to me—'Get yourself the hell out of my eyesight, Barnaby. I don't even wanna feel a breeze that touched your crooked cock.' He was always saying he didn't want me to contaminate the squad. He liked that word. *Contaminate.* They all liked it. Anyway, I'd gotten used to it, and you gotta do what the captain says, so off I went. It was one of those noisy nights where the sky was crackling. I walked a good five minutes away. I was half-unzipped behind a tree when a massive boom tore through the sky and things started falling through the trees. I could see smoke in the distance. I rushed back to the squad—I thought we were under attack—but by the time I got to where they were all sitting, I heard everyone cheering. I grabbed my bowl and sat down, eating quietly, trying to figure out what had happened. I was spooning it out and came upon these chunks of meat. But something I bit into wasn't cooked and I spit that thing out and then I moved my spoon around. . . ." Barnaby's knee, limp until now, began to tremble.

"Your spoon . . . what happened—"

"I saw him *watching* me."

"Who?"

"*Him.*" A tear sprung loose from Barnaby's eye and disappeared behind his gauze; his voice grew quiet, almost a whisper—a child's whisper. "Right there in my bowl. He was staring at me." Barnaby hugged himself and began to rock.

Willard glanced at Juliet. "What was in your mess tin?"

Barnaby sniffled. "The bluest eye I've ever seen." Juliet leaned closer to listen, mesmerized by the gruesome tale.

"What did you do?" Willard asked.

"Captain said, 'Barnaby, swallow that thing.' He had a shovel in his hand. All the guys grabbed shovels. Then Captain lifted his shovel, scooped a pile from the ground. It was all boots and arms and hands. One of the hands had a big gold ring on it. Captain set the shovel down and set to tugging it off. 'It's raining Jerries,' he laughs. I bent over and puked. Captain said, 'Barnaby, you don't have the stomach to be here. You should be eating Jerry bastards *alive*.' Then he stuck the finger in his mouth and sucked off the gold ring, holding it out on his tongue." Barnaby's face began to twitch as he spoke; Juliet felt his pulse quicken and signaled Dr. Willard. "I can't be eating people. I couldn't eat after that. I'm never hungry." Barnaby's breaths constricted to short, sharp inhalations, and Willard looked at his watch.

"O . . . kay," Willard finally said, frantically jotting something down. "That's enough for now. When you wake up, Private Barnaby, when I count to ten, your body is going to feel whole again." Willard set down his notebook and took Barnaby's hand between his own. "You'll eat and you'll talk and you'll move about normally. And you won't remember what you saw in your mess kit, you won't think about it. One, two . . ."

Juliet slowly shook her head in disbelief. She'd never imagined such a damaged man could speak in full sentences, in such razor-sharp detail. Dr. Willard was a genius. Utterly amazing. As he slowly counted toward ten, she felt her own breathing quicken, waiting for Barnaby to snap out of his Pentothal slumber as dramatically as he'd awakened with the injection.

"Six, seven, eight . . ."

But watching Barnaby closely, Juliet noticed his arms and legs gradually go limp, sinking into the mattress like cushions soaking up water, heavy and sodden. As Willard reached ten, Barnaby's mahogany-brown eye stared ahead with a haunting vacancy, as though a window had been closed.

"What happened?" she asked. "I thought he'd be awake."

"Private Barnaby?" Willard leaned close so that for a moment doctor and patient were practically nose to nose. "Christopher? Can you hear me?" Willard removed a small flashlight from his shirt pocket and shined it at Barnaby's pupil. He turned Barnaby's head from side to side. "At least his eye is tracking."

"But he's done speaking? He's still mute?" Juliet realized, sickeningly, that she might have just lost her one opportunity to ask Barnaby about Tuck. In a matter of seconds, her chance had vanished. "Is that *normal*? A patient not returning to some kind of wakefulness after that . . . ?"

"I stopped using the word *normal* when I became a psychiatrist." Willard wound the cord around the microphone and returned the recording device to its case. "We opened a door," he said. "Unfortunately, it was a wrong door, a false turn. But we'll try again. For now, let's get him back to the Recovery Tent."

The rain had let up but the ground was slick, and they had to carry the litter slowly. After settling Barnaby into his bed, they wandered outside, and Juliet began to follow Willard back to the Isolation Tent, where he had left the equipment.

Willard raised a flat hand. "I can clean up our mess. You should go get some rest."

Juliet knew that it couldn't be past nine o'clock. Had her questions been that out of line? She felt like a child being sent to bed. Doctors often socialized with their assistants postshift, and there was good reason: what they saw in the hospital was often hard to shake off. Barnaby's interview had been unexpectedly gory, and it felt wrong to simply pack up and say good night as though it had been a routine surgical procedure. She assumed they would debrief, discuss, *something*. "Did I do okay assisting in there?" she asked.

"You were excellent, Nurse Dufresne! Very helpful. A natural. We'll try again soon and see if we can draw more out of him." Willard patted Juliet's shoulder—politely, paternalistically—and he said good night.

As he walked away, something in her sank.

* * *

In the thick of a hot July day, the hospital dismantled once again. The Fifth Army was charging north toward Florence and needed doctors close behind. The convoy departed at night without headlights, as the sky above roared and growled like a monster. Somewhere ahead, German planes banged, buzzed, coughed, belched; bursts of gunfire tore through the air, dashes of silver against the velvet blackness. Juliet, seated in an open truck beside Brother Reardon, clutched her helmet and closed her eyes.

In their new encampment, she slept fitfully, awakening at the slightest rustle.

By morning, bleary-eyed, she saw a stream of casualties begin to arrive: on the first day alone, two hundred litters snaked past the Receiving Tent. Mother Hen instructed Juliet to number foreheads: lipstick 1s, 2s, 3s, 4s, and 5s indicated who most needed surgery. The plan worked efficiently, except that patients stared in feverish bewilderment at one another's numbers. Cots in the wards lay so close together that Juliet banged her knees as she sidestepped between them. Her day was a flurry of injections and bandaging, transfusions and debridements. Barnaby lay in the far corner, silent and unresponsive and, for the moment, forgotten.

With the influx of patients had come several new battle-fatigue cases: a man who chewed the inside of his mouth and kept drooling blood; a man who repeatedly struck his own face. Another patient tucked his knees to his chest and whimpered incessantly. Juliet watched Dr. Willard draw up a chair beside each of them, his notebook in his lap, spending hours at their bedsides, patting their shoulders, bringing them coffee, humming them to sleep. She wondered if they, too, had stories like Barnaby's.

Juliet still couldn't shake the night in the Isolation Tent with Barnaby. In her shallow sleep, the image of the eyeball sometimes came to her. She dreamt she was swimming in Charlesport, doing a breaststroke, as the eyeball floated toward her. Sometimes, while she was eating, she envisioned the blue eye beneath her food. She lost her appetite, merely poking at her hot meals, feasting intermittently on dry ration bars. However, she didn't know in whom she could confide, since the psychiatrist himself had put the ghastly picture in her mind, albeit inadvertently. And in the first hectic days at the new encampment, she'd barely had a chance to speak to Dr. Willard.

But when the division pushed farther north, the most critical patients were trucked south and a period of tentative quiet followed.

In a cool sliver of morning air, before the sun was up, Juliet lay awake on her bedroll while Glenda and Bernice slept. Again the blue eye had come to her in a dream. This time, she was in the chemistry lab at school, mixing various beakers, when from a froth of steam and bubbles the blue eye bobbed to the surface. The night before, she had dreamt she was washing her face over a basin of water when the blue eye appeared in her cupped hands. She woke in a damp sweat, wondering why the horrors that had rendered her patient silent were becoming her own.

Because of Tuck, she thought. *He's what is really haunting me.* She needed to find out, once and for all, if Barnaby knew what had happened to Tuck. Even if Barnaby was drugged, even if it meant angering Dr. Willard. Then at least she'd be done with the nightmarish interviews.

Juliet also decided to write to Barnaby's wife. For weeks the question of what, if anything, the army had told this woman had plagued her. Suppose Barnaby's letters had just stopped? His wife was entitled to the facts, no matter how disturbing. And news of a suicide attempt certainly bested an unexplained silence. Rising in the semidarkness of her tent, Juliet composed a single-page missive describing Barnaby's medical status, noting his auditory startle and visual tracking and other healthy reflexes, his drug-induced lapse into coherent speech, and her conviction that he would improve, though the timetable was uncertain. At the end, Juliet added a brief postscript—she had to—asking if Barnaby had ever mentioned Tucker Dufresne.

Before breakfast, Juliet took the letter to the PX and then sought out the table in the Officers' Mess where Dr. Willard was seated. She made small talk about supplies with the other nurses and then, between sips of coffee, asked Dr. Willard if he intended to conduct another Sodium Pentothal session with Barnaby.

"I'd like to assist again," she said. "I wanted you to know that."

Willard removed his glasses and cleaned them with a handkerchief. When he slid them back on, he looked at her with concentrated surprise. She felt sweat gather on her forehead. A fierce humidity had laid claim to the landscape. For days the sun had vanished behind screens of gray vapor, but the moisture never managed to gather into rain. There was a hot, jellied stillness to the air.

"You haven't been upset since our last session?" he asked.

Juliet wiped at her brow. "What do you mean?"

"No need for me to put ideas in your head."

The people seated around them began to gather their utensils and bowls; they pushed their chairs back and stood.

"Dr. Willard, you said there are a lot of locked doors in his mind. I just thought we might try another one."

"I appreciate that you're ready to pick locks and rattle doors on his behalf. Unfortunately, it's a problem of logistics at the moment. The Isolation Ward is occupied, and it would be wildly irresponsible of me to subject the patients in the Recovery Tent to his memories. They could have troubling effects on the listeners. As I'm sure you can understand."

Juliet looked away; did he know about her nightmares? Was he having the same ones?

"Well, surely there's somewhere else," she said.

* * *

The night was sweltering, the air thick and moist. Willard's tent was a mess of textbooks and notebooks; graphs and charts hung from the canvas. At the head of his bedroll, where a pillow should have been, sat a black Smith-Corona typewriter, a letter abandoned mid-sentence. Nearby, on the ground, a tin bowl held a shaving brush and razor; a Monarch Lincoln camera sat barricaded by film rolls. Clutter everywhere, but not a single personal effect—no photographs, no postcards, no souvenirs or trinkets. The only private element of the space was the distinct musk of aftershave—rosemary and cedar, she thought—a scent Juliet hadn't realized she associated with Willard.

She seated herself beside Barnaby's litter, which they had set just inside the entrance of the tent, his feet jutting out into the night. Juliet hugged her knees so as not to disrupt the space.

Willard was busy rigging the recording device. A parabola of sweat stained the back of his shirt.

"This is much cheerier than the Isolation Ward," said Juliet.

"Except my domestic organization habits leave something to be desired."

"Are these books stacked for an air raid, or are you reading them?"

"I wrote one or two of those."

Juliet thought she detected a boastful smile, but Willard turned quickly to dip the needle into the vial of Sodium Pentothal. He passed the needle to Juliet.

"We're going to give you another injection, Christopher."

The day before, Juliet had removed and redressed some of the bandages on Barnaby's face, and she could now see the bridge of his nose and a section of forehead. His eye was open, motionless and vacant as usual, but as she slid the needle into his arm, his eyelid fluttered.

"Private Barnaby, do you feel relaxed?" Willard asked.

"Hmmmm . . . very relaxed."

"My name is Dr. Willard, I'm your doctor here, looking after you. Can you do me a favor and raise your right arm? Excellent. Your left? Wonderful. Can you touch your face for me?"

Barnaby raised his fingertips to his chin.

"I got bandages."

"Yes, bandages from when you were shot in the head. I wanted to talk about the day you got injured. The day you were shot."

"It *burned*."

"The bullet?"

Barnaby winced.

"Okay, if you could, tell me what happened *before* the bullet struck you. Let's say the hour before."

"I had such rotten luck, pulling the short straw. I had nothing but rotten luck since I got to Italy."

"Why were you pulling straws?"

"For the forward observer. 'TP' patrol, we call it: *target practice*, 'cause that's what Germans use you for. You're sniper bait. Wandering right up there in the German lines. 'Go tell me if Jerry ate beans or sausage for dinner,' Captain says. 'Follow the sound of the gunfire and locate Jerry's exact position.' I sure as hell didn't wanna go. But I didn't have a choice. Short straw. Those are the rules. A few of the guys in the squad reminded Captain that I'd been seeing eyeballs in the trees, that I wasn't eating. But Captain said fair is fair, I got the straw, and he wasn't gonna chuck a thousand-year tradition of drawing straws on account of one yellow belly."

"Where was this?"

"I never saw maps. All I'd been told was there were two parts to Italy: mountain Italy and flat Italy; you go up or you go across. *Mountaly* and *flataly*. This was in *flataly*. In some forest. North of

Rome. Thick tree trunks, thick leaves. There were acorns or walnuts on the ground. They were crunching underfoot, loud as thunder."

"Were you alone?"

Barnaby pushed himself upright, his eye alert. "See, I heard
footsteps. The others were supposed to hang back until I radioed in
the German position. Nero and Jensen were doing a second patrol,
but went in a different direction. Captain Brilling is famous for
going forward with his men, said he would never ask a man to do
something he wouldn't do himself, but he wasn't coming with me. I
tried hard to keep myself calm. I lugged my rifle through trees, trying to be mouse quiet. But the twigs and acorns kept crunching and
my legs started shaking. My teeth were clacking so hard, I wedged
two pieces of gum in my mouth. I was alone, you see, all alone with
who knew how many Germans taking aim. . . .

"The Germans were supposed to be across this stream, on
the other side of a blasted bridge, hiding out with a machine-gun
encampment, but the fog was so thick I couldn't see a bridge. I was
walking through a cloud, giant trees rising up out of nowhere. It
was so foggy, I suddenly thought I might be dead already. I couldn't
tell if I was moving forward or backward. Finally I bumped into
a rock and sat on the ground but I couldn't breathe right. I was
sucking in the fog, my lungs gulping it down like I was drowning.
I was making too much noise and I knew that big blue eye could
see me."

"The blue eye?"

"From my mess tin!"

"It's all right, Christopher," said Juliet, stroking his arm. Would
the vision ever leave him? Could such a horror be erased from the
mind?

Barnaby's knee shook, and Juliet looked to Willard, worried
this might mark the end of the session, worried that the Pentothal
would wear off and she'd lose her chance to ask about Tuck.

"His pulse is still steady," Juliet whispered, truthfully.

Willard nodded, wiping his brow with a handkerchief. "Tell us what happened next, Christopher."

"I sat there 'til the fog lifted. I don't know how long went by. A few hours, I reckon. It was getting dark. I couldn't see anything but dark branches overhead. But I could hear an owl hooting so loud it was like he was sitting on my head; frogs were croaking, and those footsteps, crunch, crunch, crunching across those acorns. Then guns were firing. Before I knew it, the ground was exploding.

"I ran 'til I felt water on my feet and realized I was in the stream. I moved left, but I heard a bang, and water came pouring down on me. I turned right and heard this *snap-snap-snap.* It sounded like laughing; that's what a machine gun sounds like, bullets laughing at you. And they were calling my name, *Barnaby, Barnaby,* so I went underwater. I stayed under 'til my lungs were fit to burst and came up gulping. The air filled my lungs so fast I thought I'd choke. Then the fog was lifting and across the way I saw a row of Germans, flat on their bellies, guns pointed at me.

"I moved left and right but the bullets kept coming. Finally I crawled out of the water and stopped moving."

Juliet thought this might be a break in his tale, a chance to ask about Tuck, but Willard interjected: "Where was *your* pistol? Did you fire at the Germans?"

"I don't think so."

"Why not?"

"I kept seeing the whole thing like it wasn't me. Like *I* was that big old blue eye staring down. And they kept shooting but they weren't hitting me, like they didn't really wanna kill me, just wanted to scare me. But I *wanted* them to hit me, I *wanted* it to end."

A look of surrender glazed Barnaby's eye, and his voice softened, drifting into a child's bedtime meanderings. "I just lay down, closed my eyes, and thought of home. I wanted a moment of peace before I died. I thought of Tina. She's got a baby coming. I told her I loved her, and suddenly all the noise stopped. Then I felt that heat. Like a coal poker through my brain."

"Did you *shoot* yourself?"

"It wasn't me pulling the trigger."

"Then who did?"

Barnaby whispered: "*The blue eye.*" His chest rose abruptly and his lungs began to pump hard. Juliet felt his pulse quicken.

Dr. Willard set his pen in the open spine of his notebook. "Okay, Private Barnaby, when I count to ten, you're going to return to consciousness—"

"Christopher." Juliet rose to her knees. It was now or never. "Christopher, did you ever know a man named Tucker? He was in Sergeant McKnight's unit."

"Tuck-er," Barnaby said slowly. His head turned from side to side, as though he were looking for someone. "Tucker!" he yelped. His chest heaved and his hands clutched at the litter. "Forgive me!"

Willard's hand landed leadenly on Juliet's shoulder and pulled her away. "Enough." He rubbed Barnaby's back and resumed counting while Juliet penitently placed her hands in her lap. She wanted desperately to interrupt his count, to ask Barnaby more, but stopped herself. At ten, Barnaby's eye flickered to alertness before glazing over with its familiar blank stare.

"Christopher, can you lift your right arm for me?" Willard asked. "Christopher, can you lift your left arm? Christopher, can you hear me? . . . Christopher? . . . Christopher?!"

Willard tossed his notebook to the ground.

"I'm sorry," Juliet whispered.

Willard shook his head, staring at his recording device. "Attachments to people from home are quite strong," he said, "even in this mess. I assume this Tucker is a boyfriend? A fiancé?"

"My brother."

He looked up. "Brother."

"I know it wasn't the appropriate time."

Lifting his notebook from the floor, he mumbled: "Understatement."

"I thought it might be my only chance."

Willard took a slow, deep breath as he studied her. He pushed a tuft of hair from his glasses. "Your brother is dead? Missing?"

She paused. "Missing."

Willard's gaze traveled in rapt deliberation around the cluttered tent. In all his work exploring the suffering of men at the front, did he have any idea, Juliet wondered, the effect it had on their families back home? Did he understand her desperation? The sense of responsibility she felt to her brother?

A gravelly sigh slowly wrested its way out of him. "Nurse Dufresne, I'm far from perfect, but I try my best to be a compassionate man. I'm sorry for what you must be going through. It must be awful. I won't question you further on this subject—not for lack of caring, but because I believe in maintaining a professional emotional distance. The work we do is emotional enough. That said, please understand that these sessions are crucial to rebuilding this man's emotional and mental health." Willard gently laid his hand on Barnaby's forehead. "He's *drugged,* he's vulnerable. As you can see, I walk him carefully through a sequence of events, I follow where his mind takes us; we open doors slowly, cautiously. You can't yank him into a different line of questioning; it could be harmful. I truly wish I could help you, and I wish Barnaby could help you, and perhaps he can once he is recovered. But right now he can't even help himself."

"It won't happen again."

"Good."

She had said it firmly, yet she doubted its truth. Her mind was already sifting and speculating, wondering why Barnaby had screamed Tuck's name and said, "Forgive me!" What did Barnaby want Tuck's forgiveness for?

"Come," said Willard, signaling Juliet outside. "He won't go running anywhere in the next ten minutes."

The night air offered a faint respite from the muggy tent. Willard patted at his pockets until he found a flattened pack of cigarettes. He lit one and walked ahead of Juliet toward a table outside the mess tent. He sat with his back to the table, so that Juliet was compelled to sit beside him.

"That discussion could have brought him back to the realm of consciousness. It means there's even more to unlock—perhaps a lot more." Willard studied his cigarette. "This will take a while. Eating an eyeball . . . I'd love to say it was a nightmare, but there's one thing I've come to learn through all this: The human mind doesn't invent the worst. Nightmares are mundane compared to what actually happens up there." He turned to her. "I'd be remiss if I didn't ask: Are you certain you're comfortable with what you're hearing? I wouldn't hold it against you if it was too much."

Juliet longed to tell him about her nightmares, but what if he thought her too fragile for the work?

"I'm comfortable enough," she said, and from the slow, sad nod he offered in response, Juliet wondered if she had marooned Willard with his own discomfort, if he, too, was haunted by the blue eye.

They heard footsteps and turned to see Mother Hen approaching, swinging her flashlight. "Oh, the bloody heat. I thought *Africa* would kill me. This," she said, wagging her tongue to taste the night air, "it's like the air itself is sweating." She thumped onto the opposite bench and in politeness, Juliet and Willard pivoted to face her. Mother Hen's eyes moved suspiciously between them and she glanced at her watch.

"Your shift ended four hours ego, Nurse Dufresne."

"I was working with Dr. Willard. We got Barnaby speaking again."

"I see."

"Nurse Dufresne has been invaluable," Willard said. "Barnaby is the most stubborn case I've seen."

"Well, I hope the progress moves rapidly. There's a racket from above about a court-martial. Major Decker has been getting a lot of pressure." She pulled a cigarette from her pocket and Willard extended the flame of his lighter.

"I doubt it will come to that," said Willard.

"I have come to the conclusion these days that anything can happen." Mother Hen removed a folded paper from her pocket and flattened it on the table. "This crap was all over the hospital perimeter."

The Girl You Left Behind
The Way of All Flesh

When pretty Joan Hopkins was still standing behind the ribbon counter of a five-and-ten on Third Avenue in New York City, she never dreamed of ever seeing the interior of a duplex Park Avenue apartment. Neither did young Bob Harrison, the man she loves. Bob was drafted and sent to the battlefields of Europe thousands of miles away. Through Lazare's employment agency Joan got a job as a private secretary with wily Sam Levy. Sam is piling up big money on war contracts. Should the slaughter end very soon, he would suffer an apoplectic stroke.

NOW JOAN KNOWS WHAT BOB
AND HIS PALS ARE FIGHTING FOR!

Joan always used to look up to Bob as the guiding star of her life, and she was still a good girl when she started working for Sam Levy.

But she often got the blues thinking of Bob, whom she hadn't seen for over two years. Her boss had an understanding heart and was always very kind to her, so kind indeed, that he often invited her up to his place. He had always wanted to show her his "etchings." Besides, Sam wasn't stingy, and each time Joan came to see him, he gave her the nicest presents. Now, all women like beautiful expensive things. But Sam wasn't the man you could play for a sucker. He wanted something, wanted it very definitely. . . .

Poor little Joan! She is still thinking of Bob,
yet she is almost hoping that he'll never return.

"I used to think," said Mother Hen, her face slack, pulling a flask from her back pocket, "that the sheer magnitude of war—the blood and the bone and the loss of life—would somehow erase all of those smaller concerns of heartbreak and betrayal, lust and covetousness. Or at the very least, idiotic prejudice. Scapegoating the Jews? Half the doctors who stitch these boys back together are Jewish, and yet this filth"—she jabbed her finger at the leaflet— "will have its power. I thought the sight of death and the fear of death would make saints of us all, would strip us bare of all want and worry except staying alive and saving lives, and we would rise to the occasion of discovering our own greatness. Just like all the boys who enlisted—they enlisted believing they were deeply courageous, expecting to prove themselves heroes. And here they are, weeping in their beds at what they have now learned of themselves, of humanity. Are they not, Dr. Willard?"

Willard nodded.

"Death, it seems, only makes us all the hungrier to live deeply and fully," she continued, "which, in turn, means chaotically and cruelly. I don't understand. It's as though we insist on leaving our mark, no matter how messy. All those urges that once seemed fleeting and superficial turn out, when we are faced with the possibility of slaughter, to be the very essence of us. My nurses finish assisting an amputation, feeling the ruin of a man's life in their hands, and then rush off to fix their hair and find husbands. Men sitting in foxholes, fighting to save the whole of Europe and civilization, can be brought to tears by *this* printed rubbish—the thought of girlfriends back home fucking their bosses. Such extremes of emotion coexist within the human beast. At times, I confess, it overwhelms me."

Mother Hen gripped the table and swayed, though whether this was the effect of alcohol or sentiment, Juliet couldn't tell.

"The human mind," said Dr. Willard, "is more unknowable than the entire ocean, or all the space between the stars." He smiled. "It's why I will always have a job."

"Especially here." Mother Hen stubbed out her cigarette. "So when Private Barnaby spoke, dare I ask what he said?"

"Quite a lot," answered Willard, exchanging a brief look with Juliet. "But it's hard to know yet what is essential. We'll get him saying more."

"The poor creature," said Mother Hen.

They all sat awkwardly for a minute, listening to the cacophonous pulse of crickets and tree frogs, that primal bleating of insect and amphibian sounding out over the night long before there were wars or humans to fight in them.

Willard stubbed out his cigarette. "We should probably get Barnaby back to the Recovery Tent."

They said good night to Mother Hen and carried Barnaby's litter across the encampment. In the Recovery Tent they settled him into his bed, and Willard lifted Barnaby's clipboard and wearily shook his head. "I didn't like what she said about the court-martial. I want him saying more. And soon. Maybe next time we'll try reading him some of those letters again. How far back do they go and when is the most recent?"

Juliet took the envelope stuffed with letters from beneath his bed and shook the contents free. She began unfolding each of the pages, and Willard reached for Barnaby's musette bag. Juliet was arranging them chronologically when Willard said, "Also, a token from his wife could be useful." He was waving a small white glove.

Pearl's white glove.

CHAPTER 8

A RUMBLING OUTSIDE her tent woke Juliet. It sounded like the earth coughing up crust, a guttural gagging of the ground. For a moment she wondered if she'd dreamt the noise. In the dark she groped for her helmet, and then across the tent a flashlight came on. Bernice was sitting upright, her eyes wide and her chin extended as she turned her head slowly from side to side, straining to listen. Her thin lips shone with Vaseline.

"I don't hear a plane," said Bernice. "And I didn't feel the ground shake, did you?"

Juliet touched the ground. "I don't think so."

"A bomb *shakes* the ground."

Juliet scratched the inside of her ear; she thought she heard something outside, a distant whine, a faint whimper. An animal? A child?

She turned, instinctively, to look at Glenda's bedroll.

"Where is she?" Juliet asked.

As Juliet and Bernice rushed out into the humid night, figures in bright white underwear were spilling out of the nearby pup tents. The sky was lit by a low full moon. Everyone was swinging flashlight beams in nervous, haphazard arcs, uncertain of what to do next. Juliet and Bernice joined a group of nurses from the next tent, all knuckling sleep from their eyes, yanking out hair curlers to fasten on their helmets. As the distant whimpering grew louder, something in its uneven undulations, something in the broad, haunting silences between moans, made it clear they were listening to a human. Animals cried out in pain, Juliet knew. Humans cried out in fear of their pain; it was a sound she had come to know well.

Huddled together, the nurses moved cautiously. From nearby tents, groups of ward men and doctors and engineers converged. Soon four distinct bands were traveling the wide row between tents, cylinders of light sweeping the ground around them like electrified particles on the rim of a molecule. The groups veered slightly left, then right, mostly silent, trying to determine the source of the cries, until someone in the lead called, "On the hill!"

One by one people spilled through the narrow gaps between tents, rushing the hospital's perimeter. At the thin line of trees marking the edge of the encampment, Juliet stopped. Beyond the trees a wide hill arched in the moonlight.

A shirtless engineer, a backpack slung from one shoulder, stretched his arms ramrod straight, trying to hold everyone back. "It's a minefield!" he yelled.

The swelling crowd fell silent, and, as if in answer to his assertion, from the hill beyond came a high-pitched *Help!* that collapsed into sobs.

Juliet knew the voice immediately—Glenda's.

Bernice gripped Juliet's hand.

Someone had plugged in a surgical lamp and now shined it toward the hill. In the dissipated light, Juliet could see a trail of clothing snaking up the hill: an olive-drab jacket, a nightgown, lace-trimmed panties, a large brassiere. At the end of the trail, perhaps twenty yards beyond the tree line, she made out the shadowy figure of Dr. Lovelace, in blood-splattered long johns, suspended over Glenda in an awkward push-up.

"Stay exactly where you are!" the engineer called. "EXACTLY. These are *Schü* mines."

The engineer opened his backpack and put together a long contraption with a metal disk; he snatched a dozen pebbles from the ground and stepped forward slowly, swinging the mine detector in wide arcs, tossing pebbles ahead of him like horseshoes.

Along the tree line, the spectators began to assemble in an instinctive half formation. They mumbled and whispered.

"If he sets off a mine, won't they get hit?" Juliet asked Bernice.

"*Schü* mines explode at ankle height," she whispered. "It's the Bouncing Bettys that spray that nasty shrapnel."

As the engineer moved forward, his flashlight lit the stranded figures and Juliet could see that Dr. Lovelace's chin was tucked to his chest, though it was hard to tell if he was wounded or simply trying not to move. Lovelace watched the engineer's movements intently, though Glenda, beneath him, had turned from the crowd.

"Poor things," Bernice said.

"Crap luck," someone else muttered.

"Fucking Jerry land mines."

"Goddammit." Major Decker's voice boomed behind Juliet. "We've got a whole division, five miles from here, about to hurl themselves into the Jerry lines. They count on us not to be blowing ourselves up."

By now the engineer had moved ten yards up the hill, the mine detector beeping wildly as he marked his path with white tape. "It's a sea of shrapnel," he muttered to himself, but in the silence they could all hear him.

"Hold on, Glenda," called Mother Hen from somewhere in the crowd. "We're going to get you out of there."

Suddenly, an explosion sounded and the ground beside the engineer spit a funnel of dirt, showering the grass. Juliet ducked behind a tree, pressing against the trunk. She felt her face knock something hard and splintery and pulled back to examine a sign: CAUTION—AREA ABOVE NOT SWEPT FOR MINES.

As Juliet emerged, she saw the engineer, halfway up the hill, curled on his side, clutching spasmodically at his leg. From beyond him came Glenda's sobs.

"It's okay," Lovelace was softly telling her. "Don't worry."

"Listen up," the engineer huffed. "We're going to have to try"—he swallowed heavily—"to pull ourselves down. It's too dangerous for anyone to come get us."

"Her femoral's draining," called Lovelace.

You could bleed to death from that artery within minutes. Painfully. Glenda no doubt understood what was happening to her. She was exsanguinating—a deceptively clinical word.

"Can you walk?" the engineer asked.

"My knee's sprained, I think, but I can move. I just have to slow her bleeding. Jesus, she's gushing. . . ."

Bracing himself with one arm, Lovelace reached up and tore off his shirt and pressed the shirt to Glenda's hip. Even at a distance, Juliet could see the cloth darken with blood. Lovelace used his long johns to roughly brace his knee.

"We've got to pull ourselves down," called the engineer. "But follow the path where you came."

"I can't," Glenda whimpered.

"Sure you can. Come on, kiddo," said Lovelace. "You just gotta climb up on my back. Okay? Hold the shirt tight against your hip. If you're on top of me, the mines can't get you."

The engineer tucked himself into a ball and began to shimmy down the hill. "Once you get to my position," he called behind, "follow the tape."

Dr. Lovelace flipped over so that his back hovered over Glenda's chest. "Grab on, Glen." Slowly, Glenda slid each of her trembling hands around his neck. She wrapped her leg around his, and Juliet saw that Glenda was still wearing her shoes.

"Up we go." With audible strain, Lovelace flipped himself onto his hands and knees; with Glenda on his back, his knee wobbled, then steadied. Lovelace threw one arm forward, then the other, slowly crawling down the hill like a wounded, two-headed creature.

At the hill's base, the engineer had reached the first piece of tape and came to a stop. Panting, he scanned the spectators, as though looking for someone to carry him the rest of the way.

"I got you, Lieutenant Nelson."

It was Jim Bailey, the cook from the Officers' Mess. A big man, he took one stride forward and swept the engineer over his shoulder like a sack of flour. Bailey clearly wasn't one for drama; he did this quietly and quickly. Medics rushed the engineer away on a litter, followed by Major Decker.

Lovelace, gleaming with sweat, focused his gaze on the line of white tape. He tightened his face with renewed determination and tentatively raised his injured knee, but as he set it down, he wobbled. Glenda, atop him, keeled leftward. He swung his arm back to brace her, but Glenda was already toppling.

She tumbled through the grass, bumping against rocks and picking up speed before coming to a rough stop. Far from the white tape, far from the tree line, she pawed at the ground, tearing up grass, trying to pull herself toward Lovelace. Dirt darkened her face, blood smeared her body. As she tried to wiggle forward, she caught sight of her splintered pelvis, the pulpy wreck of her flesh, and her mouth fell open in a soundless gasp.

"Glenda, we'll send help," Mother Hen called. "Dr. Lovelace, proceed along the white tape. You're too far to help her and too injured to carry her. Follow the tape and let us get you medical attention."

Glenda's tear-filled eyes were fixed on him.

Dr. Lovelace, his face pale and expressionless, took a hesitant step forward.

"*Clifford?*" She scratched weakly at the ground and let her face drop. Her cries were quiet now, the cries of hopelessness, and for a moment no one could move, not even Lovelace.

"Heavens, we can't leave the girl!" The stocky figure of Brother Reardon, in a pair of snug gray pajamas, sprung to the front of the tree line. He worked his thumb over the large crucifix at his chest, and looked pleadingly at the sky.

He began following the line of white tape, then cut left toward where Glenda lay weeping. He tore pages from a magazine to mark his trail and every few steps looked at the ground with an expression of meditative concentration, proceeding right or left as though by divine guidance.

"Look," someone beside Juliet whispered. It was Dr. Willard— when had he arrived?—pointing at Dr. Lovelace. While Juliet had been watching Brother Reardon, Lovelace had made it past the tree line. Medics were attempting to roll him onto a litter, but he refused. He sat firmly on the ground, eyes fixed on Glenda.

Juliet returned her gaze to Brother Reardon, who was inching toward Glenda with tiptoe-like steps. At his approach, Glenda weakly raised her head. She blinked slowly, disbelievingly, as finally Brother Reardon drew up beside her, removed his pajama shirt, and laid it over her bare torso.

Juliet's chest swelled with happiness. "You're okay, Glenda," she muttered. She felt Dr. Willard take her hand.

Brother Reardon knelt, and with great care and studious maneuvering he eventually lifted Glenda off the ground. As he stepped forward, the moon bathed them in a strange blue glow, so that they appeared momentarily unearthly, a hazy scene from a book of myths. *Here was the image that had brought them all to this ruined land,* thought Juliet. *Selflessness.* And yet, as he carried her the last few yards down the hill, stumbling under her weight, not a single spectator budged. Like the basest of animals, they clung to their safety.

"Hail Mary! Hail Brother Reardon!" the crowd cheered as Brother Reardon passed the tree line. Applause broke out as he set Glenda on a litter. Glenda looked up groggily, her face ashen, smiling when she caught sight of Juliet: "Tell Momma I'm okay now."

"I'll tell all of Texas," said Juliet, kissing her forehead.

Dr. Lovelace limped over. "You'll be okay, Glen, I promise."

Glenda turned and closed her eyes.

As Glenda was carried off, Brother Reardon leaned his back against a tree and descended jerkily, inch by inch, until he was sitting on the ground, his legs out straight. He studied his knees and Juliet could see that one of them was shaking. He wiped his face with his forearm, and traces of Glenda's blood smeared his cheeks. For a moment no one seemed to know what to say; he had done what none of them dared to do, and it didn't occur to them he needed help. Finally Dr. Willard crouched beside him, and gestured Juliet to his other side.

"Reardon," said Willard, "you've probably taken a dozen vows against this, for which I have endless respect, but tonight it's a medical necessity. . . ." He put his arm around the chaplain. "Let's get you a drink."

For weeks, the scene replayed itself in Juliet's mind: the geyser of dirt, Glenda's childlike cries. It wasn't the blood that haunted her but the look on Glenda's face when she thought she'd been left for dead. Juliet recalled the body of the German soldier they'd found by the lake: What had it been like for him to die alone? Without a hand to hold or a face to look at? Without a comforting voice? The presence of another person humanized the moment; alone, one faced a bleak animal's death. The *pain* of death had always frightened Juliet, but she saw now that solitude wrought the greater horror. Had Tuck been left somewhere, abandoned?

She tried to keep busy with work. The hospital was short one nurse since Glenda had been sent home. After Glenda had been under full anesthetic for hours while her femoral artery was reconstructed and massive tissue damage repaired, Dr. Mallick walked solemnly into the Officers' Mess to inform the staff that she would likely never walk again. Glenda spent several days in the Recovery Tent, her expression unchanged, Juliet thought, since the night she lay bleeding in the grass.

"My life is over, sugar."

"Don't say that."

Juliet had carried Glenda her dinner tray: a bowl of beef and potatoes crowded by a cup of wine and a block of butter pecan fudge Juliet had received from home. Juliet brought the radio so they could listen to Axis Sally. Glenda hummed happily to the dance songs, but when "Lili Marlene" came on, she sang an English rendition, her voice low and tormented, as though singing a dirge:

> Underneath the lantern
> By the barrack gate,
> Darling I remember
> The way you used to wait.
> 'Twas there that you whispered tenderly
> That you loved me;
> You'd always be,
> My Lili of the lamplight,
> My own Lili Marlene.

Glenda flicked off the radio. Her eyes seemed to swallow sorrow. "Who's going to want me like this?"

Juliet's tongue went dry. "There are good men out there," she said, but quickly looked away in embarrassment. What on earth did she know of men? Of life? Day after day she tended captains and corporals who had faced death, men who had stormed enemy lines, while she faced nothing but injections and bedpans and bandages. She told them all to piss and eat, to take their medicine, as if they were children. Because she was *healthy*; because the hidden curse of injury and illness was an unspoken demotion within the ranks of humankind. The mere wholeness of Juliet's body bestowed on her an authority entirely unearned. The guilt of this shook her. After all, *she* was the child here, Glenda had always known that; but if Glenda thought it now, she was too kind and forgiving to dispute the platitudes of someone who had not yet owned up to her own mortality.

Glenda smiled gently. Her face, without makeup, was pale and lifeless. "Perhaps you're right."

The morning Glenda was loaded into an army truck, the nurses all handed her bottles of nail polish, tins of hot cocoa, silk scarves, charm bracelets, rollers and hairpins—items they deeply coveted. Juliet offered up a pewter frame she had bought in Naples and a leather scrapbook. At the moment of departure, Glenda mustered up her former exuberance, dramatically blowing kisses and promising to write, but Juliet suspected she'd never hear from her again. Patients usually wanted to leave their injuries, and any reminders of how they happened, far behind.

If Lovelace and Glenda ever spoke after the night on the hill, no one knew of it. As far as Juliet could tell, during the few days both were in the Recovery Tent, Glenda refused to look at him. Her chilliness seemed to anguish him, and he returned to work before his knee had fully healed. After regularly pressing Juliet for updates on her progress, on the day of Glenda's departure he asked Juliet to give Glenda a letter. Glenda stared fixedly at the envelope before tearing it in half and handing it back to Juliet. Juliet tucked the pieces into the side of Glenda's bag.

Mother Hen seemed to take Glenda's departure hardest. At midnight, she popped into all the nurses' tents, checking each bedroll, and for the rest of the night, in a robe and helmet, she dutifully roamed the perimeter of the hospital, her flashlight searching for clandestine lovers. The staff took to jokingly calling her "the lady with the lamp"—Florence Nightingale's famous title—but were silently grateful for her concern. By morning, Juliet saw Mother Hen perched on an oil drum, her eyes narrow with sleeplessness, meditatively smoking a cigarette.

For days after Glenda left, people spoke of her constantly, exchanging stories in the mess tent of the playful touch she had with patients. Juliet told the story of their trip to Lago di Vico— how, using up all of her occupation currency, Glenda had bought the ridiculous alabaster elephant from an Italian woman desperate for money. Someone related how at Anzio she had donated her own blood to save a patient. But as the fighting for Pisa intensified, casualties streamed in faster than the hospital could accommodate, and it seemed to Juliet that Glenda's story, like so many others, was lost in the noisy sea of misfortune.

July pressed on. An unremitting heat hammered the days into a blinding white sameness. Juliet shuffled between the Supply and Recovery Tents, her boots scratching at the dry ground. Thick black flies buzzed through the wards; gray mice, gaunt and possessed, scampered endlessly across the Officers' Mess.

By day's end, bats wheeled and tumbled against the luminous pastels of dusk. On occasion, one swept into the Recovery Tent, madly circling the sea of patients until, to cheers and applause, it escaped back into the night.

The capture of Pisa was proving difficult. The Germans had set up an observation post in the Leaning Tower. A tiltin' Hilton for Jerry snipers, the patients said. But the division had been ordered to protect the landmark at all cost, so artillery had been withdrawn and the soldiers were fighting hand to hand. Hundreds of replacement soldiers had joined the division and were experiencing the first shocks of combat.

In the Recovery Tent, Captain Alan Jarvis spent his day constructing a twelve-inch replica of the Leaning Tower from wet scraps of bread and old oatmeal; before bed, in one violent stroke, he would smash his replica, only to build another tower the next day.

Private Vance, beside him, had been burned on the top of his head; wispy thatches of brown hair snaked along his pink and tender scalp. Throughout the day, he sat in his bed examining a butane lighter, slowly tilting the flame upside down.

Dr. Willard spent hours at their bedsides and with the other battle-fatigued patients. By the time he came by to see Barnaby at the day's end, his glasses were smudged and the tidy side part of his morning hair was lost beneath jagged brown curls. He looked fatigued himself. Drawing up a chair at the foot of Barnaby's bed, he sat and craned his head from side to side, massaging his neck. He set his elbows on his knees and clasped his hands beneath his chin, gazing at Barnaby's quiet form with glazed weariness. His notebook lay on the ground.

"Still nothing?" Juliet asked.

Willard shook his head. "It doesn't usually take this long."

"Is there anything else we can do?"

Willard sighed, vigorously rubbed his face, and looked up with ruddy determination. "Let's meet tonight," he said, "to discuss our next move."

"I've been reviewing my notes," said Willard, "and as I read over the transcript from our last session, I am tempted to say the Germans shot him, but the medic found Barnaby's pistol in his mouth."

The mess tent was empty but for the ruins of a party: empty green wine bottles and overflowing ashtrays. A large cardboard drawing of what appeared to be a donkey had been abandoned on the ground, alongside several blindfolds. Juliet lit a candle and sat beside Dr. Willard, who had spread his papers over the yellow crumbs of hardtack.

"Maybe one of the Germans made it across the stream and got hold of his pistol?" she asked, standing to fill the kettle in the corner from a Lister bag. She lit the kerosene stove.

"The Germans would have shot him at a distance with their own guns. And everything in Barnaby's mental framework suggests a suicide attempt, everything but the fact that he doesn't recall it." Willard tapped his pencil on his papers—"We know *who* did it; the question is *why*."

"Well, is being scared out of his mind an option?" said Juliet. "If he thought he was going to die anyway, it's not that outrageous."

"Or," said Willard, "there *were* no bullets or grenades. No Germans."

"A hallucination?"

"What are the chances of five Germans firing machine guns at him and not even scratching him? He didn't have a single wound other than the bullet lodged in his head." Willard began pawing through his papers. "And it's odd that he thinks the blue eye shot him. It's possible, though I can't know for certain until he's fully conscious, that we're looking at a schizophrenic break. A break that perhaps began when he bit into that eye."

The water came to a boil, and Juliet stood to mix the coffee, letting the spoon clack loudly as she uneasily worked through the possibility of Barnaby's schizophrenia. What if, after all her waiting and hoping, Barnaby were to regain consciousness and offer up only deranged nonsense?

She set down the cups brusquely. She had foolishly pinned her hopes on a comatose and questionably sound man.

"So what do you do if Barnaby doesn't get better?"

"I'll work with him as long as it takes," said Willard.

"You're convinced you can make him better?"

"I am," he said.

His voice wavered, but she wanted to believe him. She sipped at her coffee and studied his face in the candlelight; he seemed lost, lonely. Each day he listened to the pained recollections of men's most horrific encounters, more intimate and disturbing than a hundred surgical procedures. How did he manage it? How did he fend off the nightmares? The daymares? Were it not for her determination to find out what Barnaby knew about her brother, Juliet would have already quit. But Willard persisted, forging alone, day after day, into the miserable landscapes of other people's memories. She wondered if anyone else saw it, if others appreciated the selflessness of his work. No, he didn't cross mine-fields like Brother Reardon, but he was heroic in his own way. Quietly heroic.

"You know, Dr. Willard, I don't even know where you're from."

He looked taken aback. "That's because there's no need for you to know that."

"*That's* considered a personal question?"

He smiled. "Well, it certainly isn't professional."

"But you asked me where I was from. That day at the lake."

"I was considering you for this position; it was professionally relevant."

"How is that relevant?"

Willard scrawled something in his notebook and then began examining his transcript papers one by one and putting them in order.

"I can do that," said Juliet.

"You can sit right there and drink your delectable army-issue coffee. You're not my secretary."

"Well, it would be nice to know *something* about you. Tell me something professional, then."

Willard closed his notebook and took a sip of coffee, registering his full repugnance. "Mark my words, this godforsaken coffee is the reason we're seeing so many mental breakdowns."

Juliet laughed, and Willard smiled, and a conspiratorial warmth spread between them, as if they were passengers on a train talking into the night while the rest of the compartment slept. "Something professional . . ." Willard nodded thoughtfully. "Okay, since you've asked nicely.

"Once upon a time, three years ago, when the war began, I was barely out of medical school. I was one of several doctors commissioned to act as advisors to Dr. Marshall Black Sullivan to write guidelines for the Selective Service Advisory Board. The job was to design questions and descriptions of behavior to ensure the mentally ill were excluded from service. The War Department made it clear: they wanted an army of quality, not quantity. 'Weed out the mental weaklings,' they told us. No low-grade morons, psychopaths, eccentrics, emotionally unstable men, sexually perverse, or passive-aggressive men, or even those resentful of discipline. After weeks of meetings, Sullivan announced the guidelines for a psychiatric draftee interview: 'What do you think about the war?' 'Have you suffered a nervous breakdown?' 'Do you like girls?' Sullivan, who, I was quickly learning, was a bit unfit himself, insisted the interviewees be buck naked. I resigned on the spot. Of course, the board followed Sullivan's guidelines. Any idea how long the average interview actually lasted?"

Juliet wasn't sure if the question was rhetorical but she wanted to show her interest. "Ten minutes?" she offered.

Willard shook his head. "Three. *Trois. Drei.* And pretty soon one out of four draftees was 4-F, sometimes just for nail biting. Then a group of Harvard physicians claimed they could detect unfit soldiers by physical proportions: something idiotic about wide hips correlating to cowardice. There was an actual formula about, pardon me, *pubic hair.* I guess I should have done something, but I was a novice in the field, a kid as far as they were concerned; I didn't think anyone would listen. I went about my hospital work and began studying phobias—I'd had a near-crippling phobia of snakes as a boy and was fascinated by where such things came from. So I began conducting Pentothal interviews with patients who couldn't understand the roots of their deepest fears—and I had unprecedented success. Then we entered the war, and by the middle of last year the Selective Service board was up the creek. Casualties were into the hundreds of thousands, and the army needed replacements. The idea that one quarter of young American males were mentally unsound finally struck them as absurd, and they fired Sullivan and called me. My team nixed over half the original draft interview questions and arranged for actual psychiatrists to be stationed at the replacement training centers to monitor soldiers. But then another problem came up: too many soldiers in North Africa were getting discharged for 'constitutional inadequacy'—neuropsychiatric incidents were literally *triple* the number from the Great War. When Patton slapped those soldiers in Sicily, everyone started questioning the whole idea of battle fatigue. The army decided that either the diagnoses were wrong or treatment was inadequate. They wanted 'maximum utilization' of the soldiers. So they shipped some doctors—not my team—to evac hospitals. One in Tunisia got seventy-eight percent of psychiatric casualties back to combat duty after forty-eight hours by plunging them in ice baths. A hospital in Tripoli sent ninety-three percent of mental patients back into the lines within a month."

Willard drew his cup close and stared desolately at the contents.

"I was suspicious as hell of the numbers. In the wrong hands, psychiatry can be more impressionistic than a Monet. I needed to see *firsthand* what was happening. So I demanded to go to Monte Cassino, where the fatigue cases were breaking all records. Those boys were shaking, weeping, banging their heads on the ground. Many couldn't speak. That's when I started using Sodium Pentothal again. The first time I made the mistake of doing the interview in the Recovery Tent, with the nurses and ward men and doctors *watching*. Can you imagine? The patient emerged calm, but the staff was in tears."

"It's some gruesome stuff," said Juliet.

"And yet you've handled yourself pretty well."

"Have I?"

"You strike me as being entirely too hard on yourself, Nurse Dufresne."

"Like you?" she asked, smiling.

He paused. "Perhaps. . . . Anyway, Monte Cassino was a nightmare, of course. It became clear to me then that any sane, strong man could break down under completely normal combat circumstances. Every break manifested itself differently. And these were breaks that didn't heal quickly. I rested these men, talked with them, medicated them, fed them with my own hands. I got them to stop shaking and weeping. And when they looked as good as new, I sent them back, just as I was ordered to do. But it didn't work."

"They came back?"

"Psychosomatic illness. *You* mentioned it my first day here, remember? Mental illness manifesting itself physically. Did you know that almost eight-five percent of gastrointestinal cases at the front have no organic pathology? You can get rid of the bellyaches, the shaking, the paralysis, the muteness, but that doesn't mean you've cured the illness. You stop the shakes, send the soldier back, but he shows up at the hospital again—suddenly mute."

"Like Barnaby."

"Like Barnaby. Because these men don't have *irrational* phobias. What they're afraid of is very real. The products of firsthand experience. In some ways, you could say they're more sane than we are."

"So why try to cure them if they'll just get sent back?"

"*That* is the fateful question. The war is here, and the army needs bodies. What do we do? Force the broken ones back in and hope they'll end the war faster. Sounds heartless, right? But if I don't cure the Barnabys and get them back to the front, more men die in the long run. For every torn and tattered man I send back into the lines, there are three more back home I might have spared. There is no 'right' in this work, only degrees of 'less awful.'"

Willard paused, sat back. "The army couldn't get enough replacements in Italy, so they had me set up a psychiatric hospital here. Now they want psychiatric units in the *field hospitals* so we can send boys back in after forty-eight hours. They don't understand these 'cases' are human beings who are going to suffer mental instability long after this war is over, long after all the generals hang up their uniforms. The human mind didn't evolve to exist under combat conditions. Now . . ." He turned his empty coffee cup upside down. "You asked for information and you got an hour-long graduate-level lecture. I hope my long-windedness will deter you from future inquiries."

But Juliet hadn't minded; it surprised her how intently she had listened and how many more questions she still had. It was a feeling she'd previously associated only with books—a hunger to sink headlong into a subject, a person's voice. She wanted to keep talking, and yet the lantern was sputtering.

"Everybody else here wants to tell you every little thing about their lives back home the minute you meet them," she said.

"I suppose my job is trickier than the rest. By its very nature, it's so personal that I have to enforce other boundaries. I have to be a trusted authority, with a veneer of self-containment, or I don't think I could do anyone much good."

"Veneer," she repeated. "So you do get lonely?"

"Now, that, dear one, is a personal question."

Willard said it jokingly, but the words *dear one* surprised Juliet; even Willard seemed uncomfortable with his phrasing.

For a moment, neither of them moved.

Finally, Willard leaned into the table and hugged his papers. As he rose he gathered them clumsily to his chest. "Good night, Nurse Dufresne."

"Good night, Dr. Willard."

He hurried toward the tent exit, but as he was about to leave, he turned. With an expression of amicable defeat, he said, "For what it's worth, I'm from Chicago."

CHAPTER 9

THE AMBULANCE WAS heading north, climbing into the pine-and-poplar-covered mountains. Juliet sat beside Dr. Lovelace, who was driving. They'd been ordered forward by Major Decker after the division's medical clearing company called to say a colonel needed surgery and couldn't be moved.

As the ambulance navigated the winding roads, Juliet felt a sharp chill; though it was still summer, it felt more like winter here. She pulled a blanket from the back, perforated with cigarette burns, and begrudgingly wrapped it around her shoulders. The temperature had dropped fifteen degrees since they had set out, a fact she almost mentioned to Dr. Lovelace, but then thought better of. Since the drive began, a thick silence had divided them. Glenda's absence loomed uncomfortably in the vehicle; *she* should have been the one riding beside him, assisting him. Lovelace drove quietly, methodically, nothing like the man who had wildly chauffeured everyone to the lake a month earlier; he seemed a cold and saddened version of himself. Juliet wasn't sure what she could say to him that wouldn't sound trite.

Instead she looked out the window at the pulverized stumps of trees along the road. The air was gray and cool and there wasn't a person in sight. They eased the ambulance across the noisy planks of a makeshift bridge. Below them, the piles and splintered wood of the original bridge bobbed in the current.

At the command post a sentry directed Juliet and Lovelace to a small stone building used as the battalion aid station. Juliet was happy to finally stretch her legs, happy to be away from the confines of the hospital.

But as they stepped inside, she clutched the door frame to orient herself. On a cold stone floor, a dozen men lay side by side, writhing and whimpering, their cries pouring into one another. It sounded like a swamp of screams. Against the far wall, two men had been propped up on a metal table, staring mutely at their bloodied legs. A pair of medics crouched over a patient in the corner, tossing forceps and gauze between them. Nearby, a man with a Red Cross helmet furiously pumped at the chest of the patient beneath him, intermittently blowing into his mouth. Without looking up, he called to them, "Colonel Muskegee's against the right wall."

The colonel was tall and broad shouldered and stared calmly up. At first glance, Juliet couldn't see what was wrong with him. His lips were thin and dry. His eyes moved from Lovelace to Juliet. "I want to live," he whispered.

Dr. Lovelace gently lifted his head off the stretcher, revealing, behind the left ear, a mess of gray pulp. The smell of burned brain tissue nearly made Juliet gag; she quickly dug through the surgical bag to find the Novocain and scalpel. Lovelace's hands snipped and sutured, quick as wings, while Juliet kept her hand on Muskegee's wrist. "His pulse is dropping," she warned.

"Okay, double-vein him. Adrenaline. Then plasma." Dr. Lovelace moved quickly but calmly, bandaging the man's skull.

Juliet noticed the patient beside the colonel, watching the surgery, nervously fingering the back of his own skull. From litters surrounding them came the words *doctor* and *help*. Juliet glanced around the room at the blank and weary faces, men staring at giant hooks hanging from the ceiling—she had not noticed them before. Christ, were they in a butcher shop?

"Thank bloody God!" the battalion surgeon exclaimed. The man whose heart he'd been pumping finally doubled over, coughing.

Then Juliet felt a hand on her shoulder: Dr. Lovelace was shaking his head. He began wiping down his surgical instruments, setting them back in the bag. He stood, quietly moving to another patient.

"How'm I doing, nurse?" the colonel asked. A silver star was pinned to his jacket.

"Good," she whispered.

Then he died.

At 1600 hours, they began heading back to the hospital. Dr. Lovelace drove and Juliet sat quietly, her head resting against the window. Three patients had died in an hour, and she was numb, out of emotion as if out of breath. When Lovelace said, "Roadblock ahead," Juliet barely raised her head.

A line of troops, hunched beneath swollen packs, stood across the gray road, motioning them to stop.

"A bit late for sightseeing," said one of the soldiers.

Dr. Lovelace began to explain where they had been, but the soldier cut him off: "Let's not get ahead of ourselves. Orphan?"

"Annie," Juliet answered flatly.

The soldier's demeanor suddenly changed; he grinningly tapped the hood of the ambulance. "Camp with us and make your way back in the daylight. This forest is crawling with Krauts. They've been snatching up uniforms from dead GIs and moving around like they're one of us. You sure as hell don't want them to get their hands on you."

Climbing into the back of the ambulance, Juliet and Lovelace tried to determine which supplies they needed for the night. Juliet stuffed some blankets and ration bars into her bag and stepped down onto the road. She didn't care where she slept, so long as she didn't have to hold the hands of any more dying men for the night.

"Sure as shit, is that Juliet Dufresne?"

Juliet almost didn't recognize the hulking man covered with mud. "*Beau Conroy?*"

The cold, the fatigue, the months away from home, Tuck's disappearance—it all came rushing powerfully at Juliet, a wave of longing and exhaustion, and she tumbled into Beau, her arms outstretched, pressing her cheek against his chest.

He patted her back. "Hey, there. Hey. It's gonna be all right."

Juliet wiped her eyes and looked up. "I never . . . I just never expected to see someone from home."

Beau stared at her; tears were pooling in his deep green eyes. "Come on," he whispered, throwing his arm around her. "Before these guys call me a pussy."

As they followed the troops through the pine forest, Beau walked beside her, occasionally stepping ahead to take her hand. The moon cast a silver light over the towering trees. The air was cold, stinging Juliet's cheeks, crawling through the fabric of her shirt. They clambered across the crackling limbs of fallen trees, sloshed knee-deep through chilly puddles, hiked along a rise of limestone, the soft white rock crumbling beneath their boots, until finally, at the entrance to a small cave, the soldiers all loosened their packs.

"Home sweet home," Beau announced.

The men drew sticks for guard duty, and Beau snapped his disbelievingly in two. "I'm the tallest guy here, and somehow I always pull the short stick." He yawned, and Juliet saw that he had lost a molar. As if suddenly recalling the gap in his teeth, he quickly closed his mouth.

"Want company?" she asked.

"Sure you don't want some rest?"

"It's not every night I get to see someone from home."

The soldiers dragged their packs inside, laid down their bedrolls, and wiggled themselves, fully dressed, into sleeping bags; they used their helmets as pillows. Lovelace settled in beside them.

At the mouth of the cave, Juliet and Beau arranged a bedroll and sat on it side by side, staring out at the night. He set his rifle on his shoulder and shook his canteen, the last few sips of water sloshing around.

"All yours," he said.

"I can do better." She dug in her bag and found the medical brandy.

"God, I love you."

Beau took a long sip and rubbed the back of his hand across his wet lips. Juliet sipped a pinch and leaned against the rock wall. She unlaced her boots.

Slowly, and with great effort, Beau tugged off his own boots. He peeled back layers of what appeared to be newspaper, unleashing a rank smell of mold. Blistered toes, purple and blue, poked through his damp frayed socks.

"Beau, that's trench foot."

"I can walk all right; I just can't seem to wiggle those damn little piggies. You'd think the army'd give us decent boots." He blew into his palms and rubbed his toes.

"Here, let me."

"I can't ask that of you."

"I'm a nurse, Beau."

He shook his head, dazzled. "You're a nurse now. Unbelievable. Jesus, Juliet, yesterday you were just Tuck's little tagalong sister. I still can't believe it's *you*."

She worked her thumbs gently along the darkened flesh, massaging the edges of the blisters, trying to get the circulation going.

"So how is Tuck, anyway?" Beau asked. "Last I heard, he'd gotten into some scuffle at a rest hotel."

Juliet paused and carefully set one foot down and lifted the other. "He's missing. That's all the telegram said. Missing. Since last November."

"Crap, Juliet, I'm sorry. Where?"

"Here in Italy. I think somewhere near the Volturno."

"They say the Volturno was bad." Beau nodded solemnly into the night. His expression made her sad, and she set down his foot.

"What kind of scuffle?" she asked, wiping her hands.

"The drunk kind, I'd assume. The blow-off-steam kind. I just heard a story, that's all, and recognized the name." Beau dug through his pack for a K ration tin. "Labels wore off these things, so this could be breakfast, lunch, or dinner. But let's call it dinner, 'cause I'd like to buy you dinner."

Juliet watched his fingers, red and blistered, fumble with the lid. The tin kept slipping from his hands, and she could see his frustration. After several more tries, air hissed into the can and he pulled back the lid. He dumped half the contents into a bowl for Juliet and kept the rest for himself. "GI caviar," he said, plunging in his spoon. He shoved the beans into his mouth. Juliet examined her beans and thought of mentioning Private Barnaby, explaining that he had Pearl's white glove, that he might soon come to consciousness and be able to tell her something about Tuck. She considered confessing that she'd come all this way looking for her brother. She was tired of carrying the burden of it all.

"So what do you hear from Myrna?" Beau asked.

"Zilch."

"Well, if you ask me"—he thumbed a bean from his chin into his mouth—"they were never very serious."

"I think she's pretty much in mourning. Everyone back home thinks Tuck is dead."

Beau stopped eating and considered this. "You know what? No way. Tuck's a survivor. He'd want us to keep a positive attitude. He never got flustered before a game like the other players. He won because he was determined to win."

A vision of Tuck and Beau came to her: sitting together on a bench after a long practice, staring into their upturned helmets, deep in concentration, discussing strategies. They might have been there now, a few years out of high school, home from college, tossing the ball across the field for old times' sake. This vision lay so close to the surface, this alternate version of their lives, that it startled Juliet. Would they ever get back to that? Or would they always have the feeling of a life glimpsed, hoped for, and somehow lost?

Beau was watching the workings of her face.

"How's your cheerleader?" asked Juliet.

"Oh, do not get me started on the whoring, duplicitous ways of Patty Sinclair. The guys said if I mention her name one more time, they'll hand my balls to the Jerries. I'm one hundred percent done with that witch."

Juliet shrugged. "Women."

"You're one yourself, you know," he marveled. "A real grown woman."

Juliet blushed; she liked that he thought of her that way.

As they finished their beans, thick snores echoed from the cave. One of the soldiers noisily tossed and turned. "You sure you don't wanna sleep?" asked Beau.

"With that orchestra playing?"

He smiled and blew on his hands and tucked them beneath his armpits. "Then lemme teach you how we pass the hours. The game is called Lives. You tell me where you see yourself ten years from now, then I do the same. Usually there's a few of us, so we can vote on who told the best life. I'll go first, so you see how it's played."

"Let me guess. Three girlfriends?"

"I could barely handle one! Hear me out. They say there's gonna be loans for GIs after the war and I'm gonna take that money to start my own garage. Anyone can fix a car, right? But I'd be giving something extra. You come in for an oil change, but we give the car a wax job, too. New brake pads? You get some windshield wipers. You gotta have an angle, right?"

"Absolutely."

"So where are *you* gonna be? Teaching in a nursing college somewhere?"

Juliet was stumped; she had not imagined a life beyond the war, beyond finding Tuck, for quite some time. "I think I'd like to live in a city," she said, "a big city. A place like New York or . . . Chicago." Her stomach fluttered at the word.

"No, no, no. Too cold. Too far. Up there, they think Southerners speak a foreign language. I'm gonna have to forbid that."

"I thought this was my fantasy!"

"Within reason! What about Atlanta?"

"Chicago it is," she said. "And I'd like to be a professor. In a scientific field. Maybe chemistry."

"Oh, boy, we'll never work out," he laughed.

"Beau, I think we're butchering this game."

"Not at all. We're adding exciting new dimensions. Now, where's that brandy?" Beau took two long swigs. "So, there will undoubtedly be a husband. But the important question is: Is he going to be a dull doctor? A boring lawyer? Another professor of, *gag*"— he jabbed his forefinger at his open mouth—"*chemistry*? Because some of those thinker types, they don't know how to make women happy, not in the important way. A man who works with his hands, he knows a thing or two."

"You haven't changed," said Juliet, smiling.

"Just a little frostbitten around the edges. Anyway, you still have to pick a husband."

"Frankly, I never used to think anyone would want to marry me."

"Maybe not when you were thirteen. But don't be crazy. You're a lady now. A smart, classy army nurse. You'll have guys lined up to propose."

"We'll see."

"So"—he took another swig—"let's review: the extent of Juliet's wild and adventurous life fantasy is . . . a chemistry lab in a cold northern city. Correct?"

"I guess."

"Good, 'cause that means you win! And you know what the winner gets?" He leaned over and kissed her. His lips were cold and moved over hers with an oily, curious intensity. She could taste the beans and the brandy.

"Thought I'd get that in before you run off to Chicago."

"It was much nicer than the first time."

"Oh, that. Sorry. I was an asshole."

"Yup. Asshole."

He reached out and traced her birthmark with his fingertip. "I like it, you know. It's unique. You've gotten so pretty."

"That's sleep deprivation talking."

"You don't even know you're pretty. It's why you're so nice. Crap, I shouldn't have told you."

Tears came briefly to Juliet's eyes; he had said something she'd always wanted to hear but hadn't known it. Someone thought she was pretty. She'd always thought she was too smart to want such things. Yet it moved her now. Maybe he was lying, maybe he was tired, but it made her happy, and she leaned against his shoulder. She wanted to lose herself in the bulk of him.

She closed her eyes and thought of the colonel who died that morning; she thought of Glenda being loaded into the army truck; she thought of the day she waved good-bye to Tuck at the bus depot. It seemed that everything could vanish, at any moment. *This* could vanish. This comfort with Beau, this one chance, could be taken from her.

Taking a long, deep breath, she pressed her head against his chest. His heart beat strongly. She let her fingers travel across his arms and could sense his body flexing, coming to life. She opened her eyes and looked up at him. As he slowly reached for a button on her shirt, she nodded.

"You were my first kiss," she whispered.

He smiled. "You were mine."

He slid his hand across her stomach and up her chest. She looked around for a moment, into the cave, at the sleeping men. "Will you get in trouble?"

He kissed her neck and pressed himself against her, and she felt the full weight and warmth of him. He reached for the buckle of her pants and pulled her farther outside.

"Gunderson," Beau called into the cave. "Gunderson."

The man who had been tossing and turning sat up on his bed-roll.

"Gunderson, you owe me one. Take over."

It was not what she had expected. It hurt and it was messy and now she felt sticky and cold between her legs. But the sharpness of it, the insistent bluntness, the strangeness of his body inside hers, made her feel like an entirely different person. *Juliet would never do this,* she kept thinking. And soon everything else fell from her thoughts except this idea of the her before the act and the new her. She had thought little about Beau. It seemed that being so close to another human being, you would have to think about him, but she hadn't. She had closed her eyes and thought about herself, her body, what was happening inside her body, as though she were entirely alone.

After Gunderson was sent back to sleep, Beau settled on his elbows, readjusted his rifle, and looked at the stars.

Juliet leaned back beside him and wished she could tell him what had just happened to her, as though he hadn't been there.

He kissed her head and let his lips linger on her scalp.

"I'm gonna ask you something, Juliet. . . . How do you save the world from evil?"

"No idea."

"You take out an ad in the classifieds. Wanted: brave young men to defeat the forces of evil in the world. Every boy in every high school across the country is going to sign right up. What you don't say in the ad? Expect to live in mud and shit and freeze your asses off while you watch your friends bleed to death. Expect frostbite, crappy food, bad attitudes, no sleep, shitty maps, old weapons, and lousy leadership, all while a psychotic enemy pursues you night and day. If you manage to survive, you get the honor of knowing you helped save the world from Nazi maniacs. But you think that any-one fifty years from now will bat an eyelash over it?"

"They'd better," said Juliet.

"Growing up I never thought about all those guys who fought in the Great War. Not once. But I think about them now, all the time. All of Italy, all of Europe, the ground we're sitting on, is filled with the bodies of guys just like me, who did exactly what I'm doing, thirty years ago."

His eyes were red, fixed on a point outside the cave. His nose had begun to run, and he wiped it clean. The stars clustered thickly overhead like coins in a wishing pond. Had all those men, decades earlier, once made wishes?

"I really hope Tuck is alive," Beau said.

Juliet was silent.

"I'd just like to make it out of here so I can get home to my grandma," Beau said. "She's eighty-eight. I'd like to get home so she doesn't have to sit in that house by herself for what's left of her life."

"You'll get home," said Juliet. "You will."

Beau nodded firmly. He clutched his rifle close and blinked with intense alertness.

"Goddamn straight I will."

When Juliet and Lovelace returned to the hospital the next morn-ing, Juliet found Dr. Willard seated at a picnic table pecking at his typewriter. Beside him, a Coca-Cola bottle sat like an archaeological find, a cross section of beverage and ash and cigarette butts. The sky had turned gray, and in the distance the thunder rumbled, the serrated edge of a storm.

"You're back, then," he said, studiously typing several words and forcefully hitting the return carriage.

"Major Decker sent us into the mountains, and we got stuck overnight."

"You and Lovelace." He did not look up. But she wanted him to. She felt changed, she felt womanly, and wanted Dr. Willard to see it.

"We camped with troops," she said. "I assumed you were told."

He began typing another line, hitting the return carriage twice before pulling the page from the machine and setting it tidily on the table to examine his work.

"How's Barnaby?" she asked.

"Yesterday was an eventful day here." He patted the sheet he had typed. "I have good news, and god-awful news."

"Well, give me the god-awful news first."

"Captain Brilling is pushing to start Barnaby's court-martial proceedings next week."

"*Next week?*"

"I'm petitioning to buy some time, but I had not expected it to come to this."

"Well, what can the good news possibly be?"

"He *spoke*." Willard watched her face as though she were slowly unwrapping a present. "Without Pentothal."

"He's awake?!"

"Well, snapping in and out of consciousness; but he's experiencing moments of real lucidity, finally. Brief, but conscious. His eye is now opening on its own and tracking motion, tracking sound, actively taking in what's going on around him. Earlier yesterday, when I went to check his vitals at 9:28, he said good morning."

"I can't believe it!"

"That was all. 'Good morning.' But it means he is slowly climbing out of his mental cave. He knew who I was, he knew it was morning. That is, right now, miraculous progress considering where we started." Willard spoke quickly, and Juliet saw how happy he was to share his news. "Go see for yourself. You'll notice the difference in his stare. If he says absolutely nothing, don't take it personally. His speech will come in bursts right now. Lasting a few seconds at best. It's a little like staring at the sky, trying to watch for a shooting star. It's easier to just stumble into it. It'll come more frequently in time, though."

In the Recovery Tent, Juliet headed straight to Barnaby's bed and dropped her bag. An olive army blanket had been tucked beneath his long arms. His eye was closed, flanked by the steep ridges of white bandages.

"Hi there, Private Barnaby, I'm your nurse. Do you remember me? I've been taking care of you for a few weeks. My name is Juliet Dufresne."

His eye remained closed, so Juliet sat beside him and eased off some of the gauze, soaping the edges of his chin and patting it dry. She rubbed Vaseline into his stitches.

Suddenly, he moaned, the sound of a child roused from a nap. His eye opened and sleepily directed its gaze at her face. He reached up and touched her cheek, his fingers traveling slowly toward her birthmark; his eye sparkled with amazement.

"You're the sister," he said.

CHAPTER 10

IN THE UNCOMFORTABLE days that followed—hoping, impatiently, for further moments of Barnaby's lucidity and for a coherent explanation of what he knew—Juliet sought distraction. She worked long hours and after dinner found herself drawn to the hospital's entertainments—the movies and plays and impromptu dances she'd formerly avoided. Since her night with Beau, she felt newly confident, finally entitled to join all the socializing.

The late-July nights were radiantly black. Insects thrummed against the tents and dead gnats stippled the surface of every drink. Drinking was unbridled now—no one had had a furlough in weeks, and the news from France, albeit triumphant, wrought a gloominess throughout the hospital.

Normandy, Bayeux, Cherbourg, Saint-Lô, Caen—each night, the names of the French towns and cities taken by the Allies crackled from BBC Radio. The staff and patients gathered by the radio, listening intently, angrily, not for the news itself but for news of *them,* for some momentary tribute to the one hundred miles of fortified Italian terrain they'd conquered in the last month, for some scant recognition of the hills and valleys littered with bodies, the rivers clotted with their division's blood. They began calling Italy "the Forgotten Front."

When the radio had been switched off, they all spilled into the recently assembled Rec Tent. News that Bob Hope and Marlene Dietrich had visited hospitals in France prompted Major Decker and Mother Hen to schedule extensive diversions. Several ward men had gotten hold of a copy of *Macbeth,* and one night it was passed from hand to hand while each man read aloud his part. One of the cooks had a banjo, and accompanying tambourines were made from ration-tin lids; from empty cigarette packs and shrapnel maracas were fashioned. Twice a week, movies were projected onto a large white sheet—*The Maltese Falcon, Fantasia, Ali Baba and the Forty Thieves.*

The night of *Lassie Come Home,* the entire staff except Bernice crowded the tent. She explained to Juliet that she liked only movies in which a woman renounced things she deeply desired, or in which a man had to convince those around him of a looming disaster. She did not like comedies or romances or movies with happy endings, which she said gave people false expectations about life.

Juliet wasn't in a mood to argue. She'd just left the Isolation Tent, where Private Eddie Fishwick had been moved. A bullet had pierced his vocal cords, but after surgery he developed septic shock. It was clear he wouldn't survive. For days he'd been writing furiously. At all hours Juliet could hear his pencil scratching away, pages fluttering. Mute, he handed stacks of his writing to Juliet, his hazel eyes unnerving in their clarity. But the pages held only scribbles—nothing legible. What, she wondered, did he so desperately want to communicate? Were they notes for his loved ones? Were they confessions? Questions? "I'll put these somewhere safe," she said, lacking the heart to tell him his dying words were gibberish.

And now Fishwick could barely work his pencil across the page. He drew faint, uneven lines, mere dashes and arcs, but his eyes sought Juliet's for signs of comprehension. His skin had taken on a gray translucence. As she left the Isolation Tent that night, he'd shaken his pencil at her; all she could say, guiltily, was "I'll come check on you later."

She was becoming strangely accustomed to this—the feeling of ineptness. Where she had once believed the task of nursing was knowing exactly what to do, here she found, again and again, that the challenge was understanding what she could not do. It was quite simple, really, to rush to an injured man; to walk away was another matter entirely.

In the Rec Tent, she squeezed onto a bench with Major Decker, Dr. Willard, and Mother Hen; in front of them sat a row of patients, crutches laid at their feet. Ration crates lined the sides of the tent where the ward men sat beating out a drumroll with their boot heels. The overhead lights flickered off, and the tent quieted as a preface scrolled on the white sheet:

The author of *Lassie Come Home* was a man of two countries. Born in England, he survived the First World War as a British soldier, only to die in the Second World War, killed in the line of duty in the uniform of the country he had adopted . . . America. With reverence and pride, we dedicate this picturization of his best-loved story to the late Major Eric Knight.

"To Major Knight," echoed through the tent.

Then Juliet watched as the young Joe Carraclough romped with his collie. "Ain't nothin' wrong with lovin' a bitch!" a nearby patient joked. But when Joe came home from school and learned that his destitute parents had been forced to sell Lassie, the tent fell quiet. As Lassie lay in her cage, whimpering, Juliet suddenly thought of Tuck— trapped, somewhere far from there, alone—and looked away.

When she heard cheers around her, she glanced up to see Lassie escaping. Juliet desperately clutched the bench as the ragged dog swam across rivers, limped up mountainsides, wrestled other dogs, until, finally, after hundreds of miles, on the verge of death, he scratched at the door of Joe's cottage. As Lassie collapsed in young Joe's arms, Juliet's chest tightened, and a tear slid down her cheek.

"You're my Lassie come home!" cried Joe.

After "The End" wrote itself across the white hospital sheet and the MGM music blared, Juliet looked beside her at Major Decker and Mother Hen, their faces wet with tears.

Finally, Brother Reardon stood. "Would someone please tell the quartermaster that if the army is going to send us these movies, they had best urgently provision us with Kleenex!" Then he dramatically blew his nose, and everyone laughed.

One by one, the patients limped and hobbled out of the tent. A voice sang out: "Oh, you're my Stubbs come home!" Another declared: "Ogden, go home!"

Outside, the sky was a dome of black pierced by sharp points of light. Juliet located the glowing dot of the North Star. She found Orion's belt, Cassiopeia, the Little Dipper. She remembered staring up at the night sky with Tuck on their front porch the night before he left for Fort Branley. She had said that wherever he went they'd be under the same moon, the same stars. She pointed out every constellation she knew. "Pretty names," Tuck said, "for scalding masses of fire."

The hoot of an owl drew Juliet's attention to the jagged tree line in the distance and the snow-capped mountains to the north. She felt unexpectedly light, vaguely euphoric. It was the first time in months she had cried, and it had cleansed her of something.

As she ambled through the clean, crisp air, an image of Tuck came to her—older and wearied, mounting the front steps of their Charlesport home. She imagined hugging him, stroking his scarred and stubbled face. She imagined walking with him to Raven Point, where they would lie in the tall grass and discuss everything that had happened in their time apart. She would describe the hospital and all of the people she had met, glossing over the gory deaths, just as he would gloss over combat stories. Finally, he would explain the meaning of his strange last letter, and thank her for coming so far to look for him.

Again Juliet heard the owl, and below that, mosquitoes. As she approached her tent, the mosquitoes grew louder. Or were they bees? Juliet stopped; there it was again, a low, distant buzz. A white blur in the sky caught her attention, and she hit the ground.

As the siren droned, she pressed her helmet tight to her head and set her face against the grass. She lay still until she heard a stampede; others were racing to the Recovery Tent, and she forced herself to stand and follow the throng of doctors and nurses all stumbling in.

"Get them under the fucking beds!"

"Nurse, help!"

"Cut them down! They're stuck!"

"Me, over here! Hey, help! I can't move!"

"Someone get his legs!"

"Don't leave me!"

The buzz of the airplane grew louder, and Juliet raced to Barnaby, pulling him down from his mattress and shoving him roughly under the bed. The ward men dashed from bed to bed, slashing slings with knives. Juliet tore at someone's sling with her teeth. Suddenly, the ground shook. Juliet lost her footing and banged her head on something metal.

"Help."

Disoriented, Juliet looked up and saw Private Leo and Private Dunlap, burn victims, bandaged head to toe in their beds, too fragile to be moved. Brother Reardon was fastening his helmet on one of the men, and Juliet began to do the same, but suddenly she was slammed to the ground. An arm tugged her beneath a bed. She smelled smoke and soil and the stench of bedpans. She closed her eyes. In the blackness she heard the siren, the buzz of the plane, anxious voices. "Are you okay? Is everyone safe?" Then she remembered Private Fishwick.

Juliet tried to squirm out from beneath the bed but felt the arm hold hers firmly.

"Not yet." It was Dr. Willard. "You're bleeding."

The siren faded, and Juliet became aware of a dull pain near her chin, the metallic taste of blood.

"But this is a . . ." She wanted to say "hospital," but her jaw ached.

She heard beds scraping, and suddenly people were reaching out from beneath the mattresses. Their arms were slick with plasma and glucose, their faces crusty with vomit. A man beside her rubbed dirt from his eyes and examined the gauze dangling from his chest wound.

Juliet waded through the patients and stumbled outside. In the darkness, other figures were wandering about, wobbly as sleepwalkers, their faces dirt-blackened. The air seemed charged, pulsing, as though millions of electrons had broken loose from their atoms.

Juliet moved briskly across the encampment, coughing on smoke. Just before the Isolation Tent, she sidestepped a crater. The tent's wall looked as if an enormous bite had been taken from the canvas, and she climbed through the jagged opening.

In the dark, her foot slid into a hole.

"Shit."

Juliet extracted herself and limped forward, her hands extended to feel the way.

"Private Fishwick?"

As her eyes adjusted to the darkness, she saw what looked to be a figure on the bed, split in two; in the middle was a wet and pulpy heap of innards.

Juliet moved closer and saw Fishwick's face; his eyes were strangely calm and his nostrils flared with each strained inhalation. She could now see that he was, in fact, pinned beneath another body—someone mangled and bleeding, lying facedown.

Fishwick 's eyes desperately searched out his papers, and with his hand he tried to write something in the air.

Juliet stepped forward and turned over the body on top of him. Her heart shuddered; it was Mother Hen.

* * *

Dear Juliet,

Pearl and I received the letter explaining your trans-
fer and must say that while we miss you terribly, we both
have immense respect for the work you are doing. It must be
exhausting—I recall all too well the long hospital days. But I
am sanguine you will come out of this experience, grueling as
it may be, with a greater appreciation for life. We both com-
mented on how you already sound so much more grown-up.
I'm glad the conditions are safe, and hopefully you can get to
some dances and mixers and grow in other ways as well. Your
mother was quite social during her time as a nurse—thank
goodness, because she found her way to shy old me.

Little has changed here since you left except our Victory
tomatoes did not fare well this season. Pearl thinks we should
focus on summer squashes, so I am leaving the planting to her.
We had a bad thunderstorm a few weeks back and had to cut
some loose branches off the oak beside the house. Chicken pox
went through the elementary school, and for days my waiting
room was crowded with itchy children.

I'm not good at letters, you know that, so I'm going to stop
here. Pearl will write the next one and try to send you some
chocolates. I know you are limited in what you can say, but do
tell us more of your whereabouts and what is happening there.
There is little news of Italy these days.

Love,
Papa

Juliet dipped each of the pale hands in soapy water. The fingers
were stiff, and one by one she pried them apart and worked a towel
in between. She filed the nails, blowing dust from the half-moon

cuticles. Then she laid the hands palms down, one atop the other, below the collar of the olive drab dress shirt.

She stepped back.

Mother Hen's eyes were closed, her face was washed and powdered—except for the blue tint to her lips, she might have been resting.

That morning, Bernice had stitched and washed the body. Another nurse had pressed the uniform by arranging it in the sun beneath an assortment of books. The final touches fell to Juliet—which at the start seemed simple enough, except that she had never touched the corpse of someone she *knew*.

For the first time in years, Juliet thought of her own mother. Juliet had been three years old when her mother got pneumonia. Thinking it would frighten her, Tuck and her father would not let Juliet into the room once her mother had passed, and had kept her away in the final days. So Juliet's memory of her mother had always been of the beautiful, healthy woman in all the mantel photographs. A woman who might return any day. But Juliet now grasped the shuddering fact of what Tuck and her father had witnessed. Death was a vague concept until you felt the cold, limp hand of someone you knew.

Juliet lifted off Mother Hen's helmet, revealing thick auburn hair fastened with two jagged railroad tracks of bobby pins. One by one, Juliet pulled loose the pins, segments of hair springing to life. Slowly, she ran her fingers through the strands. She dipped a comb in water, combed her hair, and then neatly refastened the bobby pins.

You were saving a patient, she thought. *A dying patient.*

Juliet recalled what her father had told Tuck: "You realize, of course, that grenades have no sense of justice. That bullets and bayonets care nothing for morality. Being right doesn't protect you from having your brain blown to bits."

Grenades were just the tip of it, though; there was no justice anywhere. She saw that now. How many men had died in the hospital because they'd come to stop the Nazis? Noble causes, selfless acts—none of it mattered. Nothing could be trusted. What could be expected from such a cold, indifferent universe? *Forgive me,* Barnaby had said. What if the man she was desperately trying to save had actually harmed her brother? The thought made Juliet momentarily nauseous. She knew nothing, she realized, not even whether she was on the right path. She'd come all this way and had no more information than on the day her father had received the army telegram. Suddenly Juliet tilted back her head and stomped her foot. "What *happened* to my brother?" she shouted.

Her face had gone hot, tears clouded her eyes, and Juliet breathed heavily in the silence that followed. In the thick air of the tent, she looked all around as though expecting a response, expecting *something,* though she could not have said from whom.

She wiped her eyes. She sat very still.

Then slowly, wearily, she began to collect her things. In an hour, Graves Registry would come. She stepped outside into the wreckage of the hospital, wandering past smashed garbage pails, the splintered shower stall, the torn ruins of the Isolation Tent, still tangled with Mother Hen's bloodied clothes.

Outside Willard's tent, Juliet heard his typewriter.

She shook the canvas flap.

"Yes?"

She stepped in and lingered at the threshold. She had not been there since the night they had worked with Barnaby, since the night he scolded her for asking about Tuck.

He looked up from his typing. "Come." He patted a space on the ground and shoved a stack of books against the wall. "How's your jaw?"

Juliet touched her face. "It hurts when I chew."

"You're eating at least."

"Some."

He stared at her, as though expecting her to speak, to explain why she was there, but she could not.

"Do you want to go for a walk?" he asked. "Get some fresh air?"

Juliet shook her head.

"Do you want to get some hot food?" He drew his hands together. "Or a drink! I probably have some Scotch hidden around here somewhere. . . ." He began pawing through the clutter of his tent, lifting notebooks and Dopp kits, digging through his medical bag.

"This is either single malt," he said, waving a bottle, "or engine oil."

Juliet gently pushed the bottle away. "May I just sit here?"

Willard moved close. "That's perfectly okay."

The Allies finally reached the Arno River, the lower half of Florence was taken, and the hospital moved again. At night, beneath bright sprays of white phosphorous, the convoy crept in darkness along the river; brown water churned over rusted trucks and tanks, eddied around the splintery ruins of bridges. Here and there, bloated corpses bobbed with the current, the smell of rot congealing the night air. Lone helmets slid like turtles.

By morning, they were once again pitching tents, the clack of hammers echoing through the valley. It was early August, and yellow wildflowers had turned the fields the color of dirty gold. Here and there, faded clay-tiled roofs poked into the sky. The sky was a bright blue, a swimming-pool blue, and it was possible to see in the distance the hazy outlines of the Apennine Mountains.

Monte Altuzzo, Monte Battaglia, Monticelli Ridge—the Appenines were the Allies' next target. For this effort, the Fifth Army was now assisted by bands of Italian partisan fighters. Alfonso and Pico, Juliet's Italian patients, each boasted a gunshot wound to the arm. It was Alfonso's eighth wound, Pico's fifth; intricate white scars webbed each man's shoulders and chest. Alfonso and Pico were all that remained of their original partisan group. Alfonso was tall and lanky, Pico short and compact—but they shared a passionate loathing of Mussolini, *fascisti,* and any foreign man who preyed upon their country's women.

Alfonso was a skilled huntsman; each morning he set out from the hospital with an ancient revolver, and by the afternoon returned with a half dozen rabbits slung from his back. Sitting on a crate, he lit a fire and skinned his prey, and by dinnertime offered his pot of steaming rabbit stew around the ward. He spoke often of his parents, and told Juliet he worried that if his mother learned of the deaths of the others in his partisan unit, she would assume the worst. He hoped to get a letter to her.

At night, the air raids continued: sirens wailed, followed by the drone of planes, the pounding of bombs. But the fighting went well, and throughout the day few casualties arrived.

One afternoon, Juliet was working in the Receiving Tent when the Senator was carried in. She moved to the stretcher and snipped open the side of his trousers.

"Isn't this exactly where you got hit the last time?" she asked, examining the blackened flesh of a small bullet wound. It looked like the hole a cigarette burns through fabric; the flesh around it was pristine.

"How many lives you think I got?" he asked.

"Not nine."

"Meow." He rolled his tongue and his head lolled sleepily. "It's like I got a bull's-eye on that leg. Another Purple Heart for the field jacket. Hey, you don't seem glad to see me. What's it take to get a little lovin'?"

"For one, try harder not to get shot."

"You're a tough nut." He giggled. "Me? I'm just a nut."

"Did they give you morphine at the aid station?"

He sipped from an invisible glass. "Champagne for the brain!"

"Munson, how many fingers am I holding up?"

He looked at her seriously. "Twelve."

"Get some sleep."

In this transitory quiet, Juliet was able to spend more time with the few patients in the Recovery Tent. The days were sunny and pleasant; gentle breezes circled the tent. The cooks dug potatoes from a nearby field and at every breakfast served beautiful hash browns. The crossing of the Arno had bolstered the troops, and for days the men debated which river Caesar had crossed. They wanted to know if the Rubicon was the Arno; they wanted to have crossed the same river Caesar had.

Barnaby, too, was still there. At the far end of the tent he lay silently in his bed. Since his initial burst of lucidity, he had said nothing more, although Juliet could now feed him with a spoon, and he would sip water from a cup. His dark brown eye would track nearby conversations, but he made no effort to communicate and gave no indication, when Juliet brought him meals or when she sponged his body before bed each night, that he recalled who she was, that he had ever recognized her.

Strangely, this didn't bother her. After Mother Hen's death, she had stopped pressing Dr. Willard for further Sodium Pentothal interviews, because it now seemed entirely likely that after months of her hoping Barnaby might know something useful about her brother, he would eventually tell her something she didn't want to hear. In his silence, she still had hope. And since the court-martial proceedings had been stalled, she told herself there would be time, when she was ready.

Beside Barnaby, a private first class named Bruce Coppelman had arrived with a wound to his forearm, and because he'd been in Able Company, everyone referred to him as ABC, or Alphabet. Juliet liked Alphabet. He was an artist and knew all about the

Renaissance and Italian art; at night, when it was too dark to read, he would describe for the entire tent the frescoes and sculptures scattered throughout the valley, the wondrous feats of human creativity that had taken place six hundred years before their tanks rolled in. His wife in Canton, Ohio, was also an artist, and after each meal he asked Juliet to help write her a letter.

Juliet often wrote letters for the men with arm or hand injuries, signing them from "Somewhere in Italy." But Coppelman assured Juliet his wife would know exactly where he was and what he was doing; they had devised a code, he said, before he shipped off to Basic Training. Juliet wondered if Tuck's cryptic letter might have contained some kind of code beyond "Miss Van Effing." She studied it for hours one night, circling every third letter, then every fourth letter. She tried reading words backward; she read sentences diagonally. Still, it made no sense to her, and she once again resigned herself to defeat.

Beside Alphabet lay Second Lieutenant Lester Cross, an accountant from New York who had undergone a four-hour mending of the femoral artery. He was mostly bald, his head gray and gleaming, with wisps of black hair tucked behind his ears. The afternoon he came out of surgery, he immediately began asking Juliet about the injections he was receiving.

"Good God, it must cost the army a fortune to keep me in here every day!"

"It does," joked Juliet. "So get better soon."

When Cross saw the X-ray machine wheel by, he jabbed his forefinger toward it. "A contraption like that—come on!"

Cross spent hours discussing maneuvers and operations with other patients, trying to calculate how many $18.75 war bonds it took to pay for a half-track and a tank. On a thick ledger he was figuring the cost of the war. He claimed gasoline costs alone would plunge the United States into bankruptcy.

When Cross spoke, the patient across the aisle, Private

Wilkowski, stood on his bed and pressed his finger to his lips, saying, "Shhhhhh. They can *hear* us."

Wilkowski had thick, carrot-colored curls, threaded with wire-like gray hairs, though he couldn't have been a day over twenty-one. He was pale and gaunt, and ash-gray circles rimmed his eyes. He did not sleep. He did not lie down. He smoked for hours on end and continually counted and studied the cigarettes he had not yet smoked. Each morning and evening he recited unsettling quotes from books no one had ever heard of. He'd been in combat for only two months, since the push from Rome, but had the haggard, hateful look of the men Juliet had seen entering their second year of fighting.

Of particular concern to Wilkowski were the constant rumors of Germans impersonating American soldiers. With each newly arriving patient in the ward, Wilkowski hobbled over and fired off a stream of incensed questions: Where did the Red Sox play? What team was Lou Gehrig on? Who wrote "The Star-Spangled Banner"? He regularly tested the nurses and ward men on the Founding Fathers and refused much-needed medication.

He had suffered a pancreatic disruption from sniper fire when racing from a foxhole where the two other soldiers suddenly gave off what he called "a stinking Jerry aura." One of them, Wilkowski said, looked like Adolf Hitler.

His mother back home in Pennsylvania wrote him regularly, though Wilkowski did not appear to reply. After several extensive interviews, Dr. Willard told Juliet that Wilkowski had once sung in his church choir and volunteered at his local library bringing books to the elderly. Juliet shook her head. It was hard to imagine a kind boy inside the madman interrogating her every day.

"Why don't they just ship him home?" Juliet said. "If he goes back to the front, he's going to end up taking a shot at one of our soldiers."

"Only if he's not cured."

"You think you can cure *him*?"

"A sane man is trapped somewhere inside of him, and yes, I

believe I can cure him. Absolutely. Besides, he doesn't want to go home, so the army would never send him. He loves being in the infantry, loves killing Germans. He actually *wants* to fight. It's combat exhaustion, minus the exhaustion. My hope is to work with him a few more weeks. If I can get him to relax, he might sleep, and if he sleeps, he might be able to shake the paranoid delusions. But without Sodium Pentothal, I can't find out where all this started."

The day Wilkowski was scheduled for his injection, however, he overheard Willard speaking German with a POW in the ward. Wilkowski threw off his bedsheets: "Get out, Kraut! Get out!" He pulled at his hair, saliva bubbling from his mouth, and hurled his body repeatedly against the tent's canvas wall. Eventually, two ward men had to restrain him.

That night, when Juliet made her final rounds, his dinner tray lay untouched beside his bed. A fly buzzed madly over the gelatinous soup. His eyes were red from weeping and he rolled an unsmoked cigarette between his fingers.

"'Darkness rises in the unseen night, and the ghosts of those forsaken and forgotten claw at the recesses of our minds until we bleed.'" He looked ahead blankly. "A. R. Turnley, *The Death of All Souls.*"

"At least have some water," she pleaded, handing him a glass.

He poured the water down her dress.

"German water," he said. "From the German's lover." He let his eyes half close in exhaustion. "Rest in peace, Germany."

Juliet stumbled away, amazed that Willard believed he could cure the man. Wilkowski was far worse in the head than any other patient she'd seen. But when could you say a person was truly ruined—damaged so hideously that he could never return to his former life, his former self? She saw it all the time with bodies: amputees, cripples, the blind. Physical injuries wrought clear changes; gauging wounds of the mind was complete guesswork.

"Nurse Dufresne," Cross called from across the tent, "how

much dough are they throwing at you to work in this circus?" It was getting dark, and the crickets chirped loudly; it was the hour when the men spoke eagerly, as though afraid of nightfall.

"Not enough," Juliet answered, toweling her dress dry.

"Me? I'm making one-third what I raked in back home, with the added bonus of bullets flying past me all day. No G.I. Bill of Rights is gonna make up for that kind of a pay cut. But I'm collecting every scrap of Jerry junk I can get my hands on. Watches, Lugers. Even pulled a gold brooch off a Kraut I nailed and sent it home to my mom for her birthday. I figure it's worth at least five hundred. Of course, back home, I've got money in the stock market. Forget war bonds. You wanna get fat off this war? Head for Wall Street. The longer the war drags on, those stocks are gonna soar. So I've devised a sure thing, assuming I make it home to cash in. How about you, Berenson, what were you?"

Private Berenson had pulled his sheet to his waist and stared dreamily at the top of the tent. "Plumber," he said.

"Hey, Donner, what were *you* before all this started?"

Lieutenant Donner set his book in his lap, and everyone looked over to hear his answer. He was the most taciturn of the patients.

A slight grin lit his face: "Happy."

"Big day today," said Juliet, pulling a stool beside Barnaby.

Peeling back the gauze, she soaped the toughened ridges of his scars. She snipped the strand nearest his eye and pulled out each stitch, one by one, dropping the short black threads into a metal bowl. Pink zippers of flesh stretched across his cheekbones, encircling his mouth.

He was watching her, his gaze shifting between the tweezers and the tray.

"How are you feeling, Christopher?"

His eye blinked several times, but his mouth remained firmly closed.

"Well, I'm sure you've heard the good news," she said. "Dr. Willard managed to stall your court-martial proceedings." The intensity of his stare unsettled her; she removed the last stitch and hastily lathered petroleum jelly over his cheeks. "There—all done. You've got enough Vaseline on you to catch flies."

She lifted her tray and stood to leave, turning back. "Look, I know you hear me, and I believe you understand everything I'm saying. I'm Tuck's sister." Nerves gripped Juliet's stomach, but she pushed breathlessly on. "I just want to know what happened to my brother. I want to know why you said 'Tuck, forgive me.' I want to know why you have his white glove."

Barnaby slowly shook his head, and Juliet knelt.

"No, *what*?" she whispered. "Are you trying to tell me something?"

He laid his cheek, thick with Vaseline, against his pillow, and gazed dreamily at the far wall of the tent. "Please, wake up," she said. "Just come back to the world and talk. We'll take care of you." But Barnaby's face remained limp, his stare vacant, and Juliet had the same feeling as when she'd ranted at the sky after Mother Hen's death—forsaken.

The next morning, a letter arrived for Juliet:

Dear Nurse Dufresne,

Many thanks for taking the time to write, and I appreciate your good intentions, but I must confess, when I first opened your letter, it seemed the worst of insults.

"Your husband has been injured, by his own hand, it is said. But we are investigating his actions fully, and his physical recovery has been nothing short of miraculous."

Nurse, please understand, my husband died almost six months ago here in the States working for the army at a munitions depot. I already suffered the trauma of the official army notification, two months pregnant, no less, and have had all the bad news about my husband that I can take for a lifetime.

I can only assume that you are writing to me about my brother, Christopher Barnaby. Your mistake was an innocent one. No doubt I'm the only girl writing to Christopher! And you were quick to assume . . . I've always believed in truth telling, and I want to reciprocate for your honesty in writing. What I'd like to say is that Christopher isn't the marrying kind and never will be. Whether this helps your understanding of him, I can't be certain, but I offer the information just in case, and trust you have his care as your top priority. If he suffered some kind of mental break, please know that it must have been an extremely difficult place for him. Christopher is an idealist, but also a very sensitive soul. He always was. Guns and firefights aren't for him. He's a talker, a thinker. I wish he'd never gotten it in his head to enlist. I was worried he wouldn't belong, but there's no stopping a man with duty in his heart.

As for the name Tucker Dufresne—Christopher never mentioned him, though he didn't much write about anyone in his squad. I didn't get the sense he liked them much, though that's not too unusual. He liked to write about justice and liberty; principles usually made him happier than people.

Sorry I can't be of more help.

I'll pray for him daily, but in the meantime, please give him my love and write if anything changes. Christopher is amazingly strong, in his own way. I don't know what I'd do without him. Send him home as soon as you can.

Tina Barnaby Emmons

CHAPTER 11

JULIET DIPPED THE comb in the metal bowl of water and parted Dr. Willard's hair. Unfolding the cloth, she found surgical scissors.

"Will these do?"

"I just hope no one's performing a celiotomy with the barber shears," he said. "You're kind to do this. I only asked out of desperation. Patients expect me to look generally clean-cut."

The day was hot and bright, and Willard was seated outside his tent; a threadbare towel lay across his shoulders over his khaki shirt, and Juliet stood behind him. She began trimming the back of his hair just above his neck, blowing the cuttings.

"Dr. Willard, I want to ask you something . . . well, and tell you something. It's personal, and I know you don't like that sort of thing, but it bears on our professional work. With Barnaby. I think you should know. It's sort of about my brother."

"Tucker Dufresne?"

"Yes."

"And this relates to our patient?"

"It does."

"Proceed."

She let the scissors dangle. "Tuck was reported missing in action almost a year ago now, here in Italy. And the thing is, just before he went missing, he sent a letter to me that sounded somewhat strange; well, it sounded almost delirious, and he mentioned a woman named Ms. Van Effing, which was a name we used to signal each other that something was wrong. So I decided to enlist. . . ."

"Please don't tell me you decided to ship here to Italy to see if you could find him."

Juliet was silent.

"Nurse Dufresne, I wouldn't be much of a friend if I didn't tell you you're on a wild-goose chase."

"That's what I thought at first." She stepped in front of him. "Private Barnaby *knew* Tuck."

"I'm sure dozens of soldiers in the division knew your brother."

"Dr. Willard, that white glove. The one you thought belonged to his wife?" She crouched, reaching for his hands. "It belonged to *Tuck*. Our stepmother gave it to him before he shipped over."

"I'm not sure that means anything for our patient or for your quest."

Juliet herself was uncertain what it meant, but it couldn't be ignored. What if Barnaby's breakdown and Tuck's disappearance were connected?

"You don't think it's strange," she said, "that they served in the same squad but Tuck never mentioned Barnaby? He mentioned all the others."

"On the long list of things I find strange about this war? Come on, Juliet. That doesn't even graze the bottom." He must have seen her eyes widen in anger: "I see where your mind is leading you and I'm trying to spare you: it's a dark and endless passage."

Juliet stood impatiently. Having finally decided after months of secrecy to share the entire truth with someone else, she'd expected, if not practical support, at least some compassion, something more than Willard's cold circumspection. She turned away from him and in a rush of frustration confessed what she had meant to withhold, what she did not yet fully understand: "I think there's something with Barnaby we didn't realize. That I didn't realize. I got a letter from Tina." She looked back.

Dr. Willard immediately stiffened, shifting in his chair. "And how, exactly, did that come about?"

"I wrote to her."

"Nurse Dufresne."

"Dr. Willard, she's not his wife; she's his *sister*."

"Cousin, aunt, next-door neighbor—it doesn't concern you. You shouldn't have written."

"I'm sorry."

"I'm sure you're sorry. People who do things they shouldn't are always sorry afterward. But they keep doing them! I need you to respect the work I'm doing here"—he pulled the towel from his shoulders and let it fall to the ground—"and if you can, try to maintain, challenging as it might be for a girl, some slight semblance of professionalism. We need boundaries in this work, or it simply doesn't work. And we need it to work; the stakes are very high. So we must have clear lines—lines that do not, under any circumstances, get crossed."

"I understand."

"Then please stop using my patient for your own ends. And make no mistake, that's what you're doing. Your job is to take care of him: to help him recover from his physical injury, and to assist me in trying to help him regain some shred of mental and emotional stability. He is not a clue in your investigation or a piece in your personal puzzle. He is a human being, one who needs a great deal of help right now or he may be put to death—by our own army. Are you registering the severity of the situation?"

Willard's anger was frightening, his disapproval unsettling—she realized now how much his closeness, his respect, meant to her.

"But I thought they postponed the court-martial until you had spent more time with him and given a full report. Until he was at least speaking."

"In a sane and rational and just universe, certainly. Not in this one. Because they count on me to get hundreds of soldiers back to the front lines, they occasionally grant me a wish. I bought Barnaby a week, two more at best. They are essentially humoring me."

"I had no idea."

"I didn't burden you with these details because, as I said, boundaries matter. These are *my* professional worries, not yours."

Juliet lifted the towel from the ground and folded it several times. She could not bring herself to look at him. "I'm embarrassed."

"Oh, come now, people do reckless and impulsive things in the name of love, and I can see that you love your brother. I truly hope you find him. But I can't help you. My plate is overflowing here; you know that. For the past week I've been struggling to make sure Private Wilkowski doesn't starve himself to death out of fear. I am Barnaby's only advocate and his only ally. My obligation is to him. And that far supersedes any personal fondness I may have for you. Now, if we can agree we've come to a peaceful understanding on this matter, and you trust my anger has passed, and I trust you with surgical shears pointed at my head, would you be so kind as to finish my haircut?"

He straightened his glasses, sunlight glinting off the lenses, and looked toward the green hills beyond the encampment. She saw now that he would never allow her to question Barnaby about Tuck. He had closed that door, and she couldn't blame him. She'd been taking advantage of her role as Barnaby's nurse, rifling through his belongings, interrogating his sister. What was wrong with her? She had no other options; that's what was wrong. No other leads. And her brother had asked for her help.

Juliet draped the towel around Willard's shoulders. She moved behind him and clipped carefully at the hair on the top of his head.

"In your entirely inappropriate and unprofessional correspondence with Private Barnaby's sister," Willard said, gazing at the hills, "did you learn anything that might be of use to us?"

"She said Christopher wasn't the marrying kind. And she wrote it, well, as if she thought it was absurd I had mistaken her for his wife. Said she'd be the only girl writing him."

"I see. Anything else?"

"Not really."

"So, this *suggestion* as to Barnaby's lack of interest in women . . . do you think it has any bearing on our work with Barnaby? Or on what happened to him at the front, or why he turned his gun on himself?"

Juliet considered the question. "It sounded like Captain Brilling hated him, and like the men in his unit had strange feelings about him, so maybe it's related."

Willard nodded slowly, a cautious gesture acknowledging the scissors above him. "A respectable speculation."

Juliet continued working, the noon sun bright in her eyes. Sweat gathered on her forehead, and she paused to wipe it with the back of her hand. She heard a surge of voices and saw people spilling out of the mess tent, pausing, as they plunged their dirty bowls in the water barrels, to take in Juliet and Willard. She was the only nurse he ever spent time with, the only member of the hospital he socialized with, and she wondered what they thought was going on. *She* wondered what was going on.

Eventually she lifted the towel from his shoulders and shook free the clippings. "Much more civilized," she said, stepping to the front of him. "I'm sure they'll finally all stop calling you Tarzan."

Willard grinned. "I should be so lucky."

She wiped clean the surgical shears, rewrapped them in the cloth, and set them back in the bag. She zipped the bag closed, debating her next words.

"Dr. Willard, please don't get angry or think this is personally motivated. But I'm just wondering. . . . This semicoma, where he sometimes speaks and sometimes seems to listen, then stops for a week: it's so *strange*. And it seems to go on and on. Don't you ever wonder if, well, it's possible he's faking?"

"Every minute."

The Germans, it was said, were fortifying a new defense: The Gothic Line stretched from the Adriatic to the Ligurian Sea, zigzagging through the Apennine Mountains. One hundred miles long and eight miles deep, this belt of foxholes and box mines and barbed-wire entanglements was meant to stop the Allies from reaching the Alps, keeping them out of Austria. The news was daunting. After covering 150 miles in its two-month summer campaign, the US Fifth Army had begun to falter. The constant rearrangement of battalions made it difficult for the men to understand how they were to conquer the Apennines before winter. The British Eighth Army, which had been advancing along the coast, was said to be preparing for a separate offensive; they were being heavily reinforced, while supplies to the Fifth Army had slowed. Patients in the hospital had begun to fear that their units, still fighting just five miles north, were decoys.

As Juliet made her rounds one afternoon, the Recovery Tent buzzed with further rumors that two American divisions and the French Expeditionary Corps—the mountain-climbing Goumiers who had so impressed Lovelace—were being entirely withdrawn from the Italian front.

"We're a holding action now," said Cross. "Just watch. They'll ship the first-class old pros to France and send us even greener grass."

"You really think they're gonna send us *anyone*?" asked Alphabet.

"They'd sure as hell better," said Cross. "My platoon is down to twelve."

"You know why this is happening?" Alphabet said. "This all goes back to *Rome*. This is because Clark pulled a *Patton*. You see, the Germans should have been cut off at Rome. And they would have been but for the ego fuck-party going on in the pea brain of Mark Clark. Clark got all hot and bothered at the thought of being the first general since the sixth century to take Rome from the south. And as the story goes, he timed his entry into Rome so he could be there with his photo corps during daylight. To hell with military strategy, the man wanted good photos! While he was holding press conferences, he let the Jerries retreat to the north, and we're still fighting them. We'll be fighting them all goddamned winter."

"Let us heretoforth refer to the capture of Rome as *Operation Whatthefuck*," said Cross. Across the tent, patients applauded.

"Clark," whispered Wilkowski, worrying the edge of his bedsheet, "has German blood."

Cross looked sadly at Wilkowski. Wilkowski's orange hair was wild and unkempt, and he had the hungry, desperate eyes of an alley cat. He had not bathed in weeks, and the air around him was sour and fetid. No one came near. The patients had finally begun to ignore his ranting; they had real fears to contend with.

"You notice how they never send the tanks in first?" Cross continued. "Since when do men clear the way for tanks? Since tanks cost more than a hundred and fifty men. It's cheaper to lose men than the tanks."

"In the Great War," said Alphabet, "they used to send birds into tunnels to see if there was gas."

"Canaries," said Cross. "That's what we are."

Silence filled the tent, and Juliet brought her hands together with a sharp clap. "How about writing some letters? Anyone need a hand?"

"A hand, an arm, another eye," Alphabet laughed.

"Amputee jokes," sighed Juliet. "My absolute favorite."

* * *

The street was quiet, and the sun was fading. The low, gray buildings on either side of them shadowed the street, and their boots echoed along the cobblestones. In the distance, the dome of the cathedral fought the setting sun with a yellow blade of light.

This was the southern end of Florence. Major Decker had issued Juliet and Willard twenty-four-hour passes, insisting they take advantage of the lull in fighting to recuperate. Even he seemed to think they were something of a couple. They had spent the morning visiting the evacuation hospital shadowing their field hospital, inquiring into the status of the patients they had transferred. They visited several stores commandeered by the army to sell nonessential provisions. They bought wool socks for the cold weather ahead; Willard purchased a leather-bound notebook and a new ribbon for his typewriter. They purchased fresh bread and chocolate and oranges and picnicked in the Boboli Gardens before wandering through the Palazzo Pitti. It was the first sightseeing Juliet had ever done; she was in a European city, wandering centuries-old royal buildings, and it humbled her. Everything in her new life would have once seemed improbable to her younger self, tucked away in her bedroom in Charlesport. Much of what happened had been arduous and gloomy, but now she was a tourist in Florence! Juliet felt adventurous and romantic, as though she had entirely stepped out of herself.

She and Willard wandered happily and by the afternoon had said nothing of the war, of Barnaby, or of the hospital; together they marveled at the beauty of Florence, as though strangers on a walking tour. Willard knew a great deal about the history of the city, and Juliet enjoyed listening to him. He explained that the first opera in the entire world for which any music survived had been performed in 1600 right there in the Palazzo Pitti, where they were standing. He touched his heart and gazed silently at the frescoed ceiling of the Galleria Palatina; he closed his eyes and let his head sway, as though hearing the music. He told her about the lives of

Verdi and Rossini, his favorite composers. He said that his dream as a young boy, long before he knew anything of medicine, was to become an opera singer. He seemed a different man here: relaxed, talkative, passionate about art and music. He, too, had stepped out of himself, and Juliet felt something contracting between them. The reserve had vanished; they walked side by side, their elbows brushing, their steps occasionally synchronized.

But as they left the Palazzo Pitti and the sun began to set, she had the awful sense that the day was slipping from her, that this feeling—this happiness at escaping herself and the war, this sense of intimacy with Willard—would vanish. She wanted to walk slowly, to hold on to everything. She wanted to taste the air and listen to the sound of their footfalls. She wanted to study the way Willard would half gesture at the façade of a building while she offered a *hmmm* of agreement. It felt as if they had always been that way, and she wanted it to go on forever. She had never known that a single day with a single person could seem like the entirety of your life. Nightfall loomed like a small death, an agonizing departure from a moment she knew she would always long for.

Now they were dutifully making their way to the home of Alfonso's parents, an errand they had promised the partisan fighter that morning. In the darkening street, reminders of all that had happened and was happening began to flood Juliet; the war took hold of her like a hand gripping her shoulder. From gray doorways hollow-cheeked children emerged, tattered clothing hanging off their shoulders, cigarette butts jutting from their lips. "Hallo, *Americani!* Any gum, chum?" Barefoot, they pattered alongside Juliet and Willard, tugging at the hem of Juliet's coat until she emptied her pockets of the chewing gum and caramels she had grabbed from the PX before she left. One child unwrapped his caramel so quickly that it fell in a puddle. The others ate their candies with the wrappers on, crackling noisily. Ahead of them, an old woman paused on the street, hitched up her moth-eaten skirt, and peed.

Juliet was relieved when they arrived at the small wooden door. "I think it's this one," she said.

Willard knocked, and after several moments, the door creaked open to reveal an old woman, her gray hair pulled into a tight bun.

"Signora Gaspaldi? We're friends of your son. *Siamo amici di vostro figlio*—Alfonso."

The woman smiled, gap-toothed. *"Il mio Alfonso!"* But as her eyes took in the red crosses on their armbands, she clasped her chest.

"Oh, no, he's fine," said Juliet. *"Sta bene."*

Juliet offered the letter. "He asked us to give you this."

Snatching the paper, the woman hollered back into the house, *"Peppino! Peppino!"* She shoved the envelope between her lips, and tugged Juliet and Willard inside. The room was large and bare and dimly lit. At a small wooden table, she pulled back two stools of differing heights. Once again she called for Peppino, and a gray-haired man came lumbering down the stairs, hooking the strap of his suspenders over one shoulder.

"Sono amici di Alfonso." She shoved the envelope at Peppino. *"Una lettera da Alfonso."*

Juliet watched as Peppino lit the nub of a candle and held the envelope close, examining both sides. With his blackened forefinger he opened the seal. Signora Gaspaldi hovered behind: *"Che cosa dice?"* she asked.

The woman couldn't read, Juliet realized.

"È vivo, lui ama l'Italia, combatterà fino a sconfiggere il nemico ed allora verrà a casa," Peppino explained, then placed the letter in his pocket. He turned to his guests. *"Amici di Alfonso? Medici?* We make the dinner. *Vino, subito."* Peppino signaled Juliet and Willard to follow him through the kitchen, ducking beneath copper pots and pans. In the small yard, the sun cast a weak orange glow across the ground. Juliet expected they might see a chicken coop—

something related to dinner. Instead, Peppino grabbed a trowel and probed the bare ground with the tip.

"*Dottore?*" He handed Willard the trowel, then sat on the stoop, gesturing for Willard to dig.

"This is what I call singing for our supper," said Willard, winking at Juliet.

Willard turned over shovelfuls of soil until the metal met with a clang. Peppino drew together his hands in one swift clap, waved Willard aside, and began clawing at the dirt. He grinned as he extracted a straw-covered jug of wine and a jar of black olives. Then he nervously signaled for Willard to cover the hole, while he dragged Juliet inside, his bounty hugged to his chest.

Signora Gaspaldi was working the thick handle of a wooden spoon around a steaming copper pot. The sweet smell of cooked onions filled the kitchen. Juliet helped set out plates and utensils, and within a few minutes Willard returned and they were seated at the small table. Bowls of large white beans, shiny with olive oil, appeared before them. Yellow pasta, long and thick and gnarled, lay beneath a mound of browned onions. The beans were meaty and delicious, the pasta rich and garlicky. Peppino and Signora Gaspaldi poured the wine liberally for Juliet and Willard and drank eagerly and happily themselves. Between sips, Juliet chewed on the black olives so that the wine wouldn't rush to her head. She already felt a little tipsy. She watched Peppino reach his fork across the table and spear the remnants of pasta on Signora Gaspaldi's plate. She, in turn, plucked his leftover beans. Juliet wondered how long they had been married, what it would be like to spend every day with another person, growing old together, raising children.

As dinner ended, Signora Gaspaldi set a small, dog-eared album before Juliet and Willard.

"Alfonso?" Juliet asked, looking at a baby photo.

"*Sì.*"

After two or three pages, she came upon photos of another baby. "And this?"

"Marco," said Signora Gaspaldi, her eyes filling with tears. *"Marco amava Mussolini. I fascisti. É morto."*

"I'm so sorry," said Juliet.

Willard drew his stool close to Signora Gaspaldi's and put his arm around her; she cried into his chest. Peppino, who seemed familiar with the scene, withdrew and soon returned with acorn coffee. Juliet sipped at the bitter drink and looked at Signora Gaspaldi's red eyes and thought of her father, and of Pearl, and even of Pearl's dead husband from the other war. She thought of the two empty bedrooms looming above them, and of the letters they so dutifully sent to her, asking for news. Juliet hadn't written in weeks and promised herself she would write as soon as she got back to the hospital.

Juliet and Willard helped clear the plates and explained that they were headed to a rest hotel run by the Fifth Army, but Signora Gaspaldi insisted they stay the night. She looked from Juliet to Willard. *"Morosi, sì?"*

"No, not *morosi,*" said Willard.

A blush crept across Juliet's face. "Not at all," said Juliet, but the mistake made her happy, confirmed what she had been feeling: this thing between them was not in her imagination. Juliet's heart began to swell.

As though their denial was of no consequence, Signora Gaspaldi waved her hand and led them up the narrow stairs. At the end of the corridor, she showed them a small, dark room. The air was cold and musty, and the walls were bare but for a faded Italian flag and a wooden crucifix. A wide metal bed sat in the center of the room.

"La stanza di Alfonso e Marco." She bowed her head apologetically. *"Una stanza privata."*

Signora Gaspaldi lit a row of candles in empty wine jugs lining the floor, and yellow light wavered across the room. She disappeared and brought them a pitcher of water with glasses and set them by the door. She threw back the covers on the mattress and removed a hot brick wrapped in a towel. She patted the mattress excitedly: *"É caldo."*

"I'll take the floor," Willard said when the signora had left.

"That's worse than a bedroll on the ground."

"I'll be fine." Willard stood facing the door. "Go ahead and get yourself comfortable."

Juliet sank into the ancient mattress and tugged off her boots. She tried to remove her pants as quietly as possible, but the sound of her zipper cut awkwardly through the room. She recalled Glenda undressing that day at the lake, her slow, languorous performance. Even with his back to her, Juliet still felt nervous. All her prudishness returned. What had happened with Beau seemed miles away, another lifetime. With Willard it was different. With Willard it mattered. She pulled the covers to her chin.

"All clear," she said.

Willard turned and unbuttoned his shirt; his chest was pale and tubular. With his pants still on, he knelt to blow out the candles. "Well, good night then."

She didn't know what she had expected, but it was certainly more than this. She wanted to tell him about Charlesport and her father. She wanted to ask him about his parents, about Chicago, about his childhood. She wanted this thing between them named, acknowledged. But Willard had shrunk from her. Juliet lay in the dark and listened to him heel off his shoes and arrange himself on the floor, his belt buckle scratching the wood. He readjusted several times before lying still for a while, but she did not think he was asleep. The sounds of pots clanking in the sink downstairs rang through the room.

"That was a nice day," she said into the darkness.

"Very nice."

"You know a lot about opera."

"To the great misfortune of those stuck in conversation with me."

"Oh, I liked it."

He was quiet, and for a moment she feared he was finally going to sleep.

"Dr. Willard, are you sure you're comfortable? We're supposed to be getting rest, after all."

"I appreciate your concern, but I'm fine."

Was he really going to say nothing more? Did he feel nothing between them? Had nothing happened in that long, wonderful day? Juliet felt as though an enormous weight were suddenly pressing against her chest; tomorrow they would return to the hospital, to their normal routine. Everything she had felt would vanish. She needed to say things, to ask things—questions she could ask only here, under the blanket of darkness.

"Dr. Willard," she began, "how come you're the only doctor in the whole hospital who doesn't seem determined to get cozy with all the nurses?"

He was silent for some time; Juliet heard Signora Gaspaldi and Peppino coming up the wooden stairs, opening a door across the hall.

"I explained to you my belief in boundaries. The need for professional distance."

A bewildered anger slowly rose within her, shook loose all her decorum. She would finally say what she had been thinking for weeks, and say it in a way too intimate to ignore. Her hand tightened around the edge of the sheet and she spat out a single word, a word she had used only a few times in her life, a word she had a right to use with the man she had wandered through Florence with, a man she had worked beside for almost three months: "*Bullshit.*"

He cleared his throat. "I have absolutely no reason to lie."

Willard's composure enraged her. How could he talk to her

with such condescension? Juliet shook her head, rustling the pillow. "Left and right," she stated, "everybody is coupling off."

"Well, what of it?" His pitch, finally, had risen to exasperation, and Juliet had the sinking feeling she had driven him away. The day was lost; any feeling he might have had for her was lost. Her true fear simply tumbled out of her:

"Dr. Willard . . . is it *me*?"

"God no, Juliet." She heard him turn from side to side, his knees and elbows knocking the floor. He lay still and seemed to ruminate on something, exhaling lengthily. "For Chrissakes," he finally whispered, "I'm married."

Juliet sat up. She blinked in the darkness, her head fuzzy. Had she heard him right?

She was waiting for him to say more, to retract, to explain. How had she never imagined . . . ?

She hoped he was at least looking toward her, that he wanted, in his moment of confession, to see her. She wanted still to feel their connection. But in the darkness she could make out nothing. Instead, she felt the arrival of a new presence, a vague and shadowy figure lurking in the room, hovering between them.

A wife.

From across the hall came the soft melodious syllables of Signora Gaspaldi's prayers. Beneath that she could hear Willard's breathing. If his thoughts were with her, or someone else, Juliet didn't know. She slowly let her face drop into her pillow.

They rode back to the hospital the next morning in mostly an awkward silence.

"You don't wear a ring," Juliet said quietly, speaking to the road ahead.

"And I don't carry around photographs or talk about my life at home. It's how it has to be, for my work."

"But I'm not a patient."

"No."

Willard gripped the wheel, and she could see white spots of bloodlessness fill his knuckles.

"Well, you're married and you're from Chicago," said Juliet, tapping out a drumbeat on the dashboard. In the painfully bright light of morning, her embarrassment had mounted. "I'll get started writing your biography as soon as we get back."

"I understand that you don't like my rules. *I* don't necessarily like my rules. But they serve us well."

"How?"

"It would be reckless for us to start having long, personal conversations. That's how it all starts."

"*What* starts?"

Willard turned to look at her quizzically, and the jeep slowed as he eased his foot off the gas pedal. He smiled gently, somewhat disbelievingly, as though touched by her question. "You're so young," he said, shaking his head. Once more, he pressed his foot on the accelerator and looked around at the pale hills. Between the hills, oblong evergreens, velvety green, stood in dark clumps. "It's a nice day," he said, "a beautiful day, and I thoroughly enjoyed my time with you in Florence. You are an excellent travel companion."

"Thank you," she said, but she felt she had lost something. She wasn't so young; she wanted him to understand that. She did not want to be a travel companion.

"I'm not a virgin," she blurted.

Willard's face went deeply red. "Sweet Jesus, girl." He spoke to the roof. "That's exactly the kind of personal thing I shouldn't know."

"I had sex in a cave. With a soldier. *Recently*."

Willard's eyes widened and he began to laugh. "Juliet, did you inject yourself with some of the Sodium Pentothal? Try to rein in *some* of your thoughts. Especially while I'm driving."

"Agree you won't talk to me like I'm a child."

"For the record, I outrank you not just in years but also medically *and* militarily. But if it will stem these confessions, yes, we're agreed."

As they pulled into the hospital encampment, they saw a crowd of nurses and doctors milling noisily outside Major Decker's tent. Two military policemen stood nearby at full alert, and Bernice seemed to be arguing with them.

Juliet and Willard both stepped from the truck, leaving behind the Palazzo Pitti and their talk of opera, leaving behind their whispers in the dark, shedding their awkwardness and embarrassment with each brisk step toward the commotion, resuming their respective roles as doctor and nurse so seamlessly that no one would have guessed what had passed between them.

Juliet rushed over to Bernice. "What's going on?" she asked. Willard came up beside her.

"It's Private Barnaby," Bernice answered. "The MPs are taking him away for the court-martial."

CHAPTER 12

SEPTEMBER BROUGHT THICK rains. The air was gray and cool, and the earth was endlessly moist—Juliet could taste it. The leaves in the trees were wet and gleaming and shook overhead like a jungle disturbed. A knee-deep fog rose from the ground and caused Juliet to move from tent to tent as though wading through clouds. Mud sucked defiantly at her boots. For balance, she walked with her arms extended, as if trying to take flight.

Barnaby had been gone almost two weeks, along with Dr. Willard, and no one had heard anything about the court-martial proceedings. Amid endless speculation, anger was mounting. To the other patients, Barnaby's trial had come to symbolize the injustice of the entire Italian campaign. They were *all* mute, in some respects, *all* doomed. In his act of self-destruction they saw the wretched madness they could, at any moment, be driven to.

Juliet felt a growing anxiety about his trial, a deepening melancholy, sharpened every morning as she walked past Dr. Willard's empty tent. In such haste to gather his notes and records, he left with Barnaby without saying good-bye. What if he never came back? It hadn't occurred to her she might not see him again.

Juliet slept poorly, a chill clinging to her scalp. Visions of the blue eye returned, meandering hideously through her dreams, and as she woke in the dark and tugged on her clothes, the nightmares still clung to her. It was still black outside when she arrived in the Recovery Tent to begin her shift, that strange, fragile hour when those who had been awake all night encountered those who had just awakened. To the familiar stream of exhausted faces and bloodshot eyes Juliet said her hellos; clipboards were handed over, notes reviewed; then they were gone, those nurses and ward men who seemed to live in the underworld of the night.

Beside the nursing station Juliet drank her coffee and stared at the two long rows of cots, the sleeping, blanket-tangled figures. She dreaded these first hours of her rounds when, one by one, the patients woke; there was always a moan or a gasp of despair as they groggily patted their stumps and their bandages, having dreamt they were whole.

The fighting had intensified near Il Giogo Pass, and amputations resumed with disconcerting regularity: *Divide deep fascia. Retract. Divide muscle. Retract. Cut periosteum. Saw bone. Sever nerves.* One afternoon, while Juliet was assisting a surgery, a thought came to her as she stared into the bucket of limbs: Would she recognize her brother's arm if she saw it? His hand? It had seemed at first a purely scientific question, but the full dismal weight of it quickly hit her. She realized she no longer believed she would find him. Day by day her hope was faltering. Barnaby was gone, half of the division in which Tuck had been fighting was shipped to France, and she knew no more about his disappearance than she did before she'd come to Italy. All she knew was that injury and death were beginning to seem strangely normal; the shock of the blood and gore had faded, and she felt a numb detachment from the bodies. *Bodies,* that was how she thought of them now, or parts of bodies: *the perforated intestine, the fractured tibia.* "The collapsed lung wants someone to write a letter for him," she heard herself tell Bernice one day.

The days were a blur of surgeries and admissions; litters arrived covered with raincoats, and Juliet worked swiftly, calmly, until one afternoon, in the Receiving Tent, looking down at a man whose face was a bleeding pincushion of shrapnel, her whole body suddenly stiffened. Hesitantly, she read the man's tag: Technical Sergeant Beau Conroy.

She stumbled. She had been eagerly awaiting a letter from

him, had been composing one to him. She had never imagined this.

She touched part of his earlobe, the only area that wasn't blackened with blood. "It's Juliet," she whispered. "It's okay. We're gonna get you fixed up."

Beau's eyes were firmly closed, the lids slick with blood, but at the sound of her voice he strained to sit up, swinging his head as though searching out her voice. His breathing accelerated, rasping with panic.

"Beau, try not to move. You might have internal injuries."

Juliet set about mixing the plasma, rigging the intravenous drip, but her hands began shaking. She inserted the needle and watched the plasma slide through the tubing. She carefully washed the blood from his face, and his eyes slowly opened. He blinked at her, stunned and miserable; she wanted to throw her arms around him but feared it would harm or terrify him. She lifted his hand and kissed his fingers. As the ward men came to carry his litter into surgery, the wounds she had washed began to seep, tears of blood running down his face.

For the next several hours, Juliet tried to stay calm, keeping busy with new admissions, tending several battle-fatigue patients. A captain from the 2nd New Zealand Division arrived, sitting upright and cross-legged on his litter, waving to and fro like demented royalty as he was carried into the Receiving Tent. His teeth were missing, and Juliet was told he had pulled them out one by one that morning in front of his entire regiment. High on morphine, he seemed amused and dazzled by her questions, but through his toothless swollen gums he spoke only backward: "End never will war this. Die to want just I. Her love I mother my tell." Another man, a lanky lieutenant who kept his hands hugged tightly around his abdomen, claimed he was pregnant. Trying to lose herself in the darkened labyrinths of their minds, Juliet took careful notes, notes that if Dr. Willard ever returned, she could give to him. All the frustration she had felt toward Willard—all her anger and embarrass-ment—vanished. She missed him terribly.

Italian civilians were streaming in, cold and hungry, fleeing the fighting at the edge of the mountains. A young woman Juliet's age appeared in the tent clutching a baby to her chest. She wore a gray man's overcoat. Her hair was black and tangled and she communicated in frantic tones that she had been eating only boiled grass and could no longer make milk for the baby. As evidence, she pulled one of her breasts out and twisted the nipple quite hard. Juliet quickly mixed powdered milk for the mother and infant, but the infant wailed and batted at the cup. Again and again the mother tried to urge the cup into the infant's mouth. The woman finally held out the child and asked Juliet to try. Juliet had never before held a baby. Its bones were light and fragile; it blinked at her suspiciously from its gray, unhappy face, but as Juliet settled on the floor of the tent, she was eventually able to ease spoonfuls of milk into its mouth.

Boy or girl? she asked the mother in Italian. A white line of milk crested the woman's mouth.

"Una ragazza."

Bernice found Juliet like this, late in the day, feeding the dehy-drated girl. "There's a Private Munson who came in this morn-ing," Bernice whispered. "A bullet struck his pocket watch. He's got springs and hands and shards of crystal all over his organs. The infection is spreading fast. He asked for you."

Juliet returned the baby to her mother and rushed outside to find the Senator as his litter was being carried into the Recovery Tent. She walked alongside. "Hey there."

His eyes flickered open as he said, dry-mouthed, "Nurse Dufresne." His face was white—corpse white. Sweat speckled his forehead. A lat-ticework of tubing covered his abdomen. "I'm not doing so hot."

"Leave the prognosis to the doctors."

Juliet helped the medics ease him onto the mattress. "I'm start-ing to get the feeling you like this place," she said.

His head began slowly turning left and right, searching the tent. "Barnaby," he said. "I wanted to talk to Barnaby."

"He's gone. . . . Oh, God, sorry, not dead. In Rome. For the court-martial."

The Senator's head collapsed onto his pillow. "Bastards."

"Who are bastards?"

"*Everyone.* You know what I like? I like fairness. I like give-everyone-a-fighting-chance. Look, I need to tell you something." He gestured her close, and his breath was hot against her ear. She could smell the rot of his infection. "About that last night he was sent out as scout. Brilling would kill me, but"—he glanced somberly at the tubing on his stomach—"I have a feeling he won't get the chance." The Senator coughed, and Juliet handed him a cup of water. She knew she should tell him to conserve his strength, but she desperately wanted to hear what he had to say.

"We were drawing straws and Barnaby drew first, 'cause it's alphabetical. But right off he got the short straw. So no one else ever drew. But I had this hunch, you know? Barnaby was *always* drawing the short straw. Always complaining he had the worst luck. And after the patrol went out, I looked outside the tent in the trash. Poof. A goddamned pile of short straws."

"Why didn't you say something?"

"You see a complaint box around here? I just can't see blaming a man for trying to kill himself when he was sent forward to get killed. They were shits to him. He told me once that his squad hung him from his pack on a tree branch—for five hours. They dropped snakes down his shirt. Said he thought his shoulders would snap out of their sockets. Then someone found some field mice and covered him with K rations and stuck the mice on him. They wanted him dead. His pulling that trigger was a formality." The Senator took another sip of water, and it seeped from the corner of his mouth. His eyes struggled to stay open.

"Do you want to sleep?'

"Uh-uh."

"Do you want me to write a letter home for you?"

"Not this moment."

"Can I do anything?'

"I think I'll just lie here awhile." His chin glistened with saliva and he looked at the ceiling. On the edge of the blanket his fingers tapped out a pattern, careful at first, then rapid, and she was about to ask him if he played the piano when his fingers stopped. His eyes were wide and unblinking and she felt for his pulse.

Another, she thought.

She remembered the ride from Naples, how he'd boisterously arranged card games, how he'd flirted with her. At the top of his bag, a letter had been set. Blood crusted the edges.

Dear Pop,

It's morning here, and I'm all alone, in a dugout. I was awake through the night, but had to wait for daylight so that I could see the page. I'm not afraid. You taught me not to be afraid, and I've been thinking of you and hearing your voice, all these dark hours. I was remembering one of our fishing trips, when you caught three trout, and I caught nothing, and you told me I had to learn to be okay with nothing at times; that you couldn't get to times of something without times of nothing. This is a time of nothing, but I'm holding strong.

I got your last letter and read it many times. It made me thi

Juliet set the letter back down. *Interrupted,* she thought. *Everything, everyone, interrupted.*

She wandered mutely from the Recovery Tent as the rain began to fall again. At the Surgical Tent, her scalp cold and damp, she asked Dr. Mallick about Beau.

"He's stable. We cleaned up his face. But the blast tore his large intestine and collapsed his left lung. I can't say what'll happen with that lung. Oh, and one of his legs had to go . . . right at the knee. Trench foot turned to gangrene."

Juliet remembered the night in the cave. How she'd rubbed his blistered feet, how his cold fingers fumbled to open the ration tin.

"How long before he comes to?"

"A couple hours. Maybe three."

"I'd like to be there."

"Well, don't worry about timing it exactly. You'll know because you'll hear him screaming all the way to France."

She meandered through the hard, cold rain, her thoughts tangled, and at the outhouse she stepped inside and latched the door shut behind her. *Scream,* she thought. That's what she wanted to do after all this time: she just wanted to scream. She held her breath and pressed her hands against the wooden walls, pushing hard, wanting to break the structure. Blood rushed to her face, and she imagined a long, primal shriek coming out of her, something warped and wordless, something honest. A scream to name every loss she'd ever felt. But Juliet released her breath and slumped forward in defeat. Even from in there she'd be heard, and she couldn't bring herself to burden the others with a sadness they no doubt felt themselves. What if all the nurses went off shrieking in the outhouse after a bad day? While the men missing limbs lay quietly in their beds. . . .

A sinking loneliness took hold of her, a sudden desperate homesickness. She missed Tuck and her father. She even missed Pearl. She missed feeling safe. She missed days when nothing happened, those long, rambling afternoons of sun-warmed daydreams. She missed matters of inconsequence: her silly pink bedroom and her posters and the dogwood tree outside her window. She missed *life*. This was death, death was everywhere and all around her; she was living in a cemetery. And like those corpses of former centuries, buried with bells on their fingers in case of error, she wanted to ring the bell and bang on the coffin and say, *Let me out. I'm not ready to be here. It's all a mistake.*

She had come to find her brother, but she no longer thought he was anywhere to be found. Now she was stuck.

A knock on the door interrupted her thoughts. "Just a sec," called Juliet, pressing hard at her cheeks as though to hold herself together. "It's all yours, Helen," she said as she stepped into the rain.

Slowly, Juliet made her way back to the Recovery Tent to finish her rounds. She tried not to think of Beau and of Munson. She tried not to think of Barnaby hanging from a tree with mice crawling over him. An unusual stillness had settled over the tent; the dozens of men lying on litters were entirely silent. "Everything okay in here?" she asked.

"*Shhhhh.*" One of the men gestured to the corner, where the young Italian woman, sitting on the ground, slept with her back against the green canvas of the tent. The baby was asleep on her chest, its face nestled in the hollow of her neck, gently gurgling. There was a beautiful synchronicity to the rise and fall of their chests, to the soft whisper of their deep, exhausted exhalations. Four empty milk cups sat beside them.

The men in the tent clearly had been watching this scene for quite some time.

"That's a pretty baby," one of them said softly.

"Pretty eyes," another whispered. "I think they were blue."

"Nah, green. Like an oak tree."

"Well, green eyes can change," the man beside Juliet whispered. "I got a little brother who had green eyes and then at one year old they turned brown."

"Boy, the poor little critter was hungry. She'll sleep for ten hours now, just you watch."

Juliet moved toward the sleeping figures and collected the empty tin cups. She gazed at the baby's serene face. They had all been that once, she thought. Munson, Beau, herself. All the men around her. They had all been that small, that helpless, that unformed. And they would all, in time, return to that end—some by nightfall. The cries and the babbling would come back; the primordial bewilderment would take hold; and they would leave the world the same way they had come into it.

A slight bleat came from the baby, and the woman, without opening her eyes, slid her hand behind its head and shifted it higher on her chest. She kissed its scalp and the baby sighed.

What any of them would have given at that moment, thought Juliet, for their mother.

CHAPTER 13

THE NEXT MORNING, sitting in the mess tent, Juliet looked up from her oatmeal to see a girl in the entrance, a boy laid across her arms. His foot was a tangle of muscle and tendon, bleeding in a cylinder of trickles as though from a just-stopped showerhead. The boy stared at the blood, his face marbled with dirt. As he quietly wept, his lips puckered in fishlike motions. The girl, no more than twelve years old, surveyed the tent, her brown eyes darting from nurse to nurse until they lit upon Major Decker's stripes.

Major Decker had already risen from his chair, rushing past the crowded tables to carefully lift the boy from the girl's arms. Juliet recalled that he had a young son.

"Nurse Dufresne," he called, "come help stabilize and prep this boy."

In the pre-op tent, Juliet explained to the fraught girl in clumsy Italian that the boy would need a blood transfusion. The girl explained this to the boy, splayed on a stretcher. She stood on her toes and watched him intently, trying to monitor everything being done. She waved her arms as she spoke, and from the rapid stream of heavily inflected Italian Juliet made out that the boy's name was Dante and that he'd stepped on a land mine while playing. *"Il pericolo é dappertutto, Dante!"* she scolded. *"Non possiamo piu giocare!"*

Over the girl's tattered pink dress a canteen knocked and sloshed against her hips. An empty bandolier hung across her like a sash. She wore a pair of men's boots, unmatched and much too large, fastened snugly about her ankles with gauze. She looked part gypsy, part mercenary fighter.

Her name was Liberata, she told Juliet, and she explained quite matter-of-factly that their parents had been killed during the American bombings. She was now a *Partigiana,* Liberata claimed: a partisan fighter.

She inspected Juliet's work rigging the blood and plasma bags. She barked a series of rebukes at Dante—*"Tu non mi ascolti! Hai fatto una cosa stupide! Non ho potuto proteggerti!"*—and told Juliet that since Dante was a soldier, it was essential to the war effort that he receive unsurpassed care. He drew maps, Liberata urged; he had important information about the landscape; he knew where the Germans would hide munitions. He would lead the Americans through the countryside, if only they would save him. The girl was a tornado of movement and indecipherable proclamations. When color seemed to fade from the boy's cheeks, Liberata grew still.

She crouched on her knees. "We will work," she said. "We will scrub the floors. We will clean the toilets. The men can do their things to me. Please, save my brother. Please."

Juliet shuddered: What was happening beyond the hospital? What was happening to the Italians? What in God's name was happening to the children?

"You don't have to do anything; they'll take care of him. The surgeons have fixed this hundreds of times." Juliet knelt so that she was face-to-face with the girl, and violated one of the strictest codes of nursing. "He'll be fine," she said firmly. "I absolutely promise."

Liberata worked her lips until tears covered her cheeks, and Juliet drew the frightened girl closer and tighter than she'd ever held anyone before.

"*Grazie,*" Liberata whispered.

When the ward man arrived to help carry Dante into surgery, Liberata followed, holding her brother's hand tight.

In the Surgical Tent, Juliet saw that half of the hospital's doctors and nurses had assembled around the operating table. Dr. Mallick, their best surgeon, the man she had pegged as the least sentimental, brought his face close to Dante's and touched his chin. "*Coraggio,* little man," Mallick whispered.

Juliet loved them all, this band of colleagues; she wanted to tell them that, that she was honored to know them, but no one did that sort of thing. It was a hospital, it was their job; by temperament they scrutinized their failures and discounted their successes.

Liberata kissed her brother's face, whispered something in his ear, and followed Juliet slowly through the gray morning light to the Recovery Tent. At the sight of the men, Liberata once again assumed her soldiery composure. She made her way up and down the center aisle, studying the triangulation of legs in casts, the bright white bandages worn like crowns; the coldness of her expression made Juliet wonder what the girl had seen during the Allied bombings.

Only when she sat on the edge of an empty bed and pulled from her pocket a small wristwatch, an object that Juliet supposed belonged to Dante, did Liberata's expression slacken.

"Hey, little one, your brother's gonna be A-okay," a nearby patient said.

The men passed her caramels and chewing gum, bottles of Coca-Cola. They carried comic books to the edge of her bed. But Liberata sat staring at the tent entrance, keeping vigil. Juliet remained beside her, her hand almost going numb on the girl's back until an hour later the ward men finally carried in Dante, his small stump bandaged below the knee.

Liberata sprung from the bed. "*Mio fratello!*" She assaulted him with noisy kisses.

"*Fratello!*" the men cheered.

Brother Reardon came by soon after, seeking out Juliet: "Major Decker just got word from HQ. Dr. Willard will be coming back to the hospital soon, in case"—he smiled—"it matters to you."

The thought lifted her spirits—Willard was returning!—and she settled happily beside the children, who had begun to sort through the comics and candies. Brother Reardon pulled their two beds

side by side, wheeled several intravenous apparatus stands around
the corners, and draped a sheet on top to create a tent. For hours he
sat inside the tent, playing cards with Liberata and a sleepy Dante;
he pulled out a harmonica and sang "Beer Barrel Polka" and "Bar-
racks' Blues." Juliet brought the children cups of milk and chocolate bars. When the darkness of late afternoon filled the tent and
Dante fell asleep, Brother Reardon stood to leave. Liberata looked
drowsy, and dazzled. Chocolate stained the corners of her mouth.
"You should get some sleep, too," Juliet told her in Italian.

Liberata clutched Juliet's fingertips.

"We will work," she whispered back in Italian. "We will scrub
the floors. We will clean the toilets. Please, let us stay here."

Juliet's throat tightened. She wanted to break the rules once
again, to tell her what she wanted to hear, but this time it would be
a blatant lie.

"I don't think it's possible," said Juliet.

Liberata nodded, wiped at a tear in the corner of her eye.

"Then we will continue fighting," she said.

After weeks of rain, the air was dry and cool and the sun shone plac-
idly. The leaves in the trees had begun to turn, and from the hills
overlooking the encampment, flags of yellow and orange waved
intermittently. The grass was tall and noisy and tangled with dan-
delions; plump daffodils nodded in the breeze. There was something soft and ancient in the light; it looked like the amber of relics,
of primordial ants and Neolithic mosquitoes.

News came that the Fifth Army was going to make a final push
into the Apennines, and the hospital was again ordered to dismantle.

Throughout the morning patients were loaded into the backs of
ambulances. Ward men collapsed the cots and dragged them nois-

ily in stacks of four outside the Recovery Tent. Beau lay silently in his bed, watching all of this. His lung had collapsed and he was too fragile to be transported. Soon he lay alone in the empty green tent, while outside a group of engineers mounted ladders and slackened the canvas, and the walls slithered gently to the ground. They eased apart the wooden frame so that the poles dropped outward away from Beau.

Alone on the large wooden platform beneath the bright noon sun, Beau watched as Juliet said her long good-byes to Dante and Liberata and the other patients. As the trucks and ambulances pulled away, splashing through puddles, spewing mud, Juliet felt the knowing weight of his stare. Juliet and Brother Reardon had been assigned to stay with Beau until a rear medical unit arrived, or until, as Major Decker instructed, "his condition changed." She knew Beau would not last the night. Together they watched the convoy snake along the narrow road toward the distant crown of mountains. After months of their being surrounded by scores of people, there was something unsettling about being left there alone, just the three of them. All that remained of the hospital were several ward tent platforms and a dozen rusted metal trash drums. Where the pup tents had been, rectangles of grass were pale and flattened, shadows abandoned by their objects.

There was a slight chill in the air, and Juliet and Brother Reardon lifted their musette bags onto the platform beside Beau and erected a small tent around his cot.

"We'll just wait here until the evac hospital catches up with us," said Juliet, fastening the final stake.

"Keep the front open," Beau said, "so I can see the sun. The sun . . . looks so . . . pretty."

Each of his breaths was a labored gasp. His lips were crusted white, as though he had washed up from the sea. He looked nothing like the football player she'd kissed outside her school, nothing like the man she'd made love with. She felt a strange anger as she looked at him, as though this weakened, ruined creature had stolen that other Beau from her.

"Hey, Juliet . . . remember how you and Tuck once saved that raven? Cher Ami? He told me about that. . . ."

Juliet nodded and rested her hand on his knee.

As the afternoon grew dark and cool, she laid a blanket over him and lit a small stove. She fed the stove with the broken plank of a tent platform. There were dark circles beneath his eyes. She heated a can of soup and slid spoonfuls into his mouth.

"This wasn't . . . supposed to happen," he said, broth dripping from his lips.

"I know."

"I wanted to go home."

"You will."

His deep-green eyes bored into her, as though all the life left in him had gathered in his stare. "Tell me I'm dying . . . so I can tell you I'm afraid."

She could not lie to him, not after everything. "You're dying, Beau." The words split open something inside of her. Something she knew she would never repair.

He nodded slowly. "I'm afraid."

"It's okay."

Brother Reardon drew close on the other side. "'You will sprinkle me with hyssop, O Lord, and I shall be made clean,'" he said softly, "'you will wash me and I shall be made whiter than snow.'" He anointed Beau's eyes, ears, lips, hands, and feet. "You have nothing to fear, my brother. This body, this vessel, is no longer serving you, but your spirit is well. Do you hear me?"

Beau looked sadly around the tent, at the empty corners of the canvas, at the stove's orange flame; he strained to lift his head and glimpse the snowcapped mountains.

"Crap. I *like* all this," he said. "I like life."

"I know." Juliet felt sickened by the magnitude of her ineloquence.

Beau's eyes seemed to whiten and moved wearily between Juliet and Brother Reardon. His breathing quickened, and he tried to cough, his face blanching with exertion.

"Can you hold me?"

Juliet was grateful for the request; she had no idea what more to say. He was the only one leaving, going somewhere that no one around him had gone. She gently wrapped her arms around him and set her head on his chest. His lungs rasped and rattled—the sound of a frightened bird caged within his ribs. She nestled close and hummed a song, or not quite a song but some notes she thought sounded pretty. Soon the movement of his chest stopped and the tent was silent, but she stayed there awhile.

Eventually she was aware of Brother Reardon lifting Beau's wrist. "He's gone."

Juliet sat up slowly, as though from an interminable sleep, and let her forehead fall into her hands.

"Come on," said Brother Reardon, taking her elbow. "Let's get some fresh air."

They stepped from the tent into the blue light of the evening. The sun, low and orange, was dipping behind the mountains.

"He is with Our Father now, Juliet. He is at peace."

Juliet nodded politely, but she did not have Brother Reardon's faith. Instead, as she sat and kicked at the grass, her own vision came to her, a wish: she wished that all the ghosts of all the men and boys who had died in the war—and the wars before this—were standing there in the field, invisible to her and Reardon, arms outstretched, welcoming Beau. Patting him on the back, uttering their obscene, affectionate epithets, those sobriquets of soldiery love. She imagined Tuck welcoming Beau, and for a moment she felt so cracked by sadness that only gravity held her together.

"Juliet?" Brother Reardon rubbed her back. "Are you okay?"

She stood and wiped off her pants. "I guess we should bury him and find somewhere to sleep."

The lavender sky was slowly darkening. A field of crooked white crosses, blue in the dusk, fronted the small stone church. They hauled their musette bags inside, swollen and heavy with what they had been able to carry of Beau's belongings. The inside of the church was cold and dark; it had the raw, wet smell of a barn. Juliet struck a match and saw that empty ration cans and dead black flies littered the floor. A half dozen beds of hay, browned and uneven, lay at the foot of the altar.

"We'll at least be safe here," said Brother Reardon. He eased his bag off his shoulders and dropped it on the floor. A rodent, roused by the thud, scratched and scampered across the dark floor, banging into several ration tins.

"They want our food, not us, right?" said Juliet.

"So I'm told."

Brother Reardon clicked on his flashlight and, noticing the empty basin of holy water, poured what was left of his canteen into the basin and blessed it. He walked to the altar and swatted away a sheet of cobwebs; with the hem of his shirt he dusted, then righted the toppled Madonna.

Juliet set down her bag and lit a kerosene lamp. A jumbled mass of splintered pew planks and rotted tree branches stood beside the door. The few pews that were spared had been turned on their sides, pushed together to form a table at the edge of the church. She set the lamp on the table, and the light spilled across three dog-eared copies of *Stars and Stripes*. A large, dusty Bible lay open to the first page, where someone had penned *Kilroy was here.* She flipped through the strange soft pages, hundreds of them; she'd read so many books, but never this one.

"I have to confess," she called across the darkness, "I haven't spent much time in churches."

"In their defense," Brother Reardon answered, "they usually look a lot better than this."

"I feel like an intruder."

"The intruders are the ones we *most* want to enter churches!"

"Well, I'm not much of a sinner, I'm afraid. It's just that my father is an atheist."

Brother Reardon shined his flashlight at her. "I never took you for much of a sinner."

"You can tell by looking?" she laughed.

"Secrets of the trade."

He had stuffed one of the hay beds inside a knotted hospital sheet and was noisily shaking it and smacking it, trying to purge the lumps. He set it on the ground and signaled Juliet over. He began to arrange another bed for himself, whistling cheerfully as he stuffed in the fistfuls of hay. It was hard for Juliet to imagine how he kept himself together; he had held the hands of so many dying men.

"So how does a person become a monk?" she asked.

"How or why?"

"Why, I guess."

He smiled. He set his bed beside hers, and they sat with the kerosene lamp perched above them. "You fail at everything else—miserably. I'm kidding, but only a little. I was a terribly lazy and confused person, bouncing from job to job after high school. I sold tickets at the movie theater; I apprenticed with a watchmaker; I was briefly a stage actor, playing Oberon in *A Midsummer Night's Dream*. Everything seemed so transitory to me, so meaningless. I simply couldn't muster the energy to do things I didn't truly believe in. I was always distracted by larger questions: Why are we here?

Why are we as we are? Who is watching over all of this? I hadn't been raised with any answers. My father was an atheist as well."

"Your career choice must have shocked him."

"Sadly, he was too piss-drunk to notice."

"I'm sorry."

He turned to adjust the lamp, and she sensed the admission had embarrassed him. Reardon was like Willard in this way; he felt he always had to be the listener.

"So you knew that man from home?" he asked. "Our last patient?"

"He was a friend of my brother."

"Not easy, I know. But what a gift for him to have you there at the end."

"I suppose."

"Your brother, he is in the army as well?"

"He was," said Juliet. "I think he died."

It was the first time the words had come to her, the first time her fear had pushed so unexpectedly into conscious thought. A rush of sadness tightened her chest. Brother Reardon's gaze lingered on her, and in the yellow light she saw that he understood.

"It's terrible, the not knowing," he said.

"At first I loved the hope, the possibility that he'd come home. Now I hate it. I want to smash it out of me. I can't bear the endless disappointment." It felt good to unburden herself of the feeling she had carried for months.

"Even if he isn't with us here anymore, Juliet, he is with Our Father. Perhaps you don't believe in such things, but that doesn't mean it isn't true."

"Tuck was eighteen when he went missing. He's my older brother. But now I'm eighteen, almost nineteen. I feel like I'm leaving him behind."

"No one is left behind," said Brother Reardon. "Ever."

"It would be nice to believe that."

"There's time yet to convince you." He smiled, his pale face half-eroded by the darkness. "And I'm good at my job."

The heaviness of the day pressed on her head, weighed against her shoulders, and she yawned. "In the morning?"

"In the morning," Brother Reardon agreed.

Juliet and Brother Reardon rose early and carried their bags to the main road. The air was cold; the light was grainy. The mountains ahead loomed like distant cities. They had been walking for an hour, pausing every few minutes to readjust their bags, when they heard a supply truck rumble to a slow stop behind them.

The driver, Rufus, happily smacked his meaty hand against the door. He was thankful for the company. Juliet and Brother Reardon climbed into the back and sat atop white pine crates. The truck smelled sharply of gasoline and rainwater; gray morning light streamed through bullet holes in the canvas.

As he drove, Rufus yelled into the back about how he'd heard things up ahead were in one hell of a tangle. Although it was hard to hear him over the churning of the engine, his story came to them in snippets, and Juliet soon made out that he'd spent most of his time far behind the lines as a quartermaster, but that Earl, the main driver, had been killed by a land mine two days earlier. Rufus was jowly and plump in a way Juliet hadn't seen in months; the soldiers at the front were all muscle and sinew, the Italians were sharpened and shadowed by hunger. A band of fat hung over the collar of Rufus's shirt, and this made Juliet irrationally angry.

"What are you seeing in the hospitals?" he asked. "I heard there's everything from gangrene to trench foot. I ain't never seen gangrene."

"If you've seen bad trench foot, you've seen gangrene," said Juliet. Her mood was dark. At daybreak she'd felt a brief relief, a welcome distance from Beau's death. But now she sat in the truck staring at her bag filled with his things—his letters, his comic books, his Zippo lighter, his boots; it would all be shipped home to Charlesport, to his grandmother, to this woman who had outlived every member of her family, including her grandson. Juliet thought of writing her a letter, since she had been there at the end, but what on earth could she say? *Your grandson was afraid, he was in pain, he asked me to hold him. . . .*

The truck lumbered onward, and the air felt cool. Rufus drove like someone nearsighted, hunching uncomfortably forward. Every few minutes he lifted an enormous map from his thighs, studied it closely, and then swatted it back down. Juliet could tell by the motion of his head that he was still talking, but the engine strained so loudly that most of what he said was lost in the racket. Their silence seemed of no concern to him. Like all of them, she supposed, he just needed to talk.

The hospital was now encamped in the mountains; the olive Red Cross tents had been pitched in tidy rows over what seemed to be the base area of a former ski resort. The poles and wires of an abandoned funicular climbed into the white mist. A large stone building, Gothic and alpine, had been commandeered as the Officers' Mess; it looked as if it had once been a grand hotel, but the windows, all smashed, were covered with white hospital sheets, which billowed in the cool breeze. Rufus pulled the truck beside this structure, and on the front porch Juliet saw a crowd of nurses and ward men.

Before driving off, Rufus asked Brother Reardon to bless him and then to bless the entire truck, and Brother Reardon complied. Then he and Juliet headed straight for the stone building, where she spotted Dr. Willard and Barnaby, seated together at a table.

"You're back," Juliet said, trying to suppress her grin.

Willard nodded, perfunctorily.

"They let Barnaby go?"

Juliet dropped her bag and moved beside Barnaby. His chesnut hair had grown in thickly, and he wore a black eye patch where the bandages had once been. There was a new alertness in his stare, and he raised his hands from his lap high above his head to show that he was handcuffed.

"He's *communicating*?" she said.

"Some," said Willard. "More so than ever." He stroked Barnaby's head, as though comforting a child. "As a reward, they sentenced him to death."

"I failed him," said Willard, staring into his coffee that night. They were seated in the back of the old stone building; there was a fireplace at the far end where a fire had been lit, and they had drawn up two metal chairs. Willard poured Scotch into his coffee. "The proceedings were ridiculous. All officers. More brass than a candelabra."

"Lovelace is saying the army hasn't killed anyone for desertion since the Civil War," said Juliet. "I'm sure Barnaby will just go to prison."

"That's not an assumption I'm comfortable making. Besides, having him sit in a cell for years is hardly consoling—his mind will lock up further." He took a long sip of his coffee and raked his hand through his hair. "How are you? How have things here been? How was the patient?"

Juliet didn't know what to say about Beau. "I'm eager for a new line of work," she offered, but something in her voice cracked.

He put his arm around her. "Me too."

They sat silently, looking briefly and curiously at each other, then at the fire. She wondered if he'd missed her as well. Somewhere above them was a billiards table, and the balls clacked intermittently as a lone player practiced his game.

"It was strange being at the hospital without you," she said. "I didn't know if you were coming back."

He slowly pulled his arm away, leaned back, and crossed his legs at the ankles. "I'm right here. Pessimism and all."

She felt his refusal once again to engage in any talk of feelings; but there were more pressing matters.

"Anyway, while you were gone," she said, "one of the men in Barnaby's unit came in as a patient. He made a deathbed confession. He said Brilling had it in for Barnaby, that he made him draw the short straw and go forward alone. He didn't say it, but I think it was, you know, about Barnaby being different. It might help with his case."

"I'm not sure right now what I could say that would help. I tell them a soldier was picked on by his commanding officer, bullied by a captain, lost his mind, and attempted suicide? If Brilling *fired* at Barnaby, that's one thing. Brilling not liking Barnaby is irrelevant. The men in that courtroom don't have a clue what it's like for soldiers at the front. They make policies, decisions; they offer sweeping judgments. They are strategists, and when they veer toward moralizing, they veer toward evil. They've never sat in a dugout all night thinking they would die."

She thought of Munson's letter to his father, of his final night alone; she wondered if his father had learned of his son's death yet.

Willard misunderstood her silence. "Fine, maybe Barnaby's being 'different' cost him some points with Captain Brilling. Let's even posit that Brilling arranged it so Barnaby would have the most dangerous jobs; that makes Brilling an asshole, but we hardly need a military tribunal to establish that."

"First-class asshole," said Juliet. "*He* should be court-martialed."

"You're forgetting the West Point Benevolent Protective Society. They'll never touch him. Besides, it has nothing to do with the matter at hand—Barnaby's shell shock."

"Unless even the tribunal hates Barnaby because he's *different*."

"I think they hate weakness, or what they view as cowardice, in any form."

"Well, what now?" She stood to poke at the fire, trying to rekindle the fading embers.

"I've issued an appeal on medical grounds, arguing that he obviously wasn't fit to stand trial. He couldn't speak for himself. I've contacted colleagues back in the States to make statements against the army punishing the mentally unwell. But it will take time."

"How long do we have?" Juliet asked.

"He's scheduled to be removed from my custody in two weeks. That's two more weeks to work with him. After that, I don't know what they'll do."

"And you no longer think he's faking this semicoma, somehow trying to save himself?"

"If that was his strategy, by now he's realized it is *deeply* flawed."

CHAPTER 14

MORNINGS, JULIET AWOKE to clumps of snow weighing darkly on the canvas above her. The balls of her feet were icy and numb, and beneath her blanket she rubbed them briskly. She reached beside her for her winter uniform and wriggled into its stiff, thick layers without moving far from the warm shadow of her sleep. She trudged across the frosted encampment while the engineers, pitched on ladders, swept snow off the tents' red crosses. The granite peaks looming beyond were beautifully striated, columns of dark gray broken by long ellipses of luminous white. The morning sun shone against them and lit the whitened encampment with a stunning incandescence.

As Juliet climbed the stone steps of the old hotel and entered the mess hall, the nurses and doctors greeted her from the long tables with hunched, wintry hellos. In the cold, they all turned in on themselves: they pulled blankets tightly around their shoulders; they clutched coffee cups as though in prayer and let the steam bathe their faces. At the back of the hall, a modest fire blazed in the fireplace, and those who had finished eating drew close, hugging their knees, staring at their bare toes. The stone ledge of the hearth was carpeted with socks.

Juliet ate a quick breakfast and hurried back across the snow, already snaked with the gray slush of footsteps.

In the Recovery Tent she nodded at the nurses on duty and moved quietly to Barnaby's cot. Before the start of her rounds each day she now spent twenty minutes alone with him. She sat on the end of his bed and tried to rub the cold from his hands. She read aloud letters from his sister and related the news reports; when all else failed, she hummed. She needed this time, this portion of morning when she was accountable to no other patient, to no other cause; guilt had crept into her thoughts and dug an impassable trench—she had craved Barnaby's recovery only for news of Tuck, and she was trying to atone. As she sat beside him, she recalled how Brilling had tried to make him eat the eyeball. She recalled what Munson had told her, that he'd been hung from a tree and covered with K rations. All along she had thought fate had brought him to her because of Tuck, but now she saw another reason. Barnaby had been picked on, and *she,* of all people, understood such torments. She knew now, deep in her bones, the life he had led. The loneliness, the self-loathing. The possibility of his execution filled her with a horrible sickness.

The appeal was stalled, and Willard had managed to buy a few extra weeks convincing the army that his study of Barnaby could prevent other desertions, which were rampant with the final push into the icy mountains.

The good news was undercut, however, by the continued reemergence of Barnaby's motor skills. His general alertness had persisted, and then one morning Juliet found him at the back of the ward, sitting up in bed, his legs over the side of the cot. He said nothing; he barely nodded in response to her questions—"Can you hear me?" "Do you know who I am?" "Do you know where you are?"—but he took the spoon from her hand and devoured the entire bowl of oatmeal. He lifted the cup of water, drinking greedily, entirely unaware of the significance of what he'd done.

The next day he made his bed and dressed himself in his khakis. His boots were shined and his laces tied; he sat on the edge of his bed expectantly, and she wondered where he thought he was going.

These improvements seemed to her further proof of the injustice of the universe. Was Barnaby recovering only in time to understand his looming punishment? Witnessing Barnaby's daily feats, the staff shook their heads with heartbroken bewilderment. Major

Decker stopped by to commend Barnaby on his recovery, but as he turned to leave, his eyes glazed over with defeat. Each morning Juliet restrained her enthusiasm as she reported Barnaby's progress to Dr. Willard. Together they tested Barnaby's reflexes and made notes. Willard had been consumed with the paperwork surrounding Barnaby's appeal, but now he wanted to arrange an immediate Sodium Pentothal interview. He felt that only a statement from Barnaby, cognizant and articulate, could change the army's mind. If Barnaby had come this far out of his coma, he might be on the cusp of conscious speech.

"One more door," Willard told her. "Let's try to open one more door."

Juliet guided Barnaby up the wide stone staircase; in the hallway they followed the wavering light from one of the rooms.

She found Willard seated on a queen-sized sleigh bed gleaming with lacquer. The mattress was bare. A small kerosene lamp sat on the stone floor, and near it Juliet saw an oblong stain of blood. The size of an arm or of a lower leg. The rooms on the upper level had been the site of a firefight; her eyes traced the wallpaper until she spotted three bullet holes in a near-perfect triangular arrangement. An ornately framed mirror hung above a wide wooden dresser; the sole jagged remnant of glass now flashed in the half dark. The white sheet covering the broken window blew in on a gust, and she saw that the room had a spectacular view of the moonlit mountains.

"Shall we start?" Willard dragged a green armchair beside the bed and gestured for Barnaby to sit. Barnaby stroked the armrests and surveyed the room until he happened on the bullet holes.

Juliet crouched before him, rolling up the thick sleeve of his winter shirt. "Don't worry about that. We're going to go away from here for a little while," she said, sliding the needle into his arm.

She watched the familiar flutter of Barnaby's eye, the slackening of his mouth, the dip and rise and dip of his chin as he keeled, like a boat, toward semislumber. They waited nearly a minute until his eye opened fully and he stared straight ahead.

"Christopher, it's Dr. Willard." Willard, seated on the edge of the bed, leaned toward Barnaby. "We've talked before, and we've talked a lot about you not feeling right, and it's important to me that we find a way to get you better. So I want to find out exactly when you started having trouble. I'd like you to tell us about the time you were shot in the shoulder. When you first came to the hospital, months back. Okay?"

Barnaby's long figure sank into the chair. He nodded slowly, as though part of a perfectly normal conversation. "Well, we were somewhere near the Volturno. We'd been walking for days. My helmet weighed a hundred pounds. My pack straps were eating into my shoulders; I was bleeding through my shirt. The platoon got orders to clear out some town. Make sure Germans weren't hiding in the buildings. Clearing a town is leapfrog business, and my squad had to go in first over this old wall with deep ditches on either side. It wasn't an easy climb, and I kept losing my foothold. Three of us were over when Geronimo, right beside me, pumping his fist for us to move in—boom, collapsed. I saw the black dot on his forehead before he started bleeding. Sniper fire.

"The rest of us made it over the wall, Sergeant McKnight shouting for us to spread out. Spread out—they tell you that all the time in training but all you wanna do when you're out there is bunch up, stick together. Three of us made a dash from the wall to the house where the sniper was firing from. He must have been alone, 'cause as we got close, he hung a white rag out the window. McKnight shouted something in German and the sniper dropped his gun out the window. Pretty soon he came out, hands over his head. He was the very first German I'd ever seen. He looked small and fairly normal. I remember thinking, if he were wearing a different uniform, you'd never know he was German.

"The rest of the squad was coming around the back of the house. Pretty soon, McKnight and Rakowski began shouting at the German. They'd been fighting alongside Geronimo well over a year, since Africa, so they were frothing at the mouth. . . . 'You fuckin' Jerry devil . . . Geronimo was a good man.' The German puts his hands behind his head, biting at his lower lip, and gets down on his knees. He's looking at the ground, and his helmet tilts forward over his eyes, but he's too scared to move it. '*Nicht schießen,*' he says. '*Nicht schießen.*' He keeps repeating that in these short, stabbing whispers, like he's talking to himself, talking to God. Sergeant McKnight's watching him, kicking at the dirt, that vein in his forehead getting fat. He orders Rakowski and Dufresne to take the Jerry to the rear, so they each grab an elbow and haul the German off the ground and start heading back toward the wall."

At the name "Dufresne," Juliet's neck tensed. Her hands went cold. She looked to her lap, staring at the thick weave of her khaki pants, the brown stitching along her zipper, trying to tune out everything in the room, listening carefully to Barnaby's words, holding each detail in her mind like a pebble plucked from a riverbed.

"McKnight's looking at me. 'Stop batting your fucking eyelashes at every Jerry,' he says. Just as Rakowski and Dufresne get close to the wall, McKnight signals them to let go of the sniper. So the German's standing there all alone, his helmet still tilted, and McKnight trains his rifle on him. McKnight's just waiting, waiting for him to start moving, and finally the Jerry takes one step, then another, and soon he's walking, walking faster, staring at the ground, breaking into a run, and I hear a gun go *pop*. Dufresne ran right over to the sniper, crouching to see if he was alive.

"As he walked back to the rest of us, he shook his head.

'I'm getting tired of that shit,' Dufresne shouted, throwing his gun down. He hadn't slept in days. McKnight said it wasn't a committee and ordered us to move out."

Juliet heard Willard lift the lantern. He held it close to Barnaby's face, then shifted it toward Juliet. He studied her expression, which she was rapidly losing the power to compose. Her cheeks felt hot, her eyes moist. Her desperation must have shown. For months Tuck's voice had been fading from her memory; she'd had trouble even picturing his face. But here he was, vivid and alive, in the half light of a ruined hotel suite. She nodded pleadingly for Willard to continue.

Willard slowly turned back to Barnaby: "So you knew Tucker Dufresne?"

Barnaby worked his thumbs nervously over the green velvet of the armrests. "I owe Tucker."

"What for?"

Barnaby shook his head, sharply. "It wasn't what they said."

"What did *they* say?"

"Lies. Nothing but lies about what he did."

Willard looked down for a moment, evidently disturbed, then returned his stare to Barnaby. "Okay, explain to me what happened next, Christopher."

"McKnight ordered me and Dufresne to check this field past the town. We had to stay low, crouching in the grass. I followed Dufresne; those were the orders. He'd been with the squad longer and always knew what he was doing, never got in harm's way. He told me not to get trigger-happy—one pop from my rifle, and Jerry would know right where we were. But pretty soon there was gunfire, and out of nowhere the whole field started shaking, the ground spraying dirt. Dufresne started crawling faster, and I was just trying to stay still, but he said to keep moving, he could see a dugout ahead. I wanted to hide under my helmet, but Dufresne was shouting, 'Move your ass, Barnaby,' so I started moving and the next thing I knew, I felt this awful heat in my shoulder. It felt like I was pinned to the ground. 'I'm hit,' I called. 'You gotta keep moving,' he yelled. But the ache in my shoulder was coming on strong, so I set my head in the grass and closed my eyes. I was getting ready to say a prayer when Dufresne yanked me by my legs, pulling me along the grass. Musta been forty yards. Bullets kept flying over us—you could hear them when they came close—but pretty soon we did a roll-tuck into the dugout.

"'Jesus, you shouldn't have done that,' I told him.

"'Probably not.' He was tired, I could see. Afraid, too. I think we'd both wet our pants from fear.

"He poured sulfonamide on my wound, then tore the sleeve off his shirt and tourniqueted my arm. I couldn't move much, and I asked him how long he thought they'd keep shooting. 'Days,' he said. 'Minutes. Doesn't matter. Anyone crosses that field, I shoot.'

"Dufresne was like that. Tough as nails.

"But the firing continued all around us, and we had no idea where the rest of the squad had gone. There was no one to cover us. So we sat there, talking low. . . . It was the first we'd really talked but we had to fill the hours—we talked about comics, cars, family stuff. He kept his eye on the field. That whole day went by, then the night. Dufresne was right. We were pinned there for two days, grenades getting lobbed just a few feet from our dugout. I was getting weaker, feverish. We were down to the last of our canteens. We kept thinking the squad would come looking for us—we were exactly where they'd sent us—but nothing. Dufresne was getting mad at McKnight. Had they left us for dead? We ate what we had, only taking small sips of water here and there so we could stay alert. We talked ourselves awake, talked about everything that ever happened to us. On the second night, I woke in the dark and realized the shooting had stopped. I was feeling so weak, I grabbed our last ration bar, took a bite, then whispered Dufresne's name to give him some. But he was gone. You can't imagine what that feels like. You come over here belonging to something, you're a part of something: your squad, your battalion, your army, your country. You can do all these things you'd never wanna do because there are others there with you. You're in this shit together. Then suddenly you wake up, alone, in some dark, human *nowhere*. You don't belong to anything but the earth beneath you. You hope with everything in you that God above is watching, but Brilling always said God would think I was an abomination. I thought I'd been forsaken. I sat there crying in the dark, preparing to die alone, but as the sun came up, I saw Dufresne's white glove sitting in my lap. It was like seeing a cactus in the desert. No one ever touched Dufresne's white glove. It never left his jacket pocket. But I knew he set it there for me, a sign that he'd gone to get help. That's the only thing that kept me alive, knowing I hadn't just been left there. Knowing Dufresne was coming back for me.

"My shoulder was aching and I was still losing blood, so I closed my eyes. Soon I heard voices. Footsteps came toward me, and I felt my heart hammering. I got my breathing real still. I felt my body being turned about—I kept my eyes closed and stayed silent, thinking it was the Germans. Hands patted down my jacket; someone took off my watch, my dog tags; then everything went still. I don't know how much time passed. My shoulder went numb. My head felt light. I passed out.

"Next thing I knew, I heard a thump and felt something heavy pressing against me. Then there was dirt on my face, falling in my nostrils, my mouth, and I started coughing. I felt hands on my face, brushing off the dirt.

"'Shit, he ain't dead!' he laughs. It was Kirkland from the platoon.

"I could barely talk, I was so weak, but I asked about Dufresne. They said they hadn't seen anyone else. I said he'd be headed back there to find me, that he'd gone to get help. They said no way in hell. They said the Germans had retreated in the night and the area was clear and he'd show up soon enough.

"At the field hospital they stitched me up. The company commander was there. Brilling. I showed him the glove, explained Tuck had left me with it and that I knew it meant he was coming back. I said they had to go look for him. Brilling got the wrong idea."

"Wrong idea?"

"It made him crazy, that glove. He said I'd taken it from Dufresne. It made him crazy that Dufresne had saved me. Brilling had lost so many men it was starting to eat away at his mind. It was like he blamed himself for every death. He started saying maybe Dufresne had deserted, Dufresne was insubordinate, and I said I knew he'd never do a thing like that. And he asked me how I knew Dufresne's mind so well. Dufresne left me that glove, I knew that. Someone else in the squad said they'd heard Dufresne's voice in the night, shouting in the field. I thought about the possibility that Dufresne had been killed trying to get me help and I started to cry. I was still stretched thin from living alone in that dugout. The crying made Captain even angrier."

"What exactly did the captain say to you?"

Barnaby invoked a haunting baritone that filled the darkened room: "'Quit crying, you fucking pansy ass.'"

Willard removed his glasses and rubbed the corners of his eyes. "Did you talk to anyone about what happened in the dugout? About their trying to bury you? Did you see a psychiatrist?"

"I never met a psychiatrist 'til you."

Willard's jaw clenched; he shook his head. With a final, defeated jab of his thumb, he clicked off the recorder. "When I count to ten . . . One, two, three . . ." He stopped, looking at Juliet, at the tears brimming in her eyes.

He turned his gaze to the broken mirror and blinked in long, silent contemplation. He cleared his throat. "Christopher, Nurse

Dufresne is here, and she'd like to ask you a few more questions. About her brother."

Juliet clasped Willard's hand in gratitude, and he set down his notebook and walked to the window. Hands plunged in his pockets, he studied the mountains through the billowing gap between the window and the sheet. Juliet moved to where he had been sitting. She had waited months for this chance.

"Christopher. The first day we spoke to you, I asked about Tucker Dufresne. You said 'Forgive me.' What were you asking forgiveness for?"

"That's what Rakowski said he heard. Tuck saying 'Forgive me' somewhere in the dark. Those were the last words anyone heard from Tuck."

Having hoped for months that somehow those two words were the missing link between Tuck and Barnaby, Juliet was now stumped.

"And they have no idea who he was talking to?"

"Rakowski didn't see a thing. Just heard Tuck's voice."

Juliet wrung her hands. "Did he seem *okay?*" she asked. "Not when you last saw him, but before that, in the time you spent with him. He sent me a letter and sounded troubled."

"It was hard to know Dufresne's mind. By the time I got there, he was always off eating cold rations by himself. I don't think the army suited him. Didn't really suit anyone decent. He liked to do his own thing, cut his own trail. He had a temper about things."

She remembered what Beau said about Tuck getting into a fight in a rest hotel. Her heart sank; she hated to think of her brother unhappy, lonely. Why hadn't he shared more of his troubles with her?

"Did he get my letters? I wrote him every day."

"Oh, did he love those letters. He'd go off near a tree and read them over and over again. It gave him his peace. We talked about that the night in the dugout. Both of us had sisters writing up a storm. I told him all about Tina and he told me all about how you were a prodigy with science, winning prizes. He bragged about how you'd thrown off college to become a nurse. He said you were growing up fast, he could tell from your letters. He said you'd all been best friends but that maybe the war would make things different. He hoped you'd never know what he'd done over here."

Juliet felt her stomach weaken; she could not bring herself to ask the next question: *What had he done?*

Willard looked back from the window to see if she meant to continue, and Juliet shook her head. Crossing the room, he once again began his count. As Barnaby blinked himself out of the haze, Willard crouched and tested his reflexes.

"Christopher, can you tell me your full rank and division? Christopher, can you tell me where you are from?"

Barnaby was silent.

"Christopher, can you tell me where you are now? Can you tell me your sister's name?"

As Willard pressed on, testing and challenging Barnaby's muteness, Juliet's mind plunged into a swirl of speculation.

Tuck, she thought, *I would have understood and forgiven everything.* And yet she hadn't asked Barnaby what he meant; she hadn't wanted the details of what Tuck had done. Perhaps she already knew the answer. Day after day she'd watched the bodies carried in on litters. She'd helped carry some herself: American soldiers maimed and dismembered at the hands of Germans. Some twenty miles north, wouldn't there also be a German field hospital? Where a young German nurse like herself would stare at the blood and gore inflicted by the Americans? By men like Tuck and Barnaby and Munson and Beau? He'd done what they'd all done: He'd shot and stabbed and charged and strangled. He'd lobbed grenades. It was the thing they never wrote about in their letters, the thing they never *could* write about, and it was everything; in between the details of food and weather and camaraderie, they never said, *Dear Mom and Pop, I've become a killer.*

Willard, disappointment evident in his expression, began lead-ing Barnaby to the doorway. Barnaby had refused to speak, and Willard gestured impatiently for Juliet to join him. She touched the side of the bed, the green chair, the wooden floor. Tuck had been conjured up in that room, and she did not yet want to leave. But with great effort she finally stood and took Barnaby's other arm.

In silence they crossed the long, dark hallway; they made their way down the stone stairs. On the ground floor, the light of the fireplace briefly warmed and lit them, and as they passed through the mess area, the nurses and doctors drinking hot chocolate at the long tables looked up eagerly, wondering if progress had been made. Willard shook his head perfunctorily, trying to rein in his despondency, and they continued out into the cold, black night.

A wet wind swept through the encampment, and the tents around them rattled and flapped. They led Barnaby back to the Recovery Tent and carried their gear to the Supply Tent. There, Juliet began placing things one by one into the metal cabinet. Her motions were jagged, unsettled. She was trying hard to compose herself. She wanted to get it done with and go back to her bedroll and curl up and sob. Willard stood at the threshold, staring for a long while at the starless sky.

"All done here," she called, sealing the cabinet.

Willard slowly stepped into the tent and arranged two crates side by side.

"Sit," he said.

She held her hands in her lap and did not look at him. She did not think he could possibly understand the despair she was feeling. He stared ahead as though carefully measuring his words.

"That's not what you wanted to hear, I'm sure," he said. "Are you okay?"

"You're not going to lecture me about focusing on the patient at hand?"

He smiled gently. "Shoot me if I do."

She felt her self-possession falter; tears began to rush her eyes. It no longer mattered if he understood; she just wanted to speak, to get it all out of her. "Just hearing about him . . . just hearing another person, a person who knew him, speak his name . . . It's all I have now, and it was wonderful, and horrible. . . . I'd give anything for another minute with him, another second. But I don't think . . . I think it's impossible. Barnaby was the last person to ever see my brother. And he knows nothing. Absolutely nothing. I thought I'd made my peace with not knowing, but now . . . To come this close and still not know if he's alive or dead. And it's still all so strange. It's just so odd that Tuck never mentioned Barnaby in his letters. Not once."

Willard listened carefully as she spoke, responding with slow, measured nods. Then he cleared his throat. "I have to ask, is there any chance your brother was . . ."

She knew what he meant. "No."

The swiftness of her denial seemed to displease him. "Because it could be a piece of the puzzle. It could even factor into Barnaby's despair. Guilt over Tuck's risking his life to save him. Perhaps there was an intimate emotional connection."

Juliet looked at the ground and thought of what Beau had said that night in the cave about Tuck and Myrna: *If you ask me, they were never very serious.* She thought about his endless stream of insignificant girlfriends. Did it mean something? Was there something about him she hadn't grasped? But after everything else, did it matter now?

"God, Dr. Willard, I don't think so, but nothing feels certain anymore."

"Well, we know your brother didn't like McKnight killing prisoners. Perhaps that was the reason for his fraught letter."

"They really do that? Kill prisoners?"

"And worse, I'm afraid."

A dark shadow of possibility crossed her mind: if that was what the Americans would do to a prisoner, what might the Germans do? Her great hope that Tuck had merely been captured suddenly seemed terribly grim.

"Whatever befell him, Juliet"—Willard put his hand on her shoulder—"the worst is probably over. I know this feels as though it is all happening now, as you hear about it, as you think about it. Tuck is through it. *You're* feeling the trauma of it, not him."

She was grateful for his words. It was as though her mind had erected a chamber of thought, brightly lit and thrumming, in which anything terrible could befall Tuck, in which every awful scenario endlessly played out. She finally wanted to shut it off.

"Did you know that if you prompted Barnaby about that first episode," she asked, "he might talk about Tuck?"

"It had crossed my mind."

Willard stood and shifted toward the tent flaps but made no headway. For all his bombast and talk of regulations, thought Juliet, he couldn't stop himself from helping a person in need.

"Thank you," she said.

He offered a half smile, fighting a blush.

"Will that session help the appeal?" she asked. "Will it help Barnaby with anything?"

"Doubtful. I suppose I'm learning what it feels like to be sent in to fight a battle that's impossible to win. I find out my equipment doesn't work, I was given the wrong maps. Barnaby should have seen a psychiatrist during his first admission. You can't leave a man in a dugout, bleeding to death, and then nearly bury him alive without asking him how his mind is holding up. You can't just send him back into the lines."

"We only treat the ones who come in here and don't want to kill anymore. But they *all* sound mad."

"It's impossible to ask men to do what they do out there and not have it change them."

In a flash, what Tuck said to Sergeant McKnight came back to her: *I'm getting tired of that shit.* Had Tuck been part of something similar before? "I think the killing—I think the violence—I think it drove my brother mad."

"He wouldn't be the first."

"God, I hate it here," Juliet said quietly.

"But I'm so glad you *are* here."

She stood and faced him; his kindness had moved her, and she felt an impulse to touch him, a *right* to touch him. She stepped toward him now, stepped into him, as if he were a room that belonged to her. He did not retreat. She set her cheek against his chest and he placed his hand on the side of her head and they stood like that for quite some time. In the silence of the tent, she could hear his breath. She did not want to speak. She did not want to move. She felt something rise within her, something eager and aching; the thought pulsed and throbbed, and she shifted her head, slightly, suggestively, so that her face titled upward. *Please, please, please kiss me,* she thought. *Lift my chin and kiss me. I think you are wonderful, kiss me.* His hand remained on her head but he made no motion to change position, and slowly, nervously, Juliet looked up, hoping she might see in his face some reflection of her own yearning. His eyes had closed, but she could not tell if it was from longing or exhaustion. She moved her mouth close to his, so close she could feel his breath on her face, and suddenly his lips pressed into hers. Their mouths moved eagerly, hungrily. His hand roamed her hair. She felt him press into her, begin to lift her, and then as quickly as it had begun, he pulled away.

"I'm sorry," he said. He flattened the front of his shirt, then began to straighten hers.

"It's okay," she said.

She was aware of him shaking his head apologetically as he stepped away; he said nothing more as he hurriedly left.

*   *   *

As the division continued its assault into the mountains, patients arrived who had been stranded for days on ice-crested peaks, their faces blistered with frostbite, their limbs gangrenous and rancid. Word came that entire battalions were pinned in the mountains, stranded without food and ammunition, fighting for the fifth straight day without sleep. The wounded arrived on makeshift toboggans hauled down ice-lacquered cow paths. Patients were blue-lipped, frostbitten, drunk on morphine. They spoke of peeing on their rifles to loosen frozen chambers. Many, having received hasty amputations at the front, arrived with stumps bandaged with shirts and pants.

Some nights, when Juliet couldn't sleep, she lay thinking of all the legs and arms buried across Italy. How many bodies could be stitched together from them? She imagined an army of creatures like Dr. Frankenstein's, zombies sewn together from every nationality—a German leg on an Italian torso with American arms—all limping across Europe, trying to end the war. *Throw down your weapons!* Waffen runter! Getatte le armi!

A bone-chilling cold had arrived, sharp winds hurling through the mountains. Since trucks couldn't navigate the terrain, mules carried supplies to the front: they left loaded with food and blankets and ammunition; they returned strapped with the musette bags of men who had been killed. Something had been done to the mules to make them deaf so they wouldn't startle at the sound of gunfire. Juliet watched the animals lope through the snow as they were led past the encampment, a look of calm detachment in their eyes. She thought, *That is the way to survive this; I'll stop listening, I'll stop looking.*

The mood throughout the wards was grim. The quartermaster complained that he hadn't been properly supplied for winter and advised the staff to write home for gloves and long underwear. Patients shivered in their beds; the doctors came down with head colds. At breakfast, Juliet stared at rows of raw, blistered noses, sets of puffy and swollen eyes. First the hospital ran out of tissues, then toilet paper. So Juliet cut up old bedsheets, the ones too blood-stained to be used on beds, and distributed the strips to patients and staff; they said nothing of the dark red splotches.

Word had come that Barnaby was going to be transported to the division stockade, and MPs now stood guard outside the Isolation Tent, where Captain Brilling had ordered him sequestered. Juliet was still in charge of bringing his food, but she'd come to dread mealtimes; she avoided his stare and moved as quickly as possible, afraid that at any moment Barnaby would return to full conscious-ness and she'd be forced to explain everything. Afraid he would tell her he was frightened, that he, too, would ask for her help. What could she possibly do?

She had failed them all: Tuck, Barnaby, Beau.

Juliet volunteered to work nights; she wanted to disappear into the nocturnal underworld, where the patients slept and dreamt and breathed peacefully, where no one was in pain, where no one was afraid. She sipped brandy throughout her shift, and before turning in at dawn, she smoked a cigarette by herself in the raw, cold air on the hotel's front porch. A wisdom tooth coming in made it painful to eat, and she had begun to lose weight.

"You look awful," said Brother Reardon, joining her in the mess hall one afternoon. A red scarf was knotted at his neck. "Really, a complete and total mess."

"Thanks."

"I mean, you need to eat. Here." He slid her a bowl of chicken broth, and she distractedly worked her spoon around the edges.

"They're taking Barnaby tomorrow," she said.

"I must admit, I didn't think this would happen."

"I've lost almost a thousand patients in four months, but this bothers me more than all of them put together. We *saved* him. I nursed him back to health, and they want to kill him."

Brother Reardon gestured toward the soup. "Starving yourself won't help him."

Juliet lifted a spoonful, blew on it, and then shoved it in her mouth, only to find the soup was practically icy. She broke a cracker in half, dropped the pieces into the bowl, and studied their flotation. "I just don't think what he did was so awful. His commanding officer pretty much set him up to go crazy. Wanted him to have his face blasted to bits, no matter who did it. They all seemed to want him dead."

"Why would anyone want that?"

She studied the concern on Brother Reardon's face; she liked him, but she was not certain what his reaction might be. "He's different."

"Different?"

"Not like the average man. I'm not sure you would understand."

Brother Reardon looked away thoughtfully, then brought his palms together and set his clasped hands firmly on the table. "I pray daily they will commute his sentence."

"And that the war will end? And that violence will vanish and we'll all be wonderful, sensible creatures? That we can look after Dante and Liberata? That everyone who died senselessly will come back to life and grow old with the rest of us? There is too much to pray for, don't you see? And none of it helps. If there is a God, he just doesn't seem to care. . . . Sorry, Brother Reardon. I overstepped. I'm just at the end of my rope."

He narrowed his eyes and reached for her hand. "I understand. What I can do, in addition to praying—and what I'd very much like to do—is spend the evening with Private Barnaby, alone. You and Dr. Willard have gone to great and admirable lengths to deal with the well-being of his mind, but I'd like to address the well-being of his soul before it's too late. Would it be all right with you if I looked after him in my own tent tonight? You can fetch him in the morning. I've asked the MPs and they'll grant me custody."

"You think *he* believes in God after all he's been through?"

Brother Reardon clutched the ornate crucifix hanging from his neck. "It's at precisely these times the Lord makes Himself known."

That evening, Juliet visited Willard's tent. She wasn't on duty. It was after dinner, and the soft noise of a musical quartet drifted across the snowy encampment from the old stone hotel. It was the first night of entertainment in weeks, an attempt to distract everyone from Barnaby's situation. She had not been alone with Willard since their kiss.

"Brother Reardon has Barnaby for the night," she said.

"I heard."

"May I come in?"

"Of course."

He was reading, his back half-turned to her, his feet crossed on his desk. His typewriter had been covered with a large piece of felt and piled with two stacks of notebooks. A tidily packed duffel leaned against the side of the tent.

"You're going with him in the morning?"

He pulled his feet down and turned to face her. He closed the book in his lap. "At 0800."

Her eyes roamed the charts on his wall. The statistics of battle fatigue, desertions, suicides.

"Are you coming back?"

"I don't know. It's not up to me."

She sat on the end of his bedroll and hugged her knees. "I wish I could go home. Tuck is dead, they're going to kill Barnaby, you're abandoning us."

"You know very well it's not up to me where the army sends me."

"We might never see each other again."

"That's a possibility."

"Does it bother you?"

He set his book back on his desk and pressed his hand contemplatively on the cover. "Yes, it bothers me."

Juliet tried to assemble her courage. She had already lost everything and didn't want to lose this, him. If only she could shake him, force him to admit what was happening between them. She planted her palms on her thighs. "Well, I've decided I'd rather embarrass myself and say everything than wake up tomorrow and realize I no longer have a chance to say any of it."

"You should never feel embarrassed in front of me. I'm your friend."

Her mouth slackened into a sulk. Juliet had no guile, no powers of seduction. Everything she felt was rising hotly to the surface. "Friend," she repeated flatly. "But we *kissed*."

"I'm sorry."

"I don't want you to be sorry. I want you to acknowledge what it meant."

Willard removed his glasses, rubbed his eyes, and looked up at her with a pleading tenderness she had not before seen. "*Juliet* . . . You do know, I hope, that I'm perfectly capable of administering Sodium Pentothal injections and monitoring vitals. I'm even able to trim my own hair." He looked back at his desk, shaking his head at his own admission. "I enjoy your company very much—perhaps too much. Maybe I shouldn't say that; maybe I can only say it now that I'm leaving. Maybe I shouldn't have indulged those feelings. But I'm human."

"Feelings." The word made her wildly happy. "Explain."

"I don't think I can."

"You can explain *everybody's* mind but your own."

His eyes brightened with amusement, and for a moment things felt pliant and playful. But his smile quickly flattened and he pulled his chair forward. "What I can explain is this: you are everything to me here, you know that, but here, this hospital—this war—isn't everything. Because I care about you, I refuse to look you in the eye and tell you a lie. And while, yes, I have feelings for you, I still love my wife. She writes three times a week. She cares as much about my work here as I do. She is a moral, loyal woman of the highest order. You'd like her, Juliet. Her name is Claire. She is a real person. Claire Curtis *Willard*. She's out there, in that part of the world that isn't bleeding and screaming and losing its mind. And someday, the war will be over, and we'll get to go back there. Yes, I slipped. Yes, I have feelings. But you need to understand why my feelings can't matter to me, to you, to us. Why I must only be your friend."

Juliet felt her throat tighten; she was jealous of the name itself: *Claire Curtis Willard.*

"Every other married man here makes exceptions."

"You wouldn't be an exception. You would be a change of course."

Juliet felt the air seep out of her. He was telling her everything, finally, but none of it changed the reality of his departure, the fact of his marriage. She looked at his belongings: his typewriter, his notebooks, his recording device. She stared at his face. Such indefatigable kindness in this man, such integrity. Such *love*. He loved her, she knew it. And she loved him. She felt as though she'd found an ancient arrowhead on a mountainside, as though she'd glimpsed what only God was meant to see: the particular radiance of one soul. But at what cost? For what was supposed to happen in such situations, what every book and movie and story had prepared her for—that they would live together happily ever after—was not happening. Juliet had a vision of missing him for the rest of her life.

Willard lifted her hands: "You'll forget me. I know it and it pains me. I'm a mentor, a superior. It's a situational crush for you. I'm at least ten years your senior. You'll look back one day and think, *What was I doing, chasing after that stodgy old doctor?* While I'll be wondering if I made a horrible life decision."

It was the first time he'd ever shown insecurity.

"I won't ever think that."

She buried her face in his bedroll, and he removed her jacket and laid it over her back. "Come on, rest here, and in the morning we can go see Barnaby together."

Juliet slowly curled up in a ball, turning away from him, but listening carefully to his motions. She would replay this moment, this conversation, a hundred times, she knew. He'd be gone tomorrow, and she'd have only her memory of this, this one glimpse of his true feelings.

When daylight seeped into the tent the next morning, she was in the same position. Willard sat at his desk, hair cowlicked, studying her as she stretched her arms. She recognized his clothes from the night before, and saw on the side of his face an imprint from his wristwatch where he must have laid his head.

"It's almost seven," he said. He offered her his canteen and she took a sip. He looked sad. "We should probably get going soon."

The shadow of the previous night's conversation hung over them, but there was nothing more to say. They had work to do. Juliet splashed water on her face, and Willard ran a comb through his hair. As he propped a mirror on his desk and lathered his face with shaving cream, she looked at his duffel bag. Willard was leaving, Barnaby might be killed. Tuck was gone. She was alone in the army in the mountains of Italy. The starkness of her life terrified her.

Outside, the snow had softened to slush in the night; they walked past the MPs waiting by the Officers' Mess and then made their way to Brother Reardon's tent.

Willard shook the tent flap. "It's us, Brother Reardon."

No one responded.

"Brother Reardon?"

Willard paused and then, as if understanding the magnitude of his mistake, looked with alarm toward Juliet and pushed aside the tent flap.

The tent was empty.

PART III

{ November 1944 }

CHAPTER 15

THE SNOWY HILLS glittered in the late-morning light. Juliet sat beside Willard as he drove the jeep, wheels grinding into the ice-crusted road. They had traveled two hours, heading south, snaking through the mountains, the road so rutted and curved that it looked at times to Juliet as though Willard were wrestling the steering wheel.

Cold air swept through the jeep, whipping Juliet's hair into her eyes. Her breath steamed. At the base of the mountain the winds slowed, and the air shed its icy chill. She pulled the wool cap from her head and unlooped her scarf.

The road widened and flattened into the valley. Along the road's rutted edge, women cradled babies, their faces blank as they stumbled through the snow. Old men jabbed thick branches at the frozen ground. Two women, their hair long and graying, walked with linked arms; Juliet turned and saw that they were her age.

"Where are they going?" asked Juliet.

"As far from the front as possible, I imagine."

They were studying every figure, every shifting shadow on the horizon. They had obtained forty-eight-hour passes, agreeing with Major Decker that they would try their best within that time to find Barnaby and Brother Reardon and get them safely to Signora Gaspaldi's, where Juliet and Willard had spent the night in Florence. Within hours of Barnaby's disappearance, the two MPs at the hospital had been joined by six others, all ordered by the high command to track down the escapees. Barnaby's disappearance had erased any chance of clemency, and Brother Reardon had also been charged with desertion.

Here, finally, was something Juliet could do; she could save the man her brother had meant to save. The decision came swiftly, passionately, propelled, in part, by the uncomfortable awareness that Brother Reardon had thought to do what she and Willard, despite countless opportunities, had not: to abandon the appeals and petitions and simply abscond with Barnaby. In a matter of hours, the chaplain had thrown aside all theoretical entanglements and arguments, had revealed the cold, sharp essence of the matter: the battle had never ended for Barnaby. He was being pursued and needed rescue.

Trying to reach the deserters before the authorities, Juliet and Willard scoured the landscape in their jeep. And yet, as she looked at the wet wreckage of the countryside, at the jagged expressions of the fleeing Italians, she grew afraid of the cold and the looming dark and the unknown roads they might have to travel, afraid they wouldn't find them. She and Willard spoke little during the ride, and she wondered if he, too, was registering the extent of the risk they had taken.

They crossed the field where weeks earlier the hospital had been encamped, looking for any traces of Barnaby and Reardon. They had agreed it was most likely Reardon would seek out places he knew were safe and had been swept for mines. It looked different now; frost had leached the color from everything. Beneath the bare trunk of a hulking oak tree, Willard eased the jeep to a stop. "Lunchtime," he said.

They stepped out, stretched their legs, and sat on the hood. In the distance, icicle-fringed farmhouses threw off sparks of sunlight. The winter cold was beautiful and menacing.

From his pack Willard pulled a tin of K rations, peeled off his woolen gloves, and fumbled with the can.

"How many miles do you think they might have covered?" she asked.

"I'd gauge three miles an hour on foot. Assuming they didn't hitch any kind of ride, they're probably already at least thirty miles from the hospital. They could conceivably be all the way to Rome by now, but I suspect they're avoiding the roads."

"I hope they brought food," she said. "They'll need to eat."

"You too," he said. "We've a long day ahead."

He handed her the spoon to lick clean, and they climbed back into the jeep. Intent on their task, they spoke little as they drove, instead surveying their respective sides of the road. For a long time they saw no one; it was as though they had driven off the edge of the world. Rows of gnarled apple trees, dusted with snow, marked an abandoned orchard; the rotted frames of carts and wheelbarrows lay scattered on the ground. Soon the sun began weakening in the afternoon sky. Starlings gathered on the naked trees, and Juliet thought of all the birds flying over the ruined landscape. She thought of the animals in the undergrowth, the squirrels and rabbits and foxes. What did they make of this gutted world?

By evening, the full moon cast a fine blue light over the fields. In the distance, a darkened barn stood like a block of ice. They stopped the jeep and approached on foot, their flashlights searching the eaves, illuminating abandoned nests in every corner. Willard jimmied the door open, and the smell of wet hay, sharp with vinegar, overwhelmed them. There were no animals in sight. Ration tins littered the troughs.

"This will have to do," said Willard.

He tested the rungs of a ladder and carried his pack to the hayloft before returning for hers. She followed him up to the darkened platform, where he lit a candle and flattened out their bedrolls.

"Don't knock the candle," said Willard. "We'll be cooked."

"Cooked sounds lovely. At least we'd be warm."

She recalled all those winters in Charlesport when she had wished for snow. One December she had glued cotton on her windowsill so she would awaken to a white Christmas. Tuck had once built her an igloo from sugar cubes, large enough to stick her hand in. She had longed to sleep in flannel pajamas on an icy-cold night. That life, those desires, seemed so far away now. She felt old.

"Give me your hands," said Willard. He was lying beside her and pulled off her gloves. He rubbed her fingers, bringing them, prayer-like, to his face, to blow steam on them. The gesture brought a tingle of embarrassment to her skin, and she looked toward the wall, where a patch of graffiti glowed in the candlelight. *Pfc. Ryan Fitzpatrick spent a damned cold night here, 1944.* Below that, in another script: *Beware: the mice speak Italian.* And to the left, in a childlike script: *Tell Mae West Jimmy Mahoney loves her.*

What had happened, she wondered, to the men who wrote those words?

As quickly as the thought came, she pushed it away.

"Are the winters in Chicago this cold?" she asked.

"Arctic. There's also a ferocious wind. Thankfully I don't sleep in a hayloft there." He slipped her gloves back on her hands. "Now, lie like a mummy and tuck them under your armpits."

Juliet lay back.

"We have about twelve hours until the sun is up," said Willard. "We should conserve our candle."

"Okay."

In the pitch dark, she could no longer make out his face. But she heard the rustle of hay and suspected he had turned to face her, one hand propped beneath his head. He must have been no more than six inches away. She could feel the warmth from his skin, pressing through the cold air. From somewhere above came a steady drip— the sound of ice melting off a tree. She could hear his breathing, and her own. She still longed for him.

"I'm wide-awake, over here," she whispered. "Cold and wide-awake."

"Shall I tell you boring life stories to put you to sleep? Something from awkward, lonely childhood?"

"I'm afraid I take the gold medal there. . . . So how old are you anyway?" she asked.

"Thirty-two."

"That's not so old," she said, but the number did seem wildly far from her own: she was two months shy of her nineteenth birthday. She studied the number in her mind—*thirty-two, thirty-two*—as though it contained a secret about him.

"It's old enough to remember how different the world looked at your age. How different it all felt."

"You really are a stodgy old mentor."

Willard laughed. "I suppose I asked for that. Come on, let's try to get some sleep."

She heard his head thump gently back against the wooden loft. Juliet marveled that the night before, she'd thought she would never see Willard again, and here they were, together, in the darkness of the Italian countryside. If there was, as he'd said, only the war and the rest of the world, they had somehow found a secret space in between. As she closed her eyes and tried to sleep, she wondered if any part of her, or any part of him, had understood that the decision to find Barnaby and Reardon would give them *this*.

The next day, they followed a mountain path into a woodland of towering poplars. The jeep zigzagged for hours through the cathedral of trees, branches whipping the windows, clumps of snow padding against the roof. Here and there, squirrels scrambled through the forest. Out of sight, the greedy rattle of a woodpecker's beak sounded disturbingly like machine-gun fire.

From the forest they emerged into warmer air. The snow hardened to icy pellets, clattering against the jeep as they bumped along a muddy mule path. Beside them ran an old stone wall, uneven and crumbling, upon which sat the occasional helmet, an abandoned mule harness, the soaked remains of a vulture.

"Even the scavengers have been scavenged," said Juliet.

In Firenzuola, they entered a tavern brimming with Polish soldiers standing shoulder to shoulder, stomping their beaten black boots to the strum of a banjo. Shaking the water from their coats, Juliet and Willard wormed through the smoke-filled room; at the bar, an elderly woman with one milky eye monitored the soldiers and the focus of their attention: a girl, perhaps eleven years old, dressed in a khaki man's shirt belted with a frayed rope. Barefoot, with blackened toenails, she twirled and spun, a large Polish helmet on her head falling over her eyes each time she came to a stop. For a moment Juliet thought it was Liberata, and then she realized the girl's hair was too light, her eyes too dark. What was similar was the weariness in her face.

The barkeep announced, *"Mia pronipote."*

The girl was pulling up the hem of the khaki shirt, jutting out one bare leg, then the other. Her knees were calloused.

"Abbiamo solo grappa," the barkeep said to Juliet. *"Che cosa vuoi?"*

"Grappa," answered Juliet.

A whoop rose from the crowd as one of the soldiers swayed and collapsed into his compatriots. *"Józef! Józef!"* they called. Someone doused his face with grappa, and his wet eyes flashed open.

Willard studied the men's uniforms, their arm patches. "It's the Monte Cassino regiment," he whispered to Juliet. "They lived through the ninth circle of hell."

Juliet took a sip of her drink and handed the glass to Willard. He brought the glass to his mouth and surveyed the room.

Just then a group of American GIs burst into the tavern.

"The Polacks bothering you?" one of the Americans, having elbowed his way to the bar, asked the old woman.

"Abbiamo solo grappa. Che cosa vuoi?"

"What's she saying?" the soldier asked Juliet.

"She asked what you want to drink. I suggest you say grappa."

"Listen, these Polacks acting up? They better not lay a hand on that girl," said the soldier. "I've seen just about enough of that shit. I have a daughter back home, and it ain't right." The man's eyes started to tear and he gulped the grappa that had been poured. "It ain't right."

Willard took Juliet's hand. "Let's get going."

The man looked her slowly up and down. "Wait, *she's* not a child." He suddenly moved behind Juliet and grabbed her waist and pressed himself into her. "Hmmm. She can stay."

Willard moved to pry away the soldier's hands and the soldier released a canine snarl. He grabbed Willard's wrist, wrenching it hard, then abruptly let go and began to tear up again. He touched his cheeks in disbelief. "Oh, God, I'm sorry. It ain't right what I done."

Willard cradled his injured hand. "Private, there's no threat here. You're just here to have a nice time at a bar. Go find your friends."

"You're my friend." The soldier opened his arms to hug Willard. "Stay and drink with me, friend. Have my grappa. . . ."

Willard pulled Juliet through the crowd onto the street, in time to hear the sound of a shattered glass. The banjo was silenced and the angry voices of Poles and Americans tumbled into the street.

Willard shook his head as he looked, with apprehension, back at the bar.

"He was just an idiot drunk," said Juliet. "I'm okay. How's your wrist?"

Willard pulled her brusquely down the street. At the corner, he turned and faced her squarely.

"I want to tell you something," he said. "About Monte Cassino. About the Goumiers."

"The mountaineer Goumiers Lovelace always talks about?"

"Yes. The fearlesss Moroccan soldiers who managed to finally conquer the abbey. I never thought I'd tell you this because I didn't want to frighten you. But now I want you to be frightened. I need you to understand certain things about where we are and what's happening. The night after Cassino was taken, the Goumiers spilled into the villages beyond the monastery. They raped thousands of women and girls. We don't even have a full count. Some of the girls were as young as eleven. Any men who tried to protect their wives or daughters were killed. These were the victors; these were our allies. The men don't just go mute and tremble and turn guns on themselves when they go mad. They do worse. Our soldiers all know this happened, and it's only made the men more unsettled, more confused. Anyone can do anything. Do you understand?"

"Yes," she said.

"I'm not sure I did the right thing in letting you come."

"I never would have stayed behind."

As they stood in the gray afternoon looking intently at each other, two MPs briskly approached.

"Sergeant, Lieutenant, a moment. We're looking for two deserters."

The MPs produced two small photographs: Barnaby and Brother Reardon. Willard glanced at them with a distinct half-hearted interest, but Juliet couldn't help staring at the photograph of Barnaby: His hair was cropped, his face entirely unharmed. His eyes were radiant. He was a perfectly healthy and handsome young man.

"We'll keep a lookout," said Willard.

The MP looked Juliet and Willard up and down. "I assume your papers are in order?"

Willard pulled Juliet close. "We're on leave. Personal time." It felt so close to the truth, so momentarily real, that Juliet leaned her head against Willard's shoulder. As Willard reached for their passes, the MP gestured for him not to bother.

"Hell," he winked, "grab it while you can."

She wanted to remain standing like that but made herself pull away.

Outside town, they crossed a muddy field, and though the cold had turned the grass a pale and lifeless green, Juliet was certain it was the field where she had stayed with Beau and Brother Reardon a month earlier. The memory of holding Beau as his breath slipped away flooded her; somewhere nearby, Beau was buried. She might be his only friend to ever pass his grave.

Willard drove awkwardly, his wrist limp in his lap while he steered with his left hand.

A drizzle fell, the snow turned to slush, and the jeep splashed noisily along until she recognized the road where she and Brother Reardon had hitched a ride with Rufus. Within minutes they pulled up before the small church.

Inside, the Madonna, polished to a shine, gazed at Juliet from the altar. There were no cobwebs or dust, though a small spider scurried across the chipped blue folds of the statue's dress. Nearby, a tattered white sheet—a hospital sheet—lay over one of the beds of hay. Otherwise, the church was empty.

"I was right," said Juliet, dipping her hand in the full basin of holy water. "They were here."

"Past tense, Juliet."

She sat on one of the overturned pews. "I know."

"Any more ideas?"

"They've probably gone to another church."

"Unfortunately, this is Italy. There are over a thousand churches in Tuscany alone."

"Well, we have the jeep. They're on foot."

He sat beside her. "Forty-eight hours, Juliet."

But they had come this far; they couldn't turn back now. "We'll say we were robbed. We'll say we got a flat tire."

"They aren't idiots."

"One more day."

"They'll throw us in jail." Willard shook his head. "I do not want you in jail."

"I can handle jail." The pronouncement was dramatic, though in truth she had no idea what jail might be like. And she suspected Willard was actually worried about worse than jail. She recalled the Goumiers.

"You're like the boys fresh off the ships," he said. "You know there's destruction everywhere, but you don't think it can touch you."

"Touch me? It's already knocked me flat on the ground. It's why I'm sitting in a cold church in the middle of nowhere. Look, I don't think I'm invincible, I think I'm necessary. I know something bad could happen, but I'm willing to risk it. I think you are, too. Anyone can change bedpans or pass a bottle of brandy around the ward right now. We're the only ones who can help Barnaby and Brother Reardon. We knew, when we left, it might come to this, that it might take a little longer."

Willard inhaled deeply, as though breathing in everything she had said; he seemed, for the first time, humbled by her. He looked around at the church.

"Regulations give us thirty days," he said softly, "before we're considered AWOL. After that, we officially become deserters. "

"We won't need thirty days." She took his hand and urged him to stand.

CHAPTER 16

THEY BACKTRACKED, THEY sidetracked; they roamed the cold stone corners of abandoned churches; they stopped in dimly lit, smoke-filled taverns, asking patrons and barkeeps if they had seen men fitting Barnaby's and Reardon's descriptions.

In between the disappointed silences after each stop, they described to each other their experiences in Basic Training, their grueling transatlantic crossings to Europe. It seemed, somehow, that their lives had begun with the war, and they spoke little of anything else. They debated the skills of other doctors and nurses in the hospital. They ranted about the army supply system. To avoid speaking of what recriminations might await them, they spoke, restlessly, of anything else.

Every few minutes, Willard would interrupt what he was saying to warn, "Depress the clutch!"

"Dr. Willard, if you say it *calmly,* I won't freeze up."

"I've been driving since I was fourteen. I am an expert driving teacher."

Juliet grinned. "I didn't know they had cars back then."

Having bandaged Willard's wrist, Juliet had taken over the driving, and the jeep occasionally jolted and bucked as she struggled to shift gears.

By late afternoon, they had reached Pistoia, where Brother Reardon had once gone on a leave. The town was quiet and gray, and the low stone buildings crumbled into the street. From scraps of khaki army canvas and wool blankets a band of beggars and prostitutes had erected a camp in the piazza. A fire had been lit, fueled by splintered scraps of old furniture, and above it a large cast-iron pot sat on the massive front grille of a truck. Nearby, a one-armed man prowled with a large net. Beneath the arches of the gateway, he halted to watch the pigeons above. He dipped into his pocket and scattered bread crumbs. A dozen pigeons swooped down, and in one swift swing he netted four birds. The net erupted with a flutter of wings. With his good arm the man leaned into the net and, using his forearm and biceps like a vise, sealed it closed and scooped up the birds. He scampered off, his eyes darting nervously, the pole dragging along the wet cobblestones, *click click click* resounding through the square.

Children playing hopscotch shouted, *"Buona caccia oggi, Luigi!"* as he passed. In galoshes made from tire rubber, the children splashed through puddles.

"Chiesa?" Juliet asked the children.

A girl pointed to a narrow street off the square—*"Oratorio"*— then tossed a bullet casing onto one of the squares. The entire hopscotch board was strewn with bullet casings.

She and Willard walked to the small church. As they opened the wooden door, Juliet had the impression of a flurry of massive crows. But the crows were, in fact, long black robes from which the worn and worried faces of nuns peered out. Heads bowed in concentration, the nuns rushed about with trays and pitchers, cups and bedpans, moving in a constant stream, their feet invisible beneath their skirts. Around them, the beds were filled with children. A small nun, no more than five feet tall, eyed Willard's Red Cross armband and threw her head back: *"Dottori! Che fortuna! Abbiamo pregato!"* Grabbing Willard's elbow, she led them both toward a shivering boy.

"Il ragazzo non mangerà."

Juliet looked at the child, and Willard pulled back the sheet over his swollen belly. Gently, he pushed on the boy's right lower abdomen and the child burst into tears.

Juliet and Willard simultaneously pronounced: "Burst appendix."

"He needs surgery," said Juliet.

Willard raised his splinted wrist. "You'll have to do it."

"You're joking. I've never cut anyone open."

"You'd prefer to leave him?"

Intently eyeing their debate, the nun stuck her index finger in the air, whisked away, and returned with a tray of medical implements that looked as though they were meant to open nuts and shellfish.

"Let's at least get him somewhere private." Willard scooped the boy into his arms and Juliet followed with the instrument tray. The nun led them behind the altar to a small, dimly lit sacristy, where a row of dusty purple cassocks hung from ornate brass hooks. They set the boy on a bare table laid with a white sheet.

"What do we have in the way of antibiotics?"

"Sulfonamide," said Juliet.

"Good. But all we have for anesthesia is Pentothal. We'll have to make that work."

When the Pentothal had quieted the boy's sobs, Juliet washed her hands and the instruments in a basin of water the nun had brought.

Willard handed Juliet a scalpel. "McBurney's point. Two-thirds of the way from the navel to the anterior superior iliac spine."

"Here?"

"Make the cut."

Juliet took a deep breath and pressed the knife to the child's hardened abdomen. The skin parted in one smooth stroke, opening a crevasse of bright pink muscle. She had watched hundreds of incisions, but it was different making the cut herself. It seemed a violation of something sacred, exposing the body, revealing its fragile and hidden machinery. She stared for a moment, stunned by how thin the skin was, what a delicate organ held a person together.

"Keep going." Willard handed her the scissors, and she carefully snipped the muscle.

"Do we have anything like a Kelly clamp? I think . . . Dr. Willard, I think I made this incision too medial."

"It's fine."

She continued the retraction until the peritoneum was in sight.

"Retractors?"

"We only have one. Do you see the cecum?"

"The what?"

"The cecum. Between the ascending colon and the ileum. The fat part at the bottom. It's right there."

"I thought that was called the jejunum."

"Juliet, do you *see* it?"

"Yes, I see it. I just didn't know what it was called."

For the next twenty minutes, all Juliet saw was the open abdomen before her: she retracted skin and muscle, the colon, and finally the ruptured pouch dangling off the cecum. Her hands moved nervously, delicately, snipping at the narrowest part of the appendix, until she'd removed it and tied off the last bit. She doused the wound with saline, then sutured closed the incision.

"Please get me out of here," she said to Willard, setting her forehead against the wall.

In the main room, the metal beds were crowded side by side. Beneath gray moth-eaten blankets, children lay strangely still, staring upward. A pigeon flapped noisily about the frescoed ceiling, and all of the boys and girls seemed to be tracking its motions, but their eyes were lusterless, hauntingly blank. Juliet and Willard wandered the rows, checking the foreheads and pulses of those who seemed feverish, and then Juliet saw her, in the last bed in the row.

"Liberata!"

The girl wore what seemed to be a burlap sack, and her shoulders and elbows were sharp with malnutrition. Her hair had been cut short. She turned her head weakly. Before Juliet could ask,

Liberata shoved the blanket off her lap and pointed to her right knee, where her leg now ended: *"Bomba."*

Juliet felt sick. She fell to her knees beside the bed and tried not to weep. Willard had drawn up beside her and set his hand on her back.

"Where's Dante?" Juliet eventually asked.

Liberata tightened her lips and shook her head and also seemed to fight tears. *"No lo so."*

I don't know.

Liberata brought her fist to her chest, and in it Juliet saw a large brass crucifix, the thick chain spilling from her hand. Juliet recognized it immediately.

"When was Fratello Reardon here?"

"Yesterday."

"Did he say where they were going?"

Liberata shook her head.

Juliet felt a momentary happiness: Reardon and Barnaby had been there; they were close. But that also meant she and Willard needed to get moving. Juliet dug in her pack and laid a pile of ration bars in Liberata's lap.

"Mange," said Juliet. "You need to eat, for strength."

Liberata studied the bars and one by one stashed them under her blanket. *"Per Dante,"* she said. *"Mio fratello."*

"We have to go," Willard said softly. "If they're still on foot, we have a chance of catching up to them tonight or tomorrow. But if they get a ride, we're lost."

Juliet stood, and Liberata's eyes flashed with panic. Juliet stiffened as she braced for the entreaties: *Please, take me with you, I will work, I will clean the toilets. . . .* But Liberata merely lay back, fastening her face blankly on the ceiling, like the scores of other children.

She did not ask to be saved. That was somehow worse.

* * *

As the sun set, bats wheeled in the purple sky. The mountains on the horizon were a black smudge, and Juliet now felt very far from where they had set out, from the safety of the hospital encampment.

She drove slowly, and in a thoughtful silence they strained their eyes against the last wisps of dusk, looking for Barnaby and Brother Reardon along the road. When it finally grew too dark to see, they pulled over at a small schoolhouse.

The door opened onto a small, dark classroom, barely large enough for the sixteen wooden desks sitting in tidy rows. A sharpened pencil sat at the top of each, and on the massive teacher's desk at the front of the room lay a tidy pile of examination booklets. A textbook had been left open, a pencil in the spine. Musty air rose from the stone floor. On the side wall hung a giant faded map of Italy, on which an *X* marked the town of San Vito-Cerreto and beside that, the word *domestico*. On another wall hung a blackboard; in faint chalk marks the question lay in a neat script: *Che cosa vuoi fare da grande?* Beneath, in the jagged block letters of inexperienced hands, was a list: *Vigile del fuoco, medico, insegnante, soldato, Mussolini.*

What would you like to be when you grow up?

Juliet recalled how many fantasies of adulthood she once had, the elaborate list of dramatic feats she felt destined to accomplish. All those dreams now seemed decadent and ludicrous. She thought of the boy on the operating table, and of Liberata. What had *they* imagined for their futures? What would happen to them? Who would take care of them? And what had become of *her*—the girl who once rescued a wounded bird, who traveled thousands of miles to find out what happened to her brother— that she could now walk away from injured children? That's what adulthood was bringing her, she thought: pragmatism, heartlessness. Something within her was eroding, something she knew she would never restore.

She threw down her pack and sat on one of the desks and began tugging off her boots. "I've never been so tired," she said.

"Hey, you did wonderfully," said Willard.

"If he's alive in the morning, I suppose. But we'll never know."

He took her boots from her and set them tidily on the floor. "Listen, if we don't have any luck locating them tomorrow," he said, standing before her, "we have to start heading back to the hospital."

Juliet nodded. They wouldn't find them; she saw it clearly now. Just as she hadn't found Tuck. She'd been defeated in everything. "Absolutely fine."

At daybreak the air was clear and sharp. As they emerged from the schoolhouse, Juliet stared at the empty space where she had parked the jeep the night before. She circled the nearby oak tree as though the jeep might be hiding on the other side.

"How did we not hear the jeep starting in the middle of the night?" she asked.

Willard stood silently on the steps of the schoolhouse. He scanned the horizon and then seemed to work through some complicated thought.

"Dr. Willard?"

Willard was opening her pack, yanking out several articles of clothing and shoving them into his own pack. He lifted her pack, testing the weight.

"You'll need to carry this," he said. He handed her the pack and hefted his own onto his shoulders. His motions were rough, nervous. He began walking toward the road. "Come on, Juliet. We need to start moving. *Now.* This is bad."

She followed quickly. The morning frost had crispened the grass, and there was a biting chill in the air. Everything looked different without the jeep. The trees loomed shadowy and frightening.

The distances were vast. A small brook she hardly noticed when they drove over it the night before now had to be forded; they held each other's hands and sidestepped the black ice-glazed rocks, jabbing sticks into the slushy water for balance. It was the first time Juliet had hiked since Basic Training, the first time her legs had covered distances beyond the hospital encampment. Her back ached; she shifted her pack from one hip, then the other. Her toes grew cold, and she felt a blister forming at her heel. A pain at the front of her feet finally brought her to a halt after only thirty minutes.

"Dr. Willard, I forgot to cut my toenails."

Willard, who had been nearly silent during their hike, dug into his pack and tossed her a small scissors. "Do it now; it's not getting any warmer."

She sat on her pack and tugged off her boots. "Don't watch. This isn't pretty."

"Juliet. Don't be ridiculous."

"It's cold and I'm carrying thirty pounds on my back. Let me be ridiculous."

He threw his hands up and turned, and her fingers, already numb from the cold, fumbled to snip the nails. She carried the scissors back to his bag.

"We have to keep moving," he said, cinching his pack.

"I'm sorry about the jeep, Dr. Willard."

"It's not your fault."

"Then why are you so angry?"

"I'm not angry," he snapped. He turned his back and lifted his pack. He was afraid, she thought, as afraid as she was. He knew the darkest stories of the war, stories worse than the Goumiers, no doubt. They had never anticipated trying to make it back to the hospital without the jeep.

"Now, lift your pack and come on," he urged.

Without the noise of the jeep, the landscape was hauntingly silent. Juliet could hear each of her footsteps on the ground, and she thought about land mines hidden beneath the soil. She wondered, too, who had stolen the jeep; were thieves lurking across the countryside? Would their food and bags eventually be taken from them? Willard insisted on walking ahead—so that he might trigger a mine first, she supposed—but he turned around several times a minute to make sure she was still in sight. Juliet had trouble moving as quickly as he did, and every few minutes he halted, impatience evident on his face. All their playfulness had vanished. They had lost their vehicle, lost their chance to find Barnaby and Reardon, and if they somehow managed to return to the hospital, they would likely be punished.

Only when they crossed a stream where several old women were filling buckets with water did Juliet feel her spirits lift.

"We must be near something," she called.

"We should be getting close to Massa," he shouted back. "We can try our best there to see about getting a vehicle."

They pressed ahead into a field of felled oaks, zigzagging between wet stumps. They scrambled over the fallen trunks, stirring squirrels and mice from beneath logs. Against one stump, two bundled figures lay locked in an embrace.

Willard gestured for her to veer around the figures; Juliet followed his path, but midway she paused, turning curiously toward the motionless forms. Beneath the draping of blankets, she glimpsed the pants of a khaki uniform, and in a surge of irrational hope, the last she would ever permit herself, she shrugged off her pack and slowly walked toward the men. She moved quietly around the other side of the stump until she could see their faces. Frost clung to their unshaven cheeks; their eyes were closed, the lashes ice-crusted. They were huddled together, arms linked, facing the stump, as though to avoid being seen. Juliet couldn't believe it; it was *them*.

"Dr. Willard," she yelled, taking their pulses. "They're alive."

It took four hours for Juliet and Willard to carry the men,

one by one, back to the schoolhouse. It was the only shelter they knew of. There they shoved aside the desks and laid each man on the stone floor. Juliet draped them with blankets and her own jacket.

"Jesus, they're pure blue," she said, kneading their limbs. "They need a fire and food."

Willard lit their stove to heat a bowl of water, and when it was warm, Juliet peeled off their gloves and dipped their fingers in. When some color had returned to their faces, she did the same with their toes. Tugging off Brother Reardon's boots, Juliet saw that his left ankle was swollen.

"We'll need a lot more than the rations we have," said Willard. He set his hand on her back. "I'm going into town."

Juliet looked up in alarm.

"What town?"

"I'm fairly certain we were almost to Massa before. If I backtrack, I think I can be there and back by sundown. Sooner if I can find us a vehicle there."

She didn't know what to say. He was right, and yet she dreaded the thought of him wandering into the wilderness alone. Of being left alone. They were not supposed to separate; that was the rule. What protection could Barnaby and Reardon offer her?

"What if you're not back by sundown?"

"I'll be back. You're safer here than out there with me."

She knew the men needed food; she knew their options were limited. And she saw in his face that he was not particularly eager to go.

"Come back as fast as humanly possible," she pleaded.

"Lock the door."

The hours passed in a painful slowness. Brother Reardon and Barnaby were still sleeping, and only the sounds of their snores kept Juliet company. She paced the small classroom, collected all the pencils from the desk, snapped them in two, and used them to feed the fire. Twice, she opened the door a crack and stared out at the darkening landscape. The trees, stripped bare of their leaves, stood oil black against the gray sky. But it wasn't until she began to hear the sounds of nightfall—the sharpening winds, the low, faint hooting of owls—that a weak knock finally sounded on the door. Willard waddled in, cradling eggs in his jacket; in the crook of his arm was a wine bottle. She wanted to berate him but saw exhaustion in his face. His cheeks were red from the cold. "I'm so sorry," he huffed.

A breath of raw air had come in with him, and she hurriedly closed the door. Without looking him in the eye, Juliet took the eggs, trying to mask her anxiety and anger. "Brother Reardon sprained his ankle," she said, matter-of-factly.

She cracked an egg, and with her forefinger she beat it in a cup. She added water from her canteen, then held the cup to each man's mouth, coaxing him to swallow.

"There, that'll put color back in their faces."

She laid Barnaby's head in her lap and carefully peeled his eye patch away from his tangle of blisters and facial hair. The patch was fraying at the edges; she tried not to tear the skin beneath, but one section pulled at a patch of frostbite and he winced.

"Ouch." His dark brown eye was staring directly at her.

"Dr. Willard," she whispered.

Willard crouched beside her, and Barnaby turned to look at him, somewhat sleepily.

"Hey there, Doc."

"Hi, Christopher. How are you feeling?"

He hugged himself and rubbed his shoulders. "Fucking *cold*."

Willard laughed. "Me too. Do you know where you are?"

Barnaby looked around and squinted at the chalkboard. "This looks like a schoolhouse." He looked back at Willard. "We're not at the hospital anymore?"

"We left the hospital," said Willard. "It wasn't safe there."

Barnaby slowly nodded, taking in the breadth of danger that might be lurking.

"They wanted to lock me up," he said.

"Yes," said Willard.

"We made a run for it?"

"So to speak."

"I owe you," he said.

Juliet, unable to contain herself, pressed her head to Barnaby's chest. The world seemed filled with glorious possibility.

By midnight, Brother Reardon had finally awakened and explained, in a mild delirium of fever and dehydration, where they had been since leaving the hospital. Willard listened intently, crouching over the stove, boiling an egg in a crackling C ration tin. Juliet spooned steaming food into Reardon's slack mouth, his face white and glossy with fever.

When the men had both fallen back asleep, Willard carried a cup across the dark classroom to Juliet. "I made some coffee," he said softly.

She set it down to cool and leaned back against the wall. Willard sat beside her, and they were silent for a long while.

"No luck finding a vehicle in town?" she asked.

"I couldn't even try. The MPs were there."

"Did they see you?"

"I don't think so."

"How are we going to get them to Signora Gaspaldi's?"

"I don't know," he said, and her disappointment in his answer must have shown. He brushed off his knees and stood. He began pulling a hospital sheet from his bag. "We need to black out the windows. With Brother Reardon's ankle, we're definitely stuck here for at least a few more days." Willard hung the sheet over the window, but it was sheer and torn in spots; they could both see it would hardly help. He surveyed the room, rifling through the drawers of the teacher's desk. "Plenty of pencils and paper, though. Rulers. Stencils. An abacus." He took one of the rulers and said, "Well, we can use the big map."

With the ruler's edge, he pried out the nails along the map's right side and peeled back the corner. He yanked the map from the wall, and a wooden door stared at them.

Cobwebbed desks and chairs cluttered the cold, dark cellar. Against one wall stood a supply shelf stacked with boxes of chalk and pencils, a pile of blank writing tablets, and shiny tins of assorted treats for children: cookies, peppermints, caramels, candied chestnuts. Two marionettes—one boy and one girl—dangled limply together from a hook in the ceiling.

As rain fell on the schoolhouse above, Juliet and the men made a camp in the darkness, drinking wine and feasting on the sweets. They rubbed olive oil into their blistered feet, bandaged their toes, mended their socks and gloves.

The dirt floor held the chill of winter, and for warmth Juliet stuffed crumpled pages from the writing tablets inside all of their clothing. They all lazed around, swollen and bloated. When any of them moved, it made a racket.

By candlelight, they read aloud to one another from Italian children's books. They played tic-tac-toe and told stories of their former lives. *Former* lives—it was how they spoke of things back home, with no mention of ever returning there, as though it were behind them. They had disappeared, thought Juliet, absconded from danger, from the war, from illness and injury, and from the world itself. In the cellar she felt safe; it provided the same thick, cavernous comfort she'd felt as a child pulling blankets over her head.

Willard once again related the tale of how he'd come to work for the army, adding a few new details, which Juliet savored: Willard's father, too, had been a psychiatrist, and he had a younger brother who was a concert pianist.

Brother Reardon had grown up in Pittsburgh, raised chiefly by his aunt, Beth, and had a wily boyhood of thieving and vandalism before Beth stayed up all night with him once, insisting that together they smash every car window, drain every fire hydrant, steal every purse or parcel in sight, carry off every signpost not nailed to the ground—and then the next morning she dragged him to a soup kitchen where they watched men line up for bread; then she took him to an orphanage. "We could stay and help here," she said, "or go back to running around and breaking things. Shall we ask the children what they think?" Brother Reardon said his aunt chased the devil out of him that day and set him on the path to serving God.

When it came Juliet's turn to speak, she found herself describing Charlesport, the waterfront and the old houses, her father and Pearl. She shared the story of her science-fair entries, trying her best to distance herself from the awkward girl she had once been. "Oh, there, there, we give Juliet the blue ribbon!" all the men said. She spoke of Tuck—not about the telegram or her quest for him, but about their childhood together, their lemonade stands and yard forts, the rescue of Cher Ami. She proudly described the day when, at fourteen, Tuck saved a woman and her baby from a sinking car.

Though living in a cold half darkness, Juliet thought she might never want to leave. She loved these men; she trusted these men. And they were forever bound, she knew, by the risks they'd all taken to save Barnaby's life.

Though Barnaby had recovered from his semicoma, he was oddly sparing with his words. He sipped at the wine and nibbled chestnuts, nodding along as the others told stories; he listened intently but seemed reluctant to speak about himself. It was possible, Juliet thought, that Barnaby had never been much of a talker; but she also wondered if, after what he'd been through with his squad, he'd simply grown suspicious of the world. She recalled what Munson had told her. If his own squad mates had strung him up, whom could he trust?

Barnaby sat quietly in the corner and made drawings of Juliet, Willard, and Brother Reardon. Of the marionettes that hung from the ceiling. It was unclear what he understood of the court-martial, if he knew about the death sentence. If he had any idea of the dangers that lay ahead—for all of them—if they were caught, he gave no indication.

But Willard had been counting the days, eager to get under way to Signora Gaspaldi's. On the sixth morning, when Juliet hiked to the stream to fill their canteens, a cloudless sky hung overhead. A heron swooped over the water; white egrets stood basking in the winter sun. When she returned to the schoolhouse, Willard was upstairs, studying the large map of Italy.

"The sky is clear," he said.

"I saw," she said. She noticed that his pack was now leaning by the door. "You think the MPs have moved on?"

"They had almost a week to scour this area. That said, I wouldn't be surprised if we've been added to their round-up list. If Brilling somehow heard that I didn't come back from my leave, he'll have pieced it together."

"So how do we get to Signora Gaspaldi's?"

"On foot. We need to stay off the roads anyway."

"On foot," Juliet repeated flatly, trying hard to hide her dismay. Even after days of rest, the idea of walking such a vast distance intimidated her.

"Come here and look," said Willard. He drew a line on the map, his pen gliding across the mountains. "We break it into two days, morning and afternoon increments. We rest when we need to. You'll be fine. Trust me."

"I don't have much of a choice, I suppose."

He shook his head and put his hand on her shoulder. "We used up all our choices a week ago," he said.

They slowly packed their belongings and boiled the last of the eggs. Willard scoured the nearby woods for two thick branches, which he topped with scraps of the canvas map and a pair of thick socks and gave to Brother Reardon as crutches.

As they all left the schoolhouse, Willard patted the closed door as though in good-bye: they were all sad to leave it. They had at least two days of heavy walking ahead. They set out at first along the dirt road, but soon cut toward the woods so they could follow the line of the road but were hidden from vehicles.

The sun was bright and the air was clear, and they walked together like an exploring party, pausing at times to take in their surroundings, enjoying the sun's warmth on their faces, the flutter and rustle of wind through the trees.

"We have the most beautiful mountains where I'm from," said Barnaby, surprising them all. "The Green Mountains."

"In Vermont?" asked Juliet.

"I'd like to get back there."

They were all silent a moment. A peregrine falcon fluttered loose from a tree and squawked toward the mountains.

"Well, I've seen enough mountains this past month to last a lifetime," said Juliet. "I miss the ocean."

"Tuck missed the ocean, too."

It was the first time Barnaby had voluntarily mentioned Tuck outside of the Pentothal sessions; he had listened to Juliet speak about him but said nothing, as though she were discussing a person he had never met.

"What else did he tell you?" she asked.

"That last night was the most we talked. But it was meaning-ful. He told a lot of football stories. It was like he thought it was a metaphor for life. I told him that, and he said no, it *was* life. He told some stories about your father. He talked about a place he and you used to go to hide out."

"Raven Point?"

"Maybe. Maybe Raven Point."

Juliet heard a rumble in the distance and stopped. Willard and Brother Reardon were looking south, toward the road. A camou-flaged jeep was bisecting the field; something seemed to be sticking straight up from it, and then Juliet saw it was a man perched in the back, swinging left and right, holding binoculars.

They hit the ground and shimmied out of their packs. Juliet kept her face down and listened as the jeep grew louder. The ground was cold, and she looked at Barnaby. She saw fear in his face, the same fear she'd seen all those nights he was describing for Willard what had happened at the front. And yet he managed to reach out and clasp her hand.

The sound of the engine faded, but it was a while before any of them moved.

When finally they stood and brushed themselves off, the air had cooled, and a purple light overtook the sky. They moved, without discussion, even farther from the road into the tall woods. Brother Reardon moved slowly, navigating awkwardly on his crutches over rocks and felled trees. Every few feet Barnaby plucked a stick from the ground and snapped it in two. Gloom hung over them. They trudged along, Willard in the lead, frequently pulling from his jacket the portion of the map of Italy he had cut and folded, look-ing at the setting sun in an attempt to reckon their direction. At the sudden dash of squirrels before her, Juliet's heart raced. She was grateful when, before full darkness had descended, Willard called out, "Look!" from ahead, pointing to a fissure in the base of the mountain.

"I think it's a cave," he said.

Carts and wheelbarrows cluttered the entrance; massive drills and hammers, powdered with dust, lay idle on the floor. It was an abandoned quarry. They removed their packs and settled between jagged walls of white marble.

Barnaby, however, remained standing, his pack piled high on his back. Slowly, he looked at each of them. "This is wrong," he said. "I don't need to get back to Vermont. I should surrender."

Juliet and Willard and Reardon glanced at one another, unsure of how much they should say, how much Barnaby understood of what his surrender would mean. Did he think it meant only prison?

"Absolutely not," said Willard, rising to remove Barnaby's pack.

But Barnaby backed away. "Doc, you're all limping around in the snow because of me, when you should be back at the hospital, helping the other soldiers."

"We're going to bring you somewhere safe," said Willard, exhaustion in his voice. "You and Brother Reardon can stay there for a while. We should be there within a day. Then Nurse Dufresne and I will go back to helping other soldiers."

"Prison can't be worse than being up at the front."

"You're not going to prison," Willard answered—too sharply, because Juliet could see a shadow of understanding cross Barnaby's face.

"I see," said Barnaby.

"Let's all get some rest, Christopher." Willard gently took his elbow. "Doctor's orders."

They made a small fire and took shelter from the cold, but a slight wind occasionally stirred the white dust from the floor, making them sneeze.

Juliet slept fitfully, wondering if the MPs would retrace their tracks the next day. The ground was cold and hard, and each time she drifted off, she awoke to the icy chill of marble against some part of her body. She thought she heard footsteps and opened her eyes; she saw the vague outlines of two figures and sat up, thinking Barnaby and Brother Reardon were trying to leave.

Then came Willard's voice, an anxious whisper: "Juliet, stay still."

As her eyes adjusted to the darkness, they caught the glint and glimmer of long objects.

"*Da sind noch drei. Es sind Amerikaner,*" someone said. "*Und es ist eine junge Frau.*"

A flashlight suddenly lit Willard's face; he was standing, and on either side a rifle nestled into his temples. Sweat glazed his forehead.

"*Aufstehen. Alle aufstehen,*" one of the Germans huffed.

"We all have to stand," Willard said, his voice flat.

Juliet slowly pulled back her blanket and moved beside Willard. On the other side of the quarry, Barnaby and Brother Reardon raised their hands.

The German shined his flashlight over Willard, stopping at his Red Cross armband.

"*Doktor?*"

The second German walked to Barnaby and Brother Reardon, examining the first's head bandages, the latter's silver lapel crosses. "*Geistliche und Patienten,*" he called. He signaled for Barnaby to sit on a wheelbarrow and gestured Brother Reardon toward Juliet and Willard. The Germans now stood side by side, in military stance, assaying their prisoners.

"*Ich bin Katholisch. Ich kann keinen Geistlichen töten.*"

Willard responded angrily: "*Es ist gegen den Willen Gottes, irgendeinen von uns zu töten. Wir sind alle Zivilisten, und wir sind unbewaffnet. Wir sind keine Bedrohung für Sie,*" he continued, though his voice now rattled with fear. "*Wir sind nicht mehr mit der Armee. Wir sind alle Deserteure.*"

"*Das sind wir auch, schätze ich,*" said the first German, laughing, "*aber wir sind immer noch Feinde.*"

"What's going on?" Barnaby asked.

Juliet watched the German who was speaking with Willard; he was a lanky man, almost equal to Willard in height, whose expression wavered between amusement and anger.

"*Keiner von uns ist eine Bedrohung für Sie. Der Mann hat eine Gehirnverletzung,*" Willard insisted. "*Ich bin sein Arzt, und sie sein Krankenschwester.*"

At this, the second German looked Juliet up and down, a strange smile curling his mouth.

"What's going on?' Barnaby asked again. He gripped the sides of his wheelbarrow. "I said, what's going on?"

"*Ruhe!*" The first German fired at the ceiling, releasing a blizzard of white dust.

Juliet watched as he reloaded his gun; she heard the click of the long chamber. He sneezed and wiped dust from his eyes. The other German tightened his grip on his rifle, aiming it firmly at Juliet's chest, and then he stepped toward her and grabbed her waist, letting the rifle tilt away, pulling her into him.

She heard an explosion, a shock of metal. She fell back. She heard fabric tear, bones crack; there was a snap of joints. Her own, she thought, until she heard a body thump to the floor beside her.

The German who had grabbed her lay facedown, his back a tangle of innards. Behind him sat Barnaby in the wheelbarrow, a pistol in his lap, smoke rising from the chamber. The other German lay on the floor, his head crookedly upturned, a pool of blood gathering beside him. His chest was motionless. Willard stood against the wall, his eyes fixed on a bloody hammer in his hand.

Juliet touched her chest, her arms, her stomach. She patted her face, her neck.

"You're okay," said Willard.

Brother Reardon moved slowly to Barnaby. "Why don't you give me that, Christopher."

"I'm no coward," Barnaby said angrily.

"Not in the least," said Brother Reardon.

Juliet was still touching her body, confused. She couldn't stop looking at the dead Germans. She gulped the cold, dusty air. Her chest rose and fell so forcefully, she thought it might burst through her shirt.

"Where did the pistol come from?" Willard asked.

The quarry was silent.

"From me," said Reardon.

"Where did *you* get it?" Willard asked.

"Liberata," he answered calmly. "In Pistoia. She insisted we take it. All the children carry them now."

They dragged the bodies to the corner, blood streaking the marble floor. White dust settled on the corpses, their faces ghostly, dust mixing with blood to form congealed pink paste.

God, thought Juliet, were they that close to the German lines? Or were there dozens, hundreds, roaming the Italian countryside, just as they were?

"We better undress them," said Willard. "Whoever comes across them, we'll be safer if no one knows who they are. We don't need a revenge party coming after us."

Juliet began to tug off their shirts, her hands shaking. She'd seen hundreds of corpses, but she kept expecting these would come back to life, grab her ankles, and drag her to the floor. She tried to stand as far away as possible as she pulled off the pants; from the pocket a dozen teeth clattered onto the marble floor, teeth of all sizes with gold fillings.

"Are those *human* teeth?" she asked.

"Reardon and I will take care of this," said Willard, pulling her back.

Willard plucked the teeth up one by one and shoved them back into the dead man's pocket. He unlaced and removed the muddy boots, peeled off the socks, and shook free the men's pants. He took off their identity tags. He dropped the clothing in the center of the quarry.

"They're no more German than the day they were born," said Reardon, making the sign of the cross over each body. He handed Willard the pistol, and Willard checked the safety and tucked it into the back of his pants.

Juliet turned to Barnaby, seated quietly on the wheelbarrow. "Thank you," she said.

He nodded and began packing his bag, barely looking at her. "It's what Tuck would have wanted me to do."

They headed northeast, trudging through frosted deadfall. The ground was frozen, and they held tightly to tree trunks and branches as they tested their footing on ice-crusted rocks. Juliet's gloves snagged on bark, and within hours wool fringed her fingers.

They walked in single file, in absolute silence, afraid their voices would reveal them, afraid they wouldn't hear approaching footsteps.

The image of the gun and the German kept returning to Juliet, and each time a wave of nausea forced her to stop in her tracks. For the first time she felt how quickly, how easily, she could die; a mere branch, snapping beneath the weight of snow, could take her life. The air itself, cold and silvery, seemed filled with peril. In all the tears she'd shed for Tuck and Beau and the hundreds of men who had died beside her, she had never before felt it had anything to do with her. She'd felt pity, not fear. But now she wondered: Was the darkness she saw when looking at them the shadow of her own death? She wanted to live; she knew that now in a way she had never before known. She would stay alive, yes, for no cause or reason, for no one but herself. She felt herself weighing, measuring, considering. She looked around at her friends. She cared for thes men but she did not think she would be willing to die for them. She was not like Tuck. She saw it sharply: she was kind and caring, but if the horrid moment ever came, she would save herself. It was cowardice, the most natural and primal cowardice, and she could speak of it to no one. Self-preservation was the loneliest of instincts.

By afternoon, they came upon tidy piles of white stones, the jagged remains of a long wall. Farther on, a vast basin, what might have once been a bath, yawned from the ground. Several smaller buildings looked more than a thousand years old. Cypress trees grew between what had once been houses, thick roots upheaving the foundations.

They sat on the edge of an old cistern and ate cold K rations and candied chestnuts. As the food melted on Juliet's tongue, she looked around at the ice-capped Apennines: How many peaks had they crossed these past few days? How many other people were wandering the mountains now, bands of people trying to make their way to safety? And how many thousands had walked this cold, hard ground before them? During the Great War, or the Conquest of Rome, surely friends and families and neighbors had wandered this path, sat on this wall. Here they were, creatures of yet another brutal epoch. Even if they survived all of this, she knew history would swallow them, silently, as it did everyone.

Quietly, solemnly, they packed up the scant remains of their food and continued walking. As night fell, stars piercing the black sky, they came upon a monastery. Willard shined his flashlight on a scrap of his map. "I know where we are."

Inside, the air was damp and mildewy. Willard flicked open his lighter, and a domed, frescoed ceiling came to life, cracks spidering from the center. The place had been ransacked—altars stripped bare, pews splintered, tapestries torn from the walls, stained glass splintered on the floor. After making a quick inspection to ensure they were alone, they hung blankets over the winows. The floor was crusted with bird droppings; abandoned nests clung to the eaves.

They shook off their packs and pulled out their rations.

Their food wouldn't last more than another day, Juliet estimated.

She assembled the stove and poured what was left of their kerosene. She struck a match, and a small blue flame leapt to life. Huddling close to the stove, they opened their cans.

It was a quiet, somber meal, and when it ended, Willard wandered up a narrow flight of stairs.

"With one eye in a dark cave," Barnaby whispered, gazing up at the fresco, "I'm still a good shot."

"The army's loss," said Juliet.

"The army can go to hell." He lay back, his arms crossed behind his head, and closed his eye.

As Reardon began arranging his bedroll, Juliet moved cautiously up the darkened stone staircase.

"Dr. Willard?"

At the top of the stairs she found him seated by a large bell that was green with oxidation. The rope had been cut, and bullet casings littered the floor. She settled beside him, facing the mountains. A stunningly bright moon presided over the sky.

"I'm scared," she said. "Out of my wits."

He put his arm around her. "I know."

"How on earth are we going to find the hospital? It could be encamped miles from where we left it."

"Let's get them to Signora Gaspaldi's first; after that, I'll get us to the hospital."

"You didn't say 'I promise.'"

He was silent. "I promise. But in all likelihood, Juliet, I'll be relieved of my duties after this."

"Not if we lie."

"Well, I'm not quite sure I'm up to the task of sending soldiers back to the front anyway."

He picked up a bullet casing and studied it, and she saw that he was in fact studying his trembling hand. He extended his fingers so she could see, then threw the casing into the night.

"I was never soldier material."

"No one is. Who the hell would want to be?"

"I was built for clinics and tents. For listening." He shook his head, as though disgusted with himself. "Not like your soldier in the cave."

It was the first Willard had mentioned of what she told him on their way back from Florence.

"He was scared, too, for what it's worth."

"Will you see him again?"

She could not bring herself to say that he'd died. "No, I don't think I'll see him again."

Willard nodded slowly. "Someday, Juliet, find yourself a man who hasn't been here, hasn't seen all of this. It makes us all madmen. Cowards and madmen. It's only the degree that varies."

"Even Barnaby's not mad anymore. *You* brought him back," she said. "He's speaking, he's thinking clearly. And he's safe. You're the one who *fixes* all of this, all of us."

He stood. "We should go make sure they're settled in okay."

"I think you're very brave," she said.

He began descending the stairway, and she saw the pistol bulge at the back of his pants. He looked back. "Thank you."

CHAPTER 17

JULIET RECOGNIZED THE street almost immediately, except that where children had once scampered and reached for her pockets, the wet, gray cobblestones stood in eerie silence. Shards of broken glass flashed from the gutters, and the smell of urine clung thickly to the wintry air. From the darkness of an alleyway, a cat mewled in fright.

The walk had taken them almost an entire day, and they moved slowly along the street, holding back at the last minute as they approached the house, fearing that after all this time, after the distance they had traveled, there might be no one inside. The front window had been barricaded with planks, and through the narrow blade of an opening no light could be seen.

Brother Reardon stepped forward to knock.

Juliet set down her pack and massaged her aching shoulders, bracing for a long wait, but almost immediately Signora Gaspaldi's face emerged from behind the door. Once again a look of distress overtook her, and Juliet had to assure her they had not brought bad news about Alfonso.

Relieved, Signora Gaspaldi looked them over; it was clear that the sight of all four of them gave her pause. She looked down both ends of the street and, after staring thoughtfully into the cobblestones for quite some time, gestured them inside.

The house was cold and dark. Signora Gaspaldi lit a candle and set it on the table amid a globular sea of hardened white wax. The light wavered gently across the room, and Juliet could see it was distinctly barer than when they last visited. She guessed that a good deal of furniture had been bartered for food. Shelves were missing from the walls, and there was only one stool left at the table; Senora Gaspaldi insisted that Juliet take it.

Juliet's legs tingled and slackened as all of her weight, finally, came off her feet. The sweat that had coated her back all day had begun drying, and she felt a chill down her spine. She explained as best she could, in her rudimentary Italian, what had happened; she included Captain Brilling's harassment of Barnaby; she mentioned the horrid episode of Barnaby almost eating the eyeball; she emphasized any detail that might persuade and soften Signora Gaspaldi. It was the first time Juliet had tried to make sense of the entire story, and what she settled upon, as she concluded her recounting, was that Barnaby had suffered battle fatigue worse than other men, in part because he had been badgered and hounded by members of his own squad. She said quietly that Barnaby was different—different in a way that some other men did not like. She did not want to harp on this, but she believed that a woman, and a mother, might be sympathetic to such a fact. Finally, she explained that Alfonso had suggested they bring the fugitives to her; if nothing else, *this* would compel Signora Gaspaldi to offer them shelter.

Signora Gaspaldi, who had listened intently to each part of the tale, nodded and glanced intermittently at Barnaby. She stood, holding the edge of the table, and with the nail of her thumb began to scrape at the hardened candle wax. Apprehension showed in her expression, and she looked to each of them, her eyes finally settling on Brother Reardon, on the silver crosses pinned to his lapels. She closed her eyes, her lips working through some silent thought, then asked if the chaplain would also need to stay in the house.

"Yes," said Juliet. "He's a fugitive now as well."

Signora Gaspaldi nodded resolutely, and she crossed the room with open arms and drew both men close. She whispered a prayer, and Juliet suspected that after everything she had said, Signora

Gaspaldi was simply a woman of God and could not refuse a man of the cloth.

Signora Gaspaldi disappeared into the kitchen and boiled water and served pieces of dry bread and cups of acorn coffee; she seemed happy for the company. Peppino was nowhere in sight, but Juliet did not have the strength to ask where he was. Perhaps the absence of a man in the house made the idea of harboring two men comforting. Once again Signora Gaspaldi took out the photo album and passed around the photos of her two sons; when the coffee cups had been emptied, she carried the candle upstairs and led all four into Alfonso's room.

Juliet looked around the room where, months earlier, she and Willard had slept. She looked at the pillow where she had buried her tears, and it seemed almost silly now, how upset she had been.

Barnaby and Reardon set down their bags and nodded fervently at Signora Gaspaldi.

"Grazie," they said, *"mille grazie."*

Barnaby studied the room; he touched the walls and then ran his hand along the edge of the bed, as though to make sure it was all real. He took a slow, deep, shuddering breath and walked to the corner, away from the rest of them.

Willard drew up behind him and set a hand on his shoulder.

"We can't stay, Christopher. Nurse Dufresne and I have to get back to the hospital. But I want you to rest, to relax, and to know that you're safe here. You're going to be fine. Signora Gaspaldi will look after you. Brother Reardon will look after you."

Barnaby cleared his throat and turned to face Willard. His eye was flecked red with emotion.

"I can't thank you enough, Doc."

"It's my job," said Willard.

Barnaby broke into a soft laugh. "Shitty job."

"Some days, yes. Not today."

They shook hands for several moments, and then Willard turned to Juliet. "I want you to explain to Signora Gaspaldi that this is to help pay for their food, whatever she needs. . . ."

Digging into his pocket, Willard extracted a ring—a gold wedding band—and set it in Signora Gaspaldi's hand. Juliet felt momentarily unsettled as the old jealousy, like a phantom limb, stirred and subsided. Yes, he was married; yes, she loved him. These were two immovable truths, and she understood now that they could coexist. They had coexisted all along. Nothing had been taken from her but a desire, a dream, and so many of those had been lost already, she imagined it a necessary shedding. Perhaps, she thought, what she really wanted was to have what Willard had: someone whose love she carried—a secret in her pocket, a glinting promise on her finger—someone for whom she would forsake all others, someone she would long to get home to. Someday, surely, the war would end, and they would all return to everything else. But who would be waiting for her?

Signora Gaspaldi kissed the ring and closed her hand tightly around it.

"*Sì, sì, mille grazie.*"

Willard turned to Juliet. "Come on, it's time to say good-bye."

Juliet walked to the corner where Barnaby stood and felt her body tense. Having waited so long to ask one question, she knew if she didn't ask now, she might never again have the opportunity. She didn't want a lifetime of shadowy guesses, bleak hypotheses.

"Christopher, do you think," she quietly began, "that there's any chance Tuck may be alive somewhere? That he was taken prisoner or went into hiding?"

Barnaby clenched his mouth; it was the pained expression she must have had when Beau asked her to tell him he was dying. He spoke slowly, uncomfortably. "You knew him years longer than I did, of course."

"But you knew him as a soldier. You knew him here."

"Well . . . I'd say there are men that would raise the white flag at a rustle in the trees." He paused. "But not Tuck. He wasn't one to be taken alive. And he wasn't one to desert or give up. I imagine he went down fighting. That's the best I can say." He took her hand. "It eats at me, too, the not knowing."

"Do you think he lost his mind?"

Barnaby shifted his weight from one foot to the other, looking down at the floor. "I think he lost his heart."

Somehow what he said didn't make Juliet sad. It was what she had been guessing for so long, the story her mind had finally settled on; it gave her some relief to hear Barnaby's confirmation, even if it was only a hypothesis. She needed something, anything, to help close the door to that cold, dark room of her imagination.

"When this is all over," she said, "after you see the mountains, come to Charlesport. See Tuck's house."

He gave her a long, strong hug—one that reminded her of Tuck's good-bye. She knew then that she would never see Barnaby again. "I'll bring Tina and the baby and we'll all raise a glass to him."

"Of course." Juliet stepped away, wiping her eyes.

Brother Reardon came toward her, his arms open. "You'll be in my prayers every night for the rest of my life," he said.

"I'm not sure if you made me believe in God, but you made me believe in people."

He smiled. "Same thing."

Juliet looked to Willard, and he looked at his watch and gestured apologetically toward the door. She smiled once more at her friends, and together she and Willard descended the darkened stairs.

$$\left[\text{ CHAPTER 18 } \right]$$

THEY HITCHED A ride on a mule-drawn wagon almost seventy miles, close to the base of the mountains, and then, with the last of their ration tins, they bartered for two bicycles. They had unloaded most of the weight from their packs and put on as much of their clothing as possible. They bicycled side by side, but against the wind they were unable to say much. She wasn't sure, in fact, what there was to say. They had lived the entirety of the past week together.

The sun was bright, the sky clear, and the landscape glittered with frost. For the first time in months, Juliet felt giddy. And she could see in Willard's face a levity she had not before seen. They had done it; they had gotten Barnaby to safety. They had done one absolute good. Whatever retribution they faced at the hospital would be worth it.

As she rode along, she thought about Barnaby, about the mysterious force of an individual. Against all odds, one quiet and frightened man had survived. They had given him the short straws and sent him forward for the most dangerous missions, and he had lived; he had fired a bullet into his own head and he had lived. Barnaby lived. There was some meaning in it, there had to be, but she could not yet fathom it. Why *him*? Why not Tuck; why not Beau? Why not the thousands of others? What meaning was there in his survival—or in hers, for that matter? Was there an obligation that came with living? With each adversity you suffered, with each disappointment, did you have to recognize that someone else hadn't even had the chance?

They cycled for most of the day until, at the base of the mountains, they waved down a supply truck. It was Rufus. But he did not recognize Juliet, no matter how many times she explained that she had ridden with him weeks earlier.

Since its last encampment, the hospital hadn't moved. As the truck pulled up to the old stone hotel, and Juliet looked at the large quiet porch and the tidy rows of green tents in the snow, she had the strange feeling that the past week—the days in the schoolhouse cellar, the night in the monastery, the shooting in the quarry—had all been a dream.

As they stepped down from the supply truck, Major Decker emerged from the stone building, moving briskly toward them through the snow.

Willard set their bags on the ground and began to recite what they had rehearsed the night before: "Major Decker, I apologize for our delay. Our jeep was stolen, and we ran into Germans—"

Major Decker waved away the excuses. "I don't know what you're talking about. You've been here all week. Everyone knows you've been here all week. Captain Brilling knows you've been here all week. Are we clear?"

"Yes."

"Did you make good use of your time here this past week? Did you accomplish the goals you set for yourself?"

"Yes."

Major Decker grinned; it was the happiest Juliet had ever seen him. "Excellent. Now go get yourselves some lunch."

They ate heartily in the quiet mess hall: cabbage soup with salted beef. They drank grapefruit juice. They devoured chocolate chip cookies and smiled at each other and shoved extras in their pockets. As they carried their bags outside and stood on the porch, she felt an urge to hug Willard—their arduous journey, their trial, was over. Together they had made it. But she feared if she moved close to him, she would once again want to kiss him. Instead, she carried her bag alone through the snow.

"I'll see you later," she called back.

In the green light of her tent, Juliet laid down her things and peeled off the damp, thick layers she'd worn for the bike ride. She splashed water on her face and refastened her braids. She looked around at the canvas walls and her bedroll and wondered how many more months or years she would live like this. *This* had become home. There seemed nothing else beyond it, but she no longer minded.

Even as she entered the Recovery Tent, the giddiness from the bike ride still bubbled within her. There had been a pause in the fighting at the front, and most of the beds were empty. Juliet grabbed a pitcher of water and began to make her way along the tent. Bernice looked at her from the nurses' desk; she seemed eager to know if they had done it, if they had found Barnaby and Reardon.

Juliet nodded, and Bernice cracked a half smile before returning to her paperwork.

Moving from bed to bed, Juliet checked the medical clipboards, pausing at the last patient, who lay entirely still with his blanket tucked tidily beneath his armpits.

"Wilkowski?"

He raised his head from his pillow; his red hair was damp with sweat. His face was pale and waxy. He pointed his forefinger at her. "Who—shot—Abraham—Lincoln?"

"I'm Nurse Dufresne. Don't you remember me?"

"The assassin's name!"

"John Wilkes Booth."

He threw back his blanket and swung his legs over the side of his bed. His knees were gray and knobby. "They won't let me go," he whispered. "I've been taken prisoner."

She lifted his medical clipboard. "You're not well," she said. "You're running a fever."

"They're trying to cook my brain!"

"We can bring the fever down."

She shook two aspirin into her palm; Wilkowski flicked away the white tablets.

"Not a thing wrong with me," he said, standing and bending at the knees. "Not a thing wrong except that I know the truth."

"At least have some water," she urged, setting a glass by his bed. A gloom began to collect around her. Was everything beginning all over again? Barnaby had been saved, but there was still Wilkowski, and hundreds, maybe thousands of others struggling to collect the shattered bits of their minds. She looked at the empty beds and knew soon they would be filled.

"Ah, I see Herr Willard is back!" Wilkowski, barefoot in his hospital gown, moved briskly toward the tent entrance, where Willard had just entered. "Herr Willard!"

Juliet offered Willard a shrug of apology from the far end.

"Private Wilkowski. I'm an American doctor, not a German. You know this very well. Would you like to see my papers?"

"Herr Willard," Wilkowski moaned. "I thought you'd left me. You were going to make me better." He jabbed angrily at his own stomach. "Make me better."

"I will," Willard said softly.

Wilkowski grew very still and slowly hugged himself. "Please don't leave me again."

"I won't."

Willard stepped forward, and Wilkowski tentatively laid his head against Willard's chest, blinking thoughtfully.

Juliet smiled. It seemed, for a moment, that Wilkowski's sadness had drawn some sense and logic to his surface. Perhaps he would return to them after all. Wilkowski wrapped his arms around Willard. Juliet could see the pride in Willard's expression. Finally, he was helping them—Wilkowski, Barnaby, the others that would come. Finally his efforts were paying off. Soon Wilkowski began shifting from side to side in what apeared to be a dazed, melancholy waltz, but which soon, step by step, took on the rutted force of a wrestling maneuver. Willard patted Wilkowski's back, trying, as they careened around, to steady himself. "You're okay," he soothed, "you're going to be okay." Then Willard gasped, and by the time Juliet looked up, Wilkowski was waving the pistol Willard had taken from Barnaby.

"Herr Willard, what's this?"

Willard's face went slack. "Private, set down the gun."

"Herr Willard! Here, finally, is the evidence!"

"Private, you're safe here. I'm an American, understand? You're safe now."

"Go back to Germany!"

"You're safe," said Willard. "It's all going to be okay, I promise. We will make you better. Do you hear me? We will make you better."

Wilkowski nodded as though in agreement, and then Juliet heard the shot and watched Willard fall to the ground.

It is a sunny September day, and Juliet steps off the bus into the bustling depot. From her purse she pulls a small piece of paper, directions for the city bus she should take. She makes her way through the crowd and out onto the sidewalk. A cool breeze greets her, and after hours of sitting she adjusts her skirt and slip, makes sure her blouse is tucked in neatly.

She finds the signpost indicating her next bus and waits behind several young men in suits; it still startles her to see men of a certain age in anything but khakis. The men are clean-shaven, their hair is neatly combed. But they cannot be more than twenty-five years old, thirty at best, and she wonders where they have been.

When the bus arrives, the men make a playful show of insisting she board first; she thanks them and takes a seat near the front, turning to look out the window as the bus rumbles away. The sun is strong, glinting off the wide ribbon of river; tall, gray buildings tidily line the avenue. At the eighth stop, she stands, and one of the men helps her lift her bag off.

She has been traveling for two days, and she is exhausted; but now that she is close, she begins to move briskly, excited. She double-checks the piece of paper in her purse.

Finally she comes upon the redbrick town house. There is a small front porch with a planter box of bright white flowers. Over the steps a wooden plank has been laid at an angle. She walks up the plank and rings the doorbell.

It is a while before she hears anything, but she knows it would

be awful to ring again; she sets down her bag, and finally the door-
knob turns. Fingers wrap themselves around the midsection of the
door, slowly pulling it open.

"You came," he says.

She looks down at Willard, who has clasped his hands. His eyes
are red. "You don't know how happy this makes me."

"I keep my promises," she says.

"You didn't have to hike in the cold, did you?"

"I rode on a lovely stuffy bus. And I could not have been happier."

"Come in."

He deftly backs up his wheelchair and turns it around in a flash.
By instinct, she almost reaches out to push it for him, but stops
herself.

"Can I get you some water?" he calls behind him. "Some coffee? We have *serious* coffee here, award-winning coffee."

"Water," she says. "But I'll get it."

He turns and narrows his eyes at her, with only a flicker of playfulness. "I'll pretend you didn't say that."

The old severity is back, and it makes her grin. "I'd like coffee,"
she says, "with milk and sugar."

"Better."

He is wearing a blue collared shirt, a navy tie, and pinstriped
gray trousers; this, she thinks, is more odd than seeing him in the
wheelchair. He looks like a man, not a doctor or a soldier—a normal man. He is staring at her as though the sight of her in a skirt
and blouse is equally bizarre. She no longer wears her hair in braids,
and she senses him taking this in—the curls that fall gently on her
shoulders—though she knows he will say nothing.

"It seems like you're getting around okay," she calls as he pushes
the wheelchair into the kitchen.

"Let's face it, I was never much of an athlete."

She hears the sound of the gas stove click to life, and she looks
around the living room: there are yellow flowers—daffodils—on

the mantel and a stack of records, almost spilling from their cases, loosely piled beside a Victrola. The walls are cluttered with framed photographs and paintings. Watercolors. Of flowers and bowls of fruits. Of a town house, the one she has just walked into.

"Claire did those," he says.

"They're beautiful."

"She's at the market. Getting asparagus for dinner. Chicken and asparagus, is that okay with you?"

Juliet nods, scans the seating in the living room, and decides upon the sofa. She settles in, even as Willard lingers by the kitchen.

"She's been . . . good to you?"

"Angelic, all things considered."

"Good." She feels a slight sting, after all this time, at the discussion of his wife, but tries to push it away. "I actually have a fiancé," says Juliet. "Amazing, right? Me."

She sees a look of faint injury in his eyes and she thinks, *This is perhaps all I ever needed.*

"And the lucky man is . . . ?"

She cannot resist a small jab: "Younger than I am. By a year. His name is Charlie."

Willard nods quietly, recognizing the slight. "I couldn't be more pleased for you."

The kettle begins whistling, and he disappears into the kitchen. He returns a minute later with a tray in his lap, balancing two cups of coffee, a creamer, and a bowl of sugar.

"Impressive," she says.

He carefully pours cream in her coffee and mixes in a spoonful of sugar and hands her the cup. "I've become quite domestic!"

The tension is behind them now, as it will forever be behind them, a distant memory that will pass further into the distance with every year that they know each other. In time, with each birth, she will send pictures of her three children. And one Christmas, when Willard and Claire visit, Juliet and Charlie will ask them to be godparents to their youngest son, Tucker. Claire will take Juliet aside and thank her, offering a tearful hug, confessing that she had always hoped to be a mother herself.

In time, Juliet will get a PhD in chemistry and will teach at a women's college for twenty-seven years. She will become a grandmother of six, and when her oldest grandson studies in Florence for a semester, she will demand, upon his return, to examine every photograph, without explanation. In this other life, she will speak little of her small and unremarkable part in the war. She will tuck it deep in the pocket of her soul like a shiny penny snatched from the ground. Along with the other tens of thousands who served, who quietly returned home and shoved their memories in the attic, she will eventually seem to the world a doddering relic of a bygone era. This won't bother her, though, this succession. For in the quiet moments of contemplation her later years will bring, she will begin to sense she was part of something longer than the war, larger than herself: a collective human walk, the unending march of history. Along the way, things were dropped, others picked up. Tuck had vanished, but during those long years when the world tore itself apart, Willard joined her. Together they had walked side by side; of all the human beings that could possibly exist in the past or the future, *this* man had been her fellow traveler. That was the arc of life, it seemed; the slow and grateful recognition of those who were, by chance or fate, simply *with* you.

"How is home?" Willard asks.

"My father and Pearl have been pretty wonderful. My father knew to ask some questions but not to pry. They give me space. He's started to talk a bit about his work during the Great War—as a way of filling in my silences, I suppose."

"Did you ever learn anything more about your brother?"

"No," she says. "We held a funeral for him last month. It was my idea. It helped, I think."

"He'd have been amazed to know the lengths to which you trying to find him."

"I did hear from Barnaby," she says. "First I got a postcard from his sister a year ago—from Florida, of all places—saying, 'Thank you, everyone is well.'"

"Florida," says Willard. "He's a free man again, I guess."

Juliet had heard nothing from Barnaby and Reardon until the Armistice was signed; she had no way of returning to Signora Gaspaldi's from the hospital, but Alfonso eventually let her know that his mother said her friends were well and on their way home. That was all.

Willard, even from the hospital back in the States where he was recovering from his injury, had continued to petition against Barnaby's sentence. Eventually Barnaby's court-martial was struck from all records. The embarrassment of his escape was too great, the story of his trial so barbaric, that the army had decided it was better to list him as missing in action.

"And then I got this letter from Barnaby," says Juliet, "three months ago."

Dear Nurse Dufresne,

It's been a long time since we said our good-byes in that small, cold room in Florence, and I wanted to say thank you once again for all you did for me. You saved my life, as did your brother, and I will forever be indebted to your family and never know what brought me the luck of finding both of you in my life at its two darkest moments.

But for the past few years, a few things have been eating at me. I've discussed them with Tina, and she thinks the truth is best. She said you were intent on letting her know the truth of what had happened to me, and it seemed you'd come a very long way to find out some truth about your brother. I told you s best I could everything that happened. And everything I believed. I don't know what I said during those sessions with Dr. Willard. Maybe you already know some of this, but from what you asked me that last day, I wasn't so sure.

But you asked me that final day if I thought your brother had lost his mind. You wanted to know what kind of soldier he'd been. If he was happy. The truth is I don't know. What I do know is that the man he was in that dugout with me, when he saved my life, was not the man he'd been a month earlier.

I will forever honor the memory of Tucker Dufresne, and count him a hero among the men I met in the war, and yet he was once responsible for an incident that makes it hard for me to think of him as the same man. Near Naples, in what they first thought was a joke, Tuck and Sergeant McKnight strung me up from a tree. They hung me from my pack. I won't go into any detail as it won't help your understanding of things, except to say it quickly became much more than a joke, and they did something bad to me. That is the truth. I don't know why he did it. But I suspect it speaks to his mind, or what the war may have done to it.

So the question is: Had he lost his mind when he did that, or when he saved me? He never much spoke to me in between, not wanting much to do with me, so I can't really answer that.

I think the war has left us all with a lot of questions. I don't sleep that well, and suppose I never will. But there's a thing about the white glove that sometimes eats at me. Tina was the one who first mentioned it a while back, when I told her about them stringing me up from the tree. You'll recall that Tuck left me in that dugout in the dark of night; so maybe he had to rummage for his things and the glove fell from his pocket. Maybe he didn't want to risk running across a darkened field with a piece of bright white fabric. So it's possible, I have to concede, that it wasn't a signal, that he never meant to come back. *It's possible when Rakowski heard him shouting "Forgive me," it was for leaving me there to die. . . . Or maybe he was apologizing for what he'd done to me and what he'd done in the war. Maybe he wanted it all to end, just like I did. That's a feeling I know. You don't mind dying when you feel like you've already been killed.*

I write this as a confession, I suppose, because these are the things I wouldn't say to you back in Florence. Things I hadn't really even thought through. I was scared; I didn't know who my friends were. Didn't think I had any. I only knew that you'd come looking for your brother and would look after me if you believed he would have wanted you to. And it's what you'd come to believe. And besides, if he'd returned alive one day, what would you hold him accountable for? But I know now you would have protected me no matter what I told you, that you are kind and decent, and I'm sorry for whatever I withheld.

And the truth is: I still believe he left the glove for me as a sign he meant to return. I believe he meant to save me. And I believe he regretted his treatment of me and he finally saw me in that dugout as a fellow soldier. Brilling and the others didn't think he was coming back for me, but they were wrong.

We all have to walk away from those years with some way of putting together the pieces. We're all assembling our stories; I see the world around me assembling its story. Well, I've told you my entire story, the one that helps me sleep.

Forgive me if these thoughts are unsettling. It is all I have left to say on the subject, and I figured I should do it now so you can put it all behind you.

I hope you are healthy and happy and have come to realize what good you did during those dark months. I often think of all you and Dr Willard did for me. May the angels watch over you.

Christopher Barnaby

"I wanted you to see it," she says, "because you're the only other person in the world it would mean anything to. And now I want to tear it to shreds."

"You loved your brother, Juliet."

"But did I know him? You're the psychiatrist: Do we ever really know another person?"

"People are complicated. War is complicated."

"Do I know *you*?"

"Probably better than I know myself."

She folds the letter three ways and sticks it back in her bag. She will not destroy it, but she will never look at it again. The war changed her brother, as it did all of them, and in his final moments he redeemed himself by saving Barnaby. That is her story. That is the tale she will carry with her. And when the question of the white glove comes to her in the thick of night, she will push it from her mind.

"I heard from Glenda," she tells Willard. "She married a dentist."

"My, my, everyone kept in touch with you."

"Not everyone," she says. "I wonder what happened to Liberata. The little girl. And her brother."

"I remember."

A quiet sadness passes between them. Outside, there is the sound of a car gliding down the street.

"Are you ready for college?" Willard asks. She will go next month, finally, to a women's college in Virginia.

"I'm ready to stop changing bedpans."

"I'm excited for you. You have so many great things ahead of you, so many great books. You'll read Darwin and Freud, Sophocles, Shakespeare, Thomas Mann. You'll be dazzled, Juliet. You'll hear Bach's cello suites for the first time, Handel's *Messiah*. There are so many beautiful things in the world, Juliet, so much better in life than what you've seen."

"*We've* seen."

He nods, sorrowfully. "Yes."

He looks at his watch. "Dinner is at seven. Will you need something to eat before then? I have some cheese and crackers."

"Seven is perfect," she says.

He wheels himself over to the Victrola and studies the pile of records. He pulls two records from the pile, looks from one to the other, and then, with a grin, sets one on the player and lowers the needle. He brings his hands together in childlike anticipation, waiting for the music to begin. Finally, the first few triumphant bars of an orchestra ring through the house.

"Puccini," he announces. "*Tosca.*"

He wheels back beside her, and they sit in silence listening to the music, a plaintive voice singing in Italian. It seems an ancient language from a faraway land. Outside the windows the sky is beginning to darken, and Juliet becomes aware of the lamps in the room, the soft yellow light settling over them. It is the light of a house, of a home, the glow of safety.

There is a pause between arias, and he turns to her.

"Do you like it?"

"I love it," she says.

"Oh, good." The music begins again, and quietly, almost inaudibly, he says, "I'm just so glad you're here."

"I'd have hiked in the cold," she whispers to him.

He smiles.

She will remember this moment many times in her life, and when, at age sixty-eight, Willard dies in his sleep, and Claire calls with the news, it is here, in this room, listening to his music, that Juliet will picture him.

And in the hour of her own death, at eighty-six, she will think again of Willard and of Tuck, of her father and Pearl, and of all the young men she saw pass away decades earlier. "I'm coming," she will say as her breath weakens, and her children beside her will wonder to whom she is speaking.

But here, now, they are young still, and the lamplight is beautiful, the music perfect, and they are beside each other, sitting contentedly.

"Friends?" she asks.

He turns and clasps her hand between his. "The best."

AUTHOR'S NOTE

This is a work of fiction drawing heavily on fact, and so it may be useful to note where I've chosen, for the purposes of my story, to veer from historical accuracy. The town of Charlesport, South Carolina, is a fictional locale based loosely on Beaufort, South Carolina, where I once lived; the movements of Tuck's division (noted as the 88th in the novel) are in fact a compendium of the movements of both the 88th and the 91st Divisions of the US Fifth Army; and none of the battles or troop movements mentioned are intended to correlate with the real-life actions of any particular unit. Artillery was used in the Battle of Pisa. The field hospital depicted is fictional, as are its movements, although the flyer discovered by Mother Hen is an actual German propaganda leaflet reproduced in Leon Weckstein's *Through My Eyes: 91st Infantry Division in the Italian Campaign, 1942–1945*. There were approximately fifty thousand desertions by American soldiers during World War II. Forty-nine were sentenced to death. Only one sentence was carried out: Private Edward Donald Slovik was the first and only American soldier to be court-martialed and executed for desertion (in January 1945) since the Civil War.

I began researching this book ten years ago, long before I knew what, exactly, the story would be, and along the way many texts were returned to libraries before I could dutifully note their titles. Of the books that remain in my possession, I'm deeply indebted to *Foot Soldier: A Combat Infantryman's War in Europe* by Roscoe C. Blunt, Jr.; *Reflections of One Army Nurse in World War II* by Gladys Bonine; *The War North of Rome: June 1944–May 1945* by omas R. Brooks; *Lingering Fever: A World War II Nurse's Memor* by LaVonne Telshaw Camp; *The 1st Field Hospital: The Experiences of T-4 Robert U. Shepard* by D. A. Chadwick, Robert Shepard as consultant; *My Darling Margy: The World War II Diaries and Letters of Surgeon Charles Francis Chunn, MD* edited by Celeste Chunn Colcorde; *The Duration and Six Months: Letters of a World War II Army Nurse* by Shirley Coressel; *Hospital at War: The 95th Evacuation Hospital in World War II* by Zachary B. Friedenberg; *The 92nd Field Hospital: A Surgeon's Memories of WWII* by John C. Gaisford, MD; *Roll Me Over: An Infantryman's World War II* by Raymond Gantter; *Nurses at the Front: Writing the Wounds of the Great War* edited by Margaret R. Higonnet; *Sixty Days in Combat: An Infantryman's Memoir of World War II in Europe* by Dean P. Joy; *Quiet Heroines: Nurses of the Second World War* by Brenda McBryde; *And If I Perish: Frontline U.S. Army Nurses in World War II* by Evelyn M. Monahan and Rosemary Neidel-Greenlee; *Love and War in the Apennines* by Eric Newby; *Our War for the World: A Memoir of Life and Death on the Front Lines in WWII* by Brendan Phibbs; *A Half Acre of Hell: A Combat Nurse in WWII* by Avis D. Schorer; *Bedpan Commando: The Story of a Combat Nurse During World War II* by June Wandrey; *Through My Eyes: 91st Infantry Division in the Italian Campaign: 1942–1945*; and *From Anzio to the Alps: An American Soldier's Story* by Lloyd M. Wells.

ACKNOWLEDGMENTS

A million thanks to Dorian Karchmar and Simone Blaser, and to the brilliant team at Scribner: Whitney Frick, Alexis Gargagliano, Nan Graham, and Kelsey Smith.

Along the way, this book was made markedly better by invaluable feedback from Nick Arvin, Eric Bennett, Sarah Funke Butler, Justin Cronin, the amazing Kurt Gutjahr, Krista Parris, and Dr. Sebastian Schubl. Thanks to Damiano Bellafri and Harald Franzen for lightning-fast translation services.

I will be eternally grateful for the time and space provided by the MacDowell Colony, the Virginia Center for the Creative Arts, the Hambidge Colony in Georgia, and the Allen Room at the New York Public Library. The Guggenheim Foundation provided crucial funding while I found my way with this novel.

As always, I am indebted to the kindness of the Vanderclan: Modur, Papito, Jefe, Amy, and my three-foot-tall roommate, who miraculously slept through the night so that I could write into the darkness. I hope one day she will read this and be proud.

ABOUT THE AUTHOR

Jennifer Vanderbes is the author of the novels *Easter Island* and *Strangers at the Feast* and is the recipient of numerous awards, including a Guggenheim Fellowship and a New York Public Library Cullman Fellowship. Her writing has appeared in the *New York Times,* the *Wall Street Journal,* the *Washington Post,* and *Granta* and has been translated into sixteen languages. She lives in New York City with her daughter. Visit her website at www.jennifervanderbes.com.

This interview first appeared on TheRumpus.net.

THE RUMPUS INTERVIEW
WITH JENNIFER VANDERBES

by Phil Klay,
National Book Award–winning author of *Redeployment*
April 15, 2014

Appropriately enough, given that Jennifer Vanderbes's latest novel is about a World War II–era nurse, I interviewed her in the VA hospital on Twenty-Third Street and First Avenue, where I was recuperating from a minor illness. We'd been planning on meeting for breakfast, but she was kind enough to switch plans and do a bedside interview, one only occasionally interrupted by the medical staff who were patching me up. I can testify to her excellent bedside manner, one that reminded me of her novel's psychiatrist, Dr. Willard, who takes a professional and intellectual yet emotionally engaged approach to his patients.

Her latest book, *The Secret of Raven Point*, starts off with a young girl, Juliet Dufresne, whose brother goes to fight in World War II, only to disappear in Italy. She becomes a nurse and ships off with the hope of getting close to where he went missing and possibly finding some answers. The book explores the experiences of figures not commonly foregrounded in war literature, such as support staff, civilians, and psychiatric casualties. *The Secret of Raven Point* is in many ways an exploration of alternate histories—a war novel written with confidence, knowledge, and insight, but also with a focus decidedly at odds with the standard images of World War II.

The Rumpus: When people talk about the tradition of war literature, it's often a very masculine tradition—the trench poets, then Hemingway, Mailer, Heller, James Jones, O'Brien—and it's one that tends to privilege the experiences of frontline soldiers. In 1939, Hemingway puts out an anthology of what he considers the best war writing of all time, and it's called *Men at War*. Civilians, women—they're somewhere off in the periphery, if they exist at all. Were you consciously arguing with that tradition?

Jennifer Vanderbes: I might have been arguing with Hemingway, which maybe sounds grandiose. I doubt he'd care. Hemingway always fascinated me—I think he's misunderstood. His breakout novel is about a man who is rendered impotent by the war. And if you look at the reviews of the time, nobody mentions the impotence. *A Farewell to Arms* is about a deserter. The masculine mythology he created for himself as a writer is very different from what he was actually writing about. And it allowed people to perceive him as this very tough guy writing about very tough things, when in fact, if you look at the texts, they are much more thoughtful and sensitive in dealing with more nuanced aspects of war and masculinity. Not to mention he was a serious romantic!

A Farewell to Arms is a book with a nurse who is very much an object of love and womanly devotion who doesn't do that much nursing. It's a book I love for its writing; it's one of my favorite books of all time, but there are parts of it and characters that I felt didn't get looked at. And those characters were interesting to me. So *A Farewell to Arms* might have been the only book I felt like I was actively in conversation with.

Rumpus: The other echo I see is with Pat Barker's work. One of your main characters is a psychiatrist working with soldiers with battle fatigue, though unlike in [Barker's] book, the psychiatric work is being done very close to the front.

Vanderbes: Pat Barker, obviously, she wrote three incredible novels about World War I, and she beautifully brought to light the work that was done on shell shock. What I found interesting, though, was learning that World War II had triple the rate of battle fatigue, or combat exhaustion, as World War I did. We've absorbed World War I as the war in which psychiatric trauma was paramount, and yet it was much more pronounced in World War II.

Rumpus: Is that what led you to nursing?

Vanderbes: It was probably one part research, one part personal experience. I worked as a hospice volunteer. I've worked in hospitals. I was never trained as a nurse, but being with people in that capacity was something that was familiar to me, and something that was both terrifying and a privilege.

I've always put women at the center of my novels, and I often put them in male domains. Practically speaking, the closest you could get to the front lines as a woman in World War II was as a field hospital nurse.

Rumpus: There's a great moment in the book when there's a confrontation between a nurse and a frontline soldier. A familiar trope of war writing is the complaint about the comfortable and lazy support staff versus the frontline soldier who understands the truth of war through his experience. But when an infantry captain confronts the head nurse, Mother Hen, she doesn't cede an ounce of authority.

Vanderbes: Yes. He's coming in very clearly to defy her authority and to harass a patient. Her experience has taught her that whatever happens on the battlefield, whatever hierarchy is at work, it all ends in the hospital. A patient is a patient. A patient could be a prisoner of war, too. There were a lot of morally complicating moments with German prisoners in American hospitals. What was the medical support staff supposed to do? You treat them as human beings, and maybe feel awful about it.

Rumpus: I remember talking to a nurse in Iraq who had tried and failed to save the life of an injured Marine, only to later have to care for the injured insurgent responsible for that Marine's death. It's a difficult, complicated experience that takes its toll.

Vanderbes: The experiences of the support staff are extremely complicated. In my second novel, *Strangers at the Feast*, I wrote about a Vietnam vet who had a desk job during the war and came back to a country that assumed he was going to go Rambo. The prejudice ruined his career. But in Vietnam there were something like nine million military personnel—I think less than one million served in combat. We imagine that most of what gets done by the army and navy involves guys with guns in direct combat.

Rumpus: Right, trigger-pullers.

Vanderbes: And actually there are millions of people taking part in the conflict. And having written a World War II novel, I now meet the children of veterans who'll say, "Oh, my father was in Italy" or "My mother was in a home-front hospital"—most of the time they weren't involved in direct combat.

Rumpus: And one of the things I love about this is that you're concerned not just with the combatants but with civilians as well.

Vanderbes: I wish I could write another novel that was just the Italian civilian novel. It's hard, because it's ugly and there's no happy ending. There's a reference in *Raven Point* to what happened right after Monte Cassino, which was not American troops but Allied troops—

Rumpus: You're referring to the mass rape and killings committed by the Moroccan Goumiers.

Vanderbes: And there was a book that came out recently, *What Soldiers Do*, about the rapes Allied soldiers committed in France.

I really think the conversation we've allowed ourselves to have culturally about Iraq and Afghanistan has allowed people to talk about World War II in a way it wasn't discussed for decades. For a while it was simply, "We beat the bad guys! Let's move on." The soldiers coming home—many of whom had done things they weren't proud of in order to beat the bad guys—had no outlet to discuss their experiences. But simultaneous with the conversations we're having about Abu Ghraib, we're opening up other conversations about the nature of war itself and the kind of moral compromises it generates.

The fundamental question is, who gets to tell war stories? Whose voice is worth hearing? And what truths will we permit them to tell?

Rumpus: And you're telling a very different World War II story. It's not the story where you're supposed to get a little misty-eyed and proud and a little sad in just the right way.

Vanderbes: I think I was frustrated. I enjoy war movies. But I do not enjoy the aspects of them where I feel that I'm being emotionally manipulated into patriotism. And I do feel proud of my country. But there was something missing in what I'd absorbed cinematically and in some of what I'd read—there was a story I hadn't yet experienced. It was about a good war in which people do bad things. And I certainly didn't want to write a war story in which war is a vague backdrop for characters to find love and passion. In real life, romance may be a necessary fiction to make wartime bearable, but when war is used in fiction to make *romance* bearable, I cringe.

Rumpus: I think you respect somebody by treating their experience honestly, including the uglier aspects. Anything less is patronizing.

Vanderbes: I strategically avoided large conflicts. The Battle of the Bulge. Normandy. People have written extensively about those events; people already have preconceived notions. So I took Italy after the capture of Rome—a portion of World War II that nobody, even at the time, paid much attention to because we were kicking ass in France. But there were a lot of soldiers in the Apennines, and it was a long winter. And that was a representation of what I wanted to do overall in the novel.

Rumpus: In what sense?

Vanderbes: I wanted to give name to the anonymous. It's like in *All Quiet on the Western Front*, which is just a stunning, stunning book. I don't think any novel has ever used a title so well, and has ever made you feel the insignificance of someone you got attached to through the book and made you understand that your relationship to them is not history's relationship to them.

Rumpus: Another one of the tropes in the military is the "band of brothers," which is a very real, very powerful thing. But you look at it from the perspective of Private Barnaby, a character who, because of who he is, doesn't fit into the band.

Vanderbes: This goes back to the question of men and war and the role of masculinity—war is often sold as a masculinizing experience. Barnaby was interesting as a character because he doesn't at all fit the frontline masculine stereotype. So his combat stress—also not considered part of the masculine experience—is exacerbated by feeling like he doesn't experience the camaraderie that is obviously so integral to the military experience.

Rumpus: And then there's the issue of shame, the aftermath of being involved in something that is horrific. Your battlefield psychiatrist, Dr. Willard, quotes Freud on how "savages" have purification rituals after combat, whereas we expect someone to go through military service and have nothing but unadulterated pride. And it seems like even today, we either want the veteran to be a symbol of pure heroism or a traumatized shell.

Vanderbes: Right . . . those are the only two options. Willard was a character I loved writing. Willard has his own moments of struggling with masculinity, one when Juliet has gone off and frolicked with some frontline soldier and he's left behind, just a doctor, ashamed he's not one of the guys toughing it out. But he also knows the frailty of the men at the front and has a very parental and caring relationship with his patients. And I think he firmly believes that trauma, combat exhaustion—that these are not indications of personal weakness. That these are normal responses to abnormal circumstances. And even in World War II, that idea was ahead of its time.

Coming out of World War I, the military establishment thought the guys who suffered shell shock must have been weak to begin with. So they thought they could integrate into the draft interview a psychological assessment that would weed out men prone to falling apart. And now, of course, we realize how horribly misguided and insulting that is, because it discredits the normal responses of very normal, healthy, strong men. Any man who could go through the incessant frontline killing and stride away with a big old happy smile, that's the guy I'd call psychologically damaged.

Willard has a deep commitment to getting these men back into shape—and he's morally compromised because he also understands he's doing it as part of the assembly line. How does he convince someone to not be scared of something that's genuinely scary, only to help him recover and send him right back into that terrifying situation? He has a terrible job. But everybody has a terrible job, in some ways. A terrible job in the service of a good cause.

Rumpus: I wanted to talk a little about sex and profanity.

Vanderbes: My favorite subjects.

Rumpus: One of Juliet's friends is very comfortable with her sexuality, whereas Juliet is a bit different. And of course, her introduction to the male anatomy is treating all the soldiers in Naples with STDs.

Vanderbes: I felt so sorry for her! But that's what they had a lot of nurses doing—obviously not the patriotic work they enlisted for. The propaganda posters of the time made becoming a nurse seem the noblest of acts. My favorite one reads, "Save His Life and Find Your Own."

Rumpus: There's also a really wonderful introduction to battlefield cursing in the book.

Vanderbes: "Heavens to fucking Betsy," right? It was more interesting to me to get the profanity in the voice of someone like Mother Hen, the head nurse, rather than the frontline soldiers. There's already an assumption that the guys are swearing every other word, so it's uninteresting to depict.

Rumpus: I know you're friends with the writer Elliott Holt, whose novel *You Are One of Them* reminded me of yours in some ways because both of your books are cleverly constructed anti–mystery novels.

Vanderbes: Well, it starts with Juliet wanting to find out what happened to her brother. How did he go missing? Is he still alive? I know there is a certain set of readers who will be frustrated with the novel because they like a tidy ending. The anti-mystery aspect of it really had a lot to do with the real history behind it, the nature of the war itself. It didn't feel right to go, *Oh, here's the experience of someone who shipped off and served as a nurse, and she got all the answers she ever needed and everything worked out perfectly.* That seemed dishonest to the overall experience. Juliet enlists with a certain intent, and a certain illusion, as many did. Doctors, nurses, soldiers, quartermasters— they were all disillusioned by the actual experience. Juliet's actual experience in the field hospital had to be interesting enough and important enough to become the focus of the story.

Rumpus: And of course she matures. It's a fairly simple question she starts out with, but as the story grows and grows in complexity, the narrow mystery plot can no longer contain what's happening in the novel.

Vanderbes: That's exactly it. It's too constricting.

Rumpus: I was wondering if you found it helpful in any ways, writing this book, that you weren't a veteran. Though there is clearly skepticism anytime a nonveteran steps in and tries to claim authority to speak about war, did it also free you to deal with precisely those subjects that are missing from the conversation?

Vanderbes: I think as a nonveteran and as a woman it's challenging to write about war. There's always a sense that your authority will be doubted, or at the very least not respected. Do you have to have five bullet holes in your body to write X, Y, and Z story?

Rumpus: Or, like Hemingway, the right amount of shrapnel.

Vanderbes: Exactly. The author's persona casts a certain light on the story. Sometimes women get a pass to write about certain subjects and be taken seriously. The novel *March*, by Geraldine Brooks, is about a Civil War doctor. It's a terrific book that takes the father from *Little Women*, the one missing male from a novel all about females, and places him in the war. So a woman has written about war but placed a man at the center of it—we accept that story as important and legitimate.

Pat Barker has done the same, placing men at the center of her war novels, though brilliantly challenging the idea of traditional masculinity along the way. I really love Pat Barker. And there's one thing in my novel that's an attempt to connect my World War II psychiatrist to her World War I psychiatrist—there's a blue eye that one of her characters and one of my characters both see. I liked the idea of a continuity between the wars, one horrific image, a haunting that would seem to never end.

Rumpus: And she's also writing about the aftermath of combat.

Vanderbes: In the way that Hemingway did. *A Farewell to Arms* is a hospital novel. Barker's part of that tradition. You can have a war novel about people after they're on the battlefield, and that's as much a war novel as anything set on the battlefield.